Return to Berlin

A Spy Story

By Noel Hynd

© 2019 by Noel Hynd

RETURN TO BERLIN   Noel Hynd

First Printing – October 23, 2019
Readers may contact Noel Hynd at Nh1212f@yahoo.com.

Typos are the new "fleas" of the electronic publishing world. We keep trying to eradicate them and they persist. If you find some here, feel free to report them to the publisher at Red.Cat.Tales.Publishing@gmail.com. They will be sprayed yet again.

{122519k}

Published by
Red Cat Tales Publishing LLC
PO Box 34313
Los Angeles, CA 90034

e-mail: Red.Cat.Tales.Publishing@gmail.com

**For
Patricia
With appreciation and love**

"A story has no beginning or end: arbitrarily one chooses that moment of experience from which to look back or from which to look ahead."

Graham Greene, *The End of the Affair*

*

"Everything must be paid for."
Thomas Mann

Chapter 1

Lisbon, Portugal
December 3, 1942

Looking up from his game of dominos in the airport lounge in Lisbon, William Thomas Cochrane, an American traveling on a false passport, noted the activity around the boarding gate for his flight to Geneva. Winter was the rainy season in Portugal. But the mid-afternoon storm that had pounded the Portuguese capital had now continued along its way.

At the airport, skies were clearing, as Cochrane could see through the big glass windows in lounge. The sun had returned and his journey to Geneva would soon continue. The aircraft, an American-made DC-3, sat on the tarmac in the near distance, waiting.

Cochrane looked back down to his game of dominos. His opponent was a man named Cambulat. The latter sat in a dark suit across from Cochrane and served as his worthy opponent. Cambulat had a Turkish passport. Cochrane knew because he had seen it. They spoke French with each other and had a small audience of one.

Behind Cambulat stood a man named Valdez, a Spaniard travelling on a diplomatic passport. Ever vigilant, Cochrane had noted that, too, during check-in for the flight. A passport these days didn't prove who a man was, but it did indicate who a man claimed to be, which could also be informative. For someone like Cochrane, an agent of the American FBI, now attached to the newly created Office of Strategic Services, America's spy agency, that was as good a place as any to start.

For a few minutes, there had been a second member of the small audience. A thin man in a long coat stopped by to peer over Cambulat's shoulder. He watched the game. Perhaps he had been attracted by a conversation in his native language. He exchanged a few words with Cambulat.

The man had been reading a censored copy of *L'édition,* so Cochrane pegged him as possibly a Frenchman.

Cochrane took the man's accent to be from the south of France. Cochrane tried to draw him into conversation, but the man deflected the attempt. It was amazing how much a man or woman might reveal in a casual conversation at an airport. But the Frenchman smiled and walked away. He didn't speak again.

To Cochrane's left sat Skordeno, a grouchy American who read a three day old edition of *The Times of London*. Skordeno had turned an icy shoulder to Cochrane the entire time in the lounge. On the other side of the small lounge sat two women. They looked Portuguese to Cochrane but he knew he could have been wrong. They spoke quietly between themselves, voices no higher than whispers. Cochrane couldn't catch the language. They were well dressed. Probably wealthy, he speculated.

Portugal remained neutral in the ongoing world war, but the country was a nest of spies, defectors, profiteers, and saboteurs. All walls had ears and concealed mini-cameras were everywhere. So one tried to never draw undue attention to oneself and one didn't remark aloud on newspaper headlines or accounts of battles.

More than three years earlier, Adolf Hitler had attacked Poland on September 1, 1939. England and France had declared war on Germany. It was not just the beginning of the Second World War, but also a unique time in Portuguese history. The Portuguese head of state, dictator António de Oliveira Salazar, had come to power in 1932 as a fascist and an ally of Francisco Franco in neighboring Spain. The son of a small rural freeholder, Salazar was a failed seminarian, an ex-economics professor and an oddball among the European dictators. He was also off to a good start in World War Two.

In Lisbon, just a few kilometers from the busy airport, Salazar straddled a line every day between Francoist Spain and Portugal's old ally, democratic England. His concern was to preserve the regime and to maintain the Empire. He knew that any slight mistake could compromise his national independence.

Neutrality appeared to be the best way to guarantee the strategic objectives of the Portuguese foreign policy.

There was a big casino down the coast in Estoril where the roulette wheels and card games never stopped. There was plenty of displaced royalty to keep things going, side by side with desperate refugees, grandstanding opportunists, and beautiful women selling sexual favors to put together money for exit permits. In America, the film *Casablanca* had just opened, but Lisbon was more Casablanca than *Casablanca*. Even the airport was alive with spies, smugglers, informants, and all sorts of shady people trying to remember the details of their fictitious new identities.

Both the Allies and the Axis powers operated openly in Portugal. Shots were rarely fired on Portuguese soil. That was the unwritten rule. The country, and specifically the capital, was a conduit point, a place to come from and to go to. Intelligence was gathered here, but the dirty daily business of killing took place elsewhere.

In the airport lounge, Cambulat turned over a final domino tile. He looked at it and tried to match it to a piece on the playing surface. But Cochrane's tiles had blocked his moves, as was common in a domino endgame. The Turk shook his head and smiled.

He again spoke French with his opponent. "Ah, I concede. You win again."

The two men, strangers until the flight had been delayed, shook hands.

"Another game?" Cambulat asked.

"Oh, I think I've had quite enough," Cochrane said with good humor. "But thank you for helping me pass the time."

"It was a pleasure, sir," said Cambulat. "You're an excellent player. I do envy you your set of tiles, however. Do you always travel with them?"

"I do now and will in the future. I've always coveted a handsome old set," Cochrane replied. "I travel. I have much time to myself. If I tire of reading, I play solitaire or with a stranger or with friends. Or in your case, a new friend."

"I'm flattered," said the Turk. "You have an excellent set of antique tiles. Have they been in your family for some time?"

"These?" Cochrane indicated his game pieces and the case they were kept in.

He laughed.

"Not at all," he answered. "I had some time on my hands yesterday in Lisbon and went to the flea market. Mercado de Santa Clara. It's not far from the center of the city. I found this intriguing set and purchased it for a very good price. You are free to examine them."

The Turk picked up a tile. The game pieces were ebony and bone with a fine patina of age and wear. Cochrane allowed his new friend to examine the set. Methodically, Cochrane placed the remaining pieces into a wooden box with a sliding top. The box served as the carrier. There were English and Arabic inscriptions on the box. In faded lettering, there was an English language street address in Cairo. There was co-equal lettering in Arabic, but the latter was not a language that Cochrane understood.

Cambulat handed the final piece back to Cochrane.

Cochrane put it into the case and slid the lid in place as he spoke. "This particular set is perhaps a hundred years old, carved and created in North Africa. Egypt it would appear, perhaps a decade or two before the American civil war. The 1840s. The tiles are carved from animal bones, probably a camel's, inlaid with ebony. Quite beautiful, don't you think?"

"Very much so," said the Turk. "Fascinating, sir."

The two men shared a handshake and a laugh. The Frenchman looking over Cambulat's shoulder smiled slightly, turned and sat down. Skordeno moved away in a huff.

A steward of the airline, a stout man in a suit, emerged from the other side of the boarding gate. He had a flight manifest in his hand. At about the same time, two men in Portuguese civil aviation uniforms, the captain and co-pilot of the impending flight, appeared from a private lounge in the terminal.

The aviators checked in by signing the flight documents in the steward's hand. They continued through the gate. The steward announced that the flight would depart in thirty minutes. Boarding would begin in ten. The crew was hoping to get the flight aloft before another row of thunderstorms moved through the area.

The passengers rose to their feet. They stretched and gathered their baggage.

Boarding went smoothly. They walked to the plane on the tarmac, escorted by two uniformed Lisbon police officers. Fourteen passengers boarded. Cochrane counted them. Then he took his assigned seat in the fifth row at a window. The seat next to him remained empty.

There was a shelf above his seat. He took a book from his one travel bag and slid the bag onto the shelf. The bag contained his box of dominos. There was a heavy mesh netting which pulled down and buttoned tight to deter valises from flying loose in flight.

Cochrane took location inventory of the other passengers: the two women who were together, Valdez, the Frenchman from the Midi, Cambulat and Skordeno. He settled into his seat. He already wished this mission was over. He had bad feelings about it. Hyper-jitters. They were getting worse.

At the last minute, a reed-thin scholarly looking man with round Lenin-style glasses and sandy hair boarded the aircraft. He carried a briefcase, walked to the front and spoke to a woman who was the air hostess. Her reaction to him was cordial but chilly. The man then returned to the rear of the aircraft near the exit and took a seat.

The man's appearance surprised Cochrane because he thought he had heard the gate shut behind them when the original fourteen passengers started for the aircraft. So this last man must have been a very late arrival. But it was wartime, he reminded himself. Allowances were sometime made, some ominous, some innocent. So now there were fifteen passengers. Cochrane had trained himself to keep track of small details. Often, they added up to something significant.

The plane was warm. Cochrane removed his coat and loosened his necktie. The plane's engine powered on. The propellers started up and soon the DC-3 taxied to a runway. In another few minutes it was aloft over Portugal. It proceeded northeast over Francoist Spain.

For the next two hours, the Portuguese airliner rumbled and bounced in a turbulent late afternoon sky at twenty-thousand feet. Eventually it was above the south of France. Cochrane carried a flask with moonshine whiskey in it. The booze had been a gift from a US Army contact for such occasions. He made use of it en route.

More than halfway to Geneva, the aircraft adjusted its cruising speed. The change was abrupt. Everyone noticed. The airplane turned starboard. Seconds after that, it hooked into a pattern that suggested an impending controlled descent.

Now the passengers looked around nervously. With a war raging all over the world, much less on almost all fronts on the European continent, there was plenty of cause for anxiety. A wave of it rippled through the seating area.

The one stewardess on board emerged from a seat in the forward section of the aircraft. She moved from row to row to advise passengers of a change in flight plans.

Cochrane pushed back the beige curtain at his window. The aircraft was in cloud cover. It was impossible to see the land below. There was only the whiteness of the clouds. Then his heart skipped and his worst fears morphed into a horrible realization. From one gap in the clouds to the next, he could discern the contours of a Messerschmidt about a hundred feet off the tip of the wing of the DC-3.

It was flying as an escort as well as a not-so-subtle threat. The flight had been intercepted.

Cochrane stared at the fighter plane. He could see the ominous straight-armed cross that was the emblem of the Luftwaffe. The final moments of his life were possibly coming into focus. The vision riveted him with anxiety: the compact German fighter plane with its single pilot, machine gun, neat little wings and a despicable swastika beneath the pilot's window.

He forgot about the stewardess for several seconds. Suddenly he felt her hand on his shoulder. He turned sharply, looking up into the frightened eyes of a young Portuguese woman.

"There's also another German plane on the other side of us," she said to him in French, barely above a whisper. "We have been ordered to land at Marseille."

"*Pourquoi?*" Cochrane answered.

The flight attendant shrugged.

"Does this happen often?" Cochrane asked, remaining in French.

"For me, never before," she said.

She crossed herself. Cochrane broke a sweat.

A thousand thoughts went through his mind. There was little time to process them. He reckoned that they were maybe twenty minutes flying time from Marseille, the rough sprawling industrial and port city on the Mediterranean. More recently, it was a stronghold of the pro-Vichy collaborationist government. For an American spy, Marseille was as hostile a place as any in Europe.

No matter how he looked at it, this was not good.

Chapter 2

Marseille, Vichy France
December 1942

Twenty-two minutes later the DC-3 bounced onto the tarmac at Marseille, a three point landing with the rear wheel last. The aircraft slowed on the landing strip. The plane turned toward the terminal. Cochrane saw several police cars waiting. As the aircraft moved closer to the debarkation area, he could see German soldiers, some with machine guns, standing with French police who had sidearms. The security squad was waiting for something important. There was at least one passenger they wanted from this flight. Cochrane didn't see how it could be anyone other than him.

Cochrane kept his eyes on the tarmac. The reception committee was at least twenty men, all armed. German uniforms. Vichy French. Police. Soldiers. Ominously, there were four in civilian uniforms.

He drew a breath. He was on the ground in enemy territory. He thought of his mission, his life, and his wife Laura back in New York. Now his only real hope was to do nothing except pray.

The plane stopped. There was some fumbling and banging at the access door to the plane. The door was behind him. He could hear it open. The stairs folded out. The ramp thudded onto the runway. There was barrage of agitated voices in French and German.

Cochrane prepared for the worst.

He heard heavy footsteps boarding the plane. Cochrane turned.

One man in civilian clothes boarded and held a Mauser upright and across his chest. He stood at attention guarding the door. Two others, also in civilian attire, boarded the plane and eyed the passengers. One walked to the front of the plane.

Cochrane knew Gestapo thugs when he saw them. It was quickly apparent who was in command. It was the last man who had boarded the aircraft.

The man was short, stocky, and heavy. When Cochrane heard his German, he recognized his accent and speech to be working class Bavarian: reduced speed, a lazy tongue and an avalanche of massacred consonants. Like almost all Gestapo, the man wore a civilian suit as he carried out his duties.

Cochrane had encountered such men on his previous mission to Germany. He knew that many of them were not even Nazis. But they were the ultimate ruthless bureaucrats who had no issues or hesitations when they carried out Hitler's orders. He knew to avoid them if possible and be very careful with them if they couldn't be avoided. Most had been recruited from local police units that had existed during the Weimar Republic and then been broken up with the creation of the SS.

The man wore a hat. For a moment he removed it so that it wouldn't be brushed by the aircraft's low ceiling. His haircut was German old style: the sides shaved, a few short hairs on the top and toward the forehead. He looked like an evil jack o'lantern.

One of the man's assistants made a small slip. He addressed him in a subdued voice as, "Kriminalkommissar Wesselmann." A violation of protocol: Gestapo agents were to keep their personal identity a secret except from superiors. But Cochrane caught it. The title, Kriminalkommissar, confirmed that the man was Gestapo.

Wesselmann. Now Cochrane had a name to go with the face.

And what a face. It was a face that would stay with Cochrane for the remainder of his life. Wesselmann's face was hard and expressionless, slashed by a set of thin cold lips. He had heavy eyelids above small brown eyes and a flat protruding forehead.

Cochrane looked more carefully. His hands were the broad square hands of a German peasant, broad paws with thick long fingers. He looked like a strangler. And if he was Gestapo, he probably *was* a strangler. The Gestapo was a cult of obedient force. There wasn't a man or woman within the organization who didn't hate anything that smacked of art, wit, creativity or intelligence.

Combined with an adulation of Hitler and his National Socialist Party, it was a loathsome mixture.

Again, Cochrane knew things from experience: some of these lugs from Bavaria and southern Germany were among the worst. Once, at the Hofbrauhaus in Munich in 1938, Cochrane had eavesdropped on a trio of men at an adjoining table whom he took to be Gestapo.

"The intellectuals of Germany and France," the boozed-up leader of the group had suggested to the others, "should be sent down a Polish coal mine and blown up."

"Along with the stupid Poles who work in the mines!" roared another of the group.

They all laughed and drank to the sentiment. It hadn't been meant as a joke. It had been meant as the start of a wish list.

The Portuguese captain emerged from his cockpit. He looked apprehensive. The flight attendant stood to the side. She looked stricken. In conversation with the Gestapo agent who had boarded, the pilot nodded obediently. The co-pilot was a smart young man. He said nothing. He kept his distance and avoided eye contact.

The man in the suit held up a badge in a gloved hand. Cochrane was correct: Gestapo. The flight was a Portuguese airliner going to Geneva. German fighters had forced the plane down in Vichy France. The Gestapo officer spoke German and assumed everyone would understand.

"Everyone debark," he demanded. In consternation, the passengers rose. Some tried to gather belongings. The Gestapo leader howled at everyone.

"You bring nothing!" he said. "Nothing!"

It was an order, not a statement.

"We are seeking enemies of the Reich! All others will be allowed to board again and continue!"

Cochrane's eyes widened. An even larger fear rushed through him. Standing next to the Gestapo commander, obviously in collusion with him, was the fair-haired man with the wire-rimmed glasses who had been late to board the flight. Somewhere, an evil fix was in.

The other passengers followed the orders. The Gestapo leader moved the passengers down the rear steps from the plane. The police on the tarmac herded them into three groups, four to a group. Their weapons were drawn. The two women stood separately next to each other.

A stiff cold wind whistled across the tarmac. It cut through clothing. A gray sky hung overhead like a shroud. The agent with the Mauser stood as head guard. The Gestapo leader watched, eyeing everyone closely as his two aides went from traveler to traveler inspecting passports.

Cochrane tried to keep his eyes trained straight ahead but watched what he could with a peripheral view. He was convinced he was moments away from dying. One by one, passengers were permitted to go back onto the plane. The two women were cleared first. Two men were cleared. One was told to remain. Another man was cleared and allowed to board the airplane.

They came to Cochrane. He produced his forged Canadian passport under the name of Abraham Stykowski. Despite the cold, sweat poured down his back. One man eyed the passport, Wesselmann questioned.

"You speak German?" asked the interrogator

"I speak German," Cochrane said,

"How do you speak German?"

"My grandmother was German. And I visited Germany during the degenerate Weimar years."

"To do what?"

"Banking. I was a banker."

"Which bank?"

"Morgan Guaranty Trust."

"What bank in Germany?"

"The Dresdner Bank."

"Oh?" Wesselmann's tone which had been frosty was now icy. "You're a wealthy man? Privileged class?"

"No. I work for a salary like everyone else. Much like you, perhaps."

"I have suspicions of a man who flatters," the Gestapo officer said, still icy.

"No flattery was intended. I'm telling you the truth."

The questions followed rapidly, meant to catch a hitch or hesitation or an uncertainty.

"Your name. It's Polish?"

"Polish Canadian."

"You don't look like a Pole."

"Really? How should a Pole look?"

"You have a middle name?"

"Stanislaus."

"Why were you named that?"

"After an uncle."

"Where do you live?"

"Near Toronto. Canada."

"Canada is at war with Germany."

"That doesn't mean I am."

"Good answer, Herr Stykowski," Wesselmann said. "Why shouldn't I arrest you?"

Cochrane produced a transit permit with the proper Third Reich markings and signatures. It was a forgery. Wesselmann looked at it carefully, including the paper.

"Are you Jewish?" Wesselmann asked.

"I'm a Polish Catholic."

"Really? Why do Catholics worship Mary?"

"We don't worship her. We venerate her."

"What's the difference?"

"Veneration is the honoring of a person. We worship Almighty God, our Creator."

"Good answer."

The Gestapo officer examined the passport, bending pages and holding it sideways to examine the binding. "This is very good. A professional product."

"It should be. It's authentic."

"Issued when?"

"A month ago."

"Where?"

"In Brazil. Rio de Janeiro."

"How did you get to Brazil?"

"By steamship."

"Which one?"

Quickly, "The *Sao Paulo*."

The Gestapo officer paused and checked the page with the appropriate stamps. All the fake details checked, but Cochrane felt sweat running down his back.

"From?"

"Nassau."

"When?"

Cochrane gave the date.

"And you were born where?"

"Ottawa."

"When?"

Cochrane gave an address and date. They matched the lies in the passport. Back in New York, he had done his memorization well.

"Do you still live there?"

"My family moved to Toronto in 1933."

"You have an entry stamp which permits you to visit Germany. Why?"

"I have financial business with the Reich."

"You are going where in Germany?"

"Berlin."

"Then why do you stop in Geneva and not Zurich?"

"My banking associates are in Geneva."

"Which bank?"

"Credit Suisse."

"Credit Suisse no longer has branches in Geneva."

Cochrane managed a small smile. "You can do better than that, Kriminalkommissar," he said. "Credit Suisse has branches in all the cities and all the cantons. Their headquarters in Zurich is under reconstruction. The acting headquarters is in Geneva. And they retain an office in Berlin on the Albertstrasse."

"You're a smart man," snapped Wesselmann.

"Now, *you* flatter *me*, sir."

"Maybe too smart!"

Wesselmann snapped shut the passport. Hard accusatory eye contact. Neither blinked. Wesselmann's eyes were pools of intimidation and menace.

Cochrane extended a hand for the return of his passport.

"I will be holding this," the Gestapo agent said, keeping it in his hand. From behind, one of the other agents placed his hands on Cochrane, patting him down, looking for a weapon. "You stay where you are with your hands at the height of your shoulders," Wesselmann demanded.

The Gestapo squad moved through the other passengers. They pulled aside Cambulat, the Turk. They dismissed three passengers, then pulled Skordeno out of the line. Two policemen held him, one on each arm. Skordeno didn't blink but his eyes found Cochrane's.

The Gestapo held three passports in addition to Cochrane's. They singled out the nameless Frenchman, too, the one with the Midi accent.

Ten passengers were back on the plane. Four passengers were left on the tarmac, their hands aloft. The fair haired rat with the round glasses was with the French police. The Germans arranged carefully the four men in custody. They positioned Cochrane second from the left, pushing Skordeno next to him. Cambulat was to Cochrane's right and the Frenchman was at the end. They continued to hold their hands aloft, palms at shoulder level.

Cochrane looked up to the aircraft. They were twenty meters from the port side of the plane. There were faces at each window watching the proceedings.

Wesselmann stood in front of the four passengers. The thin man with glasses left the police position. He reached into his jacket and pulled out a Luger. He strolled to the side of the four men on the tarmac and circled behind them, quiet as an eel in dark waters.

Wesselmann switched into heavily accented English.

"One of you we know to be an American spy," he barked. "Another of you is suspected. The other two arouse our suspicions. But you may be free to go when our business in finished. Now! You will have fifteen seconds. If you are a spy, you will confess right here and now. You will be arrested and interrogated. You will have the opportunity to work with the officers of the Reich and assist us. If you remain silent and obdurate, you will be shot. Here. On this spot. Do you all understand?"

Cochrane mumbled, "Yes." So did the three other men.

"Fifteen seconds begins!" the man said.

No one confessed to anything.

Fifteen seconds passed. Cochrane could sense the position of the man with the gun who had moved behind the line of four captives.

Cochrane couldn't help himself. He trembled.

He thought of his wife back in New York. If he were to be killed, as he now knew he would be, he wanted the vision and thought of the woman he loved to be his final one in this world.

"Very well!" Wesselmann snapped.

There was a quick shuffling of feet behind the line of four captive travelers. The captain of the squad gave a nod and then a signal by hand.

Cochrane could hear a second set of footsteps behind him, suggesting that there were two executioners. He heard the clicks of two handguns.

A pair of shots erupted behind him into the neck and skull of Skordeno, who had been next to him. Parts of bone and blood sprayed Cochrane's cheek and coat. With peripheral vision Cochrane saw Skordeno flail forward toward the ground, arms waving and spasming and half of his head missing, blood flooding obscenely from the shattered skull.

He saw the people in the aircraft turn their faces away.

Cochrane closed his eyes.

Skordeno's lifeless body was the last thing he saw. He closed his eyes, said good-bye to his wife when the thin man with glasses behind him raised his Luger and fired two more shots, instantly killing the suspected second spy.

Chapter 3

**Nazi Germany and The Soviet Union
Summer and Autumn, 1941**

On June 22, 1941, Adolf Hitler took his greatest gamble of World War Two. He launched Operation Barbarossa, a three million man invasion across Poland and into the Soviet Union. Hitler was confident the Soviet Union would fall to his brutally efficient armies in a matter of months, if not weeks. Stalin had purged and executed some of his best military men over questions of loyalty, real and imagined. Soviet military equipment was years out of date. The generals of the Red Army were often drunk and more often incompetent. The Soviets had even suffered great difficulty scoring a victory over pesky little Finland in 1940, while Germany had routed Belgium, Luxembourg, Holland and France the same year. The western front was quiet by the end of June 1940. Nazi Germany had triumphed everywhere. The swastika flew above fifteen European capitals. The only resistance was half-paralyzed and far underground.

There was no reason for Nazi Germany not to exude swagger and confidence. Joseph Stalin's repressive regime was corrupt and had difficulty administering the more remote stretches of the Soviet Union. "We have only to kick in the door," Hitler boasted, "and the whole rotten Communist structure will crash to the earth."

Barbarossa was magnificently efficient in its early stages. By September 1941, the Red Army was back on the heels of its muddy boots, its tanks and armies in desperate retreat, having lost two and a half million men. But the Red Army was also the largest in the world, comprising nearly three hundred divisions, and the Soviet Union was the world's largest country by area, with vast natural resources. There was room to rebound if early defeat could be avoided.

There was also Russia's most dependable historical ally: the weather. In October, the annual snows began in Siberia. In November they worked their way west.

Other allies for Russia were lurking, also. President Franklin Roosevelt occasionally flirted with the notion that he believed that the Russians and the Americans were on a path to convergence. He felt, sometimes anyway, that as the US was moving away from unfettered capitalism toward state-managed socialism, the Soviet Union might be moving from autocratic communism toward socialist democracy. The notion was overly optimistic, wishful, and not based on much, but it wasn't a bad thought. FDR was at heart a populist. Sometimes he saw in Stalin, in his words, "a man of the people," an autocratic spin on FDR's own mandate.

Roosevelt wasn't the only world leader trying to see Stalin in clear daylight. "Any man or state who fights on against Nazism will have our aid," Prime Minister Winston Churchill told the British people in a radio address on the BBC in reference to the Soviet dictator. Not many Brits disagreed.

It was impossible to truly know what motivated Roosevelt any more than it was possible to know what motivated Stalin. As went a popular Russian proverb, "Another man's soul is darkness." There was plenty of darkness in Stalin's soul, probably more than most.

Roosevelt's tolerance for Stalin was mostly strategic. Yet, Russia needed America, with its shipments of steel and low-interest loans, which Stalin had no intention of paying, far more than America needed Russia. Prior to Roosevelt's presidency, in return for recognizing the Soviet Union, Washington wanted Stalin to stop interfering in American affairs through its secret agents, anti-democratic activity and counterfeiting schemes. The United States also asked Stalin to take a more humane stance on the Ukraine, where Uncle Joe had engineered a fake famine, starving two million people to death. Stalin just laughed.

Great Britain, though, was already at war with Germany. Officially at least, the United States was still on the sidelines while Germany and Russia slugged it out.

The pressure on Roosevelt to keep America out of another European war was enormous. For years Churchill, the shrewdest of the wartime leaders, had wooed, cajoled, and flattered Roosevelt in particular and the American public in general in an effort to ally with its vast resources and manpower. He wrote FDR two or three times a week. Roosevelt offered some ships and other arms and war equipment. But he stopped well short of promising a war alliance. The mood of America would not allow it. In 1940 and 1941 the national debate had intensified between isolationists who wanted America to stay out of another world war and interventionists, who favored extensive aid to Great Britain.

In September 1940 a Yale Law School student named R. Douglas Stuart, son of the co-founder of Quaker Oats, founded The America First Committee, known as the AFC. There were several other co-founding law students, including future US President Gerald Ford. The group quickly became the largest homegrown pressure group against the American entry into World War Two.

Almost overnight, the AFC had nearly a million paying members. On the other coast there were "peace strikes" at several campuses of the University of California. Politically, Roosevelt's hands were tied. The isolationist movement was not shy about flexing its muscles.

In May 1941, Charles Lindbergh, still a national hero, spoke at an America First rally before a capacity crowd of twenty-two thousand at New York's Madison Square Garden. Those assembled roared their approval of staying out of another European war. On the other extreme, The Fight for Freedom Committee and the Committee to Defend America by Aiding the Allies were active in New York, insisting that America confront fascism. Their rallies were meager and tame, however, compared to the boisterous tub-thumping America Firsters.

The fighting on the Eastern Front between Russia and Germany was terrible beyond belief. The Germans wished to crush the hated Slavs. The Soviets threw into the battle anyone who could carry a weapon. Atrocities were everywhere. Armies slaughtered civilians by the thousands. Beheadings were routine, mass graves common. Brutal rapes happened by the hundreds. Soldiers set buildings on fire with prisoners crowded into them, then stood by, laughed and cheered. Millions of captured soldiers died of exposure, torture or mass execution.

The German army slaughtered Jews and Slavic peasants with enthusiasm, the Slavs in the initial combat, the captured Jews by hanging or by SS rifle squads that followed the army. Hitler's racial crusade against the Slavs soon backfired, however. Potential Nazi collaborators enlisted into the Red Army to fight for Stalin and defend the cities of the Motherland.

The Germans besieged Leningrad and tried to subdue the city by starving its entrapped people. Hitler ordered that the entire male population of Stalingrad, a city of one million, be killed. Similar orders were in effect for Moscow. All captured females were to be deported to Germany for labor or sexual exploitation or both. Millions of victims of the German invasion were noncombatants.

Stalingrad emerged as the focal point of the push into Russia, the battle that would decide the war. In military terms, the irresistible force, the Wehrmacht, was driving headlong toward the immovable object, Stalingrad, the city of the "Great Leader," who was portrayed in *Pravda* as a sympathetic but strong father figure, with the Soviet people as his "children".

No battle in previous history was more ferociously waged.

In house-to-house, farm-to-farm and factory-to-factory fighting, tens of thousands died, sometimes by knife or pistol. Snipers were used to great effect by both sides. The Axis forces suffered eight hundred fifty thousand casualties and the Soviets seven hundred fifty thousand. The Great Leader considered his losses necessary. The surrender of the city would have been an irreversible victory for the Nazis. The two sides fought on and on and on. Then in late November 1941 blizzards arrived. The Russian winter set in. Advancement and retreat froze to a halt.

Next for Russia, a December miracle.

Japan attacked Pearl Harbor, bringing the United States of America into the war. Insanely, Adolf Hitler compounded Japan's strategic error by declaring war against the United States on December eleventh. The US reciprocated with a retaliatory declaration of war against Germany a few hours later. The America First Committee dissolved the same day. Non-intervention was no longer an option.

"Greater good fortune has rarely happened to the British Empire than this event!" proclaimed Churchill. The United States and Great Britain had barely been on speaking terms with Stalin's communist regime. Now Roosevelt, Churchill and Stalin shared a common enemy. Hitler had blundered on a titanic scale and had accomplished Churchill's goal for him.

"I went to bed on December ninth and slept the sleep of the saved and thankful," Winston Churchill wrote much later in his account of World War Two. To the British Prime Minister, this meant one thing above all: eventual victory.

Britain was no longer alone.

It was late 1941. Uncle Sam was finally ready to roll up his sleeves and fight.

Chapter 4

Bern, Switzerland
November 1942

On a gray afternoon in November, twenty-four hundred miles southwest from the fighting in the Soviet Union, German and Italian intelligence entrenched in North Africa detected a major buildup of Allied shipping passing through the Strait of Gibraltar. The Germans dismissed the convoy of ships off the southern tip of the Iberian Peninsula as another shipment of supplies to reinforce Malta, which the British held.

Annoying, but tolerable.

The Italians were not as sure.

But by that point in the war the Germans were already ignoring their Italian allies. Then, on November 9, 1942, the phone rang at five thirty in the morning in the plush bedroom of the Fascist Italian foreign minister, Galeazzo Ciano, waking up Ciano. Ciano was married to Edda Mussolini, Il Duce's daughter, but wasn't working very hard on the marriage. He was in bed with his most recent mistress, an earthy sexually insatiable lady who had kept him awake till 4:00 AM. The phone startled him out of something between a dream and a stupor.

Struggling to come awake, Ciano was horrified to hear the guttural voice of German foreign minister Ulrich Jaochim von Ribbentrop shouting at him over the line.

Von Ribbentrop informed Ciano of British and American landings at the Algerian ports of Oran and Algiers and the Moroccan port of Casablanca.

"Air attacks?" asked the sleepy Ciano.

"No, you imbecile! *Landings!* An invasion."

Ciano had no immediate response.

"What," von Ribbentrop demanded, "do you plan to do?"

Ciano replied sleepily and nervously, but also honestly. "I have no idea," he said.

What von Ribbentrop and Ciano were witnessing, and what Hitler and Mussolini were also learning of that morning to great distress, was Operation Torch, a boldly ambitious strike by the United States and Great Britain at Fascist North Africa, where pro-German Vichy French forces defended much of the coastline.

The western Allies had transported sixty-five thousand men, commanded by Lieutenant General Dwight D. Eisenhower, from ports in the United States and England. They had done the unthinkable. They had successfully invaded North Africa.

They had beachheads immediately. In Algiers, the French Resistance coordinated its activity and had staged a coup at the same time as the landings from the sea. The Allies pushed inland and forced a surrender on the first day.

Elsewhere, Vichy French troops put up a fight. Bad weather hampered the invaders. The Task Force attacking Oran suffered losses to its fleet trying to land in shallow water. But Vichy ships were sunk or driven off. British battleships opened fire on Oran. The city surrendered. To the east, the allied forces laid siege to Casablanca, the principal French Atlantic naval base. Axis forces surrendered after eight days. They had been focused elsewhere. The Germans were bogged down in their struggle for Stalingrad and the Caucasus.

Moreover, the situation for Axis armed forces in Egypt had grown increasingly grim throughout September and into October. The British had revved up their troops under Lieutenant General Bernard Montgomery for a reinvigorated offensive against Rommel's powerful Afrika Korps. At the end of October, Montgomery's Eighth Army had attacked the Germans at El Alamein precipitating a massive battle of attrition, the second in the remote stretch of Egypt, that Axis forces had no hope of winning. Not surprisingly, Axis leaders concentrated on what was happening in the Egyptian desert.

By early November, Rommel's forces were rapidly retreating back into Libya against the specific orders that Hitler was shrieking into his telephone lines. Benefiting from accurate espionage and intelligence, Eisenhower's forces struck in Algeria and Morocco. The Allied victory at the Second battle of El Alamein was the beginning of the end of the Western Desert Campaign, eliminating the Axis threat to Egypt, the Suez Canal, Palestine and the Middle Eastern and Persian oil fields.

The repercussions of Operation Torch would remain enormous during the remainder of the war. The fallout would postpone the landing in France until 1944. At the same time, it allowed the United States to complete mobilization of its immense industrial and manpower resources for the titanic air and ground battles that characterized the Allied campaigns of 1944.

Behind the scenes, it had other repercussions.

A closely related but much quieter event transpired in Bern, Switzerland on November 9, the second day of Operation Torch. An American stepped off a train from France shortly after noon. He had been lucky to arrive. His train passed from Vichy France into Switzerland only minutes before the Germans closed the border. The Germans had taken this action the same day Allied troops landed in North Africa.

The man, Allen Dulles, looked more like a university professor or a diplomat than one of the great intelligence agents of the Twentieth Century. But in the espionage business, appearances frequently deceive.

Now forty-nine years old, Dulles was a man with a ruddy complexion, a small graying moustache, and keen blue eyes behind rimless spectacles. As he stepped from his train, he was wearing a tweed jacket with gray flannel trousers. He smoked a pipe and carried a single suitcase.

Dulles was in Bern to head up the center of the Office of Strategic Services in Europe. Switzerland remained the only neutral country in central Europe, so it was logical for the OSS to plant their headquarters smack in the middle of a continent at war.

Back in Washington, OSS Director Bill Donovan had wanted Dulles to work in the OSS office in London. Dulles argued for Switzerland where he had lived and worked twenty-four years earlier in the last months of World War One when he was attached to the US State Department. Switzerland was also the only neutral country with a common land frontier contiguous to Germany, albeit a rugged mountainous one in most areas. But it was the best point from which to observe what was going on, not only in Germany, but also in Italy and France. It was also a less difficult place to run agents in and out of all those countries.

Dulles won the argument. Thus, on November 10 the American Legation wrote to the Division of Foreign Affairs, Swiss Federal Political Department, that a Mr. Allen Dulles had arrived by train on November 9, and that he was assigned to the Legation.

The correspondence also stated that Dulles was staying at the Hotel Palace Bellevue, the top hotel in the capital. Some scurrying around went on behind the scenes and Dulles moved within thirty days to a rambling rented apartment at 23, Herrengasse, a solidly upscale sandstone building on a cobblestoned arcaded street that ran along the ridge high above the River Aare.

The building where Dulles had set up shop also had several perks that did not immediately meet the untrained eye. The building on Herrengasse was the last house of a row of adjoining fourteenth century townhouses built by the Bernese city government to house dignitaries. The street itself ended there in a cul-de-sac. The land fell sharply away beyond a low wall down to the vineyard terraces that sloped down to the Aare, which made a horseshoe bend around the ancient city walls. It was the most secure house on the block, if not in the entire neighborhood.

The vineyards afforded an ideal approach for visitors who did not wish to be seen entering the front door on the Herrengasse. After dark, the cover was nearly infallible. From the terrace outside his apartment, Dulles also had what he referred to as "an inspiring view" of the whole stretch of the Bernese Alps. Working those Alps with high powered binoculars or the telescope he kept in his study could also unveil some interesting secrets from time to time. Hence, the "inspiration" of a professional spy.

For those who might come to Dulles's front door in the evening, the spymaster wanted to give some anonymity. So he bribed local officials and had the streetlight opposite his front door turned off for the duration of the war. The gesture was mostly a ruse. His most clandestine guests came and went via the back door and the vineyard.

Normally seen while dressed in a suit and tie, the perfect vision of the Princeton graduate that he was, Dulles appeared at his own doorway a few mornings later. He was armed and dangerous; he carried a steel hammer and a small box of nails. He placed a discreet sign outside his apartment door and nailed it into place. A few neighbors emerged into the hallway to see what the gentle rapping was all about.

Allen W. Dulles, the sign said. *Special Assistant to the American Minister.*

The sign made it official. Mr. Dulles was as fond of understatement as he was of mind games. When one neighbor, a pretty Austrian woman in her thirties, gently chided him that a man so important as Mr. Dulles shouldn't be dealing with such trivial matters as a hammer and nails, he cheerfully nodded in agreement.

"Of course I shouldn't," he agreed. "You're quite correct."

Then he added, "Ah! But at least I'm not working with a hammer and sickle," he said, a twinkle in his blue eyes. The comment made the rounds of the building and local bars for the next week.

Meanwhile, Dulles hired a butler, a chef and a maid. He was soon living in upper-class European style, complete with bodyguards. Recently Dulles had been the recipient of a dump of some excellent military and naval intelligence from a source within the German government. The source promised more and named a strange price. Dulles did a lot of things by careful analysis of a situation and then proceeded by instinct.

The source, for whatever reason, was asking for a specific American agent whom he had known before the war to become a conduit for a proposed deal. Dulles recognized the name immediately. As soon as Dulles was entrenched in his new offices with secure communication, he cabled OSS headquarters in Washington.

The American's name was William Thomas Cochrane. Dulles's message to Washington was succinct.

"Figure out where the hell he is," Dulles requested, "and recruit him into the OSS without delay."

Chapter 5

New York City – Manhattan
October 23, 2019

    The two women arranged to meet in a small restaurant named Logan's in Tribeca, situated in a narrow restored townhouse on West Broadway between Thomas and Duane Streets. Logan's was a new place, but more comfortable than trendy, which was a relief to Caroline Dawson, who chose it as the venue for a meeting with a woman she had never met in person.

    Up until an out-of-the-blue phone call a few days earlier, Caroline had never even known that the other woman, Ellen McCoy, existed. But life was full of surprises. Good ones and bad ones. The trick was to embrace the former and gracefully sidestep the latter.

    Caroline knew Logan's well. She lived nearby on Broome Street, so this was a short walk. She knew the staff. The owner was a friend of her grown daughter. So there was a built-in security system, so to speak, in case the caller, this unknown McCoy woman, turned out to be a dangerous nut or a scam artist. The world was full of them, after all. New York City had its fair share.

    Caroline sat at a corner table in the rear of the ground floor. Logan's was frequented by the well-heeled clientele of Tribeca and Soho. The little eatery was surrounded by art galleries, trendy clothing places, independent bookstores and other restaurants and cafes.

    The building where Logan's was located dated from the 1800's. Much of the original brick walls had been restored. There were two rooms on the first floor. The front room was for quick bites and take-out and the cozy back room with the fireplace and the original brick walls was a space where a man or woman could come to eat, drink, or just talk with a friend over a glass of wine and not be hassled.

    Caroline had no idea if the McCoy woman would show up for this arranged meeting, though based on the call, based on past history, she strongly believed the woman would. She glanced at her watch, a vintage timepiece that was at least seventy-five years old. It wasn't valuable from a jewelry sense, but it ran and kept perfect time. Plus, it had been her mother's, which gave it all the value that mattered.

As the second hand on the watch swept past the twelve, signaling 2:03 PM, Caroline glanced up and saw a woman tentatively enter the dining area, carrying a shopping bag and looking from table to table. She was alone. The two women made eye contact. Caroline raised a hand in a polite wave and the other woman acknowledged with a smile. She walked to Caroline's table and offered a hand.

"Hello," the visitor said. "I'm Ellen. Thank you for coming."

"I wouldn't have missed it," Caroline said. "Please sit."

Ellen sat.

"Been waiting long? Am I late? I apologize if I am."

"You're fine," Caroline said. "I arrived about ten minutes ago."

Ellen McCoy was in town from the Chicago area, she said, and had been trying to set up this meeting for several years. First, of course, it had been necessary to find Caroline Dawson, the daughter of the late William Thomas Cochrane, the former spy, economist, lecturer at Harvard, and intelligence agent during the World War Two years.

"I hesitated for years about getting in touch with you," Ellen McCoy said, setting the shopping bag by her side at the table. "Some things are better left buried in the past. But I have a story to tell you. If you're willing to listen." She paused. "I'm a professor of history at the University of Illinois. My special area of interest is World War Two. I came across something fascinating involving your father."

"Can't hurt to listen, right?" Caroline said. "And frankly, I enjoy listening to an expert on anything."

"I'm sure that people find you all the time with old stories to tell."

"Actually, you're the first, the first stranger at least," Caroline said. "My mother told me more than a few. I was born in the fifties, so it's all secondhand information to me."

"Well, I was born in the late sixties," Ellen answered. "Even then, even for us, it was really another time, another world. World War Two and all."

"To be honest," Caroline said, "the war was a devastating experience for my father. Not so much to him professionally. He survived and became a lecturer about the politics of the era. Columbia and then Harvard. He did well in life. But deep down, the things he saw, the things he was asked to do for his country, and mankind's inhumanity to other people were not things that he liked or fully understood. And I know he had some deep regrets about some of the things that he did in wartime. I think it made him deeply pessimistic in the latter part of his life."

She paused.

"I don't know," Caroline continued. "My dad, William Cochrane, and I never had a conversation about it as adults. We should have but we didn't." She paused again. "He had a long career in education, the US State Department, the OSS during the war, and law enforcement. I'm sure there are a lot of stories I don't know of. Some of them will catch up with me. Some will disappear forever, I suppose."

"I understand," Ellen said. "This one's not going to disappear."

"How did you find me?" Caroline asked.

"Once I finally decided to contact you, I further researched your father," Ellen said. "I found several obituaries. I did some web searches, found some phone numbers and made some calls. I hope you don't mind."

"Not at all. I'm here, am I not?"

"So you are. Thank you." Ellen took a sip of her drink. "Do you have some time to listen today?" she asked. "What I have to tell you is very involved." She paused. "That watch you're wearing?" she asked, indicating the timepiece on Caroline's wrist. "It's beautiful. Was that your mother's?"

Astonished, Caroline answered. "Yes. It was. How did you know that?"

"I'll explain," Ellen said.

Caroline's gaze found her watch again. It was now ten minutes past two PM on a Wednesday. "I have all afternoon," she said.

Ellen hesitated, then found her voice again. "Did your father ever mention going back into Nazi Germany in 1943?" she asked.

"It doesn't ring a bell."

"Does the name Sophie Scholl mean anything to you? Her brother, Hans? Friends named Ilse and Frieda?"

"No."

"Hans Wesselmann?"

"No."

"Jean Cambulat? Michael Skordeno?"

Caroline shook her head.

"Well, then!" said Ellen. "I've *quite* a story to tell you. I don't know how you think of your father and I don't know if you'll change your opinion. I only know what I know. And I'm here to share it with you."

"Please go ahead," Caroline said.

Another slight pause, another sip of a drink.

Then, "It was late in 1942," Ellen said. "I think it all began in November of that year, just around Thanksgiving. Your father's part at least. From what I've learned, your father was in the United States Army at a very unusual posting at the time, the Signal Corps in Fort Monmouth, New Jersey. He was training for possible combat in Europe when one day everything changed."

Chapter 6

Fort Monmouth, New Jersey
November 1942

Master Sergeant Jimmy Murphy swaggered into the army mail room. Several dozen young soldiers at the US Army Signal Corps Unit had barely stopped sweating from the afternoon's drills and marching. William Thomas Cochrane, several years older than the average new enlistee, stood with a letter in his hand that he had not yet had a chance to open.

"Hey! Listen up, you no-good grunts!" the sergeant boomed. "Cochrane? Any of you dirtbags named Cochrane?"

Bill Cochrane looked up. "Yes, Sergeant Murphy," he snapped, tucking the letter away.

"Make yourself visible, Mister!" the sergeant bellowed.

Cochrane pushed his way through the other recruits and stopped in front of his drill sergeant.

"You're Cochrane?" the sergeant asked.

"Yes, Sergeant."

"Colonel Sawyer wants to see you. Now! On the double."

"The colonel?"

"The colonel! Headquarters! Get your ass moving!"

"What's this about?" asked Cochrane, who was slow to move.

The Sergeant unleashed a stream of profanities in the manner that only a career non-commissioned officer could. Then, "How the hell would I know? Think the colonel and I have tea at four each day at the fucking Ritz? He's waiting! Double time! Go!"

"Thank you, *Sergeant!*"

Cochrane, a man in his mid-thirties but as physically fit as the younger men in combat training, started a quick jog out onto the paths that wound their way past the drill fields and to the operational headquarters of the US Army Signal Corps training site.

The sun was setting. The afternoon had been warm, especially with all the gear each recruit had been packing. But now a chilling wind was setting in.

After the United States of America entered the Second World War, the Signal Corps became one of the technical services of the American Armed Services. Its components served both the Army ground forces and the Army air forces. The single training site was Fort Monmouth, New Jersey.

William Thomas Cochrane, formerly of the Federal Bureau of Investigation, had enlisted in the army a month after Pearl Harbor with the intention of being commissioned as an officer in a combat division. In actuality, he was re-enlisting, having served previously as an ordnance officer for two years. This time, after special wartime basic training, or re-training, he had once again taken the Officer's Candidate School option. If all went well, he would be re-instated to his old rank, a captain, or possibly with a promotion.

One thing had led to another and, with his background of fluently speaking French and German, plus some experience in counterintelligence work, he had had landed at Fort Monmouth for communications/intelligence training. The military complex consisted of a school for officers, an officer candidate school, an enlisted school and a basic training center at sub post Camp Wood, where future communications officers were trained.

Cochrane crossed the courtyard and entered the headquarters building. A sergeant at a desk directed him along a hallway until he came to the office of Colonel Isaac Sawyer, a no-nonsense charmingly profane South Carolinian who had been the commander of the base for the last seven months. Cochrane presented himself to the colonel's doorway.

"Come in, Cochrane," Sawyer said from behind a desk.

Cochrane entered and stood at attention. The moment had its awkwardness. Cochrane, at age thirty-six, was less than half a decade younger than his commanding officer.

"Yes, sir!" Cochrane answered.

"At ease, soldier."

"Thank you, sir."

On the colonel's desk was a correspondence. Cochrane couldn't tell what it was or what it said. He reasoned that he would find out soon enough.

"I get all sorts of commands and requests these days with a war going on," the colonel said. "Some are crazy, some aren't. Some I understand, some I don't."

Colonel Sawyer leaned back in his chair and stared at the man in front of him. "You signed on to go to basic training, then took the OCS option. Isn't that right?"

"That's correct, sir."

"But you've been in the army before?"

"Correct, sir."

"What if I told you you've been wasting your time? And ours."

A moment passed as Cochrane wondered where the conversation was going. "I'd be disappointed, sir."

"Why the hell is that?"

"I wish to serve my country in wartime," Cochrane said.

"Well, hot damn! Every decent red-blooded American male does," the colonel said.

Sawyer thought about the soldier in front of him for a moment, then continued. "You went through basic combat, the bag drill, weapons orientation, core values. Exemplary results across the board. You were in the top ten percent of officer candidates in every category. Not bad."

"Thank you, sir."

"Except two."

"Two, sir?"

"Yes. Language. You were among the top fifteen soldiers out of twenty-four hundred in linguistic skills. According to your file, your aptitude in French and German are close to a native speaker's in each language. How did that happen?"

"I studied French in university," Cochrane said. "Then I had the occasion to travel between the wars. As for German, I worked in Germany for more than a year. So I had on the spot practical training."

"When you were employed by the FBI?"

"Yes, sir."

"And this was during Hitler's ascent?"

"After he became chancellor, sir. When he was in power."

"How do you feel about Mr. Hitler? Be honest."

"To be very clear, sir, I despise the man, his associates, his supporters, his philosophy and his political party. Sir."

"That doesn't leave much, does it?"

"No, sir." A pause, and just before Sawyer spoke again, Cochrane saw fit to ask, "May I nuance my response a bit more, sir?"

"Go ahead."

"I hate the man's fucking guts, sir. I will do anything in my power large or small to defeat him, his criminal regime and all those who are on his side."

"I see. Commendable. Very commendable."

For a moment the colonel drummed his fingers on his desk.

"Then there was the other category here in Fort Monmouth where you are *not* in the top ten percent," the colonel said. "The intelligence test."

"Sir?" Cochrane asked in surprise.

"You were among the top two soldiers in our entire complex."

Cochrane remained silent.

Abruptly, Colonel Sawyer opened a manila file in front of him. Cochrane reasoned it was his service record. He kept his eyes straight ahead. He further reasoned that the colonel had already looked through it.

"Close the damned door, Cochrane," Colonel Sawyer said.

"Yes, sir."

Cochrane took three steps to his left and closed the door to the office. He returned to where he had stood and resumed the at-ease stance.

"I just looked through your personnel file," Sawyer said, his tone going down a notch. "You worked for the FBI in civilian life for several years?"

"Yes, sir. That is correct."

"And how exactly did you land here at the Signal Corps?"

"I re-enlisted in the army after Pearl Harbor but my induction was deferred till September, even at my old rank, so that I could complete cases that were in progress."

"Banking fraud, it says." There was a pause. "Maybe a lot of something extra, also?"

A pause, then, "As I'm sure the colonel read in my file, I was assigned to a case that had a bearing on the safety of President Roosevelt. The threat was real. But with good fortune and with the assist of many others from the Bureau, the case was resolved in 1940 with no harm to the President."

"You were the principal agent on it."

"There were several men and women working as part of a team."

"But you were the principal." It wasn't a question.

"Yes, sir."

"Then what?"

"Subsequently, I returned to banking and financial fraud on behalf of the Bureau. My focus was on European banking and financial systems as they affected the security of the United States."

"Fascinating. Germany again?"

"Yes, sir. Germany, Italy. France. Soviet Russia, which attempted to flood the United States and world markets with counterfeit US currency. There was also one case involving Spain."

"You speak Spanish, also?"

"Some. Not as well as French or German."

"Your file says you were in Cuba for a while."

"That's correct. After the President's third inauguration the FBI wasn't sure where to assign me. As it happened, they assigned me to a case on which I had to be in Havana for three months. This was earlier this year. Late winter, early spring."

"Did you enjoy Havana? Never been there."

"It was a mixed blessing."

"Tell me about it."

"It's complicated, sir."

"You're good with language from what I read here. Paint me a pretty picture with some words. What did you observe, what did you do?"

"Havana was a city of flourishing brothels and unchecked corruption," Cochrane began. "Major industries grew around the sex trade. Government officials received bribes and cops on the beat collected protection money. Every night prostitutes were in doorways, trolling the streets, or baring their breasts in windows and doorways. I think one Bureau report estimated that fifteen thousand of them worked their trade in Havana, sir. In addition, drugs, be it marijuana or heroin or cocaine, were so plentiful at the time that they were no more difficult to obtain in Cuba than a shot of first class rum. The island was enchanting but hopelessly corrupt. A Mafia playground and a bordello, high class and low class side by side, for Americans and other foreigners. In any case, I used the occasion to acquire some Spanish."

The colonel hunched his shoulders. "Say something about Cuba in Spanish."

"*La Habana sigue siendo una amante del placer, una diosa exuberante y opulenta de la corrupción y delicias ilegales.*"

Sawyer laughed. "Beyond the pay grade of my high school Spanish, Cochrane, you overeducated fuckhead. Listen up. Have you ever heard of something named the OSS?" the colonel asked. "The Office of Strategic Services?"

A longer pause from Cochrane, then. "Yes, sir. Of course I have."

"I assume you know General Donovan, who heads the agency."

"We've met," Cochrane said. "Professionally. More than once."

"And socially?"

"With respect, more times than I can count. Sir."

"You travel in the same circles, do you?"

"Different circles, but they've been known to intersect."

"Did you apply for OSS duty?"

"I sent a letter after Pearl Harbor. But I never heard anything."

"Till now," the colonel said.

Colonel Sawyer produced a white business sized envelope from within the folder. He handed it to Cochrane.

"This is an order that was not generated by normal channels, Cochrane," Sawyer said. "It was generated by the Department of Defense, then signed off on personally by J. Edgar Hoover at the FBI as well as General William Donovan. The general seems to be heading this new agency out of a garage in some steamy section of Washington as well as an office building in New York City. He's the only individual I personally know of who can be in two places at once. But I digress. You've been re-assigned out of this unit to the OSS. They have you in mind for some sort of special mission. Paperwork will follow giving you the commission of a major the US Army Signal Corps and an honorable discharge will also follow at the appropriate time. It's possible that you'll retain the rank of a major in case you ever become a prisoner of war, for which you might say a special prayer to Jesus H. Christ asking for that never to happen."

Cochrane was nonplussed. "I'm not following," he said

"Then I'll spell it out. You leave here tonight with the rank of a major. You need to be in New York at General Donovan's office tomorrow afternoon. Here's the address. But you're not going to be a soldier. From what I can see, you're going to be a spy."

A much longer pause, then the colonel added, "May I close with a personal word?"

"Yes, sir."

"I'm sorry I won't have the pleasure of having a man like you actively in this unit. Whenever we get the top candidates, the best people, for the Signal Corps, those Ivy League bastards with General Donovan at the OSS steal them from us. But that's to your credit. Good luck to you. You're also under instructions not to talk to any of the other soldiers here before you leave. Questions?"

"May I phone my wife?"

"Against orders for now. Talk to General Donovan first. You're married to both of them now and General Donovan takes priority."

Colonel Sawyer glanced at his watch.

"It's too late for a train or a bus," he continued. "One of the MP's will drive you to Manhattan tonight. I think it'll be Santini. He's a wop from Brooklyn so he won't get lost. Be ready in an hour. There's an officer's installation, an apartment, in New York. I don't know where but Santini will have the address. You'll stay there overnight. That's all."

"Thank you, sir."

"Oh," Sawyer said. "One more thing. Parting gift. You'll need this."

Sawyer reached into a desk drawer and produced a metal flask, stainless steel and gleaming. He flipped it to Cochrane who snatched it out of the air with one hand.

"Mississippi moonshine," said Sawyer. "White lightning from the wettest dry state in America. You a drinking man?"

"On occasion, sir."

"One of my sergeants gets it by the five gallon drum somewhere in Newark and runs it over here for the officers. Enjoy it and bring the flask back after the war."

"Thank you again, sir."

"Enjoy it in good health. Don't get killed. Dismissed."

Cochrane saluted. Colonel Sawyer returned the gesture of respect.

Chapter 7

**Fort Monmouth, N.J. to New York City
November 1942**

Cochrane returned to his barracks. He packed two duffel bags, the second of which included the civilian clothes that had followed him from basic training. He ate dinner in a private mess hall and, observing the prohibition on communication with the men in his unit, did not have the occasion to say good-bye to friends. A guard from the Military Police stayed with him and ushered him to a canvas top US Army quarter ton truck, more colloquially known as a "Jeep," at 8:15 PM. Daylight was long gone.

The driver of the Jeep was a sergeant. Sergeants were everywhere these days. While some officers disdained them, Cochrane respected them. Whatever their faults, Cochrane knew the non-coms were the glue that held the army together, so why quibble over table manners?

The sergeant's name was Santini. He was an MP, as Colonel Sawyer had promised. He was in uniform and wore his pistol on his left side. Cochrane took it to be a Colt 45. Santini seemed wired and alert.

Cochrane threw his two bags into the vehicle, gave the driver a thumbs up, jumped in and grabbed a seat in the back. Cochrane initiated a brief conversation.

Santini was a New York guy from Brooklyn, just as Colonel Sawyer had also promised. Cochrane guessed he had drawn this assignment because he knew how to drive to New York from New Jersey without accidentally arriving in Ohio.

The evening driving assignment was a bonus for Santini. The young man had parlayed it into two days of leave during which he could go home to Crown Heights and spend Thanksgiving Day and weekend with his family and fiancée. Sometimes things worked out neatly. Other times they didn't. In 1939 President Roosevelt had moved the Thanksgiving holiday one week earlier than normal, hoping to bolster retail sales before Christmas. This led to much ridicule, causing some to deride the holiday as, "Franksgiving." People still joked about it.

The Jeep took him onto public streets, then onto a two-lane road that led north. The trip to Manhattan would cover sixty miles through northern New Jersey and take around two hours. Cochrane had driven the route many times. Even at this hour, the trip would be stop and go, red light green light, passing through sleepy towns on the journey north.

For the first quarter hour, Cochrane and Sergeant Santini engaged in small talk, some gossip about the base, chat about the war in Europe, and some baseball. Santini was a fan of the great DiMaggio, but who wasn't? His whole family were Yankee fans, the Brooklyn connection notwithstanding. Santini said his dad had once met the great Tony Lazzeri, the second baseman on Babe Ruth's great teams, at a Knights of Columbus gathering in the Bronx. Lazzeri had signed a scorecard for the sergeant's father.

"Dad still has it," Sgt. Santini said. "Framed."

So it went. Then, after nonstop chatter, the driver fell silent, or mostly silent, chain smoking Camels. The nicotine fix and maybe something else, Cochrane suspected, kept him alert. The Jeep was drafty so the cigarette smoke didn't bother Cochrane, who didn't care for cigarettes but did enjoy an occasional cigar, an indulgence he had picked up in Havana.

As the conversation ebbed, Cochrane noted the route the driver was taking. As they proceeded past Middletown, Santini navigated a network of dark, winding two-lane roads. The direction remained north. Cochrane could tell by the stars. Santini drove through a stretch of orchards and rambling old houses, and one long narrow deserted road for twelve minutes at twenty-five miles per hour. There was a sharp left turn past a picket fence. Three minutes followed on an unmarked two-lane road.

No houses. No signs indicating a town, but Cochrane recognized buildings. Eventually, they were in Perth Amboy. Cochrane's attention started to drift from outside the Jeep to the thoughts cascading through his head.

General Donovan.

Mentally, Cochrane reviewed what he personally knew.

He had first me William Donovan in the autumn of 1940. Cochrane had been invited to a campaign event for Franklin Roosevelt, a nod to his work to foil a saboteur late in Roosevelt's second term. The White House was still indebted to the FBI for its work on the case. Hoover wasn't shy about showing off his best agents when they had attained a high profile success. Cochrane had spent a few minutes with the President before the event, at which Roosevelt personally thanked him for thwarting the plot against him and signed a photo. Cochrane had it in a frame on his desk in the Manhattan apartment he shared with his wife.

The event had been at the Shoreham Hotel in Washington. Roosevelt had given a short speech. Mike Reilley, the head of FDR's Secret Service detail, introduced Cochrane to Donovan, which seemed like a good idea for the future considering France, Belgium, Luxembourg, Norway, Denmark and the Netherlands had all fallen to Nazi aggression earlier that same year and Donovan was unofficially pulling together a spy agency. It was exactly the type of top secret stuff which everyone in the capital knew and chatted about openly at parties.

"You're going to need people who are fluent in French," Reilley said to Donovan. "Mr. Cochrane here speaks it very well."

"I'll need German specialists, too," Donovan had said.

"That would be Mr. Cochrane here, also," said Reilley.

"Is that a fact?" Donovan answered, impressed. Donovan turned to Cochrane. "When are you going to learn Spanish?" he asked.

"I speak Spanish, too, sir."

"How about Russian? That'll be the pain in the ass for the next generation."

"Find me an opportunity, give me four weeks, and I'll learn it," Cochrane said.

"Pretty confident of yourself, aren't you?" Donovan replied.

"That would be true, sir," said Cochrane, cementing the deal as a man Donovan could use in the future.

Donovan was almost sixty years old in 1942. Had the world been more a peaceful place, he might have entered the comfortable pipe-and-slippers retirement that many American men dreamed about. But the world wasn't peaceful and never would be. So Donovan was far from retired and as far as anyone knew, he owned neither pipe nor slippers.

Donovan, Cochrane knew, had been born into a conservative family of Irish Catholic immigrants in upstate New York. He found his way to New York City, graduated from Columbia University where he played baseball years before Lou Gehrig made the lawn in front of Low Library famous for long home runs.

In 1907, Donovan graduated from Columbia Law School and entered private practice. He soon grew bored. So he quit law and looked for something more physical. He landed in the New York National Guard in 1912 as a captain and became part of the New York's hardnosed 69th "Fighting Irish" Regiment. He fought in the war on the Tex-Mex border in 1916 when his regiment was called in to assist the US Army in tracking down the Mexican bandit Pancho Villa. Donovan's unit then became part of the 165th Regiment of the US Army. During his time leading the regiment, Donovan gained a nickname. The men in his battalion called him "Wild Bill," a nod to the legendary lawman Wild Bill Hickock.

Three times during the Great War Donovan was wounded in action. On July 18, 1918, for bravery under fire on the River Ourcq during the Second Battle of the Marne, he was awarded the Medal of Honor. By the end of the war, he was a colonel.

In 1924, President Calvin Coolidge appointed Donovan to serve as the assistant to the Attorney General as a monopoly buster. He travelled the world and entered the dark world of espionage. He came to the notice of President Roosevelt, who asked him to visit England as an unofficial envoy in November 1940. Through his meetings with Col. Stewart Menzies, the head of the British Secret Intelligence Service, as well as King George

VI, and Winston Churchill, Donovan concluded that his country needed a centralized means of assembling foreign intelligence. Donovan returned to Washington and met with Roosevelt. Not long afterwards, President Roosevelt established the Office of Strategic Services, the OSS. By June of 1942 the agency was up and running in Washington and New York with General Donovan in charge.

Donovan asked Allen Dulles to head the New York office. Both Donovan and Dulles had long had contacts in British Intelligence. Hence, it was no surprise that they opened their offices in Room 3603 of 30 Rockefeller Center on the floor immediately above the suite of Britain's MI6.

In the back of the drafty Jeep as they travelled through northern New Jersey, Cochrane reached for the envelope that Colonel Sawyer had given him. In the dim light from the stars, moon and reflected headlights of other cars, he glanced at the text and saw again the address that he was ordered to report to the following day.

Sure enough: Room 3603 of 30 Rockefeller Center.

Santini had developed a lead foot an hour into the ride. The Jeep hit a hard bump on the road, either a pothole or a tree branch or a stone. The vehicle bounced, took a short flight but stayed its course as Cochrane bounced high in his seat and hit his head against the roof of the Jeep.

"Very sorry, sir!" Santini said.

"No apologies necessary, Sergeant. It wouldn't be an official army trip without a bump or two, would it?"

Santini laughed. "No, sir. Thank you, sir."

"Hell, no one's shooting at us. We should be happy, right?"

"Yes, sir."

"I guess that's why we have ragtops, right?"

"Correct, sir!"

In the back of the Jeep, Cochrane rubbed his head. He glanced at his watch. It was almost 11:00 PM. Some rain had started. The windshield wipers worked well but noisily as Sergeant Santini dropped down a gear and drove cautiously. There was a nearly full moon. It lit the way. The cold was creeping into the Jeep. They passed some open fields, most likely farms, Cochrane reasoned. Strands of mist hung over them.

"How are we doing, Sergeant?" Cochrane finally asked, breaking a silence of at least sixty minutes.

"I'm just fine, sir. We'll have you there within another half hour. See up ahead?" he asked. "We'd be able to see the glow from the city if it weren't for the dimout."

Cochrane had already noticed exactly that. He agreed that it was odd how New York City had disappeared. But, "I'm in no rush at all, Sergeant. Just drive safely. You need to get home, too."

"Thank you, sir," Santini said.

They arrived in Weehawken several minutes later. They passed the dueling grounds where Aaron Burr had killed Alexander Hamilton. They passed over a long downhill stretch and then hit the entrance to the Lincoln Tunnel, the first tube of which had opened four years earlier.

The tunnel led into Manhattan. At a few minutes before midnight, Sergeant Santini delivered Cochrane to his overnight address, which was a small hotel in Murray Hill on the east side of Manhattan. Cochrane grabbed his two duffels and stepped out. Through the front door of the hotel, he could see a night clerk at the desk.

"You'll be okay getting to Brooklyn, Sergeant?" Cochrane asked.

"I should be there in another forty minutes."

"No falling asleep at the wheel. Right?"

"Oh, no, sir! I took some Dexedrine before we started. I'll be fine."

"Ah! I should have known. No wonder we were flying low."

"Correct, sir," Santini said with a laugh. "Very good, sir!"

The Jeep continued along. The check-in at the hotel was smooth.

Cochrane was in his room within ten minutes, opened the flask of magnolia state moonshine that Colonel Sawyer had given him, knocked back three long gulps, felt the burn and was asleep before Sergeant Santini was across the Brooklyn Bridge.

Chapter 8

**Nazi Germany
January 1933 – November 1942**

At the age of fifteen in 1933, Hans Scholl joined *Der Hitlerjugend*, the Hitler Youth, much like many other obedient German boys of his generation. His parents, liberal-minded anti-Hitler educators, were horrified.

Hans' father, Robert Scholl, insisted that Hitler and his brown battalions of thugs were marching Germany down a road to destruction. Hans didn't believe him. While the typical German might be a conforming soul, there is also the rebel German personality, the outspoken eccentric, who could be tolerated for a while. Hans was a rebel.

Hans made friends easily in the Nazi youth organization. In September of 1935, his peers selected him to represent their branch of the Hitler Youth at the Giant Nuremburg rally of the National Socialists, the Nazi party. He was in for a shock.

The anti-Semitic and other hateful diatribes at the rally disgusted him. Gradually, Hans concluded that his father had been right. When he returned home, he quit the Hitler Youth and joined a group called German Youth, *Deutsche Jugend*. The group was liberal, open minded and opposed to Nazism. The Gestapo arrested Hans and held him in jail for several weeks; no charges filed. By association, his parents and younger sister, Sophie, were branded enemies of the Hitler regime.

Meanwhile, the Wehrmacht was active. The Nazi government allowed Hans to end his confinement and be conscripted into the army. In 1939, he began medical studies while remaining in the Wehrmacht. The war began. He was sent to the eastern front: Poland, then Russia. What he saw there, perpetrated by his fellow soldiers, more than appalled him. He saw Jews and civilian Russian prisoners impaled on spikes, hanged, shot and set on fire while alive. Even out in the steppes of southern Russia, two thousand kilometers from Berlin, Jews were forced to wear a yellow star. If they didn't they were shot. Any civilian believed to be a member of the Communist party was handed over to the SS to be hanged. Farmers were tortured to find where they had hidden their grain. Their homes were torn down for firewood, their wives and daughters raped and their sons, if they hadn't fled or been conscripted into Slavic armies, executed. More than fifty thousand female civilians were deported back to Germany to serve as slave labor. Hans witnessed some of the worst parts of it, including massive bonfires made from the corpses of Russian soldiers.

When he returned to the Fatherland in 1942, he kept quiet. The army allowed him to continue his medical studies at the University of Munich. In spirit, he had moved a long way from the boy who had joined the Hitler Youth nine years earlier. He was now a young man, thoroughly shaken, and convinced that his only moral path was to actively oppose the Nazi regime.

At the time, there were many disillusioned former soldiers at the university. They formed a small but quiet minority of anti-Nazi free-thinkers. There was one whose name was Alexander Schmorell. Schmorell had been born in Russia but was a German citizen. He too was a medical student and a former conscript. He too was disgusted with what his country was doing.

In 1941, Schmorell had fought in the devastating German blitzkrieg that overran Poland and continued unchecked for many months into Russian territory. Like Hans Scholl, he was sickened by what the Nazified German army did to civilians. Back home, he kept quiet and applied to continue his medical studies, "to greater serve the Third Reich."

In the summer of 1942, Hans resumed his medical classes at the University of Munich, arriving within a few weeks of Hans Scholl. The two young men soon met. Their private conversations were tentative at first. They dropped hints to each other about how they felt politically. One could draw a very unpleasant visit from the Gestapo by trusting the wrong person. But inevitably, their private conversations drifted toward how best to resist the Nazi administration. They were in a perfect place for it. Not only had Munich been the cradle of the Nazi party, but now the university was a crucible of unrest against fascism and the party, even if those who felt that way had been forced deep underground.

Also at the university by this time was Hans' younger sister, Sophie. She too at one point had been part of Hitler Youth but had soured on it. In November of 1938, Sophie had been horrified by Kristallnacht. Many of her close Jewish friends and Jews throughout Germany were attacked by bands of Nazi thugs. Less than a year later, she was equally infuriated when the Second World War began.

Shortly thereafter, the regime forced her to take state work duty in exchange for eventual permission to attend university. She kept her opinions to herself, quietly seethed and completed her national service. In May of 1942, she began to study philosophy and biology at the University of Munich. Her brother Hans met her the day she arrived.

Brother and sister, Hans and Sophie, kept to themselves at first. Then a few weeks later, Hans came to Sophie late one afternoon. "There are some people I want you to meet," he said.

"Who?"

"Some very close friends," Hans said.

There was a basement bar not far from their living quarters. Two evenings later, again in the summer of 1942 while the war raged in Russia and while the Wehrmacht began to lay siege to Stalingrad, Hans led his sister to the noisy student gathering spot: the Rathskeller Kleindienst. At the table waiting was Alexander Schmorell. The other former soldier was now Hans' best friend. With Schmorell was Christoph Probst, Schmorell's boyhood friend and a former Luftwaffe pilot, who was now fervently anti-Nazi. He had been allowed to leave the Luftwaffe to study medicine.

Also at the table was a young man named Willi Graf. Graf had grown up a devout Catholic and had opposed the Nazi party. He believed it to be at odds with the teachings of Christ. He had been arrested by the Gestapo in 1935 for membership in an anti-Nazi Catholic youth group. He later found his way into the army as a medical orderly. He completed his tour in the army in early summer of 1942, landed at the University of Munich to continue his studies, and gravitated toward the classes of a dynamic professor named Kurt Huber.

Huber taught music and philosophy. Born in Switzerland in 1893, Huber was a learned man who achieved his doctorate in musicology in 1917. He had taught philosophy at the University of Munich from 1926 and was a respected researcher of traditional Germanic folk songs. He had published a popular book on the subject. In 1937 Huber became head of the Department of Folk Music at the Berlin Institute of Music Research. In 1938 he was denied a teaching contract at Berlin University because of his alleged "adherence to Catholicism."

Huber returned to Munich to teach in 1940. Huber fascinated his students, particularly because of his wide range of interests and lectures. As a child, he had contracted infantile paralysis. Like President Franklin Roosevelt of the United States, he remained partially paralyzed as an adult.

Huber walked with a limp and he spoke with a severe speech impediment. But his lectures were among the most popular on the Munich campus. They were tinged with anti-Nazi sentiment that many students felt to be a brave voice in the darkness. Many students saw him in inspirational terms, a hero who had risen to the height of academia and intellectual prominence despite being blackballed by the Nazis and limited by his physical afflictions. The Nazi authorities considered Huber to be cripple and therefore not a member of the master race.

In May 1942, when Sophie Scholl entered the University of Munich, Kurt Huber was one of her tutors. Willi Graf was one of her classmates. One time, during a lecture on the banned philosopher, Baruch Spinoza, Huber admonished the class, "Careful! Spinoza was a Jew! Don't contaminate yourselves!"

Knowing it was a dark joke and a criticism of Nazi thought, many members of the class hooted, cheered and applauded. Sophie was in the lecture hall that day. She noticed that there was a girl in the class who was younger than the others. She was light blonde and pretty. Aryan features, some would have said. She had applauded, also. Sophie made a mental note that the girl might be another student she could take into her confidence. She was easy to spot each time she attended: she always wore a small fur cap and a light blue scarf.

Sophie chatted with her after class one day and learned her name was Frieda. Frieda avoided questions about what she was studying, only allowing that she loved books, mathematics and music. Sophie and Frieda became nodding acquaintances, then friends.

Talk like Huber's was dangerous, however. Sophie's father by now had drawn a brief but unpleasant prison term for a casual remark to his secretary.

"The war! It is already lost! This Hitler is God's scourge on mankind. If the war doesn't end soon, the Russians will be sitting in Berlin," he had said.

The secretary was pro-Hitler. She reported him. The Gestapo arrested him. A magistrate sent him to jail for "defeatism."

Sophie told her brother about the lectures. Hans began to attend, bringing along Schmorell and Probst. They sat apart from each other, not wishing to draw attention to themselves as an emerging clique. Sophie and Frieda attended together but sat a few rows apart. The overall atmosphere in the lecture hall was free-thinking. But even the most naïve of students knew that "brown rats," Gestapo infiltrators and informers, were everywhere. Some of them, thugs posing as students, were so obvious and proud of what they were doing that they openly wore brown shirts.

On this night in early June of 1942, the young people at the table laughed, drank beer, ate cheap bratwursts and pretzels and had a shot or two of schnapps to keep things free and easy. Several friends joined them. Frieda smiled and listened. They discussed a book that was popular among the students. It was written by a shadowy literary figure who called himself Bruno Traven.

Traven communicated with the outside world through literary agents who shielded his true identity. He lived in Mexico, where the majority of his fiction was set, including the immensely popular *The Treasure of the Sierra Madre*, published in 1927, for which the motion picture rights had been sold to an American film company. So far the film remained unmade.

Many of the students felt that Traven was actually a German stage actor and anarchist named Ret Marut, who departed Germany for Mexico around 1924. Marut had edited an anarchist newspaper called *Der Ziegelbrenner*, "The Brickburner," that was published in Munich and Cologne from 1917 to 1921. The author's stories were free-wheeling, anti-establishment and free thinking, which made him a cultural hero to the students in Munich. To no one's surprise, his work was banned by the Nazis. So when the students passed his books around, they wrapped them in a newspaper or placed them in a large envelopes.

One of Traven's books that had been published in 1929 had had a resurgence in popularity this year. The book was set in Mexico. It recounted a monumental confrontation in the 1920s between a ruthless robber baron, an owner of a North American oil company, and an indigenous Mexican farmer who lived on a modest hacienda with his family and workers. The name of the hacienda in the novel was *La Rosa Blanca*. The White Rose. The name of the book took its name from the hacienda, *The White Rose*.

Hans and Sophie enjoyed their discussion group with their friends. They decided to make meetings regular. The group was informal yet had a distinct identity. They met first around one table at the Rathskeller Kleindienst, then around several tables as the group expanded.

There was now a boy named Fritz who was on leave from the Luftwaffe. There was a girl named Marie Luise, a chemistry student, and a girl named Lilo whose husband had been killed in Russia in May 1942. Lilo began storing documents and a duplication apparatus in her flat in Neuhausen-Nymphenburg. As weeks went by, some members of the group began printing single sheets of paper with criticisms of the Nazi regime. The papers were then distributed anonymously around the university and the surrounding neighborhood where anti-Nazi sentiment ran high. A girl named Ilse Kleinman was a music student at the university.

She had grown up in southern Germany, just north of the border with Switzerland and became clever overnight distributor of the leaflets. The cat and mouse game intensified with the snitches.

The summer of 1942 drifted by. Sophie's father completed his prison term. Sophie became increasingly worried about the security within the group. Her attention settled on Frieda, one of the youngest members of the group.

Frieda came, listened and laughed, but rarely said anything. One evening Sophie followed Frieda after the meeting. She was shocked to see that the young girl did not return to the campus, but rather went stealthily to a tram. She wasn't a university student at all but was coming in from somewhere unknown. Worse, when Frieda went to her tram she acted as if she was frightened of being followed. She acted as if she had a secret, a big one.

Sophie reported what she had seen to her brother. Frieda met the profile of a traitor.

Hans and Sophie didn't like the way things were going. There was no alternative than to confront Frieda and, for that matter, Ilse, too. Ilse and Frieda seemed to be friendly, as if they knew each other from somewhere else. That in itself was not just suspicious but dangerous in Hitler's nationalistic paradise.

Chapter 9

**New York City.
November 1942**

At half past two on a windy gray afternoon in November, Bill Cochrane presented himself to the offices of the OSS on the thirty-sixth floor of the art deco skyscraper known as the RCA Building in midtown Manhattan. It was four days before Thanksgiving. He entered to find himself in a small anteroom. A woman sat at a wide mahogany desk. She raised her eyes quickly as Cochrane came through the door, removing his hat. Behind the woman was a portrait of President Roosevelt. There was an American flag behind her to her right and a New York State flag to her left.

"I'm here to see General Donovan," Cochrane said before she could inquire.

"You're Mr. Cochrane?" she asked.

"I am," he said.

For good measure, he pulled his driver's license and army identification from his wallet. He showed both. She nodded.

"Excellent. Please have a seat," she said. "I'm Claudia Fekerte, General Donovan's assistant. General Donovan will be with you presently."

Cochrane chose a seat. He thumbed through a *Life* Magazine and then a *National Geographic*. Two minutes later, the intercom buzzed. Mrs. Fekerte stood and looked at Cochrane. "General Donovan will see you now," she said. "Please follow me."

Cochrane stood. Mrs. Fekerte rose and led him a door to her right, which she opened. Saying nothing else, she led him into the room. Donovan, who sometimes wore a military uniform to his office, was today in a dark grey double-breasted suit and a navy blue necktie with small polka dots. He was standing in front of his own desk, his hair grayish white, his jaw sturdy, his body firm and his eyes sharp.

"Ah ha! Bill Cochrane!" he said, extending a hand. "Thank you for coming. It's a pleasure to see you again."

The two men shook hands. General Donovan motioned to a chair and indicated Cochrane was to sit. Cochrane did.

"I'm flattered that you remember me, sir," Cochrane said.

"I remember you quite well," Donovan said, taking his place behind his own wide desk. There was a wall of books behind him. Instinctively, Cochrane gave the shelves a rapid scan. Law books, biographies and histories. Not a piece of fiction in sight. On top of the bookcase was a bust of a man's head. To Cochrane it looked ancient, Greek or Roman. Maybe Plato or Caesar.

"We met most recently at a function for the President," Donovan recalled. "Maybe a year ago. Mr. Roosevelt remains impressed with you."

"He's very generous."

"He damned well should be generous. He's alive because of you."

Cochrane often found himself tongue-tied when accorded praise, not quite knowing how to deflect it. This was one of those times. There were a few more seconds of small talk, then Donovan moved silkily into a pitch.

"I hope you weren't too in love with those dreary Signal Corps at Fort Monmouth. If I have my way, you won't be going back there."

"With all due respect, sir, you seem to be having your way most of the time these days. At least that's what I hear."

"Oh? What do you hear?"

"I hear you're establishing an American spy agency. You and Mr. Dulles. Not a moment too soon in my opinion."

"And who told you that?"

"Just about anyone who knows anything about the intelligence community."

Donovan chuckled. "Well, okay. Good. Commendable," the general said. "You live in New York now, I believe," Donovan said. "You have a lovely wife."

"Yes. We have an apartment in Manhattan. East Seventy-Second Street."

"She's a British citizen if I remember. She works at the British Consulate, does she not?" Donovan asked.

"That's right. In passport control. Your memory is excellent."

"Children?"

"No. Not yet, anyway."

Donovan offered a slight smile. "Probably not the wisest thing," he said, "starting a family in wartime. The men, the husbands and fathers, are going to be away. Who knows how long? Who knows what individual fates might be?"

"Such as getting killed or surviving the conflict?"

"That's one way to put it," Donovan said.

There was an awkward silence. Cochrane didn't help Donovan.

"Well, okay then, let's talk some turkey," Donovan said next. "This is all highly classified, as you'd imagine. When you accept the assignment that I'm going to talk you into accepting, you will be posted outside the United States 'indefinitely.' But we would like to think this might be a four or five month operation from start to finish."

"When is the starting point?"

"It started when you left Fort Monmouth."

"It's that urgent?"

"Yes."

"Then tell me about it."

A slight pause, then, "We have an opportunity that may be developing to get a treasure trove of highly classified information out of Germany. We need a man with your specific qualifications and history to go to Switzerland. Bern. The capital. You know Switzerland, right, from having been there before the war? Bern. Geneva. Zurich."

"Yes, I do," Cochrane answered.

"That's the first step. You'd have to travel under a false identity, which we will arrange here in New York. Your cover is that you're a white collar Canadian criminal. You have some counterfeit plates of American twenty dollar bills and you're willing to sell the plates, either in Switzerland or in Germany. Again, that's the cover that takes you to Bern."

"I would assume that I'm the fence in this operation. I wouldn't know how to engrave and if asked, I'd be revealed."

"Of course. Exactly."

Donovan opened a drawer on his desk, second row, left side. He reached in and withdrew a stack of American ten dollar bills, then he tossed some sample plates on top of the counterfeits.

Cochrane picked them up. He looked at the money. He looked at the plates.

"Quite good," he said. "Who printed these?"

"We did. Your tax dollars at work. At the Bureau of Printing and Engraving."

"Over on Fourteenth and C streets In Washington?" Cochrane asked.

"One and the same. You know Washington well. I like that."

"I've been assigned there more than a little."

"Of course. As I said, there's a complete set in a bank vault in Geneva," Donovan said. "If you're captured and asked to provide the plates, you'll be able to do it."

"Okay so far," said Cochrane.

"The identity you'll be travelling under will be that of a Canadian counterfeiter and confidence man named Abe Stykowski. You'll have to memorize the details of his life before you leave New York. He's a real person. You and he look a bit alike. Face. Size."

Donovan stopped for a moment and opened a pack of cigarettes. He offered one to Cochrane, who declined.

"I should stress the following, Bill. The Gestapo can be abjectly stupid, but they're also stubborn and mulish. They've been assigning people to cases who have a knowledge of North American cities and geography. Expect to be quizzed hard in that area somewhere along the line. Don't make a slip, don't hesitate to think."

"Where is the real Stykowski? There's no chance that we'll turn up in the same ball room in Geneva, is there?"

"None. He's in prison. Leavenworth. If you accept this assignment, we move him to Dannemora and place him in solitary. The cover story will be that he escaped. We'll put some fake stories in the newspapers for the Bund traitors who lurk among us. The escape will be part of your cover story if you need it."

"How long will I be in Switzerland?"

"Not long. A few days, we hope. Again, speed is essential in this operation. Your real destination is Germany, Bill. Berlin. Possibly Munich."

"Good Lord. That's the belly of the beast, isn't it? To accomplish what?"

"You are to retrieve something very important and of the highest priority from an intelligence point of view and bring it back to Switzerland. Deliver it safely to Mr. Dulles, then practically before you change your underwear, escort this asset to the United States."

"What can you tell me about this 'asset'?"

"Nothing," Donovan said. "You find out when you get to Berlin."

"Will Allen Dulles tell me in Switzerland?"

"No. Too risky for you to even have a notion until you arrive in Berlin."

"And you know what it is, my target?"

"Yes."

"But you can't tell me."

"Not 'can't.' *Won't*. You will have to pass through Vichy France to get to Switzerland. Gestapo is everywhere. If you are arrested and tortured, there is always a chance you would talk and reveal your assignment. If you don't know it, you can't reveal."

"So then I get executed and you send someone else."

"I suppose that's what would happen. Yes."

The silence between them turned uncomfortable. Donovan made it more so. "We wouldn't want you running into anyone in Berlin who knew you previously. Do you still have friends there? Contacts?"

"All of my friends fled. Or disappeared."

"I assume the Gestapo would still like to kill you. For what you did on your exit path in 1938."

"That's a safe assumption," Cochrane answered.

"Well, that's what we have to work with," Donovan said. "I won't bore you with a further reiteration of how important this could be. We consider this high risk but worth it."

Cochrane thought it over for several seconds. "May I tell my wife where I'm going or what I'm doing?"

"We would say 'no' to that."

"Who's 'we'?"

"'We' is me," Donovan said. "But 'we' are also realistic. I know a man can't help but talk to his wife, especially a woman as fine and intelligent as yours. Plus she has a security clearance, I'm told. What can I say? Be judicious."

"Thank you," Cochrane said.

"If you're in bed with the woman you love, I'm sure you don't tell spy stories, anyway," he said with a wink.

"You never know," Cochrane answered, trying to keep it light.

"Ha! Too true." More silence, which Donovan broke. "Look, I'll mince no words, Bill. You're a married man. If you are captured, you will be considered a spy. You will not be bartered. Your wife will be a widow." Donovan finished his smoke and snuffed it out in a marble ashtray. "I notice you haven't said, 'yes,' yet, Bill."

"No. I haven't."

"I didn't make the job attractive enough?"

"Nope."

There was a long pause between the two men. Beyond the pulled-down curtain in the office, the sun made a meager attempt to brighten the Manhattan skyline, then gave up.

Donovan leaned back. "Look," he said. "I know this is happening quickly. Take a day to relax. How's your marriage? Good?"

"Excellent."

"Then take a day with your wife. Maybe two days. Talk things over. Could you give me an answer Thursday or late Wednesday? Or by the end of the week?"

"I can do that," Cochrane said. "Does that mean I can phone my wife now and let her know I'm in town," Cochrane asked.

"Didn't you stay at home last night?" Donovan asked with a furrowed brow.

"No. Colonel Sawyer at Fort Monmouth told me to remain quiet until I spoke to you. I stayed at a hotel in Murray Hill."

"Apologies," Donovan said. "That's inhumane. Of course. Phone her and stay at home. God knows, a lot of the people who work for me would welcome their wives not knowing they're loose in the same city." He paused. Then, "Bill, it's your choice whether to work on your own on an independent mission as the one I'm offering or maybe end up as a battlefield communications officer after Europe is invaded. Flip a coin for your chances of survival. It's probably fifty fifty either way."

"I'll phone you in a day or two," Cochrane said.

Donovan looked at a calendar. "Give me an answer when you have it. I'll draw up whatever files you need, both to prime you on your new identity and your background. No point of your seeing anything till you accept, of course. Does that make sense?"

"It does."

"Very good. Oh! By the way," said Donovan, leaning back from his desk, and recalling something he might have otherwise neglected. "You know a chap named Irv Goff, don't you?"

Surprised, Cochrane knew the name. "Sure," he said. "He was in Spain with the Lincoln Brigade. Then he was back in New York."

"He's a friend of yours, right?"

"Correct."

"Seen him recently?"

"Maybe eighteen months ago."

"How is he doing? Do you know where he is now?"

Cochrane thought for a moment. "No. Should I? Do you?"

"Do I what?"

"Know where he is?"

"I'd heard that Irv was in North Africa," Donovan said. "Another story had it that he had contacts with some French *Maquis* fighters in the Strasbourg region. You're familiar with those chaps, I assume?"

"French resistance?" Cochrane countered. "Never met any but I know they're there."

"They're invisible until they're not," Donovan said. "Just like Irv."

Donovan spread his hands. "Ah, who the hell knows with a guy like Irv? " he said. "Seems as if he'd be a useful sort for us. If you ever cross paths, don't duck him. Tell him I was asking. Him and his Commie pals."

"I'll do that," Cochrane promised.

As if on cue, Mrs. Fekerte buzzed again. Donovan picked up the phone and acknowledged his next visitor. Cochrane took the hint and stood. Mrs. Fekete appeared at the door by herself and led Cochrane to a private exit. The private exit led him to the other side of the thirty-sixth floor which led to a separate elevator bank with a private attendant. That in turn returned him to the lobby of the RCA Building without additional witnesses.

*

There was a public communications room for AT&T and Western Union on the first of the two lower levels, commonly referred to "the telephone room under Thirty Rock." Cochrane went to it, grabbed some coins from his pocket and secured a quiet booth. He dialed his home number. Two rings and a familiar female voice answered.

"Laura?"

"Bill!"

"Who else?"

"Are you all right? Where are you?"

"I'm in the basement of Thirty Rock," he said. "I have a new assignment. I'll be home for a few days. I'll tell you what I can about it when I see you."

"Oh, my Lord!" She thought, then asked. "This assignment? How dangerous is it?"

"Dinner and a show tonight?" he asked. "No need to waste a free evening."

"You're on! Even though you didn't answer my question."

"Any requests?

"You know what I like," she answered.

He rang off. Cochrane consulted the theater directory in the New York *Times*. His wife, being English, was a sucker for Noel Coward. He walked to West Forty-Fifth Street where Coward's new comedy, *Blithe Spirit*, was playing at the Morosco Theater. He bought two fifth row tickets in the orchestra level. Curtain time was 8:30.

He left the theater and walked to Forty-Seventh Street and Seventh Avenue where he made a dinner reservation at the big sprawling Brass Rail restaurant, one of the less formal places in the Broadway area. Bill and Laura had frequently gone there before or after a show on Broadway before Pearl Harbor. They always enjoyed it.

Cochrane might have walked home to East Seventy-Second Street, but there was still the issue of his two duffel bags remaining at the hotel in Murray Hill. He hailed a Checker taxi on Seventh Avenue. The cabbie took him to the hotel. He asked the driver to wait, which he did. Cochrane fetched his bags and returned. From there the cab had an easy drive up Third Avenue to Seventy-

Second Street where Cochrane lived in a comfortable brick apartment building.

Cochrane was home by 3:00 PM.

The front door staff warmly greeted him. The elevator man took him up to the third floor where he lived. He knocked on the door. He fumbled with a key but the door opened.

He fell into Laura's arms at the door to their five room apartment.

The embrace was long and laden with emotion. With the world at war, and both of them players, who knew how long anyone would live? An epiphany was upon him. He suddenly realized he dreaded the war and this assignment. He wished that he didn't have to return to Bill Donovan's office or accept the thankless mission being offered.

He stepped into the apartment. Laura pushed the door shut.

"Come on," she said, taking his hand and motioning toward the bedroom. "You've been away too long. I'm your wife. We should get re-acquainted before we even talk."

Chapter 10

**New York City
November 1942**

In April of that year, the US Army had determined that the glow from New York City's lights was silhouetting American ships offshore, making them sitting ducks for German submarines that lurked nearby. Nazi U-Boats had sunk scores of oil tankers and freighters bound for Britain. Under an Army-ordered "dim out," which was less rigorous than a "blackout," the brilliant neon advertising signs in Times Square went dark. Apartment houses and office buildings throughout the city were required to veil windows more than fifteen stories high. Stores, restaurants and bars toned down their exterior lighting. Motor vehicle headlights were hooded. Wattage on streetlights and traffic signals was reduced.

So the Great White Way wasn't as White or illuminated as it had been in peacetime, but even in wartime 1942, it could still rise to greatness. The overall 'dim out' of the city, however, diminished the neon. There was no need to give enemy submarines off the coast or possibly enemy aircraft a way to find their way to an American target.

Cochrane was always a student of history. He was always conscious, sometime too conscious, of the history of places. It was difficult for him to believe that the most famous thoroughfare in New York, if not the world, had once been little more than a meandering former Native American pathway stretching from Bowling Green near the southern tip of Manhattan Island to Inwood at the northern end of the island. The city's original theatrical community started in the mid-eighteenth century when modest playhouses opened along Nassau, John, and Chatham Streets in what became the Financial District. The theaters of New York emigrated uptown over the course of decades.

Laura and Bill Cochrane dined at the Brass Rail, then walked to the Morosco on West Forty-Fifth Street. Comedies and musicals were playing well in 1942. People wanted to forget about the chaos of the world, if only innocently and for a few hours. Bill and Laura were in their seats several minutes before the curtain rose at 8:30 PM.

Blithe Spirit was a hit. The premier had been ten days earlier. The laughs, which everyone needed, had started right after the opening night curtain and had not yet stopped.

On the stage, a novelist named Charles Condomine, the *double entendre* of the name being part of the fun, invited an eccentric medium and clairvoyant named Madame Arcati to his house. She would conduct a séance, hoping to help him gather material for his next book.

The scheme backfired when he was haunted by the ghost of his annoying and temperamental first wife, Elvira, who had been dead for seven years. Madame Arcati departed after the séance, unaware that she had summoned Elvira. Only Charles could see or hear Elvira. His second wife, Ruth, refused to believe that Elvira existed, but then a floating vase of flowers, hilariously rigged with imperceptible wire by some brilliant stage managers, jumped into her hands out of thin haunted air. Elvira's ghost made several efforts to disrupt Charles's current marriage. She finally sabotaged his car in the hope of killing him so that he might join her in the spirit world, but it was Ruth rather than Charles who drove off and was killed.

More wonderful chaos and fun continued through the evening. Throughout, Laura and Bill laughed together, even with the invocation of death. Cochrane gave his wife's hand a tight squeeze several times during the comic haunting. He put his arm around her shoulders and she leaned to him, savoring the evening together.

The play hurtled toward its conclusion. The curtain came down.

The four stars of the show, Clifton Webb as Charles, Peggy Wood as Ruth, Leonora Corbett as Elvira and Mildred Natwick as Madame Arcati came out to take curtain calls. Laura and Bill stood and applauded, although with the witnessing of the spiritual world, hilarious as it may have been, the scent of death hung in the area.

The audience filed out.

Cochrane refused to let go of his wife's hand. They looked for a taxi, couldn't find one, but the night was brisk and clear. They decided to walk home. He wondered if the success of the show had to do with the possibility of laughing at death in a world where death lurked everywhere, from bombings, artillery, rifle squads or bayonets. Through his contacts in the intelligence community, he was even starting to hear stories about concentration camps in Europe. He hoped the stories that were reaching him were not true. But a dark suspicion told him that they probably were.

They stopped on Fifty-Seventh Street at The Russian Tea Room, which was still open for the evening. Cochrane requested a secluded table where Laura and he could talk with no risk of anyone overhearing.

They ordered two vodka drinks: two shots straight up with a small plate of black caviar and crackers on the side.

Until the 1930s and 40s, vodka had been strange, foreign, little known and vaguely seditious. Gin was the white spirit of choice for Americans. Vodka, the "white whiskey,' as some chose to call it, was a foreign interloper. Many barroom cynics labeled it a first cousin to turpentine. The Russian Tea Room had a better selection than almost anyone else in New York: Russian, Swedish and American. Ironically, just when the Soviet Russian stuff was trending, the war had cut off supplies. So now the best stuff was coming from Canada. The second best was coming from bathtubs in Brooklyn with fake printed-in-Crown Heights Russian stamps that everyone winked at. The caviar was also Canadian, the top stuff having been cut off from Persia and Russia. The drinks arrived: a one and a half ounce shot for each of them at eighty proof.

"Don't go away," Cochrane said to the waiter. "Cheers," he said to Laura.

"Cheers!" she said in return. They clicked glasses and each threw back a shot.

The waiter stood by. He looked on in amusement. "Another round, sir?" he asked.

"Damned right," Cochrane said.

"The lady, too?" the waiter asked.

"Damned right," Cochrane said.

Like the theater, the spirit of the restaurant was light. The war seemed far away. Theaters and bars were functioning quietly and efficiently in America's largest city while thousands of miles away millions of troops were preparing for tomorrow or maybe preparing to die.

They ordered a plate of blinis. It arrived. So did the second round of vodka.

"I suppose with what we have to talk about, a liberal blast alcohol would be a good idea," she said.

"I would not disagree," he said.

This time they sipped, working on the caviar and the blinis concurrently.

When the waiter was well beyond earshot, and when the blinis were half gone, he put his hand on hers.

"All right. So what did General Donovan have to say?" she asked. "You know I'm not keen on that man, but you might as well tell me what you talked about."

A beat, then. "He wants me to be a spy," Cochrane said. "Again."

"Oh, Lord," she said. She withdrew her hand in horror. She put it back in sympathy, or some emotion that passed for it. "You can't just go into the infantry and be shot at by a bloodthirsty enemy at like a normal man, is that it? Always these independent one-on-one episodes, right? What else can you tell me?" she asked.

"Not much." He gave it a suitable pause. Another sip of Count Smirnoff's best, then, "You know what General Donovan is like. He comes up with schemes and then says, 'Let's give it a try!' Sometimes he's brilliant. Other times everyone gets killed."

"I know that," Laura said. "I hear the same stories as you do, just not as many of them. Where would you be posted?" she asked.

"Use your imagination."

She grimaced. "I already have. You speak German, you have a history there. It doesn't take a bloody genius. He wants to send you into Germany."

"Yes. I also have to meet with Allen Dulles in Bern."

Laura reacted sharply. "Dulles in Bern? Good Christ, Bill! Donovan and Dulles. The two D's. Mr. Deceit and Mr. Duplicity, that's what people should call them. Or Death and Destruction. That's the top bloody table, indeed, isn't it? I might have known! Damn Wild Bill Donovan and all who sail with him," she said. "How many times is this war going to make a widow out of me? God!"

Laura drained her glass and savored the buzz.

Another suitable pause and, "I haven't accepted yet," he said.

"But you will, I would guess."

"Why do you say that?"

"Because I know you and we both know you will, even though maybe you haven't given him the formal 'yes' he wants. We both know how it works. Your country calls and you would rather be on your own independent assignment where you can assess your own information and control your own survival than be at the mercy of a bad commander who's going to blunder troops in all the wrong directions. It's that simple."

"You know me too well."

"Well, I married you, didn't I?" she answered. "I also know what some of the commanders are like. Couldn't organize a cat fight in a bag, the majority of them, but someone in Washington gives them ten thousand men to command and they think they're Caesar, Napoleon, Wellington and Bismarck all rolled into one. Phooey on them," she snapped as the blood shot to her indignant face.

"Wars aren't won, they're lost," she continued. "Whoever blunders less wins, meanwhile a generation of young men goes to the meatgrinders or Europe and Asia and the only real numbers game is whether more civilians die than soldiers. Verdun. The Somme. Gallipoli. Look at Dieppe just the other day: three thousand young Canadians dead on the beach in an utterly useless, abjectly senseless and thoroughly unsuccessful raid. But ignore me, I'm a cynical middle-aged lady with unpopular opinions."

She finished her drink. Cochrane sat patiently, not disagreeing with anything Laura said.

"Do you see the waiter?" she asked.

"Yes. To your left. Over by the giant red samovar, feeding beef Stroganoff to some tourists. Why?"

"Because we should have a third round, then," she said. "That's the type of evening we've embarked on, isn't it?"

"Fair enough."

Cochrane summoned the waiter. He ordered the third round. Laura was quiet and brooding as they waited for the drinks to arrive, which they did in short order.

She lifted her drink. He lifted his.

"I wouldn't be foolish enough to ask any more impertinent questions," she said. "To our good health."

"To surviving the war. Both of us," he said.

They drank their final round of vodka. They paid and departed.

Back out on the street, Laura leaned to him. He placed an arm around her and she buried her face on his shoulder. "Good God," she said. "I know what happens to us is small in terms of the world. But I'm going to be worried sick until I see you again."

"I won't take this assignment without your blessing," he said. "I can't do that to you."

"I don't know what to tell you," she said. "I don't see any reasonable answers. Not in this world that's run by a bunch of insane belligerent men."

Chapter 11

**New York City - Manhattan
November 1942**

It was past midnight when they stumbled out of The Russian Tea Room, the last couple to leave the dining area. The bar would be busy for another hour: local actors, musicians from Carnegie Hall, grifters, discreet call girls and those who liked to associate with them.

Laura and Bill were greeted by the night doorman when they arrived home. They stumbled into the elevator, then into their own apartment, Dr. Smirnoff's prescription working wonders on the nerves and the libido.

They went for the bedroom first, fell into the bed left unmade from that late afternoon. They made love passionately, knowing that their time as a couple might be nearly at and end, or might last several more decades.

They drifted off to sleep. A few hours ticked by.

Cochrane woke shortly before 3:00 AM, coming out of an uneasy sleep. Perhaps everything here in New York was too normal. Then again, this was a strange form of torture, being home with the woman he loved, among his books and whiskeys and newspapers, an island of calm when the world was at war, a war that he knew was waiting for him.

He couldn't get back to sleep. Next to him, Laura was breathing evenly. He put his hand on her shoulder, felt her respond, still in sleep, then pulled it away.

He rose from his bed and walked through his apartment. He kept the lights off in his living room. He went to the window and pushed the dark heavy curtain a few inches to one side. He looked down over East Seventy-Second Street. The city was sleeping, even if he wasn't.

On any night in Manhattan there was usually one respite from activity in most neighborhoods. No taxis or buses. No pedestrians, not even a drunk or a hobo. He glanced at his watch. It was 3:06 AM. Normally, the respite came to his neighborhood around now. Tonight it didn't. Why?

He gazed at the street three floors below him. A lone sanitation truck quietly cruised the street like a big peaceful tank, its lights dim. There were two men on the street in overcoats. One was walking a large dog. They stopped to talk to each other.

A surveillance team? A security detail of some sort? People watching him? A homosexual assignation? Two friends who recognized one another? None of these?

He tried to dismiss the men on the street and channel his thoughts.

What else did he know about Wild Bill Donovan's new operation? Cochrane had more on-the-street experience than most of the other people being recruited into the new spy agency. He had had experience in criminal investigation and, factoring in the episode with the spy named Siegfried that he had thwarted, he had experience in counterespionage, also.

He had heard back channel stories from peers. He knew the new OSS was informal, iconoclastic, freewheeling and nimble. Donovan was smart and cautious, but sometimes impulsive at the same time.

Several members of the OSS were officers in one branch of military service or another. But day-to-day the agency had a level playing field: military rank meant little and unorthodox ideas meant a lot. Cochrane also knew that the new American spies were mostly anti-Communist but would cut deals with the Reds, also.

Well, that made sense, he concluded in his dark apartment. If the enemy of one's enemy was one's friends, the filthy Bolsheviks were to be embraced, were they not? They were at war against the Nazis, right?

It was so quiet that he could hear the ticking of the Seth Thomas clock on his mantle.

He pondered further. He had heard tales about Donovan's people having a special place in their hearts, for example, for any warrior who had fought Fascism and Franco in Spain.

Donovan had also loaded the OSS with so many die-hard Reds that they had become a joke in Washington. To the post of Chief Latin American Division of the OSS, Donovan appointed a man named Doctor Maurice Halperin. Halperin regularly attended CPUSA meetings and altered the information which came across his desk to fit the current party line, sometimes to the point of absurdity. Halperin was secretive. He kept the door to his office locked. When the door was closed, other OSS employees - even his friends - liked to joke that, "Our dear Maurice is having another cell meeting." It was odd, even suspicious to an outsider. But no one on the inside thought it was strange.

The thought of Halperin reminded Cochrane of Donovan's mention of Irv Goff, their mutual acquaintance. Cochrane had come to know Goff when they were together at the National Police Academy in Washington in 1933. Subsequently, Goff had been a captain in the US Army and the Lincoln Brigade in Spain. He was later chairman of the Communist Party in Louisiana and New York. His exploits as a guerrilla in Spain had been the inspiration for Ernest Hemingway's novel, *For Whom the Bell Tolls*.

Donovan liked colorful characters. So did Cochrane, but not quite as much. Goff was one. He had grown up in Brooklyn and Long Island. As a young man, he had been a body builder. Goff had become famous as the "Adonis" of Coney Island's Muscle Beach. He had worked as an adagio dancer and professional acrobat before becoming an organizer for the Communist Party in New York.

During the horrible Civil War in Spain, Goff participated in Battle of Teruel, working behind enemy lines again with Communist-backed Spanish guerrillas who were attacking supply lines and blowing up railroad tracks used by the pro-Franco forces backed by Nazi Germany. He was a warrior. "Say whatever you want about Irv," said one mutual friend who knew him, "but he's built like a brick shithouse and blessed with a set of brass nuts."

No argument ensued. If you were in a fight, you wanted Goff watching your back.

In May of 1938, while Cochrane was still in Germany, Goff had commanded part of a successful amphibious operation on the southern coast of Spain. The raid resulted in the rescue of three hundred Republican prisoners held in the Fort of Carchuna. Far left or not in his political philosophy, Goff got results and that was what Donovan respected.

Cochrane and Goff and their wives had dinner in Manhattan at Luchow's on Fourteenth Street one evening in February of 1940. Goff had read all about himself in Hemingway's novel. He was contemptuous of the book. He was equally disdainful of the proposed movie version of the book, currently in production with Gary Cooper and Ingrid Bergman. By this time, Irv had soured on Hemingway, too, whom he used to call a friend. He didn't care for anyone very much this evening, present company excluded.

"The way the stupid Robert Jordan character in the book blew up that bridge," Goff complained. "The way Ernie described it? Complete and utter bullshit. How's that for literary criticism?"

"Pretty precise, Irv," Cochrane answered over wiener schnitzel and Berliner Weiss. "What part didn't you like?"

"I didn't like *any* of it! The Jordan guy did it like he was blowing a seam in a goddamn coal mine. I've blown up fucking bridges, man," said Goff, who would talk like a sailor even with ladies present. "A hell of a lot of them. You put a detonator in the explosives and then you get your sorry ass out of there as fast as possible. You'd better be twenty miles away when it blows. If the rocks and debris don't kill you somebody's soldiers or security cops will. Or maybe a pissed off farmer will shoot you just for sport. We went after bridges and railroads as much as we could in Spain. Usually the detonator would last five or six days behind the lines. You leave it there and let someone else worry about it."

"Yeah, well how about that Ingrid Bergman?" Cochrane asked, referencing the soon-to-be released movie.

"How about her, meatball?" Goff snorted. "That's bullshit, too. I never saw Ingrid Bergman in all the time I was in Spain. If I had, I might still be there."

At that point, Goff's wife elbowed him sharply. He finally laughed. The use of "meatball" meant Goff liked someone.

"Those two and a half years I served in Spain," Goff mused at the end of the evening. "Nothing as exhilarating will ever happen to me again."

"You fought the good fight," Cochrane answered. "But Franco and the Fascists won."

"Don't remind me, Bill," Goff said, his expression turning very sour. "I feel I left Spain without blowing the heads off enough Fascists."

Cochrane paused. "Did you have a personal victory, maybe?"

"Yeah. Sure! It was in Spain that I learned that all men could be brothers. Even now, wherever in this lousy world I meet a man or woman who fought for Spanish liberty I feel like I'm walking in a refreshing rain shower. I sense a kindred soul. Nothing will ever break that bond. We left our Goddamned hearts there, Bill. Our blood, our hearts and our souls. God damn it! We left everything behind except our bodies and some of us left those, too."

He leaned back, his eyes red, half from rage, the other ninety percent from alcohol. "I think Donovan feels the same way. That's why he tolerates us. Christ knows he's not much farther left than Louis Quatorze; you know, that French king with the funny hair and the castle?"

Goff shook his head.

"But you know what kills me, Bill?" he continued with bitterness. "You know what claws at my guts and busts my balls every night? Yeah, meatball, you're right. Franco won. The fucking Fascists won. And now, what the hell? What if Hitler wins? What if Mussolini wins? God damn it, what kind of world are we looking at when it's run by bastards like that?"

Cochrane didn't have an answer. Laura didn't, either.

John Edgar Hoover hated Reds, no one doubted that.

Hoover often dispatched agents with dossiers to Donovan with FBI snitch material on Maurice Halperin, Irv Goff and various Communist OSS employees. Hoover demanded that they be terminated: no regrets, no questions asked, and no explanations given.

Donovan often picked up the phone and replied, "Oh, come on, J. Edgar. I *know* they're Communists."

"If you know they're Communists, why did you hire them?"

"That's *why* I hired them, John Edgar. Because they're Communists. Now don't bother me, which is a polite way of me telling you to lay off and get lost."

If Donovan didn't hear Hoover's phone slam down after a few words like that, he considered the call a failure.

The presence of Communists in the OSS was a source of ongoing frustration for Mr. FBI. He sent his files to Franklin Roosevelt. Roosevelt spiked them with a chuckle.

Eleanor Roosevelt was vexing. She had been one of the country's most vocal activists on behalf of the Lincoln Brigade. Her close friend Joseph Lash, the author and left wing politician, made her a present of a small bronze statue of a Communist soldier in Spain. She kept it on her desk.

For Hoover, if there was anything worse than a man he couldn't control, it was a smart educated woman whom he couldn't intimidate. Hoover had an enemies list and Eleanor was near the top. Irv Goff was on it, too. Hoover's list wouldn't have been complete without Eleanor Roosevelt and Irv Goff on it. The feeling was mutual.

Cochrane knew a few of the special agents who were assigned this task of alerting the Roosevelts about Communists. He had worked with them as a peer. He tried to tell them they were wasting their time.

"Hitler tells us to do it, so we do it," one of them, a Special Agent named Jack Mayo once said. "Of course, it's pointless, Bill. But what the hell are we going to do?"

"You mean Hoover, not Hitler, right?" Cochrane corrected. "You said, 'Hitler.'"

"Oh, Did I? Yes. Of course. My mistake. Hey, don't tell anyone I said that, okay?"

In his New York apartment on this moody ghost-ridden November night, Cochrane sighed. His clunky three-in-the-morning dream vanished to wherever dreams go to hide until next time. He tired of watching the street. He released the curtain. He glanced at the clock above the fireplace. As he looked at it, it struck three thirty. From his own bar, he poured himself an Irish whiskey. Two solid fingers of the best stuff he owned.

He walked to the sofa in the living room, his mind alive with images of life and death, haunted by friends who were no longer living and some who were but who had disappeared to other corners of a tumultuous world. He settled back on the sofa. He closed his eyes, trying to find order in the sleepy overstressed chaos of his thoughts.

Irv Goff. Who knew if Irv was even alive or if he'd gotten himself killed?

Everything about the man was more than the sum of its parts, or seemed to be, except when it was less. Goff had sent Bill and Laura a Christmas card in 1940, an attractive woodcut with a snowy scene of Washington Square in Greenwich Village, wreaths on the Washington Square Arch. Cochrane had kept the card on his desk and pondered its implications well into the following March.

"Do you think there's a message here?" Bill finally asked Laura, showing her the card again. "Something about the Square? A rendezvous point, maybe? A hidden message or signal? Am I missing something? What the hell is Goff up to?"

"As Dr. Freud once said," Laura answered, "'Sometimes a cigar is only a cigar.' Maybe Irv just wanted to send a picture of Manhattan in the winter, dear. Have you thought of that?"

"No," Cochrane had answered. "I hadn't."

In his apartment above East Seventy-Second Street, Cochrane drained his whiskey glass, leaned back and almost started to snooze. "What a cesspool of a world," he thought. And I'm going to get killed for this?"

He drifted.

The next thing he knew, on the mantle in his apartment on East Seventy-Second Street, the Seth Thomas clock chimed four times, signaling 4:00 AM.

When it stopped, Cochrane heard a voice. Female. His wife's. Simultaneously, there was a sympathetic hand on his shoulder.

Then, "Bill?" Laura asked.

His eyes snapped open. He turned, startled. She was sitting next to him.

"You all right?" Laura asked.

He blinked half awake. "Yeah. I'm fine. A bit restless," he said. A beat, then, "Just doing some thinking."

She reached to a lamp and turned on a low watt bulb. "Can't imagine why," she said.

She embraced him and they kissed.

"How long have you been sitting next to me?" he asked.

"Ten minutes. Maybe fifteen. Come on," she said. "You can't worry about what you can't control," she said. "Come back to bed. You need some sleep."

"Yeah," he said. "I know."

"Listen to me," Laura said. "You should accept his assignment. I've thought about it. You'll have a better chance of surviving the war if you are left to your own resources. So do it. You have my prayers and my blessing. All right?"

After several seconds, "All right. Thank you," he said.

"Now. Make me two promises," she insisted.

"Anything," he answered. "I'll do my best."

"When you're in Switzerland, buy me a wristwatch," she said. "It doesn't have to be expensive. Just a sound watch in good taste. You pick something out that you like. I'm sure I'll like it, too."

"That shouldn't be difficult," he said. "Okay."

"That's only the first promise," she said. "The second one? You have to bring it back in person and place it on my wrist yourself. How's that? Will you do that for us, then?"

"I promise," he said.

They started back toward the bedroom. She did not release his hand.

They lay together very close as they both returned to sleep.

Chapter 12

**Nazi Germany
November 1942**

i

Despite countless speeches, statements, rants, curses and gestures to the contrary, Adolf Hitler had never won the trust or respect of his army officers. Nor had they ever warmed to him. Much of this grew from his innate sense of inferiority as a lowly ex-corporal from upper Austria during the Great War of 1914-1918. Hitler's first instinct, even as he rose in political power in Germany, was always to stand at rigid attention in the company of all these medal-bedecked old-guard Teutonic warriors. He looked at them as threats and potential adversaries, even when they now came to him to solicit approval. They rarely wanted his advice, but his approval was frequently necessary.

Sometimes he referred to them derisively as, *Die Oberschist*. The upper class. In Hitler's opinion these doddering dinosaurs who were left over from the previous war had been in charge of protecting Germany and standing up for traditional values. And they had failed.

He could have predicted it, he explained to the Nazi hierarchy. While Hitler had been slogging through Belgium and France, eventually suffering a wound in his thigh at the Battle of The Somme in defense of these traditional German values, these men were sipping Asbach Uralt far behind the lines. He knew, or thought he knew, that in the opinion of men like these, wacky little Austrians like Hitler were best suited to be cannon fodder.

Those who surrounded Hitler in the upper reaches of the Nazi pantheon, men like Himmler, Goebbels, and Heydrich, felt much the same way. Even Hitler's porky Air Marshall, Hermann Goering, was sympathetic.

"My army," Hitler complained bitterly at a party function in 1939, "is reactionary. My Navy is Christian. And my Air Force is National Socialist."

Indeed, Goering had fed a small armada of new Nazi party recruits into the Luftwaffe, the newest branch of Germany's military. The Protestants in the Navy were obedient and susceptible to Nazi orthodoxy. But the army remained a problem. It remained deeply monarchist, even to the point of continually organizing celebrations every January twenty-seventh on the birthday of Kaiser Wilhelm II, the last German Emperor and King of Prussia, who habitually wore a white glove on his withered left arm, the one that was six inches shorter than the right. Wilhelm had gained a reputation as a swaggering militarist through his belligerent speeches and ill-advised newspaper interviews, his foot never far from his mouth.

He reigned for thirty years, was forced to abdicate in 1918 and pass the rest of his life in cranky exile in the Netherlands until 1941 when he died. But the army, much to Hitler's vexation, still celebrated his birthday.

Nonetheless, many of these officers had presided over Germany's defeat. Hitler was unforgiving. Despite the fact that he had never risen above corporal, he proclaimed himself, "a genius." He told this to his ardent followers and they believed it. He felt his military skills and instincts, which he made up as he went along, based on no sound knowledge of situations, terrain or logistics, were superior to the methods taught in the prestigious academies and military schools. He wasn't shy about telling people so. He felt he should impose his instincts and strategies on these pretenders who had failed to maintain Germany's greatness. The rest of the goose-stepping German population agreed with him. They admired him. He had re-armed the nation when the generals couldn't. His true believers were content to follow him anywhere. He had a vision to restore the greatness of Germany.

Gradually, to the best of his abilities, he began to replace the professional military people, just as he had replaced intelligence and police agents who didn't appear loyal to him. For Hitler, dumb unquestioning devotion was paramount.

To rid himself of as many of the top professional soldiers as possible, Hitler used his two most powerful associates in the Gestapo: Reinhard Heydrich and Heinrich Himmler. Employing various intrigues of sexual blackmail and smears, he dishonored and discredited General Werner von Fritsch and Field Marshall Werner von Bloomberg. Von Fritsch was alleged to be a homosexual and linked to male prostitutes, a specious charge. Von Bloomberg was married to a woman half his age who had once posed for erotic photographs and worked as a prostitute when she needed money at age nineteen. After those two men were discredited, the opposition to Hitler in the army was tentative and reeling back on its heels. Everyone had something to hide and that's what the Gestapo was for: to find those dirty secrets and exploit them.

While it seemed omnipotent, the Gestapo was a very small organization. By late 1942, the time when Hans Wesselmann presided over the execution of two men on an icy tarmac in Marseille, its active officers within Germany numbered fewer than fifteen thousand. They policed a population of sixty-five million people. In Düsseldorf, with a population of half a million, there were no more than one hundred and twenty Gestapo officers on the day Hitler declared war on the United States in 1941.

Most rural towns had no Gestapo presence at all. The Gestapo was underfunded, under-resourced and over stretched. By the time Gestapo agents were sent to occupied areas in Belgium, France, and Poland, it was stretched even further. Everywhere they looked, there were enemies of the state, the vermin that dragged down the magnificent Aryan people: communists and socialists, religious dissidents, Jews, disobedient students, Gypsies, the retarded, the crippled, long-term criminals, prostitutes, homosexuals, immigrants from the east and the Balkans and juvenile gangs. Thank God, thought men like Hans Wesselmann, for someone like Hitler to lay down the law to these people.

Even though the numbers were against them, those in the Gestapo did not see their agency as being weak or inefficient. To make up for a lack of staff, the Gestapo used the vast majority of the obedient population to its maximum effect. This was the golden age of snitching, and these "ordinary Germans" took great pleasure in reporting what they might have seen or heard to Gestapo agents, even the slightest anti-Hitler utterance in a casual conversation. It was called 'denouncing.' It worked.

Once the proper purges had been made to the traditional army, Himmler and Heydrich analyzed who in the Gestapo had been most helpful in completing their tasks. One man stood out among the others. He was the sturdy young man from the countryside named Hans Wesselmann.

ii

Hans was a career bureaucrat who had elevated his profession to a crude art form. He was not intelligent or gifted. But he was opinionated and stubborn as a mule. He might have become a farm laborer but instead worked hard at school with rote memorization. The approach worked in most subjects. His goal was to get himself into the German government bureaucracy, a position which would get him a pension later in life. He had the body of a thug and learned weaponry from ex-soldiers in his family. He joined the Munich State Police in 1926.

The Munich State Police opposed the Nazis until 1933. But thereafter, the Nazis took control of the Munich police and some, including Hans, found themselves at ease with the nationalistic race-baiting philosophy of the new regime. Wesselmann had been born in Hesse in 1897. His father had been a gravedigger. In 1916, he joined the army and fought on the Western Front until he was captured by the British. He spent the rest of the war as a prisoner and returned to Germany in 1919. As a soldier, he had been awarded the Iron Cross Second Class. After a series of odd jobs and unemployment, he used his army contacts to train as a policeman. He became a cop in Berlin in 1931 and wore a uniform he was proud of.

Germany was rising again. Wesselmann went to hear Hitler speak several times. Enthralled, Wesselmann joined first the Nazi party and then the SS in 1932.

Adolf Hitler said things that Wesselmann thought but didn't dare say. The former corporal had suffered the same indignities thanks to the Communists and banking cabals and the other traitors who had sold out Germany. With Hitler, Germany could be great again. Wesselmann made a vow. He would die for Hitler if he had to. His devotion was that fervent.

And so it went until one day in 1935 when an SS drinking companion, an ex-convict named Otto Kruger, sidled up to him one evening in the lounge of a brothel. Otto asked if he could introduce Wesselmann to a special friend. Wesselmann said he had no objection.

Otto signaled with a hand to a sandy-haired man who was watching from the bar. The man nodded, left the company of a woman who was naked except for stockings, came to their table and sat down. Otto explained that the friend, Gunther, was a major in the SS. Gunther spoke easily, treated Wesselmann as an equal and showed great deference. There were a few minutes of small talk. Then Gunther mentioned that Wesselmann had come to the attention of people very high up in the Nazi party.

"As high as the office of Heinrich Himmler, himself," said Otto reverently.

At first Wesselmann thought he had done something wrong and was in trouble. Gunther kept talking. He asked if Wesselmann would consider taking a job that would have him doing something special for his nation and his race.

"Of course," Wesselmann said.

"The job is not much different than what you are already doing as a policeman," the man said. "But it will require you to be tough and uncompromising. Sometimes even brutal. Sometimes the tasks are distasteful but they must be done. Interested?"

"Definitely."

From there the recruitment was easy. Wesselmann resigned his job as a Berlin policeman and became an agent of the *Geheime Staatspolizei*, the Gestapo, the Nazi secret state police. He remained in the SS.

Hans was as subtle as a slash to the throat. He worked as hard for his new masters as he had for his old ones. He was a functionary from head to toe, wrapped up in regulations, statistics and notes, memos, regulations and civil codes. Gradually, he began to get out of the office and crack heads. His superiors unleashed him on troublesome leftists and Jews and Gypsies. Soon his personal reign of terror was well known in Munich. His skills at formal denouncements, blackmail letters, and terse quasi-literate threatening letters soon rose and expanded to medieval style torture, pistol whippings and secret executions by Luger.

Wesselmann rose quickly through the ranks. He was a key participant and some celebrated cases. There was, for example, a Protestant Evangelical minister named Paul Schneider who opposed the Nazification of Lutheran churches in Germany. Schneider was reported to the Gestapo in Berlin. Wesselmann investigated and arranged for Schneider to be banned from preaching. While many of the churches accepted Hitler, or stood by in silence, there were some who were starting to cause trouble. They needed to learn some lessons.

Wesselmann led a Gestapo team that arrested the meddlesome priest one morning at 3:00 AM. Wesselmann arranged to send him to the Buchenwald concentration camp. Guards placed him in solitary confinement. Schneider still refused to shut up. From memory he would recite passages from the Bible from the window of his cell to comfort other inmates every evening.

For this, the small Gestapo and SS contingent at Buchenwald beat him brutally. The camp commandant offered him the chance of release if he signed a declaration promising never to preach again. Schneider refused to sign. What more could one do? On July 18th, 1939, he was killed by lethal injection. He was twenty-seven. Good riddance to a noisy enemy of Adolf Hitler.

Then there was the case of a communist activist named Hanna Koch. Koch was a student of foreign languages at Friedrich Wilhelm University in Berlin when she apparently became disloyal and fell in with a notorious socialist resistance group called the Red Orchestra. A loyal neighbor wrote out a report of Hanna's deplorable activities and sent it anonymously to the Berlin Gestapo. Wesselmann was on duty that day and seized the case for himself.

Wesselmann led a raid on Koch's flat. They found an anti-Nazi leaflet she had translated into French, an article meant for slave laborers working in munition factories in occupied France. Wesselmann had many problems with women. If they weren't in a brothel, he had little use for them. The so-called educated ones were the worst. They too needed to learn obedience.

Wesselmann led the interrogation of Hanna. He tied her to a chair and stripped her to her waist. He beat her. He demanded to know who else had worked on the document.

"No one," she insisted. "I translated this myself. I found it at the university. It was probably dropped off by a German soldier who has been to the eastern front. Are you aware of the crimes our armies commit or do you prefer to not see them?"

He slapped her savagely across the upper body. It was obvious Hanna was protecting others. But the silly woman wouldn't break. During her interrogation, Wesselmann tied her with her back to a sizzling radiator pipe in a standing position. He tore her blouse off as she faced him. He beat her, the flesh of her back against the pipe as he pummeled her. He told her that she would be treated more leniently if she were smart enough to remember the names of other collaborators within the group. "Now! Answer me!" he insisted. "I insist on names!"

"That would make me as low as you are," she said. She spit in his face.

She went on trial for treason. She was found guilty and sentenced to death. Her parents appealed to Adolf Hitler for clemency, but the Fuehrer knew best what was good for the war effort. He personally refused their request.

At the age of twenty-two, Koch was guillotined at Plötzensee Prison, Berlin.

Wesselmann's superiors congratulated him on his exemplary work. They awarded him a medal. Shortly after Koch was beheaded, Wesselmann was promoted to high lieutenant, Kriminalkommissar.

In Munich in 1938, a few weeks after Kristallnacht but before Christmas, there were rumors about a small theater that was showing American movies and anti-Nazi cartoons from America. The ex-policeman took it upon himself to find out who was dealing in such prohibited material. He tracked down the theater; it was in a hidden section of a cellar beneath an auto repair shop.

Hans visited one evening when six employees were present and the screen was dark. He produced a Mauser that Himmler had gifted to him, lined the employees up against the wall and shot each of them. He calmly walked out, then returned with two liters of kerosene and set the place ablaze. Locals authorities declined to investigate either the murders or the arson.

Himmler and Heydrich were elated. They had at least found a man with no intellect, no conscience and totally without any scruples, remorse or morality. They needed dedicated men with such unusual and laudable composition. And now they had found a stellar example in Hans. They had several delicate assignments. They knew Wesselmann would be perfect.

There had also been the sordid business of a former *Frankfurter Zeitung* reporter who had become a member of the S.D. and had been stealing more than his fair share of expropriated Jewish property, fencing it, and fattening a numbered account in Switzerland with the proceeds.

Himmler brought both these cases to the attention of the Fuehrer, who personally knew the two perpetrators. Hitler, furious, ordered the execution of both men. The SS major so fond of ballet executed his final *pas de deux* one night when a violent thug broke into his home at 4:15 AM, pulled him out of bed, bound him, gagged him and hung him by the neck with piano wire from the antique pink crystal chandelier in his living room.

92

Two months later, the former reporter suffered an equally cruel fate. A small slim man, he was easy to overpower. He was surprised in bed one night by a gunman. His Turkish houseboy who was naked in bed with him was shot twice in the head and neck. The former reporter was then dragged from his apartment, bound in rope, gagged and pushed into the trunk of a small construction truck. Still alive, he was taken to the Glienicke Bridge on a sleet-filled night, tied to a two hundred pound diesel engine while still alive and struggling, and dumped into the black waters of the Havel River, which connected the Wannsee district of Berlin with the Brandenburg capital Potsdam. The Havel rarely yielded its dark bloody secrets. No investigation followed.

With these missions accomplished, Hans never missed a day at his office. He was a logical choice when Himmler was faced with an even more serious breach of security, one of people and classified information disappearing to the Allies. The same case involved a scandal involving a woman, a student in the Munich area, who was a traitor to the Reich.

Heydrich and Himmler discussed the case for a day, then came to the same conclusion.

"We'll assign it to Hans," Himmler said. "Hans Wesselmann."

Himmler agreed. They shared a drink and a laugh over the prospects.

Chapter 13

**New York
November 1942**

"Excellent!" said General Donovan the afternoon of the next day. Cochrane and Donovan were again in the office at 30 Rockefeller Center. "That's your final answer? You'll do it?"

"I'll go to Berlin for you," Cochrane said.

"Let's be clear," Donovan said. "Not for me. For your country."

"For my country," said Cochrane.

"I have a file ready for you to read," he said. "You'll have a private office here. Study the file, particularly your new identity. We'll have a new passport for you. You'll need to get to Portugal from New York, then continue to Switzerland. We'll arrange the travel. Portugal will be the easy part. From there to Switzerland to Germany will be the rough links, the dangerous ones in and out of Germany. We'll do everything we can here. Thank Laura for me personally. She's making a sacrifice, too."

"Portugal, huh?" Cochrane asked.

"Portugal," said Donovan. "Lisbon. These days the world is a better place thanks to Portugal."

Portugal was a unique venue.

The same day that France and England were declaring war on Germany, the Portuguese dictator Salazar officially declared that the alliance with England did not bind Portugal to enter the war. This decision had been negotiated with England beforehand. The neutrality of Portugal benefitted the allies. England in particular could use Portuguese ports.

"I've met Salazar," Donovan said. "He's a handsome guy, part failed monk, part bookkeeper and part mystery man," said Donovan. "He runs the country from a sparsely furnished, unheated office. He puts Portugal before all else and has to be approached that way. He's got the shrewdness and parsimonious habits of a Portuguese peasant and had the cold detached outlook of an intellectual Catholic. From what I hear, he has a signed photo of Mussolini on his desk."

Cochrane grinned grudgingly.

"The Portuguese people are grateful for not having to fight the war," Dulles said. "This gives our friend Salazar room to maneuver. He can fabricate the image of a Father, protector of the land, a savior. That's the thing about most dictators, you know, Bill. They secretly want to be loved. Sometimes not so secretly."

"I get it. May I ask you some questions?" Cochrane asked.

"I expected you to. Fire away. As many as you wish."

"Just one or two for right now. I'll wait till I see what's in the file. But I'm curious on several points. First, your contact is well placed in the Reich. And he's has been leaking material to us. Correct?"

"Correct."

"And he says he has another boatload of material."

"Correct again."

"How did you find him?"

"He found us. He contacted an American he knew before the war. A man who currently highly placed in the OSS."

"I assume that's you."

"You assume accurately."

"Have you yourself seen the information this source in Germany is giving?"

"Yes."

"And it's solid?"

"More than solid."

"How did you contact him in return?"

"I contacted Dulles, who was still in London. Dulles took it from there and contacted the gentleman in Germany. Through intermediaries."

"Could you give me a hint of the process?"

"For starters, notes in a dead drop in Berlin. A brick wall on a side street off the Kurfürstendamm. The information goes to Dulles first. Then Allen passes along what's relevant to me."

"When did you see the product most recently?"

"Yesterday. Half an hour before you came in."

"How is it getting to you so quickly?" Cochrane asked.

"High speed blips across a telephone line. Dulles has a one-time code book that matches one here and one in Washington."

"I've had some experience with such things," Cochrane said.

"I know. I remember."

"How did you get set up with that system here?"

"Good question. Follow along," Donovan said with a laugh.

The new system had to do with the lack of train service in Europe, Donovan explained. Within hours following the German takeover of Vichy France in the latter weeks of 1942, a frozen curtain had descended around the Swiss borders. There was no more commercial aviation, except between Switzerland and Germany. All that remained were single well monitored "government" flights every other day from Lisbon, Rome and Madrid, one round trip from each city.

Train service eventually resumed between France and Switzerland, but the searches at the French border were meticulous and exhaustive. Passengers coming from Germany or going to Germany were obliged to disembark from their original trains, walk a hundred meters past armed German soldiers and board connecting trains. Only Reichbahn trains could travel in Germany. Swiss trains were *verboten*.

"You'll run into this yourself when you're ready to travel to Germany, Bill," Donovan said. "It's neither easy nor pleasant."

American and British diplomats were even denied basic courier service in Switzerland, Donovan continued, so there was no chance to pack goodies into the diplomatic pouch. The only end-run that was possible was a slow and circuitous route via the Peruvian consulate in Switzerland which carried - for a "fee," which also might have been considered a black market bribe - a diplomatic pouch to its embassy in Lisbon, where a local gangster named Felix would pick it up, leave via the back exit at night, and deliver it to the U.S consulate disguised as a case of tennis balls the following day.

So far, the system worked. But who knew who was reading what? The whole system and set-up could implode any day.

Aside from dead drops and courier arrangements involving mail, radiotelephone and telegraph remained the only means of communication between those in Switzerland and those on the outside. But Donovan's people in New York and Washington and Dulles's people in Bern needed to communicate with each other quickly and efficiently. They found a way.

Typically, Dulles or an agent in Switzerland, would commence telephone calls around midnight or 1:00 AM local time on a scrambling device attached to a covert phone in an embassy, consulate or in Dulles's case, his home. The calls would go to Germany and to the United States. The early morning Swiss hours were essential to catch the end of a business day in Washington and New York. A missed day could cost an agent his or her life. German calls were made on Swiss time. Within the last week, Donovan had created a second extension for the phone system in the building at 30 Rockefeller Center. Only he and a top assistant named Bloomfeld had access.

"It's in the room next to us here, Bill," Donovan said, indicating the unused doorway to his left. "You have to walk through this office to get to it."

"And it works smoothly?"

"Smooth as a wet cough drop," said Donovan.

Now, blips, dots and dashes shot through the night skies and landed in specific telegraph and telephone devices at a unique line in a heavily guarded room in Washington or at Donovan's office in New York. The messages necessitated the OSS crew using clumsy one time code pads that had a cipher of randomly selected letters and characters printed on every sheet. Dulles's senders had to translate each message according to the cipher for a single specific sheet.

"On the Bern end of all of this," Donovan explained, "Allen Dulles is taking some steps to alleviate some of the torture and speed things up. He thinks he has a solution. Ask him about it when you arrive if you wish and if you're curious. You'll be amused. It will illustrate how he gets things done in Switzerland."

At length, Donovan handed a file to Cochrane. He assigned Cochrane a reading room in the same suite of offices. Mrs. Fekerte led Cochrane to the room. There wasn't much in it. A desk, good lighting and a good chair for reading. The windows were frosted and faced east. Cochrane could see out only through a small letter box slit in the glass. Cochrane was free to come and go as he saw fit. There was a Marine guard on duty, armed, and Cochrane was obliged to return his file personally to Donovan each time he left the premises, such as to the rest room down the hall.

There was little in the file on the actual assignment in Berlin. Cochrane would receive a more detailed file in Switzerland. For now, he was to focus on his fake new identity and the fake personal background, that of Abe Stykowski, the Canadian confidence man and forger.

The next day a photographer came by with a camera, a comb, a hairbrush and five different shirts. Cochrane was to change shirts and comb his hair differently from picture to picture. The photos were for various fraudulent pieces of identification that would be created.

Cochrane read a detailed summary of Stykowski's career and arrest, trial and imprisonment. He spent the next two days memorizing details but was able to go home and relax with Laura each night. Thanksgiving came and went. He began to dread the day that would soon come when he would have to ship out. But that sentiment was common, he knew. Millions of men would be shipping out in the next few years. That's what a war was all about.

He focused on memorization: the details of his fake life, his fake past. What the file didn't know, the file invented. If pressed, hopefully he could fake this way through. Hesitation or contradiction could be fatal not just to him but to the whole operation.

On the fourth day an "interrogator" came by to start quizzing him. The questions were rapid fire, Gestapo style. Hometown? Married? Destination? Reason to be in Germany? And so on.

The fifth day, a Saturday, was smoother. They broke for Sunday.

On Monday of the following week, a German speaking interrogator with a Hamburg accent turned up by surprise. The man wore a monocle and could have passed for a drill sergeant. But Cochrane held his poise over a three hour interrogation. The interrogator, then, staying in character, rose and abruptly left without speaking further.

New clothes were created and issued. Cochrane tried them on. Minor adjustments were made, fake labels sewn in. The clothing and a few other objects were packed in two large Canadian made duffel bags, which in turn were packed in two suitcases. Cochrane would jettison the two exterior bags when he got to Geneva, at which time his identity might again change under Allen Dulles's direction.

The OSS engravers in New York created two new passports. One was for Stykowski. Cochrane would start the trip with this one and carry it. The second was for a man named Henri Bremer. Same picture. Bremer was Canadian, also. The creators had used different pictures and had creatively retouched them, giving the impression of different men taken at different times. Additionally, there was also was a forged *documento de identidad*, purportedly issued in Madrid. Cochrane had a Cuban accent to his Spanish but many Spaniards had fled to Cuba in the twenties. The extra cards would be stitched into his luggage. He would need a knife to remove them. There were also extra needles and thread in a small packet. The packet looked like clothing repair but was actually for re-stitching the lining of his bags.

One thousand Swiss francs were also sewn into the lining of each duffel bag, the currency being accepted anywhere in the world. There was also a thousand dollars in American currency, aged banknotes of varying denominations. Finally, Cochrane received an envelope filled with Third Reich currency, including coins. As he examined it, he recoiled from the sight of the swastika on the money.

"That's a fair bit of money," said Donovan, alluding to the cash. "I hope you stay out of the casinos as you travel."

"I'm not a gambling man," said Cochrane.

"Nonsense. If you work for the OSS, you gamble. The stakes are just higher."

*

Cochrane spent his final evening at home with Laura having a quiet dinner at a neighborhood bistro on Third Avenue and Sixty-Ninth Street. It was named *La Fille du Roi*. It was run by a French couple who had emigrated to New York in the late 1930's. The couple proudly flew the French flag outside their eatery, though France had fallen in 1940. They had family in Normandy but hadn't heard anything from anyone for several weeks. They were scared, they said.

Neither Laura nor Bill told them that they were scared, too.

Chapter 14

Nazi Germany
1940s

The rise of National Socialism and the war had been impacting Frieda's life for as far back as she could remember. Her mother had been murdered due to some political activity and her father was never around due to his "obligations to the Reich." She had moved from one school to another and spent summers and holidays with an uncle and aunt who lived in the south near Switzerland. As she entered her teens, though, she grew quieter and disappeared into herself, accompanied by books and a love of music.

Near where she lived with her uncle in Bavaria, there were open fields and a little country chapel that was nearly abandoned. The chapel had an organ. It was wheezy and dated from the 1890's but it retained a warm vibrant sound. The house of worship was on the edge of a potato farm. It dated from the 1700's and still had a caretaker who also worked on the farm.

A neighbor taught Frieda how to read music and how to hold her hands at a keyboard. She picked up the technique quickly and learned piano. She spent afternoons and evenings playing Lutheran hymns, Chopin études and Beethoven sonatas. In a trash can one day she found some sheet music from the 1920's that was no longer in vogue and dangerous to own. She salvaged it and learned the jazzy and syncopated melodies of New York, Paris and Berlin of the 1920s, the wonderful stuff that German radio couldn't play anymore.

In Berlin when she stayed with her father or with her father's friends, there was a local library. She started reading her way through it. Then came the book burnings. One by one, her favorite authors were not just removed from the library but thrown into pyres ignited by the representatives of the "new Germany" who celebrated the "reanimation of the German spirit" over "decadence and moral perversion."

Into the flames went the works of Albert Einstein and Erich Kastner, a local writer of children's stories whom she loved. Sigmund Freud went into the fires, as did Stefan Zweig and Thomas Mann. She liked Bertolt Brecht and had seen some of his plays in Munich where they were first performed but now those were banned. There were Americans included: Jack London, Theodore Dreiser, Helen Keller and Ernest Hemingway, seen as "a corrupting foreign influence. And there was a special place in Nazi hell for a former German soldier who had been badly wounded in World War One named Erich Maria Remarque. The Nazis hated his seditious work, *All Quiet on the Western Front*.

"Unpatriotic," said Joseph Goebbels of Remarque's work, based on the author's own experiences in the trenches.

Goebbels personally banned the book in 1933 and had it removed from all German libraries. To sell it in a bookstore would be to invite your windows being smashed and your store being torched. There was probably no more unpopular book in Germany. Former soldiers from World War One called it, "literary treason," though few with that opinion had actually read it.

Remarque, an erudite man who had served in the German army, was no one's fool. He had fled to Switzerland in the mid-1930s. But even Helvetia was too close for comfort. In 1938 the Nazi government revoked his German citizenship. One never knew when some Nazi sorehead was going to dispatch assassins. Remarque and his wife fled to the United States and settled in New York in 1939. Almost three thousand other writers and journalists also fled Germany during the years of Hitler's ascent.

There were writers and artists of whom the Nazis approved.

One was a man named Hanns Johst who wrote a play called *Schlageter*, which was an expression of Nazi philosophy, first performed on Hitler's 44th birthday in 1933. In it there was a line, "Whenever I heard the word *culture*, I take the safety catch off my automatic."

The phrase was popular in Germany, widely attributed to many heroic leaders. To Nazi followers, people who read books were to be equated with Jews and should suffer the same consequences.

Frieda was very much a pragmatist. She was not blind to what was going on in her country and in her country's name. Far from it, she knew too well the state of the world. It depressed her, as did the stories she heard from her growing circle of friends when she visited the University at Munich.

The main building of the university was a single red-roofed structure on tree-lined Ludwig Strasse in a quiet section of Munich. The building had low rows of Italianate windows which prevented the edifice from looking like a dormitory. It bordered on Munich's artistic section, Schwabing, where dissident thought was either ignored, permitted or welcomed.

By wartime, most of the academic departments at the University of Munich had been taken over by Nazi party ideologues. The best professors had been dismissed. Many who dissented openly were conscripted into the Wehrmacht. They would be sent without proper training to the Russian front so they could "learn about Communists firsthand." The tone of the wartime university was set by a Nazi speaker at the university, Hanns Schemm, who announced the firings. He had previously presided at a book burning in Munich.

"From now on," Schemm told the remaining professors in 1940, "it will be your job not to determine the truth of anything, but rather how it advances the National Socialist movement."

Nonetheless, certain departments remained free of Nazi dogma, probably because no one thought they were important.

*

One night in October of 1942, there was a brilliant full moon in the sky above Munich. The members of White Rose abandoned the usual Rathskeller and headed for the English Garden, Munich's sprawling oddly named park which was near the university. They put out blankets, drank wine they had chilled in the nearby river and ate pretzels and pastries. Alex played a balalaika and Hans played a guitar. The weather was still mild and the war seemed far away.

"If you're a student here, how do you avoid the Nazis?" Frieda asked.

"Just avoid them. Some of them wear brown shirts even though they're students."

"No. I mean when you're taking classes," she corrected.

Sophie Scholl taught Frieda and then Ilse how to pick through the system. In doing so, she learned that Ilse had been Frieda's connection to the university, a friend she had grown up with, two years older, who had first encouraged her to come over and listen to some of the lecturers.

"You avoid classes like 'Racial Hygiene,' 'The history of Jewish Subversion of the West' and 'Folk and Race,'" Sophie said. "The names of the courses are dead giveaways."

"Focus on things like chemistry, mathematics, biology and philosophy," Sophie's brother Hans added. "Do you want to join us here? That would be great if you did."

"I don't know. That would be next year. I hardly know about next year." She paused. "I need to talk to my father."

The other students had heard references to her father before. They knew not to follow up.

Afterward, Frieda settled back, zoned out of the conversation and just enjoyed being with her friends. She dropped her guard and pulled a small brown notebook out of the bag she always carried. She opened it and started to look at rows of numbers, add them, and repeat them. It looked to the others like she was playing some sort of numbers game coupled with a memorization exercise.

Finally, Sophie noticed and tapped Ilse, wondering what Frieda was up to. Ilse laughed and shrugged.

"What's that?" Ilse asked Frieda.

"Something I'm doing for my father," she said.

"A bunch of numbers?" Sophie asked.

Ilse took the notebook from her friend's hand. The series and sequences of numbers were incomprehensible to the other students.

"What *is* this?" Sophie asked. "A bunch of meaningless numbers?"

"It's a code," said Frieda.

"For who?"

"Me," she said. "Just for me. Only I know the key."

"What good is that?" Hans asked.

"Plenty."

Frieda smiled and stashed her notebook in a secure coat pocket.

Earlier that afternoon, on a walk through Munich, Frieda happened across a Nazi monument called *The Eternal Watch*. The monument was in Koenig Platz in the center of the city. Munich was considered "The Capital of the Movement." There were Nazi shrines everywhere. The monument was comprised of several massive stone pillars that loomed over sixteen sarcophagi. The latter contained the remains of the sixteen early Hitler followers who were killed during the 1923 putsch when Hitler was little more than a troublesome local loudmouth. The police had dispatched Hitler's storm troopers with some well-deserved gunfire. Many had fallen. Sixteen had died, along with four Munich police officers. The Fuehrer, as he was known even then to those who worshipped him, was arrested and tossed into jail, serving nine months of a five year sentence in Landsberg Prison. He used the time to write *Mein Kampf* and come out of jail more dangerous than ever.

Now, in Munich in the autumn of 1942, *Eternal Watch* was Munich's most formidable monument. Frieda had stood to look at it in horror. It was ringed with motionless but very much alive SS guards in their imposing threatening black uniforms and knee high boots. They were staring right back at her, lecherous, treacherous, ominous, silent and threatening.

Anyone passing the monument was required to raise his or her arm in a Nazi salute.

Frieda hated that salute and refused to ever do it.

She had turned and run.

"Would you like to join us at the university?" Hans said, repeating the question asked earlier. The friendly inquiry pulled Frieda out of her vision of Eternal Watch.

"That would be great if you did," he said. "We keep to ourselves. We'll outlast the war. Hitler will fail or be deposed eventually," he said. "In the meantime, we steer clear of the Nazis as best we can."

One glass of wine too many, Frieda smiled indulgently. She leaned back and looked dreamily up to the moon and stars.

"Maybe," she said.

"What else would there be other than university?" Ilse asked. "A job?"

"Maybe I'd like to be like Bertolt Brecht or Erich Maria Remarque," she said. "You know. I'd like to write books and music and the rest of it."

"What's the rest of it?" Hans asked.

"Move to the United States," she said. "I think I know a way."

Her friends grinned and teased her good naturedly. Maybe she was dreamier and more unrealistic than they had thought. It didn't matter. They had accepted her. For the first time in her life, she had a close circle who understood her.

Frieda turned her head toward Sophie. Sophie had a large envelope containing a sheaf of papers, leaflets that Lilo had printed.

"What are those?" Frieda asked casually.

After a slight pause, "Anti-government messages to be posted all over Munich," Hans said. "We have to do it very carefully and not get caught."

"Oh," Frieda said.

"Want to help us distribute them?" Sophie asked.

Frieda thought about it for less than five seconds.

"Sure," she answered. "Why not? Give me as many as you can spare."

Chapter 15

**New York
November 1942**

The next morning, Cochrane packed carefully. Laura took a day off from her work at the British Consulate to assist, critically running her eye over everything Bill was taking, trying to pick out anything that looked unnatural or that wouldn't mesh with his new persona. Cuff links with initials were packed away in a drawer. No clothing with name labels. No authentic identification. At certain moments, she choked with emotion and had to leave the room.

When Bill was packed and ready, she went down to the street with him. He would need to stop by Rockefeller Center first for a final visual inspection. A soldier would drive him to the airport.

Cochrane hailed a taxi. He turned to his wife and they embraced.

"Just come back alive," she said.

"I promise," he said.

They held each other as if they never wished to let go.

"I'll see you in a few weeks," he said.

"You better."

"With your new watch."

"Just come back alive," she said. "To hell with the bloody watch."

They released each other. She stepped back. Bill Cochrane spoke to the taxi driver and stepped into the yellow cab. He settled into the back seat.

As the driver pulled away, Bill waved.

Laura waved back. She watched the cab disappear across East Seventy-Second Street. When the cab left her view, she lowered her hand, turned away, and fought back the tears.

At 30 Rockefeller Plaza, there was a final orientation with Allen Dulles and his top assistants, which included the inspection of Cochrane's luggage and travel gear. When it was over, Donovan walked Cochrane to the private elevator.

"There will be an unmarked army Jeep waiting on Forty-Sixth Street to take you to Idlewild," he said. "The man at the wheel will be a Marine lieutenant in civvies. He'll be armed. They all are these days. I don't expect trouble here Stateside, but you never know. There are a couple of American Bund members out on Staten Island who are tipping off German U-Boats as to locations of ships leaving the harbor. Hoover's people are closing in on them. Can you imagine? Our country opens its doors to these people and they betray us."

"I can imagine," said Cochrane.

"I guess you can at this point," Donovan said.

They stood near the elevator without calling it.

"Tell Allen that things are falling into place on this end. Tell him Helen Bougrat says hello. Former girlfriend who now works in my office here," Donovan said. "Translator for some Vichy French stuff we stole."

"I'll convey the wishes. Are you coming down to the street with me?" Cochrane asked.

"No," Donovan answered. "Not a good idea for me to be seen with you and vice versa. Plus there's always the chance some homegrown Nazi nut could get off a potshot."

"At you or me?"

"Yes," said Donovan with a laugh. "Maybe two potshots."

Donovan extended a hand. Cochrane accepted it.

"The other day when we were first talking about this mission, you likened it to a raid. Get into the enemy territory, grab what you need, and get the hell out as fast as you can. I liked that. A raid. Fast. Keep that in mind." Donovan finally released Cochrane's hand.

"I'll do that."

"Good luck, Major," said Donovan. May God protect you."

Cochrane was in the elevator and down to the street.

He found the Jeep easily. The ride to the airport took an hour. The Marine driver said little, but assisted Cochrane with his luggage at the Pan American Airlines depot. When finished, the driver gave Cochrane a crisp salute, guessing correctly that Cochrane was an officer.

"Good luck, sir," he said.

"Good luck to you, too," Cochrane said, returning the salute.

Chapter 16

**Lisbon
December 1942**

i

The aircraft out of New York was a Boeing 314 Clipper, a flying boat that took off from Jamaica Bay, the body of water adjoining the airport. The flight was in the air by 5:00 PM. It encountered severe turbulence in the mid-Atlantic halfway to its destination and extreme turbulence above the Azores as it neared the Iberian peninsula. During both bouts of rough air, the framework shook violently. At least one time Cochrane, who already hated trans-Atlantic flying, thought the flight was going down.

But it didn't.

It passed the Azores after ten hours, then lowered its altitude and descended through a heavy wet mist at six in the morning local time. It began a decent toward Cabo Ruivo Seaplane Base in Lisbon, Portugal.

From the window, breathing easier but exhausted, Cochrane could see the awakening ancient city below, decaying, shabby, decadent and beautiful, its history and ancient architecture frozen in place and time. The glories of empire had begun in the "Age of Discovery" and had lasted six centuries. They were in current decline. From the air it appeared as if Lisbon was in need of reinvention. But on the final descent to a water landing, Cochrane could see shops opening for the day and morning trams rattling through Lisbon's cobbled streets. Much like the rest of occupied Europe, most people needed to go about their daily routine. Cities thrilled Cochrane. Lisbon was a wonderful old city with a great history.

He also knew that Lisbon was the hub of the universe for European refugees fleeing the war. Among those who had successfully emigrated to America through Portugal were the artists Max Ernst and Marc Chagall and Arthur Koestler, the author.

With that thought in Cochrane's head, the plane hit the water and skidded to a glorious halt. For Bill Cochrane, the first leg of his impossible journey was complete and, he reminded himself, he was still alive.

ii

His connecting flight would not be leaving for Geneva for two more days. He registered at a hotel in the city and kept as low a profile as possible. On the first day in Lisbon, he took two long walks in the afternoon and one more in the evening, just to observe and to listen. It wasn't unusual to see military uniforms, Luftwaffe and RAF, Abwehr, Vichy French and Royal Navy.

He bought four books to read, two in German including a biography of Richard Wagner, the composer, and *Vol de Nuit* in French. He had seen the great 1933 film based on Antoine de Saint-Exupéry's brief novel about the early days of night flight in Argentina but had never read the book. Then he selected one in English, F. Scott Fitzgerald's *Tender Is The Night*, which he had also never caught up with. Fitzgerald had dropped dead in Hollywood two Decembers earlier. The clerk wrapped the four books in two bundles to protect them from the rain. The bookseller was pleased to receive payment in American dollars.

Cochrane knew Lisbon superficially, having visited one three occasions during his previous time in Europe. At a flea market he purchased some shirts, two ties, a belt and an extra pair of slacks, and a rugged pair of hiking pants in case he was pushed to terrain tougher than city sidewalks. All of these he chose to help him blend in. At one table in the market there was an old man selling toys and games. The man had a handsome collection of used games: checkers, dominos and playing cards.

The merchant was a small man with beige skin and a hooked nose. He was gracious and polite. He struck Cochrane as an Arab of some sort, as were many of the merchants in the market. Cochrane's attention settled upon an antique set of dominos. The merchant came to him. There was some fumbling over which language in which to converse, but the conversation quickly settled into English, Portuguese being a tongue that Cochrane had never attempted to master.

"May I examine these?" Cochrane asked.

"Of course, sir," the seller said with a slight nod.

"They're quite beautiful."

Cochrane picked up a domino tile. The game pieces were ebony and bone with a fine patina of age. The tiles had wear but were free of damage. The set was contained in a wooden box with a sliding top. The box served as the carrier for the pieces. In faded lettering, there was an English language street address in Cairo. There was co-equal lettering in Arabic.

"This particular set was carved and created in North Africa," the merchant said gently. "Egypt it would appear. Before the reign of Queen Victoria or perhaps around the time leading to the American civil war. The 1940s or 1860s. You're English? American?"

"Canadian," Cochrane said.

"A pleasure to meet you. My name is Masud. My family was from Cairo. These would have been quite common in the cafes of the City of a Thousand Minarets." He paused. "The tiles are carved from animal bones, probably a camel's, inlaid with ebony. Quite exotic, don't you think?"

"Very much so," said Cochrane. "Fascinating, sir."

"A gift?"

"No. I'm looking for things for diversion during hours of travel or hotel stays. I already have some books. These might be good."

"They may also bring you good fortune," Masud said. "In China, you know, dominos have long been used for prediction. Divination. In the West, Gypsies of the Romany empire have told fortunes with dominos from the seventeen hundreds to this day."

"In what manner do they do that?"

"I'm told that in the same way that Tarot cards have an intimately connected divinatory significance, so dominos have a mystic meaning in divination and fortune telling. It is conveyed through their comparative values revealed by their spots."

"And you can do this?" Cochrane said with a smile. "Tell the future?"

"Not always. But we can do it together."

"The future interests me, sir. How would we do that?"

"You reach to the box without looking and select a tile. If you are to have the finest good fortune, if God is to smile upon you, the domino will have dots that total a high number, preferably even. An uneven number will indicate that you are on your own and must create your own beneficial fortune, though a high number by itself suggests better luck than middle or low numbers."

"Why not just draw again if you don't like the results?" Cochrane asked.

"Night must fall and the sun must rise to the midpoint of the sky before you draw again."

"I see," Cochrane said with an amused smile. "Always a catch, right? Well, let's see how it works."

Masud smiled and watched. Cochrane looked away. He reached to the box and drew a tile. There were two sets of three dots. Six, an even number.

Masud, an excellent salesman, bowed.

"The higher the even number," he said, "the better the good fortune. Possibilities range from two to twelve. You are in the middle."

"Seven would the middle."

"I consider six the middle," Masud said with a wink. "So should you. And in the world we live in, any moderate good fortune is better than none."

"Agreed, sir," Cochrane said. "Very true. This *is* a beautiful set. How much are these?"

"What currency do you have?"

"Swiss francs."

"Most excellent. Fifteen francs."

Cochrane guessed that Masud had named a high price to be negotiated down. But why mess with good luck?

"I'll take them," Cochrane said. "You're an excellent salesman, Masud."

"And you are a gentleman, sir."

Masud wrapped the set in heavy paper and placed it in a bag. Cochrane gave a final nod and turned to go. Masud placed a hand on his arm, stopping him.

"Ah! I must tell you," Masud said.

Cochrane turned to listen.

"I must beg you to please indulge my one superstition with this set of dominos. I know the location in Cairo where these were created. Many craftsman have worked there for centuries at a market such as this one near Saints Sergius and Bacchus Church. It is believed to have been built in an area where the Joseph, Mary and the infant Jesus rested at the end of their journey into Egypt." The man raised his finger. "When you are finished with this set, if it brings you good fortune, pass it along to someone you care about, perhaps someone you love. You will be passing along the good fortune that accompanies it. Will you remember that?"

"Masud," Cochrane answered. "I would have difficulty ever forgetting that."

"Good day, sir."

"And to you, also."

Cochrane returned to his hotel, took dinner in a nearby restaurant, examined his books and dominos and slept. Already, the good fortune was working, he felt.

*

On the second day, he wandered the city again. On the second evening, he stopped for a drink in the bar at the Hotel Aviz. He lingered over several glasses of port. The Armenian oil mogul, Calouste Gulbenkian, a former petroleum engineer who had become rich from Iraqi oil, was present at the hotel, complete with two bodyguards with not-so-subtly-concealed Lugers sitting behind him while the oil baron conducted meetings. The bodyguards sat at a table behind their employer, each holding a pistol across his lap. It didn't take long for Cochrane to spot the third bodyguard, sitting by the entrance to the bar, a newspaper across his lap, watching everything, the nose of a particularly large pistol poking out from under the paper.

Gulbenkian was buying up as much of Henry Rothschild's art collection as he could cart away. Negotiations were going on at the end of the bar in the Aviz. The trained spy in Cochrane insisted that he listen in.

As he strained to hear the conversation, with hundreds of thousands of British pounds and Swiss francs tossed around like playing cards, Cochrane suddenly realized that a small jazz band was playing in an adjoining room. Perhaps the music had been going for an hour and he only noticed it now. He didn't know. He heard it only in imperfect fragments, same as the many conversations upon which he had eavesdropped.

Cochrane's old instincts started to kick in and kick in fast. By design, he fell into casual conversation with anyone who would talk to him. Everyone knew something. Less than two days on the street and it was obvious that the British and the Germans had ramped up their intelligence activities under the surveillance of the Portuguese secret police. The locals got in on the act as informers. Desk clerks, cleaning staffs and bartenders at hotels reported gossip. Prostitutes used pillow talk to extract shipping movements from drunken sailors. Rumor was rampant. The streets ran with paranoia. It was a hell of a place.

He finished his port. My God, he thought to himself, two weeks ago he was set to become a signal corps officer. Now he was right back in the midst of things, from the FBI frying pan into the OSS fire, in a place rife with spies and killers, swindlers and con men, all in the employ of some country's treasury.

Anything was possible. Anything that could happen could and would. There was no avoiding it. An attractive dark-haired English woman came to the extra seat at his table and sat down, uninvited.

"Buy me a drink?" she asked.

After a moment, "Sure," he said. "One. How's that?"

"That would be good," she said.

She said her name was Victoria, but half the women in England of her age were named Victoria. He gave his fake name. He guessed that she was maybe twenty-five, give or take. She wore a dress with a hem well above the knee. She kept crossing and uncrossing her very shapely legs and the hem kept working its way upward. Cochrane knew where the direction of the encounter would eventually go. She finished her drink and looked at him expectantly as a waiter came by.

"Would you like dinner?" Cochrane asked her.

"You'll buy me dinner?" he asked.

"I'd be pleased if you'd join me," he said.

She accepted. The same waiter served the meal.

They started a brief conversation about the war. She confirmed much of what he had gleaned about the city, already. She also mentioned where the German officers were staying in Lisbon but also revealed that they wore civilian clothes on the city streets.

Afterwards, she casually proposed sex in a nearby hotel where she had a clean room and said it would only cost twenty American dollars and she would do for him anything he desired. Nothing was out of bounds, she said. He politely declined, at which time she finished her drink with a long gulp, got up, and shot him a disappointed glance. She stepped away from the table without saying anything.

His reaction went from mild resentment to sympathy for the woman, who looked as if she had been reduced to this by the war. She had sounded educated, her accent middle class. Had her husband been killed? He wondered. But he was not in mood to betray his wife's trust or bring extra risks or complications upon himself.

"Victoria?" he asked before she was out of earshot.

She turned.

"Come here, please," he said.

She returned. He discreetly handed her fifty Swiss francs from his billfold.

She looked at the money in astonishment. She accepted it.

"Thank you," she said. The money disappeared into her dress.

"Good luck with an exit visa," he said. "Are you trying to get back to England or somewhere farther afield?"

"Dublin," she said quietly. "Or the United States, but that's probably impossible."

"I understand. Be careful," he said.

Impulsively, she leaned forward and kissed him on the cheek. Then, before her good fortune could evaporate, she turned and fled the bar.

Cochrane finished his drink. He missed Laura and his home. He set out for a short walk by the river back to his own hotel. There was a curfew. A glance at his watch told him he could beat it

At first the stroll was uplifting. In Bairro Alto, the nightlife-rich bohemian quarter, Cochrane took in a view of Baixa, the area that was comprised of magnificent plazas, wide avenues and tremor-proof Pombaline architecture that rose after the city was destroyed by an earthquake in the Eighteenth Century. The area sparkled with movement as did its surrounding hills. To his right, the Tagus River swirled ominously toward the Atlantic Ocean and who knew how many lurking submarines. Then a fog and river mist reminiscent of London rolled in as he walked. The low cloud gave a distinctly film noir atmosphere to the city.

Unavoidably, such was a perfect setting to kick his mind fully into reverse gear and force him to review the events of 1937 and 1938 when he had been in Nazi Germany the first time. He had barely lived to come back to the United States and tell about it and mumbled a prayer that he would come back again.

As he arrived back at his hotel and as he went to sleep that night, the full events of his first tenure in Germany played out in the front of his mind.

There was no stopping the events. The past unraveled before him much like the way the events had first occurred.

Chapter 17

**United States and Europe
1934 – 1939**

In June of 1934, Bill Cochrane entered the National Police Academy of the Federal Bureau of Investigation. He neared completion of the five months of training that had a dropout rate of 43 percent. He drew excellent marks in all fields: crime scene analysis, visual memory, forensic chemistry, firearms, description, identification, unarmed attack, and self-defense. From his days as a US Army ordnance officer, he knew enough about high level explosives to practically teach the course himself.

Upon graduation, Cochrane was sent to Kansas City, where he was soon going cheek-to-jowl with a gang of railroad-yard thieves. Then he was reassigned to Chicago, where he passed six weeks. Some Sicilian gorillas were edging into the funeral home business at the expense of some honest German-American undertakers on the North Side, making substantial contributions to the overall funeral industry at the same time.

Next, Bureau headquarters in Washington sent Cochrane swimming into some deeper water. He went to New York posing as a County Antrim gunrunner for the Irish Republican Army. In lower Manhattan and Brooklyn, Cochrane put together a good infiltration effort among the Jewish mobsters along Delancey, Hester, and Canal streets - Meyer Lansky, Waxey Gordon, and Whitey Krackauer - and from the nether side of the Brooklyn Bridge, Lepke Buchalter, Gurrah Shapiro, and Mendy Weiss. These were the presiding experts at running weapons in and out of New York. And there was no shortage of customers. Everyone, back in those days, had someone he wanted to shoot. Sometimes, even an entire group of people.

While he was at it, Cochrane uncovered and blew the whistle on several middle-range operations associated with the same gangs, mostly shlom jobs in the garment centers that had to do with sash weights and lead pipes massaging the skulls of labor organizers.

By mid-1937, President Roosevelt himself was concerned about access to information in Europe should the United States be drawn into another world war. The US, after all, had never engaged in espionage abroad.

He asked a Wall Street lawyer and world war hero named William Donovan to travel to Europe and study how an intelligence service might be established. And second, he launched a personal directive to J. Edgar Hoover to establish a foreign branch posthaste.

At the invocation of the word "foreign," J. Edgar Hoover remembered a letter of application Bill Cochrane had sent to the FBI in 1934. He abruptly recalled Cochrane to Washington to prepare for European service.

Cochrane traveled by the Polish liner *Pilsudski* from Washington to Bremen, working under the cover of an American businessman sympathetic to Hitler's National Socialist Party. His only orders from the FBI were, "Find out what you can, and don't get caught. More than likely, we won't be able to get you out."

*

Bill Cochrane's arrival in Berlin in 1937 coincided with a state visit by Mussolini. Cochrane was grateful for the public activity. Easier for him to move around the city and become oriented. Better for him to observe.

The old Germany, the one he had read about, was still there. The polite, orderly people, the handsome blond children. There were the quaint, aging gingerbread buildings both from the medieval period and the previous century. And there were the stark iron monuments erected to those who had sacrificed themselves "for the Fatherland" in the Great War.

But then there was the New Germany. Everywhere, particularly upon Il Duce's arrival, there were the new red and black facades. Everywhere there was a march. Everywhere there were swastikas, Hitler Youth, *Hitlerjugend*, evening parades by torchlight, and grandiose, overstated new buildings.

Once, on a hot afternoon, Cochrane fell into step with the front phalanx of marchers. Wearing a fedora, a suit and tie, he was mistaken for a plainclothes party official and seated on a podium behind the Fuehrer himself as the mad little corporal gave a rousing speech. Had Cochrane felt like sacrificing his own life, he could have shot the little lunatic in the back. In later years, he wondered if he should have.

Daily in Berlin, along the tree-lined main boulevards was a sea of long vertical banners, proudly alternating with the trees and fluttering. On long poles topped by golden eagles waved the red banners of the Third Reich with a black swastika in a round white field at the center. These in turn were interspersed with the red, white, and green banners of Fascist Italy. The displays were powerful and impressive, none more so than from the center of Berlin along the Kaiser Wilhelm Strasse leading to Hitler's new Chancellery in pink marble.

The pink glint of the seat of power suggested an incongruous touch to Cochrane's American sensibilities. In the coffee and tea shops he struck up conversations with Germans and discussed the bold new Nazi architecture. Twice Cochrane was told what everyone else in Germany seemed to know.

"Hitler likes pink," they told him.

Cochrane pondered this as he found himself an apartment. When he ceased to think about Hitler's predilection for pink, he was struck by the fact that both the United States and Nazi Germany now had an eagle as their symbol. And there, he concluded, the similarities ended.

About a week after his arrival, Cochrane faced certain disaster. There lived on a side street only a few blocks from the Reichstag a large, smiling, bookish bespectacled tailor named Kurt Kurkevics. The tailor, a Latvian, had been on the FBI payroll for the previous six months. But when Cochrane ambled by Kurkevics' home and then his shop, the tailor was nowhere to be found. The home was locked and dark, the shop boarded up. Cochrane's contact in Berlin had been uncovered and, most likely, executed.

Cochrane then improvised. He opened a brokerage house and spent his free hours lounging around the bar at the Kaiser Wilhelm Hotel. He took into his confidence anyone with whom he fell into conversation and mentioned that he had inside information on the American stock market. When investors grinned and offered money to him, he at first demurred, then accepted it a few weeks later purely out of friendship. Within two months he had cabled a million and a half dollars' worth of investments to the United States.

Fortunately, most of them turned out well. More business walked in. Cochrane considered his good fortune to be a gift from a providential God. Until he had arrived in Germany, he had never followed the US stock market. He knew virtually nothing about it, other than having overheard a friend from Chestnut Hill, just before leaving Washington, comment that everything would be going up within a year.

German friends, some in the party and some in the government, took him into private offices in buildings on the Tierpitzufer where the supreme intelligence communities were housed. Once he met Himmler and shook hands with him. Another time he was introduced to Admiral Canaris, the head of the Abwehr, or intelligence division. Canaris, Cochrane quickly learned, was a lightning rod for the few remaining anti-Hitler factions within the government. And on one grand but nerve-shattering occasion, after a performance of *Die Walküre*, the American was in the same ballroom as Hitler and Goering. Cochrane again worked his way remarkably close to the Nazi 'brain trust.' He spent the evening studying the two men in their medal-bedecked uniforms with red bands and sashes. Cochrane moved close enough to Hitler to smell the overdone Viennese cologne in which the jittery little tyrant bathed. The two men, for one fleeting dazzling moment, even established eye contact, though Cochrane felt it would be presumptuous and risky to initiate a conversation. So he did not.

Always, Cochrane was introduced as a financier willing to do business with Germany. He used his real name and actual passport. Introduced to diplomats and to those with influence within the party, a catch phrase developed. "Our sympathetic American friend," they called him. The diplomats and power brokers would nod, smile, and boast in civilized conversational tones of their plans for a new German empire, a new world order, make that, now that the Jews, Socialists, and Communists were on the run and could no longer pollute the Reich.

"I personally praise Hitler for that above all," Cochrane would confide to them. Then Bill Cochrane complicated his life. He fell for a woman. Her name was Theresia and she said she worked for a prominent man named Otto Mauer in the Interior Ministry.

It was Bill Cochrane's first serious involvement since the death of his first wife.

He first met Theresia on an evening in the bustling Rathskeller Keitel, not far from where they both worked. He was already seated when a single woman in her mid-twenties, tall, dark-haired, and with high cheekbones, took the table next to him. She wore a black skirt, a loose pale pink sweater, and around her neck, fastened with a gold pin, was a striking red silk scarf.

Cochrane spoke first, admiring the scarf. He asked her in German where she had bought it. At first, she was reserved, modest, letting him lead the conversation. But the talk blossomed. He joined her at her table.

Two nights later, they attended the cinema, followed by a late coffee. Then they shared a brandy. He walked her home. She admitted that he fascinated her because there were so few Americans left in Berlin. He told her she fascinated him because she was so beautiful, which she was.

An affair began. Some nights she would sleep over at his place. Other nights he would stay at hers.

Then, about a month and a half after it all began, Theresia spoke out in the middle of a night. It was past 2 AM. She couldn't sleep. She awakened him.

"What will you do when war breaks out?" she asked.

"Stay in Berlin. Sell securities if I still could," he answered sleepily

"Shouldn't you return to America?" she asked.

"I don't know. Why?"

"Because you should," she said. "All my friends know there will be another war. One to correct the injustices of the last war. They say the Americans will be our enemies again. Roosevelt is partially Jewish, Hitler says."

"That's ridiculous, Theresia," he answered.

"I know it's ridiculous," she said, barely above a whisper. "But we all live with all sorts of lies, don't we?"

Somewhere in the far distance, from another apartment, perhaps, Cochrane thought he heard someone playing a flute. Theresia changed the subject unexpectedly, as was her habit.

"Do you have a wife in America?" she asked.

"No."

"That's something else you should do," she said. "Marry someday. Have a family."

"Someday," he agreed.

"My husband is a lieutenant in the Navy," she said. "I haven't seen or heard from him for six months. The last time, he hinted that he was going to South America. He is in a submarine."

Cochrane listened, watching her breathe, watching her chest move gently up and down and following the glow of the cigarette until she snuffed it.

"My husband Heinrich would kill you if he discovered you to be my lover," she said, turning toward Cochrane and moving into his arms. "And he would kill me if he knew I was in love with you."

"So we won't tell him," Cochrane answered. Then he kissed her and told her that he was in love with her, husband or no husband. They made love again. He waited for tomorrow and wondered idly if he should see a special contact in Berlin. He needed something small, compact, and thirty-two caliber, in case of some funny sort of emergency.

"I have a daughter, too," she said.
"I never knew that," he answered, surprised.
"You never asked," she said.
"Where is she?"
"Away. At a school. Near Munich. Fredericka is much safer where she is," Theresia said.

Through Theresia, Cochrane met a man named Otto Mauer. Mauer was introduced as a coordinator of labor and industry within the Interior Ministry. Cochrane gravitated toward him as well as he could without arousing suspicion. Eventually, the two men became friendly.

Mauer was between forty and fifty, with brown hair that was silvering instead of graying and a narrow, unfriendly jaw. He wore thin round glasses and had an air of being midway between a dentist and an aristocrat. Cochrane, after a few meetings, began to like Mauer. Eventually, Mauer invited Cochrane to visit him and his family on their private estate south of Munich. The train voyage there was an espionage bonanza.

As the train carried Cochrane southward, he began to notice crated military equipment stacked in increasing volume from one station to the next. At Regensburg, Cochrane stepped off the train during its fifteen-minute stop, ostensibly to smoke a small cigar. It was a damp day, surprisingly chilly for that time of year. Cochrane walked the length of the platform, as if to savor the exercise.

The supplies carried Wehrmacht insignia and were barely concealed. Had Cochrane wished to look more closely, he could have learned which battalions were the intended recipients. But he did pass close enough to the crates and their military guards to actually learn some of the contents. It was the precise war equipment - helmets, rifles, blankets, and knapsacks - Cochrane reasoned, necessary to sustain a light-armored or infantry division.

Farther south, at Freising and at Landshut, Cochrane observed the soldiers who would be using the equipment. By the time Cochrane reached Munich, soldiers were everywhere. But the equipment was nowhere in view. Bill Cochrane knew he had stumbled across a military secret unknown outside the Third Reich.

Germany was fortifying for an invasion of Austria. There could be no other reason for a buildup of troops in that area. Surely, Austria, Switzerland, and Czechoslovakia were not preparing to invade Germany.

That was the good part. The bad part was that both men realized that one or both of them were under surveillance by the Gestapo. By the end of the visit, Cochrane filled a notebook with classified Abwehr information. In return, he agreed to help smuggle Mauer out of Germany.

Mauer had a final gift for Cochrane: a gift of information.

Walking together on Mauer's estate one night, Mauer was still able to confront Cochrane with the unexpected.

"My secretary, Theresia," Mauer inquired pleasantly. "You find her attractive?"

"I do," Cochrane answered.

Mauer half turned his head. "Are you her lover?" he asked, not missing a step.

"Sometimes."

"Do you ever consider taking her back to America after you leave?"

"Sometimes," Cochrane answered a second time. They were passing through the forest again. Mauer followed a path that was invisible to anyone else.

"She has a husband, you know."

"I know." The concept of cuckoldry after prying through state secrets seemed both forlorn and comical to Cochrane. He wished the topic could be avoided. "She told me all about him," he said. "He's a naval man. Been on a submarine for several months, she thinks. Down off South America and so on."

"That's what she told you?"

"Yes."

"You're a fool! Theresia's husband is a captain in the SS," Mauer said. "He has a greater predilection for adolescent boys than for fully matured women. Accordingly, he allows the Gestapo to employ his wife in certain investigative activities. It advances his career."

126

Cochrane felt a sinking feeling.

"Of course, some such assignments are not totally without pleasure."

They walked several paces and Cochrane saw his entire relationship with Theresia flash before him. The demure response when he first started talking, yet her strategic placement next to him at the restaurant.

"And you're telling me that I'm one of those assignments?" Cochrane answered.

"It's not so much that I'm telling you," Mauer concluded. "It's Abteilung Three that is telling me. I pulled the report with your name on it. I will spare you the details. She cannot decide whether or not you are a spy. Tell me," Mauer concluded as they emerged from the woods and the manor loomed in the dusk a kilometer down a hillside, "for the sake of all of us. When will you be leaving Germany? Soon?"

Cochrane felt something in the depths of his stomach and fell strangely silent. "I might consider doing just that," he said.

Mauer said nothing further.

When he returned to Berlin, Cochrane assessed his situation. He had scored a major penetration of the Abwehr. But the Gestapo had him under a microscope. Arrest had to be no more than days away.

Somewhere things had already gone wrong.

How had the Gestapo so quickly picked up his scent? How had they uncovered and murdered the tailor Kurkevics, Cochrane's only liaison, even before his arrival? Luck on behalf of the master race? Blundering by the FBI? Magic? Something was missing which precluded Cochrane completely understanding his situation.

Cochrane filed a single message to Washington. "Have contacted interesting Russian named Count Choulakoff," Cochrane cabled. "If he wishes to travel, you may wish to buy him a ticket. Fascinating man. I will remain in Berlin for some time."

The cable went to Bill Cochrane's "Aunt Charlotte," in New York. Aunt Charlotte lived inside a Box 1014 at the General Post Office in Baltimore, an FBI mail drop for Frank Lerrick's office.

Then, in Berlin, Theresia was absent from her job. Meanwhile, Gestapo agents were now on Cochrane's trail twenty-four hours a day.

On a Wednesday night, Cochrane bought flowers in a stall near the opera house and walked the seven remaining blocks to Theresia's flat. He always met her at eight in the evening. Tonight would be no different. Cochrane's babysitters remained downstairs and across the street as he climbed the stairs. When he knocked on her door, there was silence. Cochrane used a small file that he always carried and the lock virtually fainted when it first felt the pressure.

He cautiously pushed the door open. "Theresia?" There was no answer.

He set the flowers on a table and he walked to the bedroom. At first, when he saw the unclothed body, he thought she was asleep. But he knew she wasn't. Not by the scent of death in the room. And not by the impossible angle at which her neck was twisted.

He looked closer. He saw the cigarette burns at her breasts. He saw others at her lower abdomen and between her legs. He considered the pain Theresia had endured. Then he saw how expertly her neck had been broken.

Cochrane's first thought was that her killer had been her husband. He had discovered her liaison and would deal with Cochrane next. Then it all shifted into place.

The Gestapo commanders who had ordered her into an affair with Cochrane had come by for a reckoning. Why was she so slow to obtain satisfactory information from this American? Had she betrayed her commander in favor of a satisfying bed? Obviously, they had decided she had.

Bill Cochrane swept his wet eyes with his hands. He sprang to his feet. He could no longer stay in that memory-infested apartment. He left by the front stairs, closing the door the way he had found it, and carrying the flowers. He opened the door to the street and bumped into his bodyguards. They stood immobile, staring at him, and they smirked. All three were larger than he was. Typical Nazi hoods. Big, strong, and stupid-looking.

But he looked as if he did not recognize them. "Excuse me," Cochrane said. He stepped by them and walked calmly. When he arrived at the Rathskeller Keitel two minutes later, he ordered a double brandy and sat alone at a table for two.

Cochrane gradually stopped quaking. He ordered another brandy to steady his nerves, and then another and another. He wished that the liquor would make him drunk. But it did not. He was too shaken. The brandy made him more introspective.

He had begun to hate. He understood hatred but had always intellectualized it. But this was personal. These murderous lunatics in their brown and black shirts and their steel-heeled boots, goose-stepping around Berlin. This, Cochrane now knew, was hatred.

He finished his drink and gripped the lapels of his overcoat close to him. He left the café and walked into a wet cold rain.

He cursed all of Germany and fixed the day's date in his mind. His usefulness in Germany had ended. It was now important to complete the business at hand.

The following Friday morning, Cochrane took a noon train from Berlin and arrived in Stuttgart that evening, traveling with one carefully prepared suitcase.

In Stuttgart he took his dinner at the restaurant in the train station. He allowed his trailers ample time. Two followed him while the other presumably searched his hotel room.

When he returned to his hotel he was pleased to see that his suitcase had been searched and carefully repacked. But his visitor had not noted the geometric patterns with which Cochrane had arranged the suitcase's contents—a pen pointing northward, a necktie pointing southeast.

On the next day he visited Heidelberg and twice again he was searched. On Monday he traveled by train to Freiburg and checked into a hotel that was popular among party members.

After lunch Cochrane went to a variety store where he purchased a battery and some heavy wire for hanging pictures. Then he asked the proprietor whether he might have an ice pick.

The proprietor said he did. Cochrane selected one with a seven-inch blade.

Next, he purchased a new suitcase, an expensive steel and leather one with heavy, sturdy locks. Cochrane returned to his hotel and set to work, praying that he would not be interrupted. Sweat poured off his face. The game was life and death now.

From around his left leg, he removed four bars of hollow lead pipe, each about six inches long, that he had kept bandaged to his shin since leaving Berlin. From within a narrow sheath within his belt he removed twenty .22-caliber bullets. He then prepared his suitcase for his next visitors, carefully closing it and leaving it on his bed.

Cochrane used his file to slit open the false side of his old suitcase. He removed a Swiss passport. He slid it into a folio. He also kept with him the photograph of the Mauer family.

He then donned his topcoat, casually strolled down the hotel stairs, and walked out the front door. One of his bodyguards followed. Too bad they won't all be going up to the room, he thought.

He glanced at his watch. It was ten minutes after seven. He was several minutes behind his schedule. He entered the restaurant he had studied earlier that afternoon.

He darted past the astonished waiters, past the captains, and then out into the kitchen in front of a bewildered staff. He slipped through the back door into a quiet alley. But instead of fleeing, he moved toward the alley's closed end. There he stood, his back flat against the brick wall of the building, until his trailer appeared.

"Mein Herr?" Cochrane inquired. The man whirled, eye to eye with Bill Cochrane from a distance of five meters. "You are following someone?" Cochrane asked in German. Cochrane's adversary was a thick-browed man who stepped closer.

"You stupid fool," the man said in a guttural German that Cochrane fixed as Bremen or Leipzig. "You are playing games with us?"

The Gestapo agent's hand went beneath his overcoat. Cochrane saw a Luger. He bolted forward and crashed into the larger man, bringing his knee upward, hard toward the man's groin.

The huge German cursed him and pushed off with his forearms. As the Luger came out, Cochrane smashed the man's wrist with his own left forearm. Then Cochrane's right hand came stabbing upward, thrusting the ice pick into the German's stomach.

The man bellowed. Cochrane kneed the man again, harder than before. Then he knocked the gun away. He pulled back the ice pick, braced himself, and stabbed upward again, this time toward the heart. The Gestapo agent staggered for several feet, then Cochrane hit him hard from the back, knocking him down onto the garbage-strewn alleyway.

The body went still. Cochrane picked up the Luger and tucked it into his belt. He stripped the dead man of his Gestapo identification and discarded his own overcoat, which was now covered with blood. He found a taxi and went to the railroad station. At 8:22 PM he was on the last train leaving Freiburg for Zurich.

At the same moment as Cochrane's departure, two Gestapo agents tired of fussing with the locks on Cochrane's new suitcase. One of them unsheathed a knife. The blade of the knife protruded through the leather case and triggered the electric circuit that Cochrane had wound around the valise. As the case opened, the four lead pipes exploded simultaneously. The two agents were hardly in position to appreciate Cochrane's makeshift machine gun. Nor were they capable of wishing they had never laid their hands on Theresia Koehler.

Police were summoned. Within minutes all trains out of Freiburg, particularly the two that were in transit southbound for Switzerland, were ordered stopped.

Bill Cochrane sat by a window seat in the town of Mulheim, fifteen kilometers north of the frontier at Basel. He saw several dozen Wehrmacht soldiers on the station platform, carrying their automatic rifles at their waists. Cochrane knew there would be trouble. The soldiers were going from car to car.

Cochrane slid a hand beneath his coat to the Luger in his belt. He knew that they would be looking for an American. The doors to his first-class compartment flew open and he was faced with two tall, strong, but young soldiers.

"Passports! Identifications!" they demanded. Their eyes drifted across the other faces in the compartment and settled suspiciously upon Cochrane. He stared at the two young Germans, gave them a look of condescension, shook his head in irritation, and gazed out the window.

"Tell me, Sergeant," Cochrane asked in flawless German, "how much longer can we waste our time in this stinking little town?"

The corporal stepped to the sergeant's side and glared at Cochrane. "You have the insolence to ask us questions?" snapped the sergeant. "Your passport!"

The corporal made a slight gesture with his gun. Three other passengers cringed.

With a gesture of annoyance, Cochrane reached to his passport and tossed it contemptuously onto the floor at the sergeant's feet. As the corporal covered Cochrane, the sergeant opened the Swiss passport. He stared at the photograph in the passport and raised his eyes to check it against Bill Cochrane. He found a close enough match. But something was wrong with the man before him and the sergeant knew it.

Cochrane's hand went slowly to his breast pocket. The corporal eyed him.

"At ease, Corporal!" Cochrane muttered sourly.

Cochrane withdrew the Gestapo shield from his breast pocket. The eyes of the two soldiers went wide with terror.

"Now would you kindly hand me back my passport and get your asses moving through this train!"

Cochrane's other hand remained within his coat; the palm pressed against the handle of the pistol. The Luger was Cochrane's only remaining hope if the bluff failed.

"Thank you, sir!" blurted the sergeant. He fumbled the passport back into Cochrane's hands. The American snatched it furiously and drove the two soldiers from the compartment with a withering stare. The young sergeant had rattled too easily to obey army protocol: checking the name on the Gestapo shield against the passport. Had either soldier taken that simple measure, all three of them would have died.

In Zurich, when Cochrane was certain that the Gestapo was not on his back, he looked for an address that he had memorized months previously in Washington: a print shop in a prosperous residential neighborhood five minutes' walk from the lake. He found it without difficulty.

The print shop was on a side street, nestled between an antique dealer and a dressmaker. The proprietor, according to the window, was a man named Engle.

Moments later, Cochrane was in the rear of Engle's shop, the doors closed for greater security. Cochrane needed three passports made urgently and smuggled back into Germany. Engle sighed. Cochrane informed him that Uncle Edgar in Washington would handle the reimbursement.

"These passports," Engle inquired. "Swiss? Canadian? What must they be?"

"Swiss would be excellent."

"I cannot work without photographs."

Cochrane withdrew the portrait of the Mauer family from his inside pocket. With a pair of scissors, Cochrane trimmed it into three single photographs. These he handed to Engle. Cochrane next printed the address of Frau Mauer's chocolate shop in Munich.

"The passports," Cochrane continued, "must be sent by private courier from within the Reich and in an envelope that will appear to be a business correspondence. It should be marked 'Personal Attention of Frau Mauer.' And I should stress," Cochrane concluded, "that there may be a certain urgency to this order."

Engle raised his eyes slightly. "These days, Mein Herr," he said, "there is always great urgency. The world rushes headlong with great urgency. And toward what end?" The old man hunched his shoulders. He sighed. "You are in trouble with the Nazis? Gestapo?"

No response from Cochrane.

133

Engle studied his visitor. "Did you kill one? A Gestapo agent?"

"Probably more than one."

Engle arched an eyebrow. For the first time a crafty smile danced across the merchant's face. "Be careful, my American friend," he said. "Zurich is alive with Gestapo and SS. In the last day there has been a marked increase. They seem to be looking for someone." Engle's gaze alighted on Cochrane. "Maybe an American." He paused, then, "May an old man give a young man some advice?"

"Feel free," Cochrane said.

"Continue home immediately," said Engle. "Take the least predictable route. I will see that your three friends" - and here the old man glanced down to what Cochrane had written - "the Mauer family, are taken care of."

Bill Cochrane offered Engle his hand, which turned into a clasp with both of the engraver's hands. "Filthy bloody Nazis," the old man murmured. "Animals."

Cochrane boarded an express for Geneva that afternoon. It was 5:30 when the train pulled away from the station. In the dining car that night, Cochrane's attention focused on an auburn-haired woman of maybe forty dining alone. He took her to be Swiss, and twice when she looked up she saw him watching her, but against his instincts, he decided that amorous pursuits were not worth the trouble.

The next morning in Geneva, Cochrane took the first plane out, which went to Tehran, where the Gestapo crawled in alarming numbers and where he again changed passports, becoming Canadian and using an English-language bookstore as a dead drop for his new identity. He dyed his hair black, acquired glasses, and found an ill-fitting brown suit in a flea market. He flew to Palestine and enlisted as a cook's assistant on a British freighter bound to Bermuda. The vessel arrived safely, despite the hazards of submarines. He presented himself to the United States Consulate in Hamilton and talked a skeptical undersecretary into placing a telephone call to Washington. The next day, Washington brought him home, telling him that it all had been worth it, even before they learned what it all had been.

It was November 12, 1938. He had been away for fifteen months.

For the next six weeks he was debriefed personally by Assistant Director Frank Lerrick, who generally named only broad topics, allowing Cochrane to guide him through the Abwehr at Cochrane's own pace. A stenographer recorded everything, and on one day two generals from the Joint Chiefs of Staff appeared also, sat quietly, and listened. Cochrane's testimony filled three locked filing cabinets. The FBI had scored a staggering intelligence coup, so it seemed, and Bill Cochrane had done it.

"I can see great things for you in this Bureau," Lerrick concluded warmly when all questions had been asked.

"Good," said Cochrane. "Now you tell me something," Cochrane said.

"What happened to Otto Mauer? And his family? I promised to get them out of Germany."

Lerrick's face went colder than a tombstone. Cochrane lost his smile.

"Come on, Lerrick!" Cochrane snapped. "I've been talking to you for six weeks. Would you answer my one question?"

"They are alive. We got them to New York. That's all I can tell you right now."

Bill Cochrane exhaled an enormous sigh. He thought of Mauer, his lovely wife and their son. "Thank God. That's all I asked," Cochrane said.

A few days into 1939, Bill Cochrane reported for work and awaited a new assignment.

For the Bureau itself, it was the best of times and it was the worst of times, depending whose opinion one sought. The desperado bandits and bank robbers of the Depression era were gone, either dead or imprisoned or somewhere in between.

Hoover himself had garnered much of the credit. But the gangland fortunes that had been weaned on Prohibition gin and basement beer were placing a stranglehold on the cities from

Illinois to New York. The Bureau seemed outmanned, outgunned, and outmaneuvered. Or just plain outfoxed.

Two foreign agents, personally dispatched by Hoover, had returned from Moscow via Khartoum with no luggage and figurative bullet holes in their hats. Another had been buried in Rome by jubilant Fascisti, and yet another was missing and presumed dead in the Suez. It was a time when Hoover's agents were running into the ground, sometimes literally, all over the globe.

As for Cochrane's escapade in Berlin and Munich, there were two ways of viewing it:

One: Cochrane had scored a major intelligence coup. Every bit of information checked and double-checked. The FBI had penetrated a foreign spy service for the first time. The mission was a success.

Or, two: Cochrane had left Germany at the speed of light with every contact apparently compromised and scrambling for cover. How and why, he wondered. The mission was, in the end, a disaster.

Worse, the Gestapo knew exactly who the "banker" was who had befriended people in Berlin and Munich, then left a trail of blood as he killed agents on his way out of the Reich and managed to smuggle the Mauer family out, also. As long as the Nazis were in power, the memory would remain alive.

Cochrane soon found himself immersed in boring grunt work within the bureau, with few cases that piqued his interest. He was re-assigned to the Baltimore office, where First Maryland National Bank had uncovered a chamber of horrors in, of all places, their auditing room. Cochrane's reception by the other agents in Baltimore was downright frosty. It was common currency that Cochrane had scored some considerable successes for the Bureau. But now J. Edgar Hoover was wary of Cochrane's star power. So as the months passed in Baltimore, Bill Cochrane felt the final days of his youth slipping away. If his services were not appreciated, he could not give other adults lessons in common sense.

He sought a job in private enterprise. He was, after all, a banker by profession, spoke a foreign language or two, and knew he could count on the Bureau to barter him a fine letter of recommendation in exchange for his resignation. He applied for work at three New York banks. Morgan Guaranty made him an outstanding offer. That settled it.

He would move to New York. He would receive a salary that was more than fair. He would find himself a comfortable apartment and, he hoped against hope, a special woman. He would settle down, acquire an inch or two around the waistline probably, and mind his own business while the rest of the world tumbled sublimely into hell in a Fascist basket.

He had made his contribution. Who could blame him in his position for now settling on a little peace and quiet?

So on a steamy summer afternoon, he typed out his letter of resignation from the Bureau, a chore he had been putting off for several days. And it was at that moment, as luck would have it, that his secretary, Patricia, entered the room with an outlandish suggestion: J. Edgar himself was on the line, beckoning him, summoning him, no, ordering him to Washington as soon as humanly possible.

"Fine, indeed," Cochrane thought to himself, setting down the telephone and gazing at the completed letter on his desk. He looked at the calendar and made a mental note. August 3, 1939. "I'll deliver my resignation in person."

Within twenty-four hours he was assigned to a spy and saboteur codenamed 'Siegfried' who was apparently inflicting losses on Allied shipping and threatening the life of President Roosevelt. It was a case Cochrane could get his teeth into.

Cochrane tore up his letter of resignation and, in defense of his country, threw himself back into his work.

Chapter 18

Toulouse, Vichy France
December 1942

Cochrane could not control his body from trembling. He stood on the cold tarmac, an intensified rain sweeping across landing strip. The body of Skordeno lay on the ground on one side of him. A long pool of blood exited from a head wound that had removed half his skull. On the other side of him, also on the ground, lay the body of Cambulat, the Turk with whom he had played dominos. Wartime was a merciless unrelenting era. Cochrane needed no such reminders. Two dead men were reminders enough.

He drew a breath, still wondering if he were about to be shot. He felt a hand on his right shoulder. "You!" said Wesselmann in German. "Back on the aircraft."

"Yes, sir," Cochrane said. His mouth was parched. His lips could barely move.

"Quickly!" the Gestapo agent said. "There are flight schedules to maintain."

The second in command used the nose of a pistol to move along the fourth man who had been herded to the tarmac.

Cochrane started to move. Then Wesselmann grabbed his arm. "Wait! Passport again."

"What?"

"Show me your passport again. Slowly with your left hand."

Cochrane reached into his pocket and withdrew the forged Canadian passport. Wesselmann looked at the information page again and the binding, his eyes flicking back and forth from the information to Cochrane's eyes.

"Something occurs to me. You said you lived where?" Wesselmann asked.

"Toronto."

"I used to visit there," he said. "I had an uncle. Tell me two main thoroughfares in Toronto."

"Yonge Street. Marlborough Street."

"And two nearby towns?"

"Brampton and Mississauga."

"Which way is Kitchener?"

"To the southwest."

"Distance?"

"By private motor car. Maybe an hour. Or two. Depending on weather. Time of year."

"Snow. Of course."

"Are there many Jews in Toronto?"

Cochrane simmered. "I don't keep track of such things."

"Maybe you should."

Cochrane knew he was being provoked. He could me meek or anger could rise to his defense. "Why are you questioning me?" he finally asked. "If I'm delayed, I'll need to advise my contacts in Berlin. They will learn that you interfered with official business of the Reich. You will be the loser, not I."

Wesselmann eyed him again. The German retained the passport.

"There is something wrong with you."

"No, there isn't. Give me my passport."

A local police team arrived with two gurneys. They began the messy job of removing the two dead men on the ground.

"This passport is fraudulent. Or it is real. If it is fraudulent, it is the best forgery I've ever seen," Wesselmann said. He closed the document.

"I take both of your statements as high compliments," Cochrane said. "Heil Hitler!"

With a cautious hand Cochrane reached forward and put his hand on the passport. Wesselmann did not release his grip. Then he did, grudgingly. "Heil Hitler!" he said.

Cochrane took back the passport. He returned it to his pocket.

"Board the plane!" the Gestapo agent demanded.

139

Cochrane walked back to the entrance door at the rear of the aircraft.

"You're welcome," he heard Wesselmann say to his back. Cochrane did not respond. Nor did he look back at the two dead men on the tarmac. He returned to his seat and pulled down the window shade. A few moments later, he heard the rear exit door slam shut. The female flight attendant locked the door into place. She looked ashen. She exchanged a horrified glance with Cochrane but said nothing.

The aircraft's engines came to life. No one said anything. Daylight was dying. Cochrane knew they would go aloft but the back end of the flight would be at night, always risky in the winter months.

Ten minutes later, they taxied down the runway, turned and were aloft. The air was again turbulent. The attendant passed through the cabin with paper cups of water. Cochrane accepted his but at a moment when the air calmed down, he stood, opened his valise and found the flask that Colonel Sawyer had given him. He sat down and pulled a long swig or it. Then another and then a third. It helped.

"Jesus," he muttered to himself, thinking of the dead men on the runway.

The flight was a ninety minute white-knuckler. Cochrane tried to leaf through a copy of *Time* magazine, but his attention wasn't there. He had learned the brutality of the Nazi administration before the war and had witnessed it when he tracked down a saboteur in 1939 and 1940. But he had underestimated how much the brutality of the regime had been jacked up for wartime.

He raised the shade. There was darkness outside. Few lights were on the ground. He assumed there was cloud cover.

The DC-3 approached Geneva from the southwest. Cochrane was relieved when he could feel the aircraft begin to descend. He reassured himself. Pilots, he knew, loved the DC-3. It had a low stall speed and was highly maneuverable.

He saw a flash of light from the ground. It was a searchlight from Geneva. The DC-3 went into its final descent. The front wheels touched the landing strip, followed a moment later by the single rear wheel. The pilot applied the brakes and the aircraft eased into its landing.

Swiss Customs were rigorous.

All of Cochrane's papers were examined carefully. Every bit of his luggage was inspected. Swiss customs agents stamped his fake passport. He passed through to a portico where taxis awaited.

He found a taxi that took him into the city of Geneva. He planned to stay there overnight, then continue by train the next morning. If connections went smoothly, which they actually did occasionally, he could be in Allen Dulles's office in nearby Bern, the capital, the next afternoon or evening.

He remembered his instructions, which seemed like a world away and an eternity in the past. He gave the address for the Hotel des Alpes in French. The driver, a small man with a thin moustache, a red face and a gray beret, knew the hotel.

Cochrane arrived at the hotel and registered. For a few extra francs, two sandwiches and a half bottle of wine were arranged for him in the hotel lounge, even though the lounge had closed. He arranged also for the desk clerk to make sure he was awakened by seven the next morning.

Dead tired, but at least not dead, he breathed easier. The fifth floor, he knew, was a safe house for OSS operatives. That was why Donovan had steered him there. He could expect the same in Bern.

Later on the fifth floor, Cochrane examined his room. He found it comfortable and acceptable. When the hallway was clear, he examined the layout. There were two emergency getaway routes: one down the back stairs and another down an outside fire escape. He hoped to use neither.

He bathed and collapsed into a comfortable bed. He was one day into his journey. Who knew how long it might take or even whether he would come back from it alive? The horror of the two men shot dead on the tarmac in Marseille still blazed through his head. It could just as easily have been him whose brains were blown out and scattered amidst the sleet on the gritty asphalt.

He thought of his wife, Laura, sleeping soundly in the early morning in New York, he hoped. He fell asleep holding that thought and emotion. What would happen to her if he never returned was not something he wished to even consider.

When the knock on his door came the next morning at seven, he bolted upright in his bed. The night had gone too quickly. He responded groggily but fifteen minutes later was downstairs for breakfast. Another thirty minutes after that, he walked to the train station and caught the next available train to Bern.

"Next available," was a fluid term in wartime. A stationmaster made an announcement: there had been an avalanche of snow coming off a mountain or a hillside north of the city. All trains were cancelled till evening.

"Don't believe a word of it about the snow," snorted a fellow voyager in the waiting room. "The Swiss army is moving troops. They close the tracks so no one can monitor their movements."

"Oh, really? Do they move them to the German border or the French border?" Cochrane asked.

"Both," the man said. "But the border with Germany needs to be much stronger. They allow the French border to be porous. Black market. Bunch of crooks. Everyone knows that. I'm going to the cinema. It will take all day."

It did. The train didn't leave till 6:15 PM.

Chapter 19

**Bern, Switzerland
December 1942**

If a city could be bland, exciting, charming, provincial, remote and important all at once, Bern, the Swiss capital, was exactly that when Bill Cochrane stepped off the train from Geneva.

Situated on a bend in the River Aare, Bern remained in some ways a quiet city of a hundred thousand people while the war swirled around Swiss borders. The spectacular Jungfrau and several other imposing mountains looked down upon its terraced neighborhoods, ancient architecture and arcaded streets. Once upon a time, a time which was vanishing into the past, Bern had been a quiet provincial capital of a steadfastly neutral country.

The First World War had changed everything in Europe, including Bern. The Swiss capital had moved, for better or worse, into the treacherous Twentieth Century. It may have been quiet, but by 1942 Bern was a world focal point, a joyous nest of surly spies and suspicious characters from all corners of the world.

In contemporary Bern, theater and music thrived in English, French and German. Young Swiss women flocked to the embassies to work. At first food was scarce during the war, then when Americans and American dollars started to roll in, one could buy anything one wanted, and anything was available. The social center was the Palace Bellevue Hotel where congregated a lively aggregation of young expatriates, wheelers dealers, young diplomats, calls girls and mistresses, plus disgraced senior military officers with no more battalions to command. They all seemed to have money and a willingness to put the war on hold until the next morning, or the morning after that. The Palace Bellevue had nightly jazz band dances, so why not kick up one's heels? One's luck might run out the following week and be obliged to return to the real world.

Thus, Bill Cochrane settled into a Bern hotel shortly after an evening arrival, much as he had done in Geneva. The desk clerk, a young woman, looked up at him. He surrendered his passport to her for registration.

"Welcome, sir," she said. "My name is Gina."

"Hello, Gina," Cochrane said.

Gina smiled engagingly. She spoke French to Cochrane. She didn't know exactly who he was, but she knew what he was and handled it with aplomb. Before Cochrane left New York, Donovan's orientation team had given him an alert as to who she was.

Gina was thirty-one and an Italian by birth. She had fled fascists in Milan and had moved to Switzerland with the financial help of her Uncle Abraham who had wisely emigrated to the United States in 1936. Gina, in negotiating transport out of Mussolini's Italy, had put herself at the disposal of William Donovan's office in the United States. Her uncle, who knew very well how the world worked, had played tennis with Bill Donovan in Washington for several months. One evening he asked to speak to Donovan privately.

"My niece Luigina is half Jewish," he explained. "She's well educated and from a successful family of merchants. She speaks five languages, but, as you can imagine, she is in danger in Italy."

"I understand. I'm sorry to hear that," Donovan answered.

"I'm certain Gina could be of valuable service to United States," Abraham explained. He paused; the deal not yet complete. "She even knows how to use a gun. I know because I taught her myself how a young woman needs to defend herself."

"Admirable," Donovan said.

"But she needs to get to a neutral country."

"I would agree," Donovan said. "Let's see what we can do."

Donovan, seeing opportunities large and small all over Europe, put things in motion, starting with a forger in Rome who was a master at exit papers. When Gina arrived in Switzerland a month after the post tennis conversation in Washington, Dulles took over. He guided her to a friendly soul in the labor ministry who arranged temporary residence and a work permit. Another accomplice directed her to this hotel whose owner was a pro-American French gentleman named Maurice Levi. Levi loathed the fascists and was happy to do anything to defeat them. He was delighted to give Gina her job and even more delighted when she became his mistress.

The arrangement with Gina was simple. If a reservation by mail or telephone or telegram came to her addressed to her formal name, Luigina, which appeared nowhere in the hotel records, she was to give it special attention. Such had been the case with a reservation received for Mr. Stykowski.

"We'll put you on the fifth floor, sir," Gina said. "That's the top floor. I think you'll be comfortable there."

"That would be excellent," Cochrane said.

Gina oversaw the operations and had a short list of other secured services around the city. She had her eye on invisible finances, emergency identity or armaments, and discreet escorts, the type of things that a certain sort of travelling man might require. She had been promised passage to the United States once the war was won. Hence, she always knew who to expect checking in.

The dining room was closed but the night porter, at Gina's request, was kind enough to make two sandwiches for him and provide a half bottle of red Rhone wine. Cochrane accepted and was allowed to relax in the downstairs lounge, where the lights were turned back on for him despite his late arrival.

He appreciated the gesture and the food. What he appreciated even more was that Donovan's people seemed to be everywhere.

Chapter 20

Bern, Switzerland
December 1942

In Bern, Cochrane killed the next day, waiting for his pre-arranged evening rendezvous with Allen Dulles. He wore the heavy hiking pants that he had bought in Portugal. He found his way to Herrengasse toward dusk, spotted Number 23, Dulles's residence, and kept walking. He went to a small bistro for dinner, then toward 8:30 PM found his way to a low road beneath Herrengasse. He located the vineyard he had been alerted to and spotted the path through it. A cold rain began.

Punctually at 9:00 PM, he entered the vineyard. He trekked to the other side, an uphill walk with loose stones and uneven turf. But he kept the back entrance of Number 23 in view. He emerged from the vineyard under a cover of near darkness with only one small tear to his hiking pants.

The cul-de-sac of 23 Herrengasse was across a narrow street from the vineyard. The streetlamp was off near the rear entrance to the building, which struck Cochrane as both odd and convenient. He crossed a street where several dark cars were parked. Globs of sleet were now falling. The street and sidewalk were already slippery. The weather distracted him from assessing his surroundings as he walked toward a door that appeared to be the back entrance of Dulles's residence.

The space between the cars and the door was no more than twenty feet. He was halfway between the cars and the door when he heard noise. There was movement behind him. He turned sharply. In a severe shadow, the figure of a lean man unfolded out of a parked Citroen, legs first then the whole body as he stood. Cochrane looked to see if the man had a weapon but he didn't see one. The night was cold and the man's hands were in the pockets of a bulky coat.

"Bill Cochrane?" the man said softly.

Cochrane waited and didn't answer. Had he been carrying a weapon he would have reached for it. The man walked toward Cochrane. There were a few slices of light from the windows above the ground floor of the building. Cochrane's eyes adjusted quickly. As the man approached, his hand emerged from his coat pocket. At the same time, Cochrane saw the glasses and recognized the shape and the facial features of Allen Dulles.

Dulles extended his hand in greeting.

"I apologize if I startled you, Bill," Dulles said. "Precautions, you know?"

From out of a shadow close to the building wall, a large body swelled into view and loomed uncomfortably close to Cochrane. The body morphed into the shape of a big man in a leather jacket and gloves. The man must have been six feet six. Cochrane had never seen such a large individual loom into view from nowhere so quickly.

Cochrane wondered if his skills had eroded. First he missed Dulles in the car, now he had missed the security detail at the rear of 23 Herrengasse.

"You all right, Mr. Dulles?" the man asked.

The man spoke with a low voice and flat accent from the American Midwest, with forearms like ham hocks to make things even better. As Cochrane looked him quickly up and down, he saw that the left hand held a forty-five caliber American Colt semi-automatic. Cochrane recognized it as US Army issue. There was nothing subtle about the weapon; it could blow a three foot hole in a brick wall. Get any part of a man's head with that artillery and the man would no longer have much to think with.

"I'm fine, Jimmy," Dulles said. "Our guest here has come a long way. I'm here to welcome him. Thank you."

Jimmy grunted. He retreated back into the world of shadows. Cochrane assumed there was at least one other guard on the premises, around front. But he had cleared scrutiny, so what did it matter?

Dulles and Cochrane shook hands. When the clasp released, Dulles wrapped an arm around Cochrane's shoulder.

"Come on in," he said. "The door's unlocked. There's a fire going. I'd tell you that all's right with the world, but that would be a lie and you'd recognize it as one."

"Indeed, I would, sir," said Cochrane.

"Formality is not necessary. We know each other. Call me Allen. Welcome to the war."

"Thank you. I think."

Dulles arrived at the door.

"Warm up. Have a brandy. Have two or three. We have much to discuss. I've got a son-of-a-bitch of an assignment and you're the only man who can help me."

Chapter 21

Bern, Switzerland
December 1942

They climbed two flights of stairs. Dulles ushered Cochrane into an apartment that had a large foyer, lit with a copper standing lamp similar to one that Cochrane had in his library in New York. They continued into a salon. There was a sofa, comfortable chairs and two lamps. A pair of large windows faced the front of the building, probably giving a wonderful view of Bern. But it was night and the shades were drawn. In a grate, a fire was burning.

"Make yourself comfortable anywhere," Dulles said.

"Thank you." Cochrane settled into a Queen Anne chair.

"I'm having a Cognac. Martell. I don't have any of the XO, but I have some Cordon Bleu. Would that interest you?"

Dulles reached for a crystal decanter without waiting for a response.

"Indeed it would," Cochrane said anyway.

"This is from a case from the *Queen Mary*'s maiden voyage in the 1936. I had a case of it when I arrived here," he continued as he found two crystal snifters and polished them with a cloth. "I'm down to my last two bottles, I hate to admit."

"Dare I ask how the case got from the docks to here?" Cochrane asked. "Switzerland is a landlocked country, after all."

"Ask all you want. One of my MI6 friends across the street, a good fellow named Nigel, has some field people on the docks in Liverpool. When the *Queen Mary* was being converted to a troop transport," Dulles said, "Nigel asked what to do with the Cognac inventories. There was only one real answer: ship them immediately by air courier to the diplomatic staff in Switzerland. We don't want the sailors getting drunk on the expensive stuff, do we?"

"Oh, hell. No, of course not," said Cochrane. "Not when we can do it for them."

Dulles smiled. "Point taken," he said. "The Huns have closed down most of the air courier service," Dulles said. "I doubt if we'd be able to get another case. Pity."

Dulles poured. Two fingers high of the beautiful stuff into each snifter.

"They're communists on the docks, you know. Liverpool, after all. Bill Donovan loves that part. But they can be malleable. You scratch my back, I'll drive your Rolls. That's how it works in England these days, doesn't it?"

Cochrane accepted the joke and the Cognac at the same time. "I wouldn't know," he said.

"Of course you would, Bill," Dulles said. "Don't be coy with me. Cheers."

"Cheers."

"How is Donovan, by the way?"

"I thought you communicated all the time."

"We do. But you saw him in person."

"He's fine."

"Good. That's good. Wild Bill is going to be in things for the long haul. After we win this damned war, we're going to have a tiger by the tail with Stalin's people. We're going to need people to keep an eye on our Commie bastard pals. They looted half the gold from the Treasury in Madrid before the country fell to Franco, you know. Shipped it all to Moscow. Damned thieves. Cheers, again."

"Cheers," Cochrane said a second time.

Dulles retreated to the chair just across from his guest. "How's the wife? Laura, I believe? I met her once in Washington."

"Excellent. Fine. Worried sick as to what you have in store for me," Cochrane added.

Dulles set aside his Cognac. He strolled to a wooden console record player across the room. He selected a disk from a collection housed on an adjacent shelf. It was a jazz recording from the 1920's, music by Bix Beiderbecke, the great American cornetist who had died of pneumonia at the age of twenty-nine. Dulles set the disk on the turntable, put the needle on the vinyl, pushed the volume of brilliant Dixieland loud enough to cover any ensuing conversation, turned and sat.

"Well, to be brutally honest," Allen Dulles said, "she damned well should be. Worried, I mean. Laura. Your wife. Know what they do to spies in Germany if they get caught?"

"They decapitate them," Cochrane said. "I've already been warned. Guillotine, I hear."

"You hear correctly. If it's good enough for a Bourbon king, apparently it's good enough for a captured spy. That seems to be their thinking; or what passes for thinking."

"Donovan mentioned that in New York," said Cochrane.

"It bears repeating, my friend. They have a special scaffold, I'm told. The unlucky victim gets to be executed face up. The last thing he or she sees in this world or maybe any world is the blade falling. Then there's darkness pretty soon after that, I would think."

He sipped and savored the Martell.

"The Nazis are not shy about executing women, either," Dulles continued. "There's a Gestapo fellow in Bremen, I hear. A big Teutonic ape of a man with a wooden leg from the first great war. He takes sadistic pleasure in his work. He uses a whip made out of rhinoceros hide. His ex-playmates in the Afrika Korps created it for him. He takes his victims to a private chamber and apparently can take a man's head off with one or two cracks of the whip. His name is Burchhardt. At first I didn't believe the stories but so many of our people in the Bremen area have repeated the details that I'm inclined to believe it," he said, taking another sip. "That's what happens to spies in Nazi Germany when they get caught. You should know that."

"After I've travelled a quarter of the way around the world, are you trying to get me to decline the mission?"

"Of course I am. Then if you get killed I won't feel guilty."

"Would you feel guilty anyway?"

"Interesting question." Dulles pursed his lips. "Maybe for a few days. A week at most," he added with a wink.

"Then please tell me what I'm here for," Cochrane said.

Dulles drained his glass. "Fine," he said. "I'll do just that." He thought for a moment, then resumed. "You have been requested personally, by name, for this project," Dulles said. "Was that conveyed to you in New York?"

"The file I read stated that," Cochrane said. "But I don't know who it was."

"A man in the Naval Ministry. He's also a captain the SS," Dulles said. "Two roles. That means he's got quite a bit of power and a damned good share of official access. That's our contact. Does that mean anything to you?"

"It's starting to."

"Apparently you had an affair with the man's wife in Berlin around 1938, you hot-blooded scoundrel. That should make it pretty clear, I would think, unless you made an unhealthy habit of cuckolding several men who met that description."

"There was only one," Cochrane said. "His wife was a good woman."

"You recall the man's name?"

"Of course I do. Heinrich Koehler. And his wife's name was Theresia. Eventually, she was murdered by the Gestapo. I settled scores with several of them as I got out of the country as fast as I could."

"You killed a few of them from what I learn."

"That's correct."

"Very good," Dulles said. "We're at the same starting point. Herr Koehler has been leaking information to us for the last eighteen months. He is of the opinion that the mad little dictator bit off far more than his armies could chew when he declared war on the United States. So he's looking for a soft landing if he can get out of the country."

Dulles paused.

Then he said, "The flow has intensified recently and it's top shelf intelligence. We sense urgency on the part of Koehler and we'd like the flow of intelligence to continue. For it to continue, he has requested you to meet his intermediary in Berlin as soon as possible. He says he needs to put something in your hands physically."

"And what do I do then?"

"You take whatever he gives you and you guard it with your life. Next, you move the Tyrolean Alps if you damned well have to but you bring it back to me in this neutral nation in this picturesque city in this lovely room by this comforting fireplace beside which we currently sit and speak and then we can have another drink over it."

The longest pause of the evening followed.

Then, "Clear?" asked Dulles.

"Clear."

There was another silence in the room. It lasted for several seconds.

"Questions?" Dulles asked.

"Of course."

"Throw them at me."

"Since it's my life that's going to be on the line, or my head that is going to fall backwards into the executioner's basket, I'm curious on several points. First, your contact, Koehler, has been leaking material to the OSS. I'm told that the deciphering is a murderous procedure but you've taken steps to speed it up. As a matter of interest, would you mind telling me how?"

"I don't mind at all," Dulles said.

Dulles explained that he had come up with the solution in his first month at his new post. There was a growing population in Switzerland of American airmen whose planes had crashed after bombing runs in Germany and Austria. Some had managed enough good luck to find their way across the Swiss border. Switzerland being neutral, these men were seen as foreign combatants but not enemy. Hence, they were interned in camps and not returned to their units.

The camps were not nearly as horrible as the work or labor camps in Germany or Poland or Russia. But most of these men

153

hankered to get back to their units, which the Swiss steadfastly refused to allow. They would be shot if they tried to escape.

Many of these aviators were interned within a day's drive from Bern at a place named Adelboden, a vacant summer resort northeast of Geneva. The camp commandant was a blond, blue-eyed officer named with the unlikely name of Schubert who reminded the internees of every SS man they had ever dealt with. The men were put up in stripped-down resort hotels, where they were kept under constant surveillance.

The prevailing problem at Adelboden was boredom. The prevailing sport was drinking. The men could purchase their own alcohol with the small stipends they received in lieu of flight pay from the American legation in Bern. Some of them stayed drunk for days at a time. And after a while, boredom, spartan conditions, and the growing proximity of Allied fighters in France fed the urge to flee.

The obstacles to flight, however, were daunting. Some of the men took hikes deep into the mountains, escorted by armed guards who acted as guides. It was a storybook landscape: church bells chiming every hour, glacial lakes sparkling like giant jewels in the midday sun. But only an expert mountain climber stood a chance of escaping through the massive Alpine peaks that rose, like so many imprisoning walls, around the deep, pine-scented valley. And beyond the impassable ranges, in every direction, lay the Reich.

The guards explained that the mountains prevented their country from being overrun by the German army. They also maintained that more than 60 percent of the Swiss population was of German descent, and that many Swiss belonged to local Nazi groups and were not likely to assist an American on the run.

From instinct and from having dealt with the Swiss for more than twenty years, Dulles knew which Swiss were friendly to the Allied cause which were pro-Nazi. Dulles went to the Swiss whom he trusted and obtained permission to visit Adelboden. He quickly assessed that it was a miserable place in a lovely setting. Hot water, for example, was a luxury. It was turned on once every ten days at Adelboden, and then for only a few hours. Without coal to heat their quarters in cold weather, the men ate their skimpy meals of black bread, potatoes and watery soup dressed in their flight suits and gloves. They ate meat once a week and it was awful—usually blood sausage made from mountain goat.

So Dulles sent black market goods, especially liquor, some liberated from the *Queen Mary*, over to the camp commanders, including Schubert. Then he sent over better food for the guards and the captured Americans.

In return, the Swiss managed to warp the rules a little. They began to issue one-day "recreational passes" for teams of airmen. The airmen came to Bern on their passes and were trained as code readers. For an extra coal delivery that might warm the barracks and fuel the ovens for an extra week, Dulles was allowed consecutive seven-day daily passes for his code readers. Soon Dulles had created teams of code creators and readers who would visit in twenty-four hour shifts, often working two eight hour shifts with another eight hours tossed in for sleeping. Best of all, the American captives felt they were working for the war effort, which they were.

Dulles loved one time code pads and the furloughed POW's became experts. Dulles assumed everything that was sent out was also being recorded by the Germans and probably the Soviets as well. Once a Soviet friend and Dulles, comparing notes, realized that they had both been reading the same intelligence reports. What neither could figure was whether the report had first been Russian, British or American.

They worked not in Dulles's home, but rather in the small compact and eventually heavily guarded apartment on the top floor of 26 Duforstrasse in Bern.

"Twenty-six Duforstrasse is where you'll work for the next week," Dulles said. "You'll need to study the file and do a lot of memorization. Game?"

The jazz recording came to an end. Dulles held up a finger, signifying Cochrane should be silent for a moment while the music was changed. Dulles selected a new recording. Cochrane could see

155

what it was. When Dulles sat, a recording of one of Cochrane's favorites, made in Paris in the 1920's, began.

"Ah! Josephine Baker," said Cochrane.

"Yes. You don't object, do you?"

"Far from it. I'm a fan."

"Quite a talented lady," said Dulles. "She remains in France, you know, despite the war. Or at least that's her home base. She still travels. I saw her perform in Paris in the 1920s when I was attached to the League of Nations. It must have been 1928. Doesn't seem so long ago. She was spectacular."

"I envy you," said Cochrane.

"You should."

"And of course for your crazy mission into Germany, I'm game," Cochrane said when music resumed. "Why didn't Donovan give me more details?"

Dulles shrugged. We figured if you came all this way you wouldn't turn us down."

"How do we know Koehler just doesn't want a shot at me. By 'shot' I mean, 'bullet.' I suppose he has some sense of wounded honor and I did have an affair with his late wife."

Dulles shrugged.

"We can't say for certain, but it doesn't appear that way. He wants to get to either the United States or South America. Part of the price is that he send us a further boatload of material. He promises to knock our socks off. He says the delivery system will be unusual. I don't know if he has microdots or ledgers or photographs. But so far, he's been providing extraordinary information that checks and double checks."

"So it's worth it to you and General Donovan to put my life at risk. Correct?"

"That sums it up rather concisely, Bill," Dulles said. "But figure it's wartime. Every man's life is being put at risk by somebody. Or several somebodies."

"True enough."

Dulles took a final sip of brandy. His glass empty, he set it aside.

"Any other questions for tonight?" Dulles asked.

"Do you know a good watch merchant in Bern? Anyone you favor?"

"Doing some shopping? For your lady in New York, I'd bet."

"I'd like to," Cochrane said.

"There's a Swiss Frenchman named Maurice Lesser near the big clock tower. He knows me. He'll take care of you and give you a fair price on anything in his shop. He'll be the only one in the shop. Should I phone him and ask him to take care of you?"

"Yes. Thank you."

There was a pause, then Dulles spoke again. "I should mention one other factor in this before you read it in the file."

Cochrane waited.

"This was supposed to be a three man operation," Dulles began. "You were intended to have some support going into Germany. Two men. Problem is, there's a venal little Gestapo officer who's been made the principal for the other side on this case."

"And so?"

"And so, indeed! Somehow the Gestapo got wind of what we were doing. An informer, most likely. The Gestapo agent is named Wesselmann. If there had been one more day, Wesselmann might have known there were three of our people on the plane. But he didn't so you're alive and Skordeno and Cambulat are dead."

Dulles paused.

"I don't have to tell you what happened, Bill. You saw it for yourself. Poor bastards. They were good men." He paused, then concluded. "Don't forget about them if you happen to encounter the man who murdered them."

Chapter 22

Marseille, Vichy France
December 1942

In a dreary basement conference room in the main prefecture of police in Marseille, Hans Wesselmann stood at attention as his Gestapo commander, Heinrich Nussman, Klaus Barbie's former top assistant in Lyon, berated him in language that might have scorched the wallpaper had there been any. The doors were closed but the tongue lashing could be heard throughout the corridor. These grim gray rooms, including *Chambre 017*, the one used for torture, had been commandeered by the SS and the Gestapo from the local police. It did not take a genius to know not to interfere. The regular city gendarmes upstairs went about their daily business and rarely ventured to the lower level.

Had anyone peered through the thick glass of the small panel on Kriminaldirektor Nussman's office door, one would have seen the rigidly posed Wesselmann stiff, sweating and not far from a tremble. For most of the quarter hour excoriation, he remained silent. Occasionally his lips wavered and moved as he formed short simple answers or questions. The next thing he knew he was dismissed and ordered to rectify his egregious mistake by any means possible, as quietly as possible and without fail.

Wesselmann turned sharply after his browbeating. He left the room, his cheeks burning, his insides surging and his knees weak. He walked down a corridor that was even more gloomy than the meeting room. Everyone gave way. He blinked rapidly, anger and fear smoldering within him. He said nothing to anyone who passed him as he walked to his small office, Chambre 018.

Across from "018" was the torture room. Just last week, a local resistance leader named Henri Picard had been beaten and skinned alive by Klaus Barbie, who had come down from Lyon to interrogate the prisoner. Later Picard's head was immersed in a bucket of ammonia. He died shortly afterwards; his body disposed of overnight in the harbor beneath the Chateau d'If.

Wesselmann had been part of a detail of three to do the job. Well, Wesselmann told himself, he had done better than Picard. So far.

Wesselmann closed his office door. He grabbed a pack of Gauloise cigarettes and smoked one. He fell into thought. He was a man who knew his own limitations. He lacked the mental acuity with which many Germans of his age had climbed the ladder of the SS and the Gestapo. He lacked the handsome Aryan features that propelled many of his peers upwards. And he did not have the physical bulk to make witnesses cower.

What he did have was viciousness and tenacity and a devotion to Adolf Hitler, whom he considered the savior of Germany and the Aryan people. Cornered and on the brink of being disgraced among his peers, he also had the venality to slash back at whoever was tormenting him.

Wesselmann's office was no more than ten feet by eight feet. It held two metal tables and two chairs, a filing cabinet, a small bookcase and a fan that never worked. On top of the tables, which barely had any working space, were files on local informers and suspects. The single window looked through a grate up to a junk-strewn courtyard. Outside it was raining and the rain splattered the glass.

Wesselmann stood very still, then anger overtook him. He picked up a stack of snitch files and flung them across the room. He kicked a chair. This mistake at the airport was a huge black mark on his record, even though it had not been his fault.

And then there was the even worse mistake, the one for which he was upbraided by Kommandant Nussman. One of Wesselmann's sources was a street prostitute named Irena whom he patronized when he didn't have enough money for one of the fancier brothels.

Whores could be arrested if they worked in public on the streets, but many of them, including Irena, bought protection with their services. Irena had heard a story from another client, a drunken submarine officer on leave.

The story revolved around about a man in the SS hierarchy who had links to the German navy. The man was a traitor, a defeatist. He was looking to deliver to the United States a bonanza of defense information and then defect to the United States with his family.

In the pursuit of such, the man had contacted Allen Dulles in Geneva through intermediaries. Two spies were being sent to usher the man and his information out of Germany. One of the spies had had previous contact with the man during the 1930's. That was the story Wesselmann had received.

Wesselmann had seen this as a major case. If he could break it, it was a sure path to huge advancement in the ranks. So Wesselmann had investigated and pulled every string he knew of. He had the aircraft intercepted in France, had met it himself, and had terminated the two spies.

Or at least he thought he had. He had acted too quickly. He didn't have the story completely correct. Much of it was spot on, but the details about the spies was wrong. There had been three, not two. The third one had slipped past him. Wesselmann remembered him very well. He had used a Canadian passport and had a letter of passage which, now seen in retrospect, had been a fake.

Now the spy, travelling under a fake passport, had landed in Geneva and was most likely on his way to Germany. Wesselmann had reviewed the flight information and had now narrowed it down as to he was looking for.

Nussman had given him free reign and the authority. He had also given him the alternative: resolve this quickly or suffer your own sorry fate, instead.

Chambre 017, located across the hall in this dreary basement, was the alternative. Only it wouldn't be Wesselmann's head in a bucket of ammonia. It would be a set of more private body parts.

Wesselmann spent the next days digging through his files, examining angles, making phone calls, prowling through his informers among the students. Suddenly, he thought he had a connection. He understood why the SS officer was so intent on defecting and getting one member of his family out of Germany. And sure enough, once again the case revolved around a troublesome female.

Chapter 23

Bern, Switzerland
December 1942

Cochrane went for a walk in the Swiss capital. Situated on a cliff surrounded on three sides by the aquamarine waters of the River Aare, a tributary of the High Rhine, the city had, for better or worse, preserved its medieval character. The streets were cobbled and bordered by covered, arcaded sidewalks that wound along for miles. On the lower levels of the buildings were shops, cafés, bookstores, and restaurants, while the upper floors were residences.

The old town was not far from the government center. It was segmented by public fountains, old statues, towers, several bridges across the Aare and the famous Clock Tower that dated from the Thirteenth Century.

Cochrane walked toward the tower from the east. There was a slight drizzle. He stopped at a kiosk and purchased a *Neue Berner Zeitung*.

Most of the Swiss, including many who were pro-Nazi, had feared a possible invasion by Germany. So, being a cautious people who had been at peace for several hundred years, they had removed all street signs. Cochrane had been in the Swiss capital in 1938, however, and recalled enough to retain a sense of direction and location. He also knew, as did Dulles, that the clock tower, the Zytglogge, was the key landmark medieval tower in Bern. Built in the early Thirteenth Century, it had served the city as guard tower, prison, clock tower, center of urban life and civic memorial.

It had once even been a women's prison, notably housing *Pfaffendirnen,* "priests' whores," women convicted of sexual relations with clerics. The clerics were convicted of nothing, but the women were incarcerated.

Cochrane followed an unpredictable pattern on foot. He slipped in and out of three stores and one café. Finally, convinced that no one was following him, he arrived at 99 Bundestrasse, the storefront of the watch merchant whom Dulles had recommended.

He was happy to see, from the display window, that the proprietor was still listed as Maurice Lesser, the name Dulles had given. Cochrane entered the store.

There were two other customers, a man and a woman speaking French. Cochrane knew enough French to place the accent as Niçoise, which meant Vichy, but it proved nothing. They may have been in exile. There was a man behind a counter and Cochrane assumed he was Lesser.

Lesser was a short thin man with very white skin and black hair. He stood behind a dazzling counter of time pieces, contemporary and antique, ranging from the affordable to the astronomically expensive.

He glanced at Cochrane but gave no indication of recognition. Then he looked back to the items the Francophones were examining. The woman tried on a watch.

"I'll be with you in a moment, sir," Lesser said to Cochrane in German.

"I'm in no hurry," Cochrane replied in German.

Cochrane browsed. The French couple finally purchased a Gebrüder Thiel watch. Lesser followed them to the door, thanked them politely, closed the door, locked it and returned to Cochrane. At the same time, Cochrane's eyes landed on exactly what he wanted in a display case. It was a woman's watch, a recent model, an Omega Chronometer with 14 karat rose gold.

"I wonder if I might examine this one?" Cochrane asked.

The watch merchant pulled a velvet cushion from beneath the display case. He reached in and gently lifted the Omega from the others.

"Quite beautiful," said Cochrane.

"I'm sure it matches the beauty of the lady you're purchasing for," said Lesser.

Outside the sun made a rare midwinter appearance. The jeweler held the watch by the edges of its leather strap so that the

163

pinkish gold could catch the sunlight. He adjusted his spectacles to make them magnify. He was impressed by his own merchandise.

"It would match my Laura quite well," Cochrane said. "May I?"

"Of course."

Cochrane took the watch in his hand. It was love at first sight.

"I'll take it," he said. "It's for my wife."

"Excellent, sir."

"There is one condition."

"Monsieur?" asked Lesser.

"I am in the midpoint of a professional trip which will take me out of the country. The trip has some peril. This is wartime, after all. I would be happy to pay you the full price now, but please keep the watch in your safe until I return. I will also give you the name of my wife and a postal address in New York. If I don't return within six months please send it along with a sealed note that I will write. Be sure that she receives it. May I rely on you?"

"That would not be difficult, sir," Lesser said. "I can do that."

"My employer assured me that you'd take care of this."

Lesser's eyes narrowed. "I understand perfectly," he said. He reached to another spot under the counter. His hand returned with a small gift card and envelope for the occasion.

"Perfect," said Cochrane. "Thank you."

Lesser put the watch back into a case and giftwrapped it in red with a white ribbon. Cochrane meanwhile wrote out a note to his wife.

Laura, he wrote. *I will always love you. Bill.*

He sealed it. On a separate piece of paper, he wrote Laura's full name and his home address on Seventy-Second Street in New York.

The watch cost three hundred Swiss francs. Cochrane paid in cash.

Lesser placed the cased watch in a strong envelope along with the note and the address. He gave Cochrane a nod.

164

"So, to be clear, in the case of my death you'll see that the watch gets to my wife. Correct?" Cochrane asked.

"Of course, sir," said Lesser. "We have several such orders. We will take care of every one." He paused. He switched into English. "And tell Mr. Dulles I send my regards. We served together in the diplomatic corps in Vienna several years ago."

Chapter 24

Munich
January 1943

In a corridor of a university building a few days later, Sophie and Hans spotted Frieda. They confronted her. Frieda confessed.

No, she wasn't a university student. She was only sixteen and attended a fashionable but notoriously rigid secondary school nearby. The school was an "internat." Students came from all over Germany and she boarded.

"My mother is dead and my father is away to the war," she said. "They stuck me at this very formal school." She was concentrating on music and mathematics, the work of Johannes Brahms and Kurt Gödel. "Everyone there is Teutonic and strict. Girls have to lower their britches and are caned by the male masters if they don't do their assignments. I hate it! So I sneak out."

"They don't miss you?"

"They don't care so long as I come back. All the girls sneak out. With the war, everyone has more to worry about than me. Plus, I'm a good student and I'm smart. I don't get caught."

"Why do you attend Professor Huber's class?" Hans demanded.

"I came over to the university to attend a concert," Frieda said. "I overheard talk about Dr. Huber and I was curious. So I come to listen and be with likeminded friends. I love what he says." She paused. "I'm anti-Nazi, too."

"How do we know you are?" Sophie asked.

"Trust me."

"It's dangerous to trust people," Hans said.

"Very dangerous," Sophie added.

"I know. But I just trusted you."

"Can we see where you go to school?" Hans asked.

"If you want to, yes. Take the tram with me on a Saturday."

Sophie and Hans went to see Frieda's school. Over several weeks, Frieda won their trust. She became a more integral part of the group, gradually had more to say and quietly developed friends at the university. In chats with some of the students, it became clear that the girl was phenomenally gifted in math. She was an excellent pianist and, in private, could play ragtime and jazz and the other melodies considered "degenerate" by the regime.

Frieda realized that she had nothing to fear from the members of the group. She became a regular at the meetings. So did Ilse, Frieda's longtime friend, who fell into a tight friendship with Sophie.

There was a piano at the Rathskeller Kleindienst. Sometimes Frieda would play the songs of Kurt Weill, music that the Nazi regime said was anti-German and smacked of "cultural Bolshevism."

Frieda had learned the songs in several language. She developed a fluency in English and French through her love of the popular music of the Twenties and Thirties. Ilse, the music student, liked to sing and frequently joined in. Also popular among the students was the music of Al Jolson, the great Jewish-American stage and film star, whose music was banned by the Nazis due to Jolson's "race." Frieda introduced Ilsc to some of Jolson's music. Ilse was great in English. One night a big blond kid name Albert who was also ex-Luftwaffe took over the piano and Ilse and Frieda sang *California, Here I Come*, a song that Jolson had introduced on Broadway in 1921 and later recorded in Hollywood.

The lights went dark in the Rathskeller and they had the whole place as an audience. They got up on the tables and sang.

They would do routines from time to time much to the delight of the students in attendance. Sometimes police or suspected snitches would come in, just to monitor what was going on. A student from the group at the door would blow a whistle and give a hand signal. The students would switch to patriotic songs, then have a huge laugh when the opposition departed.

One Saturday night, Hans handed Frieda a copy of a book in a thick envelope tied with string. "It's a gift from Sophie and me," he said. "Read it when you can. But it's banned. So be careful."

"All right," Frieda said. "May I look now?"

"Yes. But don't show it outside this group. You'll risk a lot of trouble."

At the same time, a lively discussion was taking place across three tables. The question at hand was what to name their group. Frieda was sitting across from Sophie. Frieda gently opened the envelope and slid a copy of Bruno Traven's popular novel onto the table. Frieda smiled. She loved to read stories that took her far away and had wanted to read this book in particular.

Sophie's eyes settled upon it. She looked up.

"White Rose?" Ilse asked aloud.

"White Rose!" Sophie said, invoking the book, the hacienda and the seemingly hopeless social struggle. "That's who we are in this group. The White Rose!"

Chapter 25

Bern, Switzerland
January 1943

In Bern, Allen Dulles could frequently be found in the late evening at the Palace Bellevue, usually with a beautiful woman on his arm. Nonetheless, the flourishing subculture of professional spies in the city annoyed him. There was no secret that Dulles was a high level intelligence operative or that his residence was being used for American intelligence work. Because of the openness of what should have been a covert operation, Dulles was constantly besieged by questionable visitors.

Many visitors were legitimate. But a greater number was not. Dulles listened to almost all of those who came. They would brazenly visit German agents in the morning, the British secret service in the afternoon, and Dulles's office on the Herrengasse in the evening. They would offer to each prospective buyer their carefully prepared and sensational reports, a few of which were actually true.

Dulles had learned the hard way to listen to everyone and take any meeting offered.

In 1916, after passing the Foreign Service exam and finishing his master's degree at Princeton, Dulles left for his first posting. He became the third secretary in the US Embassy to the Austro-Hungarian Empire in Vienna. He had barely washed his laundry when the United States declared war on Germany and the Austro-Hungarian Empire. Dulles scurried to Switzerland for the first time at age twenty-three, joining the American Legation in Bern. He arrived there April of 1917.

When Dulles arrived no one knew what to do with all the extra help, so the first secretary took him to lunch one day. "I'm assigning you to work in intelligence," the man said. "Keep your ears open. There are more spies in this city than there are peanuts in a bag at the circus. Write me a weekly report so that it looks like you're busy."

In the midst of all this, Dulles fell for a blonde, a Swiss woman who was said to be a knockout. She was socially prominent and a skilled tennis player.

Dulles and his best friend, a young undersecretary at the British embassy named Robert Craigie, were in hot pursuit of the woman and her twin sister. And why wouldn't they be? The two ladies had finally agreed to an unchaperoned "tennis weekend" at a country chalet.

Late on the Friday afternoon of the planned departure, Dulles was concluding his week as the legation's duty officer. He anticipated the type of weekend any young man might dream of.

The telephone rang. A man with a ponderous Russian accent introduced himself in German as Vladimir Illich Lenin and urgently requested a meeting for that same afternoon.

Dulles assumed the caller was just another local nut case trying to get back to his homeland, looking for some sort of help. Dulles told him to stop by on Monday.

"Monday will be too late!" Lenin snapped. "I must talk to someone! Now! This afternoon!"

Dulles declined. "Come in Monday," he repeated.

The next morning, Saturday, Lenin was on his way to Russia in the sealed train provided by German officials. He arrived at Finland Station in Petrograd on April 16, 1917, where he was greeted by a large crowd of workers, soldiers, sailors, and Bolshevik supporters. Lenin proceeded to change the history of the Twentieth Century.

Hence, as the Second World War plodded on Dulles gave an audience to all of the kooks and cranks, con men and spies who wanted to bend his ear, always suspicious yet always trolling for that one little item that could turn the tide of history.

As Bill Cochrane had discovered, the apartment he had leased at 23 Herrengasse, was reserved for special clients. It too had more than a few armaments and security arrangements. He presented himself there again on his fifth day in the Swiss capital.

170

"I'm ready," he told Dulles at a mid-morning meeting, "to go to Germany."

"Good," Dulles said. "The first part of your assignment: you get yourself to Berlin without being uncovered. We've equipped you with some addressees for contacts and safe houses. You've memorized everything?"

"Yes."

"The addresses are vital," said Dulles. "If you must note them somewhere, put them into your own code and keep them well hidden. We have very few working contacts in Berlin right now, especially as it pertains to this case. Connect with your contacts. There's a small apartment waiting for you: a room and a half on the ground floor of a secure building. That's a key address. You've got that embedded in your brain, yes?"

"Yes."

"What is it?"

"125, Friedrichshain."

"Good. You have a contact who works as a waiter in the Haus Faterland, also, and one who parks his car on the Frieburgstrasse near the big station. Those are you priorities, along with our guy Stein, one of your key contacts, who may or may not be alive." He thought for a moment. "There's also a drinking place called the Tavern Wittgenstein. It's friendly to our people. Drop in at least a few times. Be seen."

"How many times is 'a few'?" Cochrane asked.

"As often as you can without being suspicious. Enough to be seen."

"I read and memorized everything," Cochrane said.

"Of course," Dulles said. "Right. Ah, look, Bill, the anti-Hitler underground in Berlin is miniscule, but it's there. Someone will find you when it's known that you're in Berlin. The trick is to be recognized by our people but not theirs, right?"

"It's a good trick when it works," Cochrane said.

"Okay. It's an inexact science. But I'm convinced. You're as ready to go as you'll ever be."

"Thanks."

"Keep in mind that our key contact will be putting more information in your hands, your care, your custody. Your mission will be to get that source of information back to me, personally. Follow? You are to bring the item here to me and present it to this office. I will vet it and then you will accompany it back to Washington. When all of that is confirmed, our contact will eventually follow. The Germans are already setting up their rat lines, by the way, their routes of escape when the Nazi roof caves in. You're not travelling with a weapon are you?"

"I don't have one, no."

"Don't carry one across the border into Germany. You'll get arrested. But you'll need one in Berlin. Once you're ensconced in a safe location, one will be delivered. Don't ask questions when it arrives."

Dulles opened a side drawer on his desk. He pulled out three cartons of Lucky Strike cigarettes. "Take these," he said.

"I don't smoke," said Cochrane.

"Of course you don't. But most of the Germans who are susceptible to petty bribes do. I don't need to explain that to you, do I?"

Cochrane shook his head.

"Use your second passport, the Henri Bremer one, to go into Germany, but use the Stykowski identity day to day, unless you need to improvise. You have a second set of transit papers, correct?"

"Correct."

"Be prepared to fight your way out of Germany again. I may be able to arrange some extra help for you while you're there, to make up for the loss of Cambulat and Skordeno. But I can't promise anything. Sorry."

"I understand."

"Oh! By the way," Dulles said. 'Pineapple'."

"What?"

"*Pineapple.*"

"What the hell is 'pineapple'?" Cochrane asked.

"What's what?" Donovan responded.

"Pineapple!"

"Sorry? Say it again?"

"What the hell, Allen?" Cochrane snapped. "Pineapple! Pineapple!"

"There," Dulles said. "Good. You've got it. That's the operational word. If someone says it to you, they're part of our team. I'm sure you won't forget it. I made you say it four times. Good luck, Bill. Be sure to come back in one piece. I'll be waiting here in Bern."

"And my wife will be waiting in Manhattan. I'll be happier when I see her than when I see you."

"That's how it should be, my friend. May God protect you."

They shook hands.

That evening, Cochrane carefully packed his suitcase for Germany, keeping the Bremer passport and letter accessible as needed. He would leave for Berlin at 11:00 AM the next day.

Chapter 26

Bern to Berlin
January 1943

Cochrane found a comfortable seat in a train compartment for six passengers. Two seats were empty. Three young men occupied the trio of seats across from him. They wore civilian clothing but had military shoes and haircuts. They were sitting hugger-mugger across the seats, laughing and pushing each other. Cochrane wasn't sure whether or not they were drunk, even at that hour of the morning. He was equally unsure if they were Swiss or German until they started to speak and laugh further. Apparently they had just spent a few merry days on leave with some Swiss ladies in Bern.

Their German was from the north of the country, probably near Hamburg. They looked like three army friends on leave. One of them had huge hands and another had a scar across the side of his neck. As Cochrane looked more closely, he saw that most of the man's left ear was missing. War wounds, Cochrane concluded. Another had food stains all over the side of his suit jacket. It looked as if he'd had a drunken collision with a soup bowl.

The train left the station at 11:23 in the morning. Cochrane pulled his book on Wagner out of his bag, the one that he had bought at the market in Lisbon. He settled in to read, keeping his eyes lowered and his ears open. It would not have been the first time that he saw or overheard something of interest on a train. Little things added up, he always told himself.

Cochrane had brought with him a Swiss newspaper. This had been an unconscious act, unthinking really. The German government was at war not just with an assortment of foreign powers but also with the worldwide free press. Cochrane had placed the copy of *Der Neue Zürcher Zeitung,* Zurich's most respected journal, on the empty seat next to him. There was a bold article on the front page focusing on the war on the Eastern front. It was not good news for Team Berlin.

The Wehrmacht had made a bold move in the east to capture Moscow. Cochrane knew as much from newspapers in New York and Washington. But now according to the Zurich newspaper, the move had officially failed. Or at best it had not yet been successful, which was the next worst thing to failure. No one in Berlin was admitting anything.

From what Cochrane had read, the Soviet forces had constructed three defensive belts, deploying newly raised reserve armies, tank divisions and rifle brigades. The defenses had stymied further Wehrmacht advances on Moscow.

Now in early 1943, a Soviet strategic counter-offensive was pushing the German armies back to the positions west of Moscow. All this while the dreaded Russian winter held on and snarled logistics for the invaders, much as it had for Napoleon in 1812. The failure to knock Russia out of the war was a major setback, terminating the goal of a quick German victory in the USSR.

The newspaper reported that Field Marshal Walther von Brauchitsch had apparently been relieved as the commander of the Oberkommando des Heeres, the OKH, the High Command of the German Army. Hitler had now re-appointed himself as Germany's supreme military commander, much to the horror of the professional army which was in no position to voice objections.

Cochrane was distracted from his book. He picked up the newspaper, stared at the article and processed its implications. If the German juggernaut failed and was locked into a stalemate, the war in the east could be endless. If the German armies were defeated, captured and collapsed – probably then to be liquidated by the Soviets – nothing would halt the westward advance of the Red Army and Bolshevism. The prospect was almost as frightening as National Socialism.

A related article in the paper also mentioned that since the launching of Operation Barbarossa in the summer of 1941 an estimated three million Soviet prisoners had died while in German hands.

Suddenly one of the German soldiers, seeing the front page while Cochrane read an interior page, got a burr up his backside. He took aim on the content of the news.

"Lies! All lies!" barked the soldier. "Fraudulent stories and propaganda!"

Jostled, Cochrane lowered the paper to see what the fuss was about. Two of the soldiers pointed at the front page headline in disapproval. The third one, the one with the war wounds, said nothing.

"What is?" Cochrane answered in German. "What lies?"

The German with only one and a half ears stood, leaned across the space between seats and brushed his hand forcefully across the newspaper.

"Lies in the cheesemaker journal!" the soldier insisted. "We are winning the war against Bolshevism!"

"Of course," said Cochrane with a nod. "Complete lies in the Swiss papers these days. Where did you fight and what did you witness?"

The German eased back and sat. "They treated us as liberators."

"Who did?" Cochrane asked.

"The filthy Poles. The degenerate Red Russians."

"The Belarusians, too," said one of his Kammaraden.

The others did not seem too sure, though the one with the soup stains mentioned that Jews and Communists controlled all of the French and English language press. This on orders from Churchill, Roosevelt and that weird de Gaulle fellow who was hiding out in London.

"Oh, I'm sure they *did* welcome you as liberators," said Cochrane, remaining in German. "How could it have been any other way? But you know, I don't think the Reich will last a thousand years as the Fuehrer has promised."

Their gazes stiffened. All six bloodshot eyes narrowed on Cochrane.

"I think it will last *two* thousand years!" Cochrane exclaimed. *"Heil Hitler!"*

176

A moment, and all three barked and hooted their approval. Cochrane folded away the newspaper. He closed the book on Wagner. He engaged them in conversation about their military experiences, where they were stationed, troop strengths, movements, shortages and means of communications.

"We shot a hundred civilians in a town named Griski in Poland," one of them said. "They were trying to surrender. Our commander told us to shoot them."

Another of them, the one with one and a half ears, laughed. "There was a well in this one Belarusian village. We threw twenty-six Jewish children down it, then threw in two grenades."

"Where was that?" Cochrane asked.

"Mogilev," the soldier said. "Our orders were to exterminate Belarusian settlements for German colonization."

"And that's what you did?"

The soldier shrugged. "What would you have done? Those were orders. You obey or get shot."

"You served the Reich and did your job," said Cochrane amiably, hiding his disgust. He reached into his bag and broke open a carton of Lucky Strikes. He flipped a pack to each soldier. The soldiers accepted the smokes and thanked him.

Cochrane nodded to the sleeve and military insignias of the soldier with the wounds. "That's your unit?" he asked.

"Yes. Thirtieth Waffen Grenadier Division of the SS."

"You must be proud. Who was your heroic commander?"

"Field Marshal Hans Seigling."

The discussion drifted. By now, Cochrane realized the soldiers were drunk. But he didn't push the conversation. He let it ramble. He tried to memorize what they were telling him. He put an extra pack of cigarettes in his pocket and returned the rest to his luggage.

"We had three teenage girls, hostages near Minsk. Blondes," the soldier in the middle chipped in, opening a pack of smokes. "The whole rifle squad raped them. Then an SS major shot them. Sadistic bastard. Wrecked our fun."

So it went. It was extraordinary how much they had to say so early in the day to a stranger.

The train arrived at Basel, the Swiss city at the border with Germany. There was a customs and immigration check. Cochrane used his second passport. The stop was lengthy but went smoothly. Then the same train continued, which was unusual. Normally, Cochrane knew, a German train would have been put into service. That told Cochrane that there was either a shortage of rail transit or a problem. He made a mental note.

There was one further wrinkle en route.

When it reached the first station beyond the Swiss border, the train eased off the regular track to a waiting area. Cochrane broke a sweat. A local police official boarded and ordered all male passengers to disembark for a passport check.

A Gestapo officer flanked by a huge soldier observed the procedure. He doublechecked some of the passports, including the one belonging to the lone North American traveler. Cochrane's forged permit for travel eased the situation. But the Gestapo man carefully put down in his notebook the particulars of the passport.

A few minutes later a local cop announced that an order had just been received from Berlin to detain all Americans and British Commonwealth subjects presenting themselves at the frontier and to report all such cases to Himmler immediately. A major search was on. They were looking for someone

For the next half hour or so, Cochrane nervously paced the platform. He considered trying to escape into the nearby forests, where he would hope to meet up with resistance members. He decided against it. They were probably twenty kilometers into Germany and the terrain looked hilly, snowy and desolate.

Finally, with the train about to leave, the gendarme rushed over to Cochrane and motioned him to climb aboard.

"Are you certain?" Cochrane asked.

The Gestapo officer was nowhere in sight, having gone to the neighborhood bistro for lunch.

"Go!" the stationmaster said. "Leave!" he whispered. "Our cooperation with these Nazi bastards has its limits!"

"You won't get in trouble?"

"Herr Arschloch went upstairs with a cheap whore," the man said. "If he reports me for letting the train go, I report him for sodomy while on duty. Who's in more trouble then, Mein Herr?"

"Good question," said Cochrane.

Cochrane tipped his hat and re-boarded the train. When he arrived back at his seat, however, the soldiers were gone. His book on Wagner was still there but his Swiss newspaper had been confiscated. The train however steamed smoothly northward toward the capital and nerve center of Nazi Germany.

Chapter 27

Stalingrad, Soviet Union
January 1943

In the brutal battle for Stalingrad, the stalemate had turned more than bitter for the Wehrmacht's Sixth Army, under the command of Field Marshall Friedrich Wilhelm Ernst Paulus. Months had worn on; the Germans were unable to cross the Don and Soviet resistance was relentless. The Soviet military had captured the airfields used by German forces, shattering the supply lines needed by any army.

Now the Sixth Army was running out of food and ammunition. Many soldiers had no clean water. Rats were everywhere. Skilled Soviet snipers were active day and night. Hundreds of German soldiers had gone crazy and thousands were wounded. Evacuation was impossible. The Germans held one makeshift emergency air strip for evacuation and the Red Army was closing in on that. The situation was so desperate that many of Paulus's young soldiers were standing on top of their trenches in order to be shot by Soviet rifle squads and put out of their misery.

On the seventh of January 1943, General Konstantin Rokossovsky, commander of the Red Army on the Don front, called a ceasefire. He offered surrender terms that were more than reasonable to Paulus's men: normal rations, medical treatment for the ill and wounded, permission to retain their badges, decorations, uniforms and personal effects. As part of his communication, Rokossovsky advised Paulus that he was in an indefensible position. Paulus could surrender his command or have the quarter million men under his command annihilated by the building Soviet forces. Those were the two choices.

General Paulus contacted Berlin and requested permission from Hitler to surrender. Hitler was inside his Wolf's Lair field headquarters near Rastenburg, East Prussia.

"Capitulation is beyond consideration!" raged Hitler in the response that came back to Marshall Paulus. "The front with

Russia is fifteen hundred kilometers. Every additional day that the Sixth Army holds out helps the whole front. It draws away the Russian divisions from Ukraine and Georgia. Continue to resist!"

The Wehrmacht High Command rejected the offer, also.

Paulus messaged back that he would obey the orders of the High Command.

Chapter 28

**Berlin
March 1943**

There are men who return to cities where they have once lived, worked or had romances and find part of their youth flirting with them from the streets and buildings, the sights and the sounds.

For Bill Cochrane, when he arrived at Berlin's main railroad station, the Anhalter Bahnhof, for the first time in four years, this was far from the case. He had no sooner set foot on the train platform after arrival than a scene before him gave him a jolt of horror.

Armed guards from an SS unit were herding two dozen elderly men and women, each carrying one small bag, toward a train that was readying to depart. Cochrane stopped to light a cigarette. A casual smoke was his way of surreptitiously watching something. With a further surge of disgust he saw that all of the docile elderly people wore yellow stars. A few wore medals from the Great War. He assumed quickly and correctly that they were Jews being deported. The group passed within a few meters of him.

Cochrane made his mental notes. He was on Platform One. As he smoked, he watched with peripheral vision and saw the destination of the captive voyagers. The guards prodded them onto the train on the next track. A sign on the platform gave the destination as Theresienstadt, which Cochrane knew to be a town in what was then Nazi-occupied Czechoslovakia. It had once been a spa. Who knew what was going on there now?

The guards took the old people to the end of the train. They pushed them into two specially consigned third class carriages. The carriages had no windows.

The final passenger was an old woman in a babushka who must have been at least seventy-five. She protested her departure, probably already knowing she would never return. She started screaming and crying, hysterically yelling something about wanting to see her daughter.

One of the guards grabbed her by the arm and neck. Cochrane's sense of decency told him to intercede. But he stopped himself. The guard shoved the old woman roughly into the last carriage. Another pushed her harder with the butt of his rifle and his foot. When she fought back they punched her, picked her up and threw her into the car. Cochrane's final glimpse of her had her falling. The guards pulled the door shut and padlocked it from the outside. They laughed.

He turned away in disgust. He felt helpless. He hated the feeling. How could he not? He continued to watch.

The guard unit fell out of formation and came back along the platform, passing close to Cochrane. Cochrane counted twelve of them. Most of them were laughing or smiling. They appeared to be proud of their work, though one young man who appeared to be no more than eighteen looked confused and stricken, as if he had trouble comprehending what he had just done. Not wishing to attract attention to himself, Cochrane dropped his half-smoked cigarette onto the platform. He had trouble fighting back the urge to say something. He turned and walked toward the exit, a deep sense of revulsion in the pit of his stomach. He slammed right into two large uniformed soldiers. One grabbed his arm. The other put a hand on his shoulder.

"You are watching something?" one asked.

Jolted, "Not at all," Cochrane said.

"Papers?" the first one asked.

As Cochrane pulled his documents from his pocket, the whistle of the deportation train screeched. The train lurched and began to move. His insides felt as if they were ready to explode. One of the soldiers looked him up and down while the other studied his papers.

"I have business with the Reich," he said.

"What sort?"

"Financial."

Cochrane watched the train roll out of the station. No one else paid it any attention. From that, Cochrane concluded that what he had witnessed was an all-too-common occurrence. He drew a breath. He knew he would be unable to forget what he had just seen.

The soldiers who had approached Cochrane stepped away for a moment. Then they came back to him. They returned his documents.

"Be on your way," one said.

"Yes, sir," Cochrane said.

The American spy emerged onto the street and into a blast of frigid wind. He drew a breath. He pulled his hat, coat and scarf close to him. So far, the previous winter of 1941-1942 had been the coldest on record in Europe, but this winter of 1942-43 wasn't much warmer.

There were shivering merchants with pushcarts outside the train station. They had trash cans burning trash for heat, creating a putrid layer of low smoke. Cochrane stopped at a cart and bought a pair of woolen gloves, then a second pair in case he lost the first. Carrying only one suitcase now, he continued on his way. Nazi slogans and victory posters were everywhere.

Cochrane had liked Berlin when he had been there. He liked the theater, the clubs and the restaurants but had loathed the politics of the Third Reich. And gradually the city had changed under the Nazis. Theaters were censored, as were artists and writers. Most of his friends had either fled or been arrested. The spirit in the dining places had changed. He knew one reason: non-Aryan owners and waiters had been barred from doing business.

Yes, the city bustled as he remembered it, though in a different way than he recalled. He recognized his old surroundings but sensed a subdued mood on the street, even though the city was bedecked with red and black banners with prominent swastikas.

Men in uniforms were everywhere: soldiers, police and who knew what sort of security? He wondered if the news of the lack of victory in Russia contributed to the mood on the street. He wondered how many Gestapo were embedded in the crowds.

Cochrane crossed the street from the train station. He knew there had been a row of hotels across from the Anhalter Bahnhof before the war. He had never stayed at any of these hotels. They were mostly for transits of a day or two. He entered one called the Zum Ritter and politely registered under his false identity. His Canadian passport bore no extra scrutiny when he provided his travel permit simultaneously.

The Zum Ritter was what he needed. A modest hotel where he had never been before and where there was almost no chance of running into anyone who had known him in the Nineteen Thirties. Nor did he need any mention of his real name.

The hotel was a temporary but brief part of his plan. He would register there and leave his suitcase. He would go out and scout his assigned location. He had memorized the locations Dulles had given him and knew his way around the city enough to find each address.

Once he was convinced that his back was clean and that the small apartment that the anti-Hitler underground had arranged was secure, he would move.

Not before. In the meantime, he would observe.

He unpacked in his room at the Zum Ritter. He moved some of his cash in Swiss francs and German marks to his billfold. He kept some small denomination of American currency, also. It came in handy. Everyone carried some if they were lucky enough to have it. Even in Germany the black market was greased by American dollars and British pounds sterling.

He felt naked without a weapon. He was anxious to obtain one. He tucked his passport into his inner pocket and proceeded. From a pants pocket, he found the smallest coin he had, a one Reichspfennig piece, a worthless piece of zinc complete with German eagle and swastika. Zinc had replaced bronze in the coinage because everything bronze had gone off to war. The coin was worth less than an American penny.

He prepared to move around Berlin. As he departed from his room, he made sure no one was watching. Then he wedged the one-pfennig piece into the slim gap between the door to his room and the door frame. The precise spot was two hand lengths below the doorknob. If the coin wasn't exactly in the same place when he returned, he would know that his room had been entered.

He went out late in the afternoon. He bought a street map and a small notebook from a kiosk. He sat in a sidewalk café and noted how often police came by and whether there was any activity on rooftops. He knew that Berlin had been the target of occasional air raids by the Royal Air Force and occasionally by American airplanes based in England. Cochrane looked to see where the air raid shelters were. If there was anything he dreaded more than being recognized or taken prisoner it was being bombed to death by "friendly" British or American aircraft.

He had already heard stories about spies behind the lines "neutralized" by their own planes. The potential of adding to the statistics on the subject was not something to which he wished to contribute.

Above all, he concluded that his first instinct was the best one: get in and out of Berlin as quickly as possible, get whatever it was he was here for and make the trek back to Switzerland.

He left the café.

It was his plan to return to the hotel, wash, change clothes and have a modest dinner. Daylight was dying. He decided to postpone his visit to the apartment address until the next day. Speed was essential in this mission but caution trumped speed. He needed to be patient.

As he walked back to the hotel however, he noticed a small crowd on the corner. He walked to it.

As he drew closer, he realized that what had drawn the crowd was the latest edition of *Der Sturmer*, a weekly tabloid-format newspaper of public disinformation that was devoured edition by edition by those who supported Hitler. It was a significant instrument of Nazi propaganda and was vehemently anti-Semitic. The paper was published privately by a vile little man named Julius Streicher. The paper did not display the Nazi party swastika in its logo, but everyone knew what it was. The billboard heading read, *Mit der Sturmer gegen Juda*: "With the Stürmer against Judea."

Copies of *Der Stürmer* were displayed in prominent Nazi-red display boxes called *Stürmerkasten* throughout the Third Reich. The display boxes allowed its fictions to reach those brain-dead readers who either did not have time to read a daily newspaper or could not afford the expense. All one needed was a low enough intellect to believe a word that was in the rag.

Cochrane knew all about the publisher, Julius Streicher. Streicher was a virulent anti-Semite and prominent member of the Nazi Party. He had been prominent in Nazi circles during Cochrane's first visit to the city. *Der Stürmer* was a sleezy central element of the Nazi propaganda machine.

The paper had an audience of half a million true believers every day. The newspaper had originated at Nuremberg during Adolf Hitler's rise to power. The first copy had been published in 1923. *Der Stürmer*'s circulation grew over time, the degree of the paper's outright lies and lunatic conspiracy theories intensifying over the years.

The paper was the mouthpiece for the downtrodden angry ignorant little man in the street. It ran daily caricatures of Jews and accusations that Jewish people used the blood of Christians in religious rituals. It also dealt in sexually explicit, anti-Catholic, anti-Communist, and anti-monarchist propaganda. Paper by paper, the mainstream press had been ridiculed by the Nazis and put out of business. There were no opposition newspapers in existence and most were stridently pro-Hitler.

As early as 1933, Streicher had been calling for the extermination of the Jews of Europe. He had given vicious fringe ideas a pseudo-respectability by putting them in print. Now his ideas were part of the mainstream of German public thought, further legitimized by a leader who embraced and expounded them. With the war going, Streicher regularly attacked recent immigrants and intellectuals. His readers cheered him on.

From the late 1920s, Julius Streicher's broadsheet had been so strident that it was even an embarrassment for the Nazi party. In

1936, the sale of the *Der Stürmer* in Berlin was restricted during the Olympic Games, rather than give visitors too good a look at what was going on in the Reich. Joseph Goebbels tried to outlaw the newspaper in 1938. Hermann Goering, whom *Der Sturmer* had libeled earlier in his career, banned *Der Stürmer* in all of his departments. Goering had a hatred of the paper after it published a completely fallacious article alleging that his daughter Edda had been conceived through artificial insemination. It was only through Hitler's intervention that Streicher was spared any punishment.

As Cochrane looked at the posted newspaper in revulsion, a young woman in her early twenties made a strange gesture at the displayed paper. Then she saw Cochrane and gave him a doubletake. At first, he feared she was someone he knew. But it wasn't. She turned and quickly stepped away.

As Cochrane moved into the small assemblage of a half dozen people in front of him, his eyes settled on a wet portion of that article. It took him a moment to realize what he was seeing and had seen. Someone had spit at the article and the paper was still wet from saliva. The spit was fresh. He guessed it was the young woman whom he had surprised and who had rushed away.

He looked at the article. It was another bit of rabid anti-Semitism, complete with a screaming headline and cartoonish illustrations. It was packed with racist caricatures and driven by an illustrated semi-pornographic story of a hairy apelike Jewish man seducing a naked virginal German girl. Cochrane bailed on the article after three paragraphs

Cochrane felt like spitting also. He turned away. He knew the direction to his assigned rooming house. He began to walk, circling twice en route to see if he could catch any followers, turning suddenly three times to smoke out any pavement teams. He went in and out of a café, reversed directions and was convinced his back was clean.

He continued on to a building at 125, Friedrichshain which was in the Kreuzberg neighborhood. The street was a narrow collection of shops, private houses and apartment buildings, middle class to working class. He did not know the neighborhood well but had no trouble orienting himself.

He found the specific location assigned by Dulles. By then it was dark. The instructions he had memorized called for him to go to that location during daylight hours and find the small apartment number 110 on the ground floor. A key would be under a flowerpot by the door. A local custodian would remove the key overnight so no intruder could take it.

Cochrane bought a small bottle of German brandy and pocketed it. He returned to the hotel, watching his back the entire time. He finished his moonshine and started the local product.

His spirits were buoyed by not being able to discern a shadow behind him. He took dinner early in the hotel refectory, then repaired to his assigned room. He lit a dim lamp, by which he read the opening thirty pages of *Vol de Nuit*. He took out his set of domino tiles and played two solitaire games.

Then he slept.

Chapter 29

Berlin
January 1943

The next afternoon, Bill Cochrane found his way back to 125, Friedrichshain.

He found the key under the flowerpot outside the door to the unit. The key was to a small apartment on the ground floor on the side of a brick building. There were stairs at the rear of the entrance foyer, and two apartments on the ground floor.

He took the key and entered the apartment. The flat was narrow, cramped and had a musty smell. The paint on the wall was chipped and stained. There had been water leakage from above. He wondered who had used the unit previously. There was a small kitchen area, a sitting room and a sleeping alcove. There was one window which had bars. It looked out onto an alley. The unit had electricity, though there was also a supply of candles, matches and two small gas lamps. It was not homey. It was gritty and rough edged: all the more reason to complete his assignment and get out of Berlin and Germany.

He inspected it carefully and departed. He wanted to keep taking different routes to throw off anyone who might follow. He decided to look for the Tavern Wittgenstein that Dulles had mentioned, the venue that might be a *sub rosa* meeting place for other people working for the Allied cause or, better, the OSS.

He took the tram to the center of the city, getting off a block from Friedrich Wilhelm University.

Friedrich Wilhelm University, like many of the German universities, had once been one of the finest in the world. The Nazis had done their best to destroy the learning systems in the country, always a goal of blind nationalists who never like the free exchange of knowledge. Men with solid academic credentials in the leadership positions of the high academies had been replaced by bigoted shills and ignoramuses with ranks in the SS. It had gone that way in Berlin, Munich, Heidelberg, Bremen and every other

German city, much as it also had in Fascist Italy and Francoist Spain. In Germany, revered seats of learning and enlightenment had been turned into branch outposts of the Ministry of Propaganda, much to the delight of all those who hated learning and intellectualism.

On his way to the center of Berlin, Cochrane saw neighborhoods that had been reduced to rubble. The British had started bombing Berlin, though most of the British bombs were still falling on Bremen, the port in the North Sea, to inhibit submarine activity. Bombing Berlin had proved difficult so far.

The tram dropped him the Mitte district in the center of Berlin. He drew a breath. He could not possibly have been in more dangerous territory as a spy. Something about having his feet on the ground in this place, not far from the Reichstag, not far from the Brandenburg Gate, a stone's throw from Gestapo Headquarters, turned his stomach to water. It was like a special form of stage fright – he had done some acting in Provincetown, Massachusetts as a much younger man – that incapacitates even the most skilled of information gatherers from time to time. He was starting to feel it. It told him to back up and walk away.

He blanked for a moment. He froze. His nervous system stalled. It was two or three seconds at most but it felt like four hours. Then he realized that he was staring down the wide boulevard and looking directly at the main building of what had many times been referred to as "the mother of all modern universities." He also saw a railroad bridge which ran close by Friedrich Wilhelm University's academic buildings.

He drew a breath and kicked himself back in gear.

He chose – foolishly perhaps – to go forward. He had come this far. He waited for traffic, crossed the street and fell into a comfortable stride.

He scoured the neighborhood, paying special attention to bars located by or under the bridge, as Dulles had suggested. He checked the names. He found nothing called Tavern Wittgenstein. What was he missing? What was wrong?

There was no one he could trust enough to ask. Asking questions would only draw suspicion to himself. Maybe later if he got desperate. After an hour, he gave up.

He ducked into a doorway and pulled his map from his coat pocket. He quickly mastered the return route by foot and tram.

It took him forty-five minutes to get back to the Zum Ritter. The coin he had left in the doorway was still in place. That calmed him.

He gathered his baggage, paid his bill and took another tram back to Kreuzberg, walking the final block, covering his back. He still detected no surveillance, though he also knew it could be an illusion.

He settled into his small flat.

There was an 8:00 PM curfew in the neighborhood, so he was sure to have a light dinner in a wine bar adjacent to his temporary new home. He returned to his flat by seven thirty, read for a while, played a few solitaire games of dominos, spent too much time worrying about Laura in New York, fought off an intense spasm of loneliness and depression and again slept.

Chapter 30

**Berlin
January 1943**

At his new location, he met his neighbors the next afternoon, the people who lived in the other unit on the first floor. The man was named Heinz Kessler. He worked as a welder in a bicycle factory, he said when they met. Heinz was also the air raid warden for the building and did some chores around the building for a few Reichsmarks less in monthly rent. Heinz had wife. She was a talkative bookish woman named Greta. She was friendly and was quick to announce that she had a job as a seamstress in a factory that made military clothing.

She was proud of her work. She stitched uniforms for the men in the Luftwaffe. Her skills focused on the gray greatcoats with embroidered cuffs that the officers wore.

A few years earlier, she had worked at Peek & Cloppenburg, a well-known department store in Berlin, she said. But things had changed, not necessarily for the better, though she did say that she was happy to have food, work and a place to live.

Greta and Heinz invited their new neighbor to join them at a small beer garden halfway down the block. Cochrane closed his new residence and used another one pfennig coin to monitor his security. He joined Heinz and Greta in the beer garden. For a few moments he felt as if it were 1937 all over again and he hadn't made any enemies in Berlin, only friends.

Cochrane gave them his fake name and identity, however, and they had no reason to question it. They met at the beer garden at half past five in the afternoon. The day had remained dull and gray. But what further impressed Cochrane – what he had not anticipated - was that from what he could see, everyone was in the heart of a nation involved in a savage war, and everyone was going about his or her daily business, even the people who spit at the posted editions of *Der Sturmer*.

"So it's a good place to work?" Cochrane asked Greta. "The factory that makes the coats?"

She said it was. She mentioned how things were scarce, despite what people said on the official radio. For part of the previous winter she had been without an overcoat. But her boss, Herr Braun, was a decent man who tried to take care of his workers. He had given Greta some heavy black woolen fabric used for making Panzer tank division uniforms.

"As part of your apprenticeship," he had said. "Let's see if you can make an overcoat from scratch. Make it to your size. It's your training assignment, then keep it."

She did, and she was wearing it as they spoke.

"Do you read, Herr Stykowski?" she asked.

"Do I know *how* to read?" Cochrane asked in mild surprise.

"My wife is asking you if you like books," Heinz interjected indulgently as he inhaled deeply on a cigarette.

"Oh," Cochrane said with a laugh. "Yes, of course. I read and I do like books. Why?"

Greta leaned forward. "My grandmother was from Estonia," she said. "I still read in Russian. You're not supposed to have Russian books in Germany, but I have a few. Maybe six. Classics. Tolstoy. Dostoyevsky and Gogol. I'm not a defeatist, you understand. Hitler is a great leader doing great things. But I read in that language. Russian. It might make me useful to the Reich at some point in the future."

"What she means is if the Red Army arrives in Berlin," Heinz said, "she thinks she'll be able to reason with the soldiers."

Greta gave her husband a playful shove. Cochrane wasn't sure if Heinz's remark had been meant as a joke. Meanwhile Greta moved to the point of what she had to say. She had recently re-read *The Overcoat*, by Nikolai Gogol. In the story the main character, Akaky Akakievich is a put-upon clerk in a government office. He spends all his money on a new overcoat which is stolen. Further humiliations follow as he tries to find the coat.

"Because the man does not have the coat," Greta recalled, "Akaky dies of pneumonia. Soon after, there are reports of his ghost haunting St. Petersburg, stealing coats from others." She laughed. "Do you know the story?"

"I *do* know it," Cochrane answered.

As she spoke, Cochrane watched Heinz's brown cigarette slowly burning between his stained calloused fingers. Her husband was indulging the conversation but had disengaged from it. Without warning, he stood up without speaking, leaving behind half a glass of pilsner. He left the table and walked back toward their building. He limped badly. Cochrane watched him go, wondering what was going on.

"He'll be back," Greta said, explaining it away. "He has a weak bladder. He goes to urinate two dozen times a day. He also doesn't like this story. How do you know Gogol's work?" she asked.

"I read it in university in Canada," he said.

"They read Russian books in Canada?"

"Some do. Some don't."

"Why?"

"It's a famous story. And some people choose to study world literature."

"Oh. I read it with friends before the war, the story by Gogol," she said. "We had a discussion group in a public *konditorei*. Some of us asked questions. Was the story about bureaucrats? About human need? Was it a satire, or a tragedy? But then an old man sitting at a nearby table got up and walked over and scolded us. He was wearing a merit medal from the Great War. The Order of the Red Eagle. It shocked us. Both that he was there, and that he had such a high award. We hadn't seen him. He just appeared. We were all a little shocked. He scolded us all for missing the point.

"'Ghosts are very real,' he said. 'None of you understood the story. The story was about a real ghost.' The old man said that he knew that ghosts were real because for years he had been in the Great War and still saw many of his friends who had been killed. Then we blinked and he wasn't there anymore. But we all saw him. What do you think?"

"I wouldn't know what to say to that," Cochrane said. For a moment, the comic hijinks of Noel Coward's *Blithe Spirit* passed through his mind. They triggered thoughts of Laura back in New York. Then those thoughts were gone and he was back to Berlin.

He tried to change to subject. "Tell me more about where you work," he said. "The factory."

"Why?"

"I'm curious."

"Curious why?"

"As a new friend," Cochrane lied.

She rambled through several details. Her factory was in the Hackesche Höfe in Mitte, which Cochrane recalled as the heart of Berlin's Jewish district. Down the street from where she worked, Greta volunteered, was a nursing home in the Grosse Hamburger Strasse. It served as a collection center for Jewish people who were being relocated. Nazi terminology slithered softly through her lips.

"Berlin has already been *Judenrein*," she said, meaning 'cleansed of Jews'.

"It is a nicer city," she continued. "There were some Jewish girls in my school classes but mostly they are all gone. Jews all over town are being taken away, including the tailor, Goldberg, across the street. He was rounded up five days ago." She shrugged. "There were some Jewish girls in my class at school in 1933 but by the time I finished school in 1936, they were all gone. When I asked my mother where they went, she got very quiet. She said she didn't know but wherever it was, she said, the Jews had brought it on themselves."

"I saw some elderly Jewish people at the train station," Cochrane said. "They were being taken to a town named Theresienstadt."

"Oh?" she answered.

"Theresienstadt is a model ghetto. The Jews are lucky to be relocated there," came a voice from behind Cochrane. "Those are Jews who served in the first great war."

"It is also departure spot for those Jews moving to Palestine," said Greta.

"You know that to be a fact?" Cochrane asked.

"It's what we are told, so it's what I say," she said tersely.

Heinz slid awkwardly back onto the chair he had vacated. The burning brown cigarette was still in progress, though it was down to an ugly stub of about half an inch.

He had a newspaper under his arm, folded. "The Yids will be happier there," he said, loud enough to be heard at adjoining table. "Palestine. Far far away. Damn Jews. Parasites!"

He spat on the ground. Cochrane wondered if he were being tested. If this conversation was bait, he wasn't taking it.

"Well, we've gotten away from the point of my story," Greta said. "I was re-reading the story about the overcoat and my employers assigned me to make a coat for myself. I needed the coat. There are many hardships in Berlin this winter and I needed a coat. But isn't that strange that this should happen when I'm reading the book again."

"Call it good fortune," Cochrane said affably.

Heinz snuffed out his cigarette in a tin ashtray. He put a copy of *Der Sturmer* on the table. Cochrane sighed. Heinz pulled out a second cigarette. Greta took one from his pack and they carefully lit both on the same match.

"The factory is staffed by girls and women," Greta said when she resumed her chatter. "And a few men too old to serve in the armed forces. My cousin Fritz works there, too, operating an ironing machine. He watches out for me."

"Who does he watch out for?" Cochrane asked.

"Everyone. I shouldn't even be talking to you."

"My wife talks too much," Heinz said. "Did she tell you about the story about the ghosts?"

"She mentioned it. Interesting."

"She should shut up," Heinz said.

"I don't mind listening," Cochrane said.

"Greta's brother was in the Wehrmacht. He was killed in Poland by a Communist militia. Partisans. He was shot through the neck and bled to death. She's been seeing her brother and talking about ghosts ever since."

"Oh," Cochrane said. "I'm sorry."

Greta went very quiet very fast. Her husband shot her a glare. Then he apparently felt bad and put an arm around her shoulders. He hugged her and she leaned in sadly next to him.

"Hitler says we will all have to make sacrifices," she said. She tried to rebound the subject. "Are you married, Herr Stykowski?" she asked.

"No."

"Would you like to meet some German girls? Many of them are lovely. Their husbands are away in the army or in prison or dead. Inconvenient for them, convenient for you."

"Not right now, thank you."

"They'd probably enjoy the sex," Heinz said.

"Not interested."

Greta looked at him strangely. Then her mouth formed a perfect "O." What were things coming to these wartime days?

"Not interested in women? Are you homosexual?" she asked.

"No, no, no!," he answered. He shook his head. "Just busy," he said.

"Are there air raids?" Cochrane asked, pivoting the subject again. "I saw some damage on my way here from the Anhalter Bahnhof, the big train station."

They looked at each other. Heinz picked up the glass he had left behind and took a long drink. His eyes met Cochrane's dead on. His hand shook slightly as he put the glass down.

Then he answered. "There are occasional air raids during the nights," he said. "But no serious attacks yet."

"Things can change," Greta said. "And they probably will."

Heinz leaned in closer so as to not be overheard.

"You should know what to do," he said. "The air raid warning is a siren. Loud. Intense. Like American fire trucks from what I used to see when American movies were shown here. When the alarm sounds many people on this block go down to the cellar. You can do that in this building. We have reinforced the ceiling to make it more secure. But there is also an informal warning system.

Everyone listens to the radio. On the government station they will say, 'Bombers coming from Hanover-Braunschweig!' When we hear that, we know that Berlin will be the target."

"Many people don't have electricity. Or you can lose electricity quickly," Greta chimed in. "They have radios with a battery and a crystal, and we had to move the crystal to tune into the station. But some people listen to the BBC. It is prohibited by law, but people do it. London always knows what was happening before Berlin. Citizens go outside and bang their pots and pans with big wooden soup spoons. When you hear the noise, listen to the radio, and wait for the official warning. Even Horace knows people are listening to the BBC."

Mention of the BBC set Greta off in a new direction: the radio. The tenth anniversary of the Nazis' *Machtergreifung* was approaching, the day that was celebrated as the taking over of power. On January 30, 1933, Hitler had been named chancellor. The SA and SS had led torchlit parades throughout Berlin to celebrate. They did the same every January 30th since. This year both Goering and Goebbels were planning to give important speeches that were to be broadcast live by national radio.

"Everyone will be listening!" Greta said with apparent pride. "Everyone!"

Heinz was right. Greta was a chatter box. Charming, but a true motormouth.

"Who's Horace?" Cochrane asked, going back one subject.

"Horace is the local *gauleiter*," Heinz said. "He's the block captain for the Nazis and the SS. He used to be a farmer. He has a deformed arm from a threshing machine. The people who listen to the BBC might save his life, too, so he doesn't report it to the SS or the Gestapo. He chooses not to know."

Heinz paused. "There is also a neighborhood bunker you can go to if the alarm sounds. It's two streets over. That's the safest place. Would you like us to show you?"

Cochrane answered, "Sometime, maybe. Sure."

"Better sooner than sorry," Greta said.

"Okay. I would," Cochrane said, picking up a hint. "That would be very kind of you. Could we do it now?"

They paid at the beer garden and stood.

"Air raids," said Heinz as he limped along en route, "will soon be a major problem. That's not being a defeatist. It's just bound to happen."

"Of course," Cochrane said. "Of course."

They walked two blocks. The afternoon had turned to evening. It was already dark.

Chapter 31

**Berlin
Wartime**

Berlin had been at the far end of the flying range of British bombers as recently as early 1940. The German capital was six hundred miles from London. It could be bombed only at night in summer when the days were longer and skies clear, though those factors also heightened the peril to Allied bombers.

The first RAF raid on Berlin had taken place on the night of August 25, 1940. Nearly a hundred RAF aircraft bombed Tempelhof Airport near the center of Berlin. While the damage was slight, the psychological effect on Hitler and the populace was incalculable. Hitler had promised the German people that it couldn't happen, that England would be punched out of the war before the RAF had the capacity to strike Berlin.

And now attacks on the capital had happened! The raid on Berlin prompted Hitler to order the shift of the Luftwaffe's target from British airfields and air defenses to British cities. It was a questionable move that left the top Luftwaffe commanders muttering. British air defenses were exhausted and overstretched. Victory was with grasp and now there was to be a strategy shift?

During the final months of 1940, there were more raids on Berlin, none of which did serious damage. The raids grew more frequent in 1941 but were ineffective in hitting important targets. The head of the Air Staff of the RAF, Sir Charles Portal, justified these raids by saying that to "get four million people out of bed and into the shelters" was worth the losses involved.

The Soviet Union initiated air attacks on Berlin on August 8, 1941.

Bombers attached to the Soviet Navy, flying from the Baltic Sea off Estonia, conducted nearly a dozen limited raids on the Reich capital with three to ten aircraft in each raid. Bombers from the Soviet army, operating from Leningrad, executed several similar small raids on Berlin. The Soviet attacks were calling cards, a preview of horrible things to come.

During most of 1941, however, the British Bomber Command's priority had been to attack Germany's U-boat ports as part of Britain's effort to win the Battle of the Atlantic. Then on November 7, 1941, Sir Richard Peirse, head of RAF Bomber Command, launched a large raid on Berlin, sending more than one hundred seventy bombers to the capital. Again, little damage was done due to bad weather. Seventy-five of the bombers crashed in Germany from anti-aircraft fire or engine malfunction. These disastrous results led to the dismissal of Peirse. Since then, there had been almost nothing from the air and the Americans were hardly even in the ball game.

But Peirse had been replaced by Sir Arthur Travers Harris, who believed in both the efficacy and necessity of area bombing.

"The Nazis entered this war under the rather childish delusion that they were going to bomb everyone else," Harris remarked, "and nobody was going to bomb them. At Rotterdam, London, Warsaw, and half a hundred other places, they put their rather naïve theory into operation. They sowed the wind, and now they are going to reap the whirlwind."

The whirlwind was coming in the form of new bombers with longer ranges, particularly the Avro Lancaster, large numbers of which were nearing completion on the other side of the channel. The British air defense industry had also developed another lethal weapon from above: the de Havilland DH.98 Mosquito.

The 'Mossy,' as its pilots now called it, was a shoulder-winged multi-role twin engine combat aircraft, its frame constructed mostly of wood. It also became known as "The Wooden Wonder." Light and nimble, it was one of the fastest operational aircraft in the world.

Originally conceived as an unarmed fast bomber, the Mosquito was adaptable. It could also become a high-altitude night bomber, a fighter-bomber, an intruder, a low to medium-altitude daytime tactical bomber, a pathfinder, a day or night fighter or a maritime strike aircraft. It also served as a fast transport to carry small, high-value cargoes to and from neutral countries through enemy-controlled airspace. The crew of two, pilot and navigator, sat side by side. A single passenger could ride nervously in the aircraft's bomb bay as needed, while hoping that the bay wouldn't open accidentally.

Such was the bold talk. Such was the great war equipment in the offing. But not much had happened since the disastrous raid of November 1941. In a world at war, anything was always possible. Berliners remained ready.

Cochrane and his two new German friends ambled the two blocks to the shelter. The evening was suddenly very chilly, but dry. Cochrane kept the pace slow so that Heinz could keep up. He shivered. There was a feeling in the air of imminent snow.

They came to a concrete building that had been built in 1941, according to Greta. This was the local bunker. It had heavily reinforced walls and could accommodate two hundred people, Heinz explained. They went in. Anyone could take refuge there during an air raid. The building contained a honeycomb of small rooms, each with a pair of bunk beds, and two benches for sitting. There were also full kitchens and bathrooms. Cochrane saw many children. The place was noisy, a barrage of voices bouncing off concrete walls and tiled floors.

"Some Germans are living here full-time already," Greta said quietly, speaking under the noise. "Their homes have been destroyed by English killers. Even though the raids were not successful, many working people were nevertheless killed or left homeless."

"I understand," said Cochrane.

"I'm sure you do," Heinz answered in a strange tone.

Heinz abruptly took three large steps. He stood away from Cochrane and Greta. It was a strange move. Cochrane watched him carefully. It appeared that he was standing guard, not letting anyone else get too close. At the same time, Greta moved close enough to Cochrane to be a dancing partner.

"When you go back to North America, you'll tell people what you have seen here, I hope," she said.

Cochrane held very still. He acknowledged nothing.

"Hitler's Germany is hell on earth," she whispered. "No one knows when it will end. The only thing we fear more than the Nazis is the Russians. Or maybe it's the other way around."

Almost imperceptibly, Cochrane gave a slight nod. Greta's eyes were trained away in the direction of her husband. But she caught the gesture.

"*Danke shoen,*" she said. "*Viel Glück.* That's all. Be careful while you're here."

She looked back to him. Cochrane glanced at her. He made no gesture and spoke not a syllable. His eyes said everything.

They walked back to their building in the dark. They said good night in the lobby.

Cochrane returned to his ground floor apartment. He heard the Kesslers' door slam and opened his own door. He saw immediately that the coin was missing.

He stepped in carefully, feeling vulnerable.

He found a light switch and turned on a standing lamp. There was no one else there and nothing had been disturbed. But one thing had changed.

On the small kitchen table there was a brown shoe box. Cochrane approached it carefully. There was no string on it, nor was it sealed. He opened it and looked in.

There was an object wrapped in brown paper. He knew immediately that it was a pistol, the only a question was what sort. It turned out to be a Mauser, German made. There was a leather holster for it, the type that could attach to a belt. There were also two packs of nine millimeter bullets, twenty-four to a pack.

He sighed. Yes, unfortunately he needed this.

Other questions posed themselves and answered themselves just as quickly. The odor of brown cigarettes hung faintly in the air.

It was unmistakable. Heinz was the local underground contact in this neighborhood, which was why Dulles had arranged this residence. Similarly, this was why Heinz and Greta had introduced themselves so readily, and, to take things one step further, Heinz had delivered the weapon in the few minutes that he had stood up from the table, disappeared and returned.

Weak bladder? Maybe? Limp from an injury in the Great War?

Most likely. Pro-Nazi and an anti-Semite?

Not very probable.

Cochrane lifted the box. He saw something else which had been placed under the box. He grimaced. It was the one pfennig zinc coin that he had used as a door marker. It was Heinz's message that Cochrane wasn't being careful enough. Cochrane needed to raise the quality of his game. Cochrane appreciated the message. Casualness or carelessness could cost him his life and doom his mission.

Cochrane loaded his new pistol. He stashed the box and hid the bullets.

He settled in at the kitchen table. He read for a while, played a few games of dominos, then quit for the day. There was a chain on his window. He set it. There was a bolt lock and chain on his front door. He put both in use.

He placed the pistol at bedside and slept, happy to have survived another day behind enemy lines. There were no nighttime intruders and, better still, no air raids.

Then next morning, Cochrane saw Heinz in the front foyer, sweeping the floor before reporting to work. As Cochrane passed, he dropped two packs of cigarettes in Heinz's coat pocket. Cochrane turned to look when he reached the front door.

Heinz gave him a wink but no smile. The message couldn't have been any clearer if it had been concealed in blips, dots and dashes as they shot through the night skies to Bern and Washington.

Chapter 32

Berlin

There was a café attached to the beer garden. It was open the next morning for coffee and pumpernickel rolls. Cochrane stopped there for breakfast, then set out to see if he could contact any of the sources that Dulles had provided.

His first stop was the building that had once been Haus Vaterland, where Dulles's files indicated they had a contact, a waiter who worked in one of the many restaurants that had prospered there in peacetime. An unpleasant surprise punched Cochrane in the face.

The hulking building on the southwest side of Potsdamer Platz in central Berlin stood gray and forlorn, padlocked with iron grates pulled across the doorways. It was sad, borderline tragic, much like the theaters and bookstores that he had patronized when he lived in Berlin. They too were now sad, shuttered and abandoned. As he stood in front of the location of such past gaiety, snow began to fall out of an iron sky. The grim weather capped a dreary mood in a city which suddenly seemed oppressive beyond belief.

Before the war, Haus Vaterland been the most famous dining place in the world. On the third floor there had been a restaurant called the Rheinterrasse. The Rheinterrasse had a diorama to give the illusion of sitting outdoors overlooking the river between Sankt Goar and the Lorelei Rock. A troupe of twenty women, beautiful and scantily clad "Rhine maidens," danced between the tables under hoops twined with grape vines. For a single young man, what was not to like?

Lighting and sound effects created hourly thunderstorms during which the diaphanous attire of the dancers got naughty and wet. The spectacle was made even more lush, as one might imagine, by glass after glass of Moselle wine and the occasional presence of a friendly water nymph at one's table to nudge along the alcohol consumption.

A mischievous echo in Cochrane's head recalled the many hours he spent there admiring the maidens. He was lucky enough to meet a few and luckier still to have one special evening in his memory: a Rhine maiden named Annalise had taken a casual liking to him and invited him to splash down at her place overnight. Then a few more overnights.

No such luck today. The contrast between the remembered happiness of the early part of his previous stay in Berlin contrasted sharply with the chilly present. Compared with the more egregious excesses of the Weimar years, the doings of the Rhine maidens had been innocuous. But now the padlocks were in place in the interest of moral rearmaments and the cleansing the German spirit.

Disappointed, Cochrane turned. He started toward his second address for the morning.

The next destination was a street named Freiburgstrasse not far from the central train station. Cochrane went there by tram and on foot. He looked for the motor car that Dulles had mentioned but didn't see it or anything resembling it.

"We have a contact who parks his car on that block. It's an Adler Standard from 1930. Beaten up. License plate ends in '99'. Leave a note asking if he wants to sell it. Use the workname you're going under," Dulles had said.

So much wasted effort. A third of the block was in rubble. The rest of the block was without electricity. Damage from the November 1941 bombing, Cochrane guessed, yet to be repaired. He had already heard some stories: a few stray bombs had fallen far off their intended targets – or had been dumped by English pilots overanxious to get out of the battle zone. There were only three cars parked on the block, and none was an Adler Standard.

One, a Mercedes, was a burned out chassis. The parts of it that hadn't been incinerated had been stripped. One was a Volkswagen with a crushed roof and shattered windows. It lay flat on the ground on its rims. All four tires were long gone.

The other vehicle was an old Ford with a tiny Third Reich flag on its front right fender. It appeared that this vehicle still functioned. Very possibly, it belonged to the Nazi gauleiter, the block captain. Cochrane strolled too close and soon had an answer to his conjecture about the car's ownership.

In his peripheral vision, Cochrane saw a window shade jerk open in a street level apartment. A man of about fifty, stout with massive arms, broad shoulders and a black armband appeared in the window. The arms were folded and the man glared at Cochrane.

Cochrane didn't acknowledge the man. He quickly vanished from the street, careful not to slip on the light accumulation of fresh snow.

He turned the corner sharply. He broke into a quick jog. Conveniently, at the next corner a tram was pulling away from a curb. He hopped on it, carefully surveying whether anyone had followed him. He paid the conductor and watched the street.

No one had followed. His back was clean.

Thank God for small stuff. He felt better about things, with the exception of the departed Rhine maidens, whom he missed.

Chapter 33

Berlin
January 1943

Cochrane took the streetcar five blocks, got off, walked three blocks to enter the route of another streetcar, boarded that one and rode for two blocks. He stepped off a block before his address, 36 Kittelstrasse, a few streets north of Pariser Platz.

This neighborhood was more middle class than the previous ones. From the way the neighborhood was decorated, he could tell that there had been a Nazi rally within the last few days, if not the last day or two. There were flags in store windows and on lamp posts. As he walked toward his destination, he saw copies of the unavoidable *Der Sturmer* on each corner, feeding their malicious fables to anyone dumb enough to digest them.

Cochrane stopped to look at the front page, not because one ounce of him flirted with agreement with any of this trash, but because it was always good to know what the enemy was saying and thinking. Even the lies promulgated by a notoriously dishonest government could suggest what was going on behind the scenes.

There were special bulletin boards that displayed the paper.

"Whoever knows a Jew knows the devil," proclaimed one article.

"The Jews are our saboteurs," proclaimed another.

A smaller article on the same page, also from *Der Sturmer*, told of a recent incident in Latvia. A heroic German infantry squad of ten had been captured by a Latvian defense militia and had been summarily been executed by a Communist-Jewish rifle squad.

"Ten more martyrs for National Socialism!" proclaimed the article. "The international Jewish rabble led by Roosevelt, Churchill and the Elders of Zion provokes us, but we are a nation of Aryan brothers and sisters! We will triumph for our fallen comrades!"

"Of course 'we' will," Cochrane muttered under his breath.

He continued on his way, changing direction twice before presenting himself at the pre-assigned address at 36 Kittelstrasse.

The building was sandstone and bleak.

Two front windows to the street were nailed in place with heavy wooden shutters. The front door was heavy and open. Cochrane looked to upper levels of the building. There were four floors above street level. Half the shutters were closed. Most were in disarray. One was linked to the old building with just one hinge, ready to crash to the sidewalk in the next stiff breeze.

Cochrane saw no bomb damage on the block. He stepped into the building.

The lobby was dingy, ill lit and needed to be swept. There was an old elevator behind a grate, a poster with a picture of a handsome uniformed Hitler, a Hitler youth calendar from 1940, and a door to a small apartment that bore a sign indicating that the caretaker lived within.

The door was half open. Cochrane went to it and knocked.

The door slid further open in response.

A graying battered man sitting on a sofa, turned, got up, looked critically at Cochrane and walked to him. The man walked with a cane, his right knee buckling with each step.

"What do you want?" he asked in German as he neared.

"I'm looking for a man named Fritz Stein," Cochrane said. "I'm told he lives here."

"Who tells you something like that?" the man asked, suspicious.

"Mutual friends."

"Stein has friends?" the man laughed. "If he has friends, his friends should give him some money. Then he could pay his rent."

"Everyone has friends," Cochrane said, trying to keep things light. "You. Me? Maybe even Stein."

"He lives in Room 302," the man said. "I haven't seen Stein for several days," he said. "You can knock. I don't care."

"Danke schön," said Cochrane.

The small rusting elevator must have been forty years old. It sat like an antique cage behind the metal grate.

"Is it safe to ride the elevator or should I take the steps?" Cochrane asked.

The old man shrugged. "Everyone who's gone up has come back down. So far. Take your choice. Easier to go up than to come down. Take your chances. I don't give a crap."

At the caretaker's doorway, just behind him, a large woman appeared with two crutches. She wore a heavy coat that was worn and soiled. Her hair was wrapped in a scarf. She watched the proceedings critically but kept silent.

At one moment, her gaze rose and crashed into Cochrane's eyes. As she leaned on her left crutch, her appraisal of him was chilly. There was something wrong with her. It took a moment, but Cochrane realized that one eye was a fake. It wouldn't focus, much less move.

"I'll try the elevator," Cochrane said.

The woman muttered something guttural that he couldn't catch. It sounded as if her teeth were missing.

Cochrane stepped into the elevator and closed the double grates. He pressed the button for the third floor. The lift gave a wicked shudder and started to ascend.

Looking down as the elevator struggled to rise, Cochrane saw the old man – probably a World War One veteran - and his invalid wife disappear between his feet.

The lift rose grudgingly. There was no light. The gears screeched. The grill rattled like frozen branches in a forest. It groaned its way to the third landing. Cochrane put his hand on the gate handle to allow himself to step out. The mechanism jammed. He forced it. The elevator shuddered again and the door opened. He stepped out.

"What a ride," he thought.

Cochrane stepped through the hallway. He felt a layer of grit under his shoes. Several doors had small German flags pasted to them, bold and red and with the swastika. He found Room 302. That door had the Nazi flag, also.

He knocked.

There was no answer. Cochrane tried the doorknob. It turned slightly, then caught. He knocked again. No response. He tried the knob again, more forcibly this time. It gave way with a snap. He pushed the door open.

"Hello?" he called in German. "*Hallo? Ist jemand zuhause?*" Anyone home?

No answer.

Cochrane stepped into the room, leaving the door open a quarter of the way behind him. The furnishings were simple. There was a table with a wooden chair, an ice box, and a small loveseat that was badly worn and covered with a blanket. A bare bulb was at the center of the ceiling. A chain hung from it for turning it on or off. Cochrane gently pulled the chain. It responded. The bulb was dim but the electricity was connected.

He walked to the ice box and found nothing in it. There were some plates in the sink that hadn't been washed. A small cloud of flies hovered. On a counter near a sink there was a paper bag. There were two apples in it. They hadn't rotted. Someone had been here recently.

Cochrane moved to the door to the next room, a narrow sleeping alcove with no light, not knowing what to expect, but fearing the worst. He glanced in. He saw no one, dead or alive, just a narrow unmade bed and a night table next to it with a clock. He walked to the clock. It was ticking. Someone had wound it, most likely within the last day. Most of these German clocks worked for thirty six hours.

There was a closet. The door was half open. He pulled it wide open. Two shirts, a pair of pants. Another heavy coat. No dead body. He was relieved.

He considered leaving a note for Stein but decided against it.

He retreated from the apartment and closed the door. He found the stairs and chose not to risk the elevator again. The staircase was unlit. When he rounded the first corner he found the steps were broken and blocked with an accumulation of garbage.

The garbage rustled. Rats.

He returned to the elevator, stepped in and took it back to the ground level. It landed with a thud and a clank. Cochrane pushed his way out. The caretaker hadn't moved. The woman with crutches remained at the door. They stood in silence. The elevator door slammed shut with a predictable clatter.

"You might want to oil this thing, don't you think?" Cochrane said. "Before it stalls with someone in it."

"I keep requesting," the caretaker said. "No one does nothing. All the oil is somewhere else."

"I imagine it is," Cochrane said. "A small sacrifice to combat Bolshevism."

The old man was about to say something in response, then thought better of it. The woman with the crutches watched him through one narrowed eye, as if she knew there was something suspicious about Cochrane but couldn't decide what. For whatever reason, they just plain didn't like him. He assumed he wasn't German enough.

Cochrane tipped his hat. He walked to the front door, down the two transom steps to the sidewalk, and walked smack into two better dressed men in overcoats who smoked and talked. But their conversation halted into silence as soon as they saw him. They turned away from him in unison the second their eyes met.

Cochrane calculated quickly and felt a surge of fear. The men had new hats, clean coats and fresh shoes. They hadn't been there when he had entered. They were police or Gestapo.

Were they there for him or were they there for Stein? Or a lucky third party? Cochrane was not about to inquire. Fifty-fifty it was he who was in the cross hairs.

Cochrane continued on his way, half expecting to feel a hand on his arm at any moment, his heartbeat quickening. When he turned the first corner, he again accelerated his pace. Fortunately the street was crowded. He removed his hat to make it harder to be spotted. The snow was helpful, also.

He continued quickly around two corners, keeping an eye out for tiny partnerships of two or three men – a Gestapo trademark – in overcoats, gloves and hats.

There was now snow on most of the sidewalks. The weather changed the pace at which he needed to move. Traffic was creeping. People moved faster and everyone was wearing extra layers.

Cochrane stopped quickly at a street vendor. He bought a gray wool cap and pulled it over his head. He bought a dark green scarf from the same man. He re-bundled himself and continued in a zigzag pattern through several blocks. Then he was lucky enough to come out on a block of Wilhelm Strasse south of Unter den Linden.

He took a minor detour since he was in Der Mitte. He searched again for a Tavern Wittgenstein. Again, futility. He might as well have been searching for the gold at the bottom of the Rhine. Where, he wondered with irony, were the Rhine maidens when he needed them? Surely *they* would have known their way around the capital. He thought wistfully of Annalise. She had been a sweet girl who enjoyed her music, cigarettes, liquor and casual promiscuity. He hoped to hell she had gotten out of the country.

He boarded a streetcar and escaped the neighborhood, not knowing when or if he would dare return.

Chapter 34

Stalingrad, Soviet Union
January 1943

During the first weeks of January the Wehrmacht had continued to hold their emergency airstrip on the outskirts of Stalingrad. But Soviet commander General Konstantin Rokossovsky again offered Field Marshal Paulus a chance to surrender.

Paulus radioed Hitler again. He spoke personally with Hitler. Members of the Wehrmacht High Command stood by in Hitler's bunker. Paulus stressed that his troops in Russia were without ammunition or food. He explained that he was no longer able to lead them because there was nowhere to go.

"I also have nearly twenty thousand severely wounded men or men in immediate need of medical attention," he said. "They are dying by the minute."

"Then they will die as founding heroes of the Thousand Year Reich!" Hitler screeched into the phone. Once again, the Fuehrer demanded that Paulus hold the stalemate at Stalingrad and fight to the death.

The call ended.

In Berlin, a furious Hitler turned to his assembled generals. Why was it, he demanded, that no one was as noble as he, the genius and infallible leader? "This Paulus is a man who sees fifty to sixty thousand of his soldiers fighting bravely to the end. How can he even talk of surrendering to the Bolsheviks?"

The question may or may not have been rhetorical, but no general was foolish enough to respond. The question hung in the room.

The situation festered for four days.

Another call came to Berlin. Paulus now informed Hitler that his men were only hours from collapse.

Hitler, seemingly estranged from reality, replied with an avalanche of field promotions to Paulus and his officers to build up their spirits. Most significantly, he promoted Paulus to Generalfeldmarschall, papers to follow by military courier. In promoting him, Hitler also explained that there was no known record of a Prussian or German field marshal ever having surrendered.

The message was clear. The Sixth Army was to hold its ground fight until their final bullets had been fired and their positions had been overrun. And Paulus was to put his pistol to his head and commit suicide. Hitler implied that if Paulus allowed himself to be taken alive, he would shame Germany's military history.

Paulus set down his phone, knowing one way or another, the end was near. A Roman Catholic, he was morally opposed to taking his own life.

He turned to his aide, a man named Wilhelm Adam. Colonel Adam was a career soldier who had been awarded the Iron Cross as recently as December. Colonel Adam was also the Headquarters commander for the encircled Sixth Army. Adam had heard the message from Berlin.

"What will you do, sir?" the aid asked.

"I have no idea what I will do," Paulus said calmly. "But I have no intention whatsoever of shooting myself for this Bohemian peasant corporal."

Chapter 35

Berlin
January 1943

Air raid sirens began wailing in Berlin at 10:28 AM.

Cochrane was on the street, about to do another morning of searching for his contacts in Berlin and for the Tavern Wittgenstein, when all hell broke loose from above. He ran toward the bunker that Heinz and Greta had shown him. As he ran, he could hear the drone of oncoming planes and then the thunderous pounding of anti-aircraft guns on the perimeter of the city. Other guns were on rooftops within the city. Bombs began to fall, first distantly, then closer, and then even all over his immediate neighborhood.

The noise was deafening.

A final bomb exploded fifty meters down the street. It rattled Cochrane's teeth as he surged with a terrified crowd into the portals of the bunker, then into the bunker and then down a flight of steps. There was electricity and dim lighting. Then the lights flickered and were gone. Darkness followed.

Cochrane moved down two flights of stairs. Fluorescent paint on the walls substituted for a lighting system. Everything else was pitch black. Cochrane went through several doors but had no desire to go deeper in the event of a cave-in. Some rooms were filled with terrified people huddled in small pockets of light punctuated by the occasional lit match.

Children screamed. Adults cried. Old people groaned. Grown men cursed.

A few people had already been injured, some badly, either from flying pieces of nearby buildings or from being trampled getting to safety. No doctors were apparent.

Just before Cochrane had entered the shelter, a bomb had hit a building on the next block, sending a shower of heavy debris, sharp pieces of sandstone and plaster, down on the street where the bunker was located. Some of it had rained down on Cochrane.

His eyes adjusted. There was some light but it was very dim.

A middle aged German woman staggered into his room and looked for a place to sit. There wasn't a place. Cochrane reached forward and guided her by the wrist. The room was loud with agitated terrified voices. Up at street level, the British bombs were pounding the German capital.

Cochrane indicated that the German woman should take his seat. She accepted but could barely sit. She was sobbing and barely coherent. She had been separated from her husband in running to the shelter, she said. He was older and slow, she said. He had suffered a shattered hip in the last world war and she was terrified he wouldn't survive this one. He had forced her to run on ahead.

Then she fell silent, looking at Cochrane. She pointed to his face where the debris had marked him. Instantly, he was aware that his left cheek was hot. It didn't feel right. His hand went to it and came away with a sticky liquid that was dark in the very dim light.

Blood.

As the realization set in that he'd been cut by the debris, she pushed a handkerchief into his hand. He used it to mop the wound and stanch the bleeding.

"English bastards!" someone cursed.

Around the room where Cochrane sat was a vast network of abandoned tunnels from unfinished underground train routes. The tunnels were now safe-havens for thousands of Berlin's civilians as the British bombs fell from the sky. The tunnels were cold and damp. The air supply depleted quickly, making breathing difficult. The air vents clanged constantly. The overhead bombings shook the walls and floors deep in the bunker.

An hour passed. Then a second. More bombers were hitting the city. The local air raid wardens assembled on the first lower level. They took in everyone they could but allowed no one to leave. The ground, walls and ceiling continued to rumble. The sirens wailed intermittently, then came to full life again toward 1:00 PM.

Toward 5:30 PM, when it was almost dark outside, those who had sought safety and refuge were allowed to go to the street.

Cochrane was one of the first civilians to emerge. On the street there was rubble everywhere. Halfway down the block, one building had been destroyed and the facades of three others had collapsed into the street. There were fires, large and small. There was crying and hysterical screaming.

The woman who had offered him a handkerchief had found her husband. The man was dead a few meters from the entrance portal to the bunker. He had almost made it but then the left side of his body had been torn open by either a bomb or debris. He went to comfort her, but an ambulance and hearse crew arrived at the same moment that he spotted her. The crew attended to her.

Blood, pieces of human bones and body parts were everywhere: on walls, on sidewalks, on cars and lampposts. Cochrane felt sick. He trudged back to the building where he was housed. Heinz stood at the door and gave him a look but said nothing.

He stepped inside. Greta was seated on a bench in the foyer, her head in her hands. He went to her. She muttered that two of her best friends had been killed, plus a child who had lived in this building on her way home from school.

Cochrane touched her shoulder. "I'm sorry," he said. "I share your grief."

He paused. She said nothing.

"I'm glad you're alive," he said.

"I'm not sure I am," she said.

Greta looked up at Cochrane with red wet eyes. She shook her head and looked away. Heinz appeared and sat down next to her. Cochrane went to his small pair of rooms. The electricity was out.

He lit a candle, sat on a wooden chair and lost himself in thought.

When would it end, he asked himself just as Greta had asked him.

There was no answer, other than the temporary one he found by drinking the last few gulps of whiskey that Colonel Sawyer had given him.

Where did it all lead? Cochrane wondered and had no answer.

The next day he learned more.

The air raid, an attack of a large squadron of De Havilland Mosquitos flown by the Royal Air Force, had coordinated perfectly with the 11 AM speech by Goering celebrating the tenth anniversary of the Nazis' *Machtergreifung*. Goering was on the radio to a huge national audience when the bombs started coming out of the sky, many of them directed at him. He curtailed his remarks and ran for cover. Anyone listening could hear the explosions and the high anxiety in Goering's voice.

Then at 1 PM, the time of Goebbels' speech, the second wave of RAF Mossies swept the German capital. Goebbels too ran for cover.

Cochrane tried to process what he had experienced and what he was now seeing on the street. These were great propaganda raids, he reasoned, much like the Doolittle Raid on the Japanese home islands had done for boosting American morale in early 1942. But from what he was hearing, Berlin had taken enormous losses, with hundreds of dead civilians, thousands of wounded and even more left homeless. The attacks on Berlin were a severe embarrassment for the German leadership who had promised that there wouldn't be any. But more immediately, there was the carnage on the street and parts of the city in ruins.

Later in the day, Cochrane found a café that was open. He sat at a table. He drank a bottled beer and forced down a bratwurst of questionable freshness. Beside him at a neighboring table, there was a German woman of about fifty in deep shock.

Cochrane noticed there was blood on her clothing. With the intention of comforting her, he lured her into a conversation. It was a mistake.

She rambled in a slow dazed voice.

"I could hear the early warning siren, but I don't remember anything at all about the bombing raid," she said slowly. "I passed out in a shelter. I thought I would suffocate. We took a direct hit from an English bomb. When I woke, it was dark. My sister's family was lying near me and on top of me. I couldn't breathe."

She paused for more than a minute. Her voice wavered and she continued.

"I asked my nephew who was lying on me to get off," she said, "but he only groaned out loud and got heavier. Wherever I put my hand it was all slippery. I felt his heart stop. I felt him die. When I managed to lift myself up, I lit a match. The top of his head was blown off."

Cochrane opened his mouth to speak but couldn't.

The woman was expressionless. She got up from her table and walked slowly away. She moved like a ghost, complete with ghostly overcoat. Cochrane watched her until she was gone. Cochrane was so dazed by the experience that he began to question his own sanity. Was the woman a ghost? Had she actually been killed in the air raid and just not yet settled into an afterlife?

He had never previously entertained such thoughts. Then he suddenly felt ill. He left money on the table, stood, walked a few meters, and felt worse. He turned and ducked into an alley, trying to keep his food down.

This, too, was a mistake. In the alley were six dead bodies, two of them children. They were stacked up without body bags, waiting for removal. He turned away from them, leaned against a wobbly brick wall, braced himself and vomited.

Later, when he returned to the building where he was staying, Heinz stopped him with more bad news. Horace, the block *gauleiter*, had not been able to get out of his own building. The building had collapsed on him and he been killed also.

Chapter 36

Stalingrad
January 1943

Winter mornings were normally dark and cold in the hours before dawn in the Soviet Union. But they were darker and colder than ever on the morning of January 31, 1943, the day after the British bombing of Berlin. The mission had taken eight hours round trip and the average age of a man on the attacking aircraft was twenty-two years old. In terms of the embarrassment to Hitler and the Nazi high command, the English boys had done themselves proud. In terms of the carnage on the ground in Berlin, well, war was war.

Deep in Russian territory, the German commander, Friedrich Paulus was in a partitioned chamber in the cellar of a sturdy brick building that the Wehrmacht had requisitioned on the outskirts of Stalingrad. A fire burned in a corner, its smoke going up a makeshift chimney. Paulus was asleep that morning and in the midst of a depressing dream.

There was a sharp knock on his door. He bolted upright in his bed and clutched his Mauser. Paulus awakened quickly into a reality darker than his dream.

"Enter!" he said.

He stood and trained his pistol at the doorway. He was ready to use it.

His top military aide, Wilhelm Adam, entered.

Colonel Adam handed Paulus a piece of paper. "Congratulations, sir," he said.

The paper confirmed to Paulus his recent promotion to Field Marshal.

Paulus looked at the meaningless promotion with no enthusiasm.

"Thank you," Paulus said. "Dismissed, if there's nothing else."

"There *is* something else, Mein Herr," Adam confirmed.

222

"What would that be?" the Field Marshal asked.

"I need to inform you, Herr Field Marshal," said Adam, "that the Russians are at the door."

"The door to this building?" answered Paulus incredulously.

"No, sir. The door to this chamber."

With these words, Adam opened the door behind him. A Soviet general named Kovalyov and his interpreter entered the room. The Soviet officer wished Paulus a good morning in Russian. He cheerfully added that every German in the building was now his prisoner. For that matter, the entire German Sixth Army was now his prisoner.

Paulus considered the pistol in his hand. General Kovalyov eyed it, also. Wisely, Paulus placed the Mauser on a table.

The Soviet general continued to speak. The interpreter passed along the messages.

"Prepare yourself for departure," the interpreter conveyed. "We shall return for you at 0900. You will depart in your personal vehicle. That is all for now."

The Russians left the room. Colonel Adam recorded Paulus's new rank in his military document, stamped it with an official seal that bore a swastika, then threw the seal into the glowing fire.

Soldiers of the Red Army closed the main entrance to the cellar and guarded it. An officer, the head of the guards, allowed Paulus and his driver to go outside and get the car ready at 8:45 AM. Coming out of the building into the cold gray day, Field Marshal Paulus stood dumbfounded at the surrealistic scene before him.

Wehrmacht and Red Army soldiers, who just a few hours earlier had each other in their rifle sights, now stood quietly together in the yard. They were all armed, some with weapons in their hands, some with them over their shoulders. The German soldiers were ragged, tattered and bloodied in light coats against the brutal Russian winter. They looked like phantoms with hollow, unshaven cheeks. The Red Army warriors looked fresh. They were smiling and wore warm winter uniforms.

At 9:00 AM sharp the commander of the Soviet Sixty-fourth Army arrived to take the commander of the vanquished German Sixth Army and its staff towards the rear. Paulus removed his wedding ring and asked permission to have it sent back to his wife in Germany. Permission was granted. He would never again, however, see his wife.

The Red Army took ninety-one thousand prisoners. Half of them would die on a forced march to prison camps in Siberia. Half of those would die in the camps. Eventually, six thousand would be repatriated to Germany in the 1950s.

The German march towards the Volga had ended in catastrophe for the invaders. So ended the siege of Stalingrad.

At the time, however, the more immediate repercussions were just beginning.

Chapter 37

**Berlin
February 1943**

    Two mornings after the January air raid on Berlin, Cochrane woke at dawn. He lay in bed for a half an hour thinking, listening to Berlin waking up on the other side of the walls of his building. Yes, he reminded himself. There was a war going on and he was in it, just like a soldier, except possibly even more so. He made a decision. He would start carrying his gun and hope he didn't get stopped and searched.

    Toward 7:45 AM, he emerged from his flat to the street, tired and hungry, and half in disbelief over what he had seen over the previous day. But there were plenty of reminders. The people who were still alive were cleaning up, just as the targeted English civilians had been cleaning up and putting one foot in front of the other in London for months. As he looked around, Cochrane asked himself again: what was the bombing accomplishing?

    He shuddered. Why did the world have to be such a violent unforgiving place? How had civilized nations devolved so quickly into barbarianism?

    Some random thoughts ran through his mind. In May of 1940, three German planes on a bombing mission that targeted a French airfield near Dijon went three hundred kilometers off course. But that didn't stop them from finding a target that looked inviting. The German aircraft bombed their own city of Freiburg am Bresgau, killing fifty-seven German inhabitants, including children.

    Hitler, seeing an opportunity not a disaster, and always comfortable with a lie that he could sell to his adoring public, blamed the civilian bombing on the British. The English had done it intentionally, he told the German people. He pledged a fivefold revenge against "the English murderers" and started to bomb English civilians. So began the Battle of Britain, the bombing campaign aimed at London. Eventually, the citizens of Berlin would have to pay the price.

But the Nazi high command remained undeterred.

"Do you want total war?" Goebbels shouted to a large crowd just hours after the January thirtieth bombing of Berlin. "Isn't that what you asked for?"

"Ja! Ja!" the crowd roared in response.

Total war was what they had asked for and total war was what they were now getting.

And so the war of terror from above was underway. The unwritten rules of war from World War One seemed forgotten: in the past civilians were not bombed. The unarmed "warriors" were therefore now delivered up to the bombs, as required by the new rules of conflict. The bombs shredded, entombed, suffocated and incinerated women and children, old people and infants, prisoners and hospital patients, friend and foe, National Socialists and camp detainees, guilty and innocent. So it went in the ugly new world.

Cochrane emerged from his small apartment. He found one store that was open. He stood in line for half an hour and bought bread and jam. He devoured it for breakfast.

People on the street talked about getting to work and dealing with a tram system that had shut down. Increasingly now, the pressure was mounting on Cochrane to find a contact with Dulles's sources. He had a choice between going back to the university area and try to find the Tavern Wittgenstein or return to the area near the Pariser Platz to find Fritz Stein.

He chose the latter. He set out on foot.

The British bombs had fallen haphazardly. Some blocks in the center of Berlin had been spared and some had been destroyed. If there had been a military target, Cochrane didn't see it. What he did see was hunger and destitution and a landscape of rubble that was already crawling with rats. He also saw more body bags than he cared to tally.

The stench of decay was already in the air. It might have stifled some human spirits, but the able-bodied Berliners continued to clean up. Many walked down the streets of their neighborhoods and passed the dreadful ruins of their stores and their neighbors' homes. Perhaps, deep down, they had been expecting as much. Perhaps, deep down, most of them still believed in Hitler and awaited the miracle that he could pull out of his hat.

Several blocks into his journey, Cochrane spotted an unusual sight: a working tram that had gone back into service, despite several broken windows. Thinking quickly, recalling the lines that had existed when he had previously been in Berlin, he realized this tram line would take him to the area of Friedrich Wilhelm University.

He took the tram. It was slow. Twice the tram stopped because rubble needed to be cleared from the street. But people pitched in and cleared it, cursing the Allied bombers that had attacked the city.

On the tram, Cochrane tuned into conversations among Berliners. No one was talking about anything except the bombings. Oddly, people discussed the event in dispassionate tones more usually reserved for Kaffee und Kuchen among close friends.

Rumors abounded.

Were some Berlin residents on the banks of the Havel machine gunned by low-flying British planes as some of the riders of the morning tram claimed? Another man on his way to work mentioned that a town north of the city had been completely obliterated. A woman said she received a call from his sister who said that her block had been destroyed. The most brutal forms of death were described. People who couldn't find doctors went to the roofs of buildings and leaped to their deaths because of unendurable burns. There were mutterings about pretty teenage German girls being raped by Jews and Gypsies beneath the ruins.

Cochrane arrived near the university around noon. The day was clear and cold, though little plumes of smoke rose from new ruins every few blocks.

He looked again for the Tavern Wittgenstein. He searched the areas under the railroad bridge and wondered if the place still existed. All he knew was that he couldn't find it.

He wondered if he should make a bold move on Heinz, talk quietly and see if Dulles could be contacted. He put the idea on hold. The notion was risky. He made sure his gun was out of view, showing no telltale bulge beneath his coat. With a sigh of disgust, he gave up on the bar and set out on foot for a second visit to for Fritz Stein's premises.

Chapter 38

**Berlin
February 1943**

    Cochrane moved quickly through the entrance hall of Fritz Stein's building. The door to the building custodian's apartment was open a few inches as he passed. Cochrane saw the man loom into the doorway, then slide away and push his door shut. Cochrane heard latches fall and click into place. He heard a heavy chair being pulled into position across the door.
    Cochrane's instincts told him to flee. He ignored them, increasingly desperate to make some sort of contact in Berlin. He took the stairs up to the third floor, stepping past the trash and the rats on the way.
    He arrived on the third floor and walked quickly toward Stein's door, the one marked *302*. He rapped sharply. There was no response. Cochrane tried the doorknob. The door swung open easily.
    Cochrane stepped in. Sensing disaster, Cochrane drew his Mauser.
    A moment passed before his eyes could focus and before he was able to process everything. The living area had been torn apart. The books from the bookcase had been ripped from the shelves and thrown to the floor. The single vase lay smashed in pieces. The plates and cutlery from the tiny kitchen were askew on the floor, the plates shattered. The single table had been turned over. One leg was broken. The chair was smashed. One window was broken. The ice box was overturned and opened.
    "Herr Stein?" he asked aloud.
    He didn't expect a response, which was fortunate: none came.
    He moved quickly to the sleeping room and stopped short. He gagged in disgust. A man, presumably Stein, was hanging in a noose that was part of a heavy rope that had been thrown over a

closet door. The victim's face was blue and there was an expression of agony remaining.

Suicide or murder? Cochrane stepped closer.

There was no chair to have kicked away. There were marks on the body. The dead man's clothing was torn. There had been a struggle. Cochrane knew from his days as an FBI special agent on assignment what to look for next.

He reached to the hanging man's hands. Sure enough, there was blood and skin under the nails. The victim had fought the men who had come to kill him but they had overpowered him.

"Jesus…" Cochrane muttered.

He put his pistol away. He had just tucked it securely into the holster on his belt when he heard the wail of sirens. At first he thought it was another air raid, but then another moment passed and he realized that the two sirens were very different. And in that immeasurably short space of time, he knew he was as good as captured. The sirens drew near and stopped.

He turned from the sleeping room, bolted through the living area and went to the hallway outside the apartment. The stairs continued upwards but he reckoned he would corner himself and die in a shootout. He ran to the stairs that led downward but could already hear several voices shouting on the ground floor. The surly superintendent was yelling that the foreigner had come again and was upstairs.

Cochrane looked for any escape route. The only thing he saw was a window that faced the rear of the building. He went to it. It was closed and locked. He drew his pistol and smashed the glass. The pane fell out. He could hear a commotion on the staircase. The garbage that littered the stairs was delaying the police. For that he was thankful.

He looked out the window. The drop was about forty feet. He would break an ankle or leg and be captured. He looked each way. There was an alley below and it led to open streets on both sides. No one was covering either exit.

To his left there was a drainpipe which led from a rooftop gutter. It was his only chance. He pulled on his gloves. He pulled himself through the shattered windowpane. He managed to grip the pipe with one hand. He leaned forward, prayed to God Almighty, lunged and caught it with his other hand. It was cold but stable.

The pipe swayed. Gravity pulled him downward. His grip slid on the pipe but eased him fifteen feet closer to the alley. He tightened his grip and slowed the descent to a stop. Then he eased down another ten or twelve feet, then a final five, braced himself and released his tenuous grip.

He softened his fall by keeping his knees agile and bent. He hit the ground, fell and got to his feet. Remarkably, he was still alive and not injured.

He looked each way, orienting himself in a narrow alley with brick walls and garbage cans. He wanted no part of the front of the building where police cars were assembled. He headed away, then heard a voice from above yelling, "Halt!"

He kept going. There was a gunshot from above that smashed into the bricks near him. Then a second shot that missed him by six or seven feet.

He whirled and pressed himself against the wall of Stein's building. He drew his Mauser, looked upwards and saw a man in a black coat pointing a pistol at him from the same window from which he had escaped.

The man was trying to get a clean shot. Cochrane raised his pistol and launched a barrage of three shots at the window. The man above him howled and his gun flew wildly from his hand. Cochrane figured one of his shots had hit the man.

Cochrane turned and ran down the alley. He turned away from the building, pushed his way through a crowd of pedestrians, weaved through some pushcarts and cut his pace to a quick walk.

He had escaped the immediate premises. But for how long?

There was a shopping district nearby. Cochrane quickstepped through it. He knew that police would flood the area. They were after him. There were no two ways about it. He was blown, his identity was known and his head was destined for a guillotine if he was captured. He could not imagine it turning out any differently.

As he moved and distanced himself from Stein's building, he scanned every store and shop that he passed. Finally he made his way to Leipziger Platz and found what he needed most. A huge department store.

The establishment had once been known as the Wertheim store. It had been the flagship of the largest department store chain in Berlin. This particular location had once been the biggest department store in Europe during its glory days of the 1920s and early 1930s. The company had been victimized by the Nazi Aryanization policies in the 1930s. The new restrictive laws forced Jewish employees from their jobs, both in management and in sales. Now the store had been renamed AWAG, an acronym for Allgemeine Warenhandelsgesellschaft A.G.

The store was a shadow of its former glamorous self. But it had dozens of elevators and a glass-roofed atrium. It offered a fleeing spy what he needed most: crowd cover, many choices of routes and a chance to change his profile.

At the same time, glancing over his shoulder, he tallied that there were at least two men on his trail, moving quickly about a hundred feet behind him. There was another team also keeping pace, a man and a woman. The woman held a yellow handbag which made her easy to spot.

Using a crowd of shoppers for cover, he quickly shoved his hat under his coat as he went through the door to the department store. With a similar gesture a few paces later, he stole a cloth carrying bag on the first floor.

He found his way up a flight of stairs to the men's department.

He loitered long enough to make sure that the two men who were following him were still behind him, probably reluctant to come as close as the men's department. When the coast was clear and when the two salesclerks were busy, he grabbed a Tyrolean hat and crumpled it to make it look used. Then he folded a brown cloth coat, common like one would see on the street, onto his arm, and ducked into the lavatory.

There were several men in the room. He ducked into a toilet stall and listened to a filthy story told by one man to another about what his wife did for him. With this as the soundtrack, he ditched his original coat into his new carrying bag, pulled the new one on, popped the Tyrolean hat on his head, and waited till two other men were exiting.

He started a brief conversation with them in German, making it look as if they were three friends who knew each other, extolling news of two great German victories in the east and casting doubt on the news of the surrender at Stalingrad, all while keeping his hand to his face to stifle the watchers if they were still on him.

Conveniently, the men laughed with him and took the bait, exchanging conversation. He amused them with a dirty joke about promiscuous English women and they all laughed together.

He thought he spotted a member of a team assigned to him. It was the woman with the yellow handbag, except she had changed her hat. The followers didn't see him: more than likely they were watching for a single man.

He peeled off from his new best friends on the second floor. He found an emergency staircase. He ran down to the street level, then saw that the stairs descended again. He took a chance, went to an empty basement and found a door that led to an outdoor set of steps that led up to the street.

The door was locked with a chain and a padlock the size of a man's fist.

Inspired, he saw a half window that led to the same set of steps. He smashed the window, broke the sash by kicking it in half, and escaped.

On the street, he thought he saw two members of a team that was following him, but their backs were to him. He also noticed that there were many uniformed police flooding into the area: not a coincidence. The cops stood around looking in every direction but, luckily for Cochrane, not knowing exactly who they were searching for.

He rounded the first corner possible and went into a small shop, which was just about to close. It was starting to rain. He bought a black raincoat and pulled it on over his other coat. He was just paying when he realized that a man standing next to him, watching him, was a Wehrmacht officer. Looking more closely, he could see the insignia of the Fourth Panzer Division.

The man was dark-haired, thin lipped, and covered with braids and badges. The military officer had a sidearm on the right side. Their gaze met. Cochrane offered him a smile. He received none in return.

There was a mirror behind the clerk's station and Cochrane looked to it, trying to escape the army's officer's attention. It didn't work. Their gazes crashed together again. Cochrane shifted his eyes slightly. There was something "off" about the man's posture. Then Cochrane saw what it was. The officer's left arm was missing, the sleeve of his uniformed pinned against his left side.

Cochrane turned back to him.

"Russians?" he asked, indicating the loss of the arm.

"French," the officer said. "Gembloux."

"Filthy degenerates," said Cochrane.

A pause, then, "You're not German?" the soldier asked, suspicious.

An inspired moment, then, "Spanish," said Cochrane. "General Franco sends you his good wishes," he added with a man-to-man wink.

"Just one thing," the officer said.

Cochrane turned.

"It gets very cold here. You should buy gloves."

Cochrane reached to his pocket and showed his gloves.

"I used to have many pairs. Now I only need one," the disabled officer said. "You'd think they'd give me a discount," he said.

Then he threw back his head, laughed and slapped Cochrane on the back. "An arm! A small price to pay for the glory of the Third Reich," he said.

"Heil Hitler," said Cochrane moving toward the door as fast as he could without arousing further suspicion.

"Heil Hitler!" The man used his one remaining arm for an awkward salute.

Cochrane was quickly back out onto the street.

He remembered the name and address of a watchmaker who had been his friend in the old days. He went to the man's shop and found it closed. It had been spared damage from the recent air raid, however.

He went around to the back of the shop. He broke in quietly and without damaging anything.

He was afraid to turn on a light, so he groped around in the darkness. He found a box of matches and a half eaten loaf of bread that the watchmaker had left in a bag on the counter, along with a jar of pickles.

The bread was a godsend. Cochrane devoured half of it. He found a wind up alarm clock and set it for 6:00 AM. He wanted to hide out and yet be gone before the watchmaker appeared, but not so early that he couldn't blend in with morning crowds going to work.

He huddled under a counter and slept fitfully, waking up three times overnight. But at least he had escaped. Or he thought he had. Temporarily.

The next morning he used the private water closet at the back of the shop and consumed the other half of the loaf of bread. He left at 7:00 AM.

He had no map, but still had his bearings. The morning had broken cloudy and gray. He found his way to one of the suburban train stations but saw police and Gestapo everywhere. He turned and ran. He wracked his head for some sort of contact from his old days, someone who wouldn't turn him in.

He was desperate. He was even afraid to return to his temporary lodging with Heinz. He figured crossing the city would be impossible.

He found a public phone and called two numbers that he could remember. Neither were operational. He wandered the city, starting to freeze and not knowing what to do. Berlin was a city at war, with no friendly embassy, no old contacts that he dared go near, and none of the connections that Dulles had promised.

He figured the Gestapo would now have staked out the Swedes, the Swiss, the Portuguese and the Spanish, just in case. And none of these would have any reason to help him. The majority of the people working in these posts were probably pro-Hitler.

He wandered back to his old neighborhood where he had lived in the 1930s. Staggering from fatigue, his eyes at half mast, he asked a man on the street when Klienstrasse was, since all the signs were gone. The man gave an honest answer, then demanded to know who he was.

Only then did Cochrane realize that the man he was talking to was a policeman. He hurried off, pretending he had not heard the follow-up question.

There were several houses that were bombed out.

With the heaviest of hearts, he selected one that had once belonged to friends. He broke in, found some food in a kitchen, ate again, then crawled to a place in the cellar where he slept for his second night on the run.

He must have made mistakes. When he rose the next morning, he had decided that he would go to the big train station and try to get out of Berlin, as far south as he could, then make a run for the Swiss border. His assignment here was shot to living hell and he would be lucky to escape alive.

But when he came to the hollowed-out door frame where the front door had once stood, he froze. The house was surrounded by police. He tried to wait it out and hope they weren't there for him, but he must have been spotted. He crouched behind a tattered sofa.

Two men from the Home Guard came in seconds later with pistols drawn.

Cochrane stood. He was about to lunge for his own gun and go out in a blaze of bullets when a third man grabbed him from behind.

It was over. He was as good as dead.

They led him outside, handcuffed him to a lamp post and for good measure, blackjacked him across the back of both legs. All hell broke loose. Within a few minutes, there was a flurry of activity and various police arrived in what must have been a dozen official cars.

A crowd gathered. Workmen. Soldiers. Pretty young women.

Cochrane figured he was down to his final days, if not hours, if not minutes. He could hear a story circulating in the crowd that he was an English spy, probably a "spotter" for the recent air raid. People threw garbage and stones. The police stood by and laughed.

Then two more unmarked cars arrived. This was even worse. The cars had government plates, swastikas and the flag of Nazi Germany on each front fender.

Two men stepped out quickly. The Home Guard cops were shoved aside and a local police captain pointed out Cochrane. He was still chained to a lamp post, as if anyone could miss him.

The two men walked toward him. The doors to the second car opened.

A Wehrmacht officer stepped out with the driver, who also looked Gestapo.

Cochrane knew this was it. Mission unaccomplished, it would be weeks before Dulles could even assume he had failed and died.

The four recent arrivals walked to him.

Three were Gestapo. The fourth was the one-armed Wehrmacht officer whom he had spoken with in the clothing store.

The soldier nodded slowly and triumphantly. He raised his one remaining arm.

"That's him," he said. "May I use your gun to shoot him?"

"Our orders are to hold him," said one of the Gestapo officers. "We have something worse in mind."

Cochrane thought he was dreaming. Or in a nightmare.

237

The Gestapo agent looked familiar. Then Cochrane realized he knew him. It was the same man who had executed two spies on the tarmac in Marseille.

Wesselmann. If this wasn't the bitter end, it was damned close to it.

Chapter 39

Berlin
February 1943

News of the surrender at Stalingrad did not reach Berlin until February second. When it did, Hitler flew into a rage. He blamed Field Marshal Paulus for the catastrophic defeat in the east that he, Hitler, had engineered. He vowed to never appoint another field marshal again, as if that would solve the problem.

What followed was perplexing. For several years, certain anti-Nazis had attempted to undermine Hitler and reform Germany. All efforts had failed. The vigilance of the various secret police agencies, most notably the Gestapo, had sabotaged all efforts. In the armed forces, many opposition groups existed but much of the officer corps had been bought off by solid pay and easy promotions. Yet with the loss of the Sixth Army at Stalingrad, many in the army could see the inevitable scenario for the next few months.

Troops would be diverted from positions in western Europe to slow or halt the advance of the Soviet Red Army. The latter would now target Berlin the same way Hitler had targeted Stalingrad and Moscow. Meanwhile, various anti-Hitler resistance groups formed and strengthened, both within the civilian population and the armed forces.

But almost all of it stayed underground with the notable exception of the universities. And again, just as Munich had played a vital part in the ascent of National Socialism, so it now played a role in civilian opposition to it.

The Hitler Youth movement, which represented itself in great numbers in the universities, had promoted Hitler's rise to power. Now in Munich, few able bodied male students remained. The student population of the university consisted of cripples, disabled veterans, females, and the brown-shirted low-brow Nazi shills who passed themselves off as student leaders. The Nazi party had planted deep spy networks within the universities but the students were adept at spotting the rats among them.

German national radio announced the defeat at Stalingrad on February third. The news ignited more anti-Nazi sentiment. The Soviet Union was happy to fan the flames. German language propaganda radio emanating from Russia filled the airwaves across Germany with the names and hometowns of German troops captured at Stalingrad. Across Germany there was increased bitterness and discontent. And while the names of the captured were being broadcast, a relentless barrage of postal notifications was returning to Germany of soldiers who had died in action on the Russian front.

Worse, anyone looking at the situation rationally knew the war had been lost at Stalingrad. With the obliteration of the Sixth Army, the westward advance of the Red Army was inevitable. Added to that, the inevitable invasion of France by American, Canadian and British troops loomed to the west. Anyone with two eyes, a brain and a sense of military history could see that Hitler and his unchecked *Deutschland Uber Alles* nationalism had dealt the country a catastrophic losing hand.

As potential open revolt simmered at the University of Munich, Gauleiter Paul Geisel of Bavaria, an unquestioning follower of Hitler, called a mandatory assemblage of the students of the university. In a vast meeting hall where all doors were guarded, Geisel ridiculed the male students who had already been injured in combat. He demanded that they drop their studies and offer service to the Wehrmacht. Then he declared that female students could better serve the German nation by bearing children than by acquiring a higher education.

"Stop wasting time reading books!" he told the female students. "Find a husband and produce a child for the Third Reich!"

That was enough to move the audience to its feet, but not in approval. The students shouted him down and drove him from the stage. Guards moved in and attempted to arrest those who had booed Geisel. The crowd surged forward. They attacked, overpowered and beat the Gestapo and SS guards who attempted the arrests and who stood at the doors to the lecture hall. The students picked up some of them and threw them down flights of stairs and trampled them. The insurrection spilled out onto the streets of Munich. Paul Geisel somehow escaped with his life.

Members of The White Rose, most of whom had been in the lecture hall, concluded that the time was now right to spread the anti-Hitler revolt across Germany. Overnight, loud bold graffiti that read *Down With Hitler!* appeared not just on the walls of university buildings but also on public buildings in Munich. Sophie Scholl bought a can of white paint and splashed the single word *Freiheit!* - Freedom! - on the exterior wall of the building that housed the main university lecture hall.

Gestapo flooded into the area the next day. They put down the demonstration, the first anti-government rally in public since Hitler took office in 1933.

But White Rose was ready with their next move. Pamphlets printed and distributed by members of the group urging open revolt across Germany appeared on February eighteenth. Sophie, Hans, Lilo, Frieda, Ilse, Alexander and maybe two dozen others scurried about overnight distributing them. They played a dangerous cat and mouse game with the Gestapo and SS. They distributed pamphlets in ever increasing bundles around the city. Supporters with access to copying machines made copies and distributed them further.

The printings spread to neighboring towns. Within a day they were circulating at universities in Bremen and Berlin and Hamburg, then to Essen, Nuremburg, Cologne and Stuttgart. In the text, there was an enumeration of crimes committed against the people of Germany. The text cited the many failures of the Nazi party and made an urgent appeal to the honor of the officer corps of the professional army to overthrow Hitler.

"We demand a return of our beloved German nation," declared the pamphlets, "from the most appalling tyranny that our people have ever endured!"

For several hours, something akin to revolution gripped Munich, just as it had in the Twenties when Hitler's storm troopers had seized the streets. On the nineteenth of February, an unprecedented event took place in Munich: a large street demonstration of hundreds of students, workers and war veterans marched against Hitler in defiance of the government. The demonstration surged beyond the confines of the university and into the city and back again in an attempt to incite an insurrection across Germany that would halt the war and bring down the Nazi government.

As the students passed one university building, a pro-Nazi block captain named Jakob Schmidt watched the demonstration. He was also the university's head porter and a major resident snitch, loyal to the Nazi party and on the party payroll. He recognized several of the students, in particular a brother and sister who had flagrantly thrown bundles of the leaflets into university buildings. Rather than confronting them, he ratted them out by name to the Gestapo. The Gestapo put them under surveillance.

In the days that followed, Gestapo and SS were everywhere in Munich. Some members of the White Rose continued to go to class and operate 'underground' at night, slipping around the city steps ahead of the government agents who stalked them. Others went in separate directions.

Ilse fled Munich, leaving her room in university housing just minutes before Gestapo arrived to arrest her. She connected with a resistance group east of Munich and made her way southward. She had access to a Swiss passport through her family if she could return home to retrieve it. She had an aunt and uncle living in Switzerland. It was her intention to rejoin her family in the south and, if possible, leave the country for the duration of the war.

Frieda, complete with pale blue scarf and fur cap, did not return to the university area of Munich. She stayed close to her boarding school. Then two days after the quasi-insurrection in Munich two men in Naval uniforms arrived at her school looking for her.

They exchanged a few words with the school's headmaster. They explained nothing other than that they had come for Frieda and had official orders in writing. Then they went to a classroom and pulled Frieda out, kicking and screaming, in the middle of a class. One man held a hand over her mouth. She bit him, drawing blood. What was odd was that they were forceful, but not brutal. They could have beaten her but didn't.

They dragged her to her room and ordered her to pack. In tears, she did.

They were taking her to Berlin "for questioning and for her safety," her abductors said to the terrified faculty. They removed all trace of Frieda from the school and took everything from the registrar's office that bore her name.

Those at the school were told not to discuss her. They should not even mention her name.

Frieda would never be seen there again. Friends who remembered her only said her name among themselves in hushed tones and with the utmost of secrecy and the height of discretion. A story soon circulated that she had been shot. Another equally uncorroborated tale also emerged that claimed she had been taken to the battlefront in Serbia to serve as the mistress to a German general.

It was only after the war that they would learn, in shock and through actual witnesses, what had actually happened, which made the unfounded rumors seem pale in comparison.

Chapter 40

Berlin
February 1943

Late on the first morning after Cochrane's arrest, new guards came to see him. They uncuffed his wrists and allowed him to visit a bathroom. The manacles remained on his ankles. The guards pulled him to his feet and pushed him through the police station.

They muscled him out the back door of the police station and into an alley. There was a guard on each end of the alley. A crowd had gathered. Cochrane kept his eyes down. He felt the hostility of the German people upon him.

The guards shoved him into the back seat of an unmarked police car. In the middle of the back seat there was an iron rail. One of the guards forced Cochrane's wrists to the rail. The guard shackled him to the interior of the vehicle. The police lowered the shades on the side windows at the rear of the car. The car door slammed closed so quickly that he had no time to resist. Cochrane could see out only through the front window.

The guards came around and jumped into the front seats. The vehicle merged into city traffic, which was light. There was rain again and visibility was difficult. The more belligerent members of the crowd, survivors of the air raid no doubt, closed in on the vehicle and threw bottles and stones. The car accelerated, bumping several onlookers as it pulled out into Berlin traffic, which was light.

The guards drove him somewhere for several hours, speaking only occasionally and in low tones. Then they stopped. The guards dragged him out of the car. He was given a quarter loaf of bread and a jar of water. His hands were freed temporarily, but his ankles were not.

"Where are we going?" he asked.

The guards laughed. One of them made a gesture of a gun to the temple. They laughed again. The guards put the manacles back on Cochrane's wrists. They pushed him back into the car. It was only then that he realized that there was a second car following. More guards, he suspected.

They drove for two more hours. They arrived in a remote wooded area. It was near dusk and there was a heavy rainstorm. Cochrane looked in every direction, hoping to take in any detail that might help an escape in the unlikely event that he was able to break free. But the rain rolled in in heavy sheets, like smoke from an aerial bombardment. He couldn't see anything that would help. They were in a rural area and Cochrane figured he would be shot there and buried without a trace or a marker. It was wartime: things like this happened all the time.

The guards led him across a short pathway through a clump of trees. Cochrane saw what he assumed was his destination. It was an old trailer, or caravan, set in a depression in the ground. Not far away was a bomb crater. The trailer looked as if it had once been yellow with blue trim but now it was just shabby and rusty. The windows had been covered with metal which was bolted into place. Like Cochrane, the trailer wasn't going anywhere. The tires were gone. It was propped up on bricks.

His jailers led him to the door to the trailer. They had keys and unlocked it. The trailer was two steps up on a pair of cinder blocks. They pushed Cochrane into the vehicle. The chains on his ankles caught and he fell, knocking his head and his shoulder as he hit the ground. The door slammed and he was in darkness.

It occurred to him that he was being held overnight way out of the ordinary field of prisoners or captured spies. Why? One part of him suggested that he was being lined up for a horrible questioning, torture and execution. He pictured the guillotine that they used: the one where the victim had to lie face up to experience the true horror of his end. He couldn't shake the image.

The thought made him feel so nauseous that he had to fight to dismiss it. Then he thought of Laura and hoped that if he were to be executed, she would do well. He prayed that her sadness would diminish over time and that she would marry again and not be alone.

There, he told himself. That would be his recurring prayer. Best to exit this world with a normal thought based on love rather than bitterness. What else could he hope for?

A night passed. He was given more water, a rotting apple and a full loaf of old bread. Twice the next day he was led out of the trailer at gunpoint to relieve his kidneys and bowels. Then he was returned to the trailer and locked up again. There was a kerosene heater outside the trailer which kept the inside just above freezing.

More time passed, all of it slowly. A few extraordinary notions came upon him. He hadn't yet been shot. He hadn't been tortured. He was still alive three days in captivity. And, strangest of all, he hadn't been interrogated. Putting all of these ideas in place, it occurred to him that he was being kept alive and not injured for a reason. That was the positive thought.

But for how long? That was the negative thought.

Granted, the reprieve could end very quickly. But so far, it hadn't.

From time to time he hallucinated or lost consciousness. On what he thought was the fourth day, his guards changed. Hans Wesselmann, looking smug and triumphant, returned with another man. They forced Cochrane into another car, a pre-war German Ford. They took him on another drive. He was again surprised that he hadn't been blindfolded.

He followed the route that his driver took. Suddenly something connected. He recognized a few buildings. They were driving through the western half of Berlin. Cochrane only had a vague idea of where he was. He had been in this area of Berlin when he had lived here. They crossed Havel River. They were distant from the center of the city, but he could see bomb damage. Houses became less frequent and the rain started again. It beat on the roof of the car.

Wesselmann drove. There was another guard who shared the front seat with him. The second man was huge. His head barely fit beneath the roof of the car. The captors smoked incessantly. They said little. When they did speak they communicated in low guttural whispers which Cochrane had trouble understanding.

First the drumbeat of the rain on the roof of the car was a problem, but so was the low quality of their speech. Like most Gestapo, they were thuggish and uneducated, reveling in both qualities. They had a loose grip on their own language.

Cochrane then recognized where they were. They were entering an area called Grunewald. It was a forest located on the western side of Berlin and on the east side of the Havel, mainly in the Grunewald locality. It was the largest green area in Berlin. Soviet and British bombs had fallen on it recently, so its tranquility and natural beauty had been deeply compromised.

The guard drove fast and kept looking at his rear view mirror. It must have been midmorning. They hit a smooth road through a stand of very tall trees and then hit a winding road that went through a ridge of tall pines.

They had continued for twenty minutes when a farmhouse came into view. The driver turned sharply into a driveway and the car felt as if it were on gravel. There was a wall of trees on each side of the driveway and an open field beyond the house. There was a dark green Opel, relatively new, in the driveway. The vehicle was in good condition.

The guards escorted Cochrane into the farmhouse through the front door. Cochrane remained in handcuffs and ankle shackles. Wesselmann stopped him in the entrance foyer and made him stand at attention. The taller guard went into the next room.

A brief conversation followed with a man in the adjoining room. Cochrane was struck by the clash between the peasant inflections of his captors and whoever waited for him. The latter man was educated and spoke in a very precise proper native "high" German.

The conversation concluded with the unseen German speaker concluding brusquely, "Bring him in."

Wesselmann grabbed Cochrane by the arm and marched him to the next room. Cochrane nearly stumbled from the brisk movement with manacles on his ankles. Wesselmann held him upright.

In the adjoining chamber, there was a severe looking man with grayish temples sitting in an armchair. The man surveyed Cochrane disdainfully as the guards hustled the captured spy before him.

The man looked military. The two guards fell into positions of attention behind Cochrane, one on the left, one on the right.

"You are William Thomas Cochrane," the man said quietly. "You are an American spy."

"I'm not who you think I am," Cochrane attempted. "I'm a Canadian businessman with business with the Reich."

The man laughed. He skipped past Cochrane's denial. He already knew the truth. No need to argue. The man had done his homework. He reached into his jacket pocket and pulled out a paper.

"Oh? Really?" the man scoffed. He held the paper aloft so that Cochrane could see it. The document was a copy of a passport control registration from the 1930s, when Cochrane had first entered Nazi Germany.

Cochrane looked at it, felt a further tumbling sensation, but didn't say anything.

"This is you, isn't it?" the man said.

Cochrane said nothing. Behind him, he heard the shuffling of his guards' feet. They were anxious to get on with things.

"Do you know who I am?" the man asked.

"No," Cochrane answered.

"Think hard. Have you ever seen me before?"

"If I have, I don't remember."

"*Would* you remember?"

"Probably."

The man laughed. A heavy silence filled the room.

Then, "You are correct," the man said very formally. "We have never met in person."

Cochrane tried to fight back revealing how fearful he really was.

"I regret never having had the honor," said Cochrane.

He was aware of the two guards behind him, shuffling even more nervously. The vision of Cambulat and Skordeno shot from behind on the tarmac in Vichy France resounded all over his psyche and set his mind on fire.

"I'm sure you do regret having never met man to man. It might have changed things. And you will continue to regret this," said the German. "But in the past we shared something of considerable value and import."

"What was that?" asked Cochrane.

"My wife," said the man. "Theresia. She had an affair with you when I was on Naval maneuvers. Repeated sexual liaisons. Don't deny it. I know everything. I am Heinrich Koehler. You know my name as well as I know yours."

Cochrane felt as if a load of bricks had dropped on him. He was too nonplussed to deny what they both knew. He also felt that this was the final nail in his coffin. He began to anticipate death in very real terms. He hoped it would be quick and merciful.

"Do you deny knowing her?" the German said with an edge.

From somewhere deep within him, Cochrane dredged up some truth.

"No. I don't deny it And I agree that she was a very fine woman. I regret that she was murdered and I regret any pain I caused you."

"Of course you do," Koehler said, without sounding as if he meant it. "We're all filled with regrets as the days of our lives come to an end. Is that not the case, Herr Cochrane?"

Cochrane did not reply.

Koehler flew into a sudden rage. "Answer me!" he roared. "Look me in the eye and answer me!"

"That's the case," Cochrane said.

"You made love to my wife many times when I was away in service to Adolf Hitler and the Third Reich. You must understand how 'dishonored' I have been!"

"I understand."

Koehler drew a pistol. He began to gesture with it.

"Since we all agree," Koehler said bitterly. "Let us get on with the execution."

Chapter 41

**Berlin
February 1943**

Koehler gestured to the two guards. They came up behind Cochrane again. They lifted him and turned him. They shoved him back through the entrance area and then outside.

Wesselmann put a hard knee into Cochrane's back. The guards dragged Cochrane into the Ford. They shoved him into the back seat, locking him to the chassis again with a metal attachment that rose from the floor and which was bolted in place.

Koehler came out of his house. He watched. He went to the Opel that stood in the driveway. There was no rain, just a mist. A quarter moon was shining. Cochrane could see the moon through the front window of the Ford and, absurdly perhaps, was struck by the notion that it was the last moon he would probably ever see.

Koehler climbed into his own car and signaled that the car with the prisoner should follow. Koehler started by driving north through the forest. Cochrane could tell the position by the moon, but he was increasingly desperate. He quietly tried to disengage from the handcuffs, even though he knew he couldn't run. All he could think of was if he somehow could get out of the car he might be able to escape into the darkness. But it was futile and the idea was an illusion.

They drove for several minutes, maybe a quarter hour. Then Koehler's Opel slowed. It found some tire tracks that led between a group of pine trees. The lead car's engine cut to a crawl. The cars pushed through some branches and thickets. Cochrane could see that the foliage had been cut away.

The cars moved into a clearing, about forty feet by forty feet. Cochrane saw another set of headlights, and then a second set. The Opel rolled to a halt and the Ford stopped next to it.

Cochrane saw Koehler step out and make a gesture to his two Gestapo assistants to hurry things along. The back doors

251

opened in the Ford. One guard held Cochrane at pistol point, the weapon to Cochrane's head. Wesselmann unlocked his cuffs.

Cochrane struggled. Wesselmann quickly whacked him in the ribs with the nose of a pistol. Oddly, Koehler saw it and barked for the man to stop. He drew his own weapon, a heavy pistol that may have been Czech.

"Control yourself, Hans, you idiot!" Koehler said to Wesselmann. "This is for me to finish!"

The Gestapo agents assembled Cochrane in a standing position. Cochrane took in what was facing him. There were two other cars. One was a utilitarian Benz, the other a newer and grander Opel.

There were three woman standing with shovels near the cars. Beside them was an open hole in the ground, unmistakably in the shape of a grave. Cochrane processed quickly. The door opened to one of the other cars. A man stepped out in dark slacks and a dark coat. He said nothing and stood with folded arms by the driver's side of the car. He wore a sidearm and had the face and build of a soldier.

Cochrane thought fleetingly that he saw a movement in the car, a head silhouetted against the rear window, but at this point it barely mattered. Then it occurred to him that the person in the car – if that person even existed – was female. Cochrane was convinced that he was hallucinating.

Then that thought was interrupted by Koehler. He spoke Russian to the three women. Cochrane realized the women were slave laborers, captured and now in forcible service to the Reich, as were thousands of other Russian and Polish women. They had been brought here to do some dirty work: literally, to dig a grave, presumably Cochrane's.

Koehler took charge of the situation. He drew his pistol. He asked for the keys to Cochrane's handcuffs and ankle cuffs. Wesselmann tossed them to him. Koehler made a good catch with his free hand.

He ordered the three female diggers to go with the Gestapo drivers. They were to return to a work camp in Berlin. Koehler gave the address aloud.

"I wish to stay and watch while you shoot this swine," Wesselmann said.

"Your wishes are as meaningless to me as bird shit, Kriminalkommissar Wesselmann," Koehler said. "Your orders are to return these women to their labor brigade. That is all. Dismissed!"

Wesselmann hesitated and glowered. Then he turned. Koehler spoke in Russian to the three frightened laborers. The three women obediently went toward the battered Ford, carrying the shovels.

"Leave the shovels, you idiots!" Koehler said in Russian. "Drop them!"

The women dropped their tools. They piled into the back seat of the Ford, happy to escape this place with the open grave. The Gestapo men looked at Koehler as if something was wrong. He stared them down. "I'll finish things here myself," Koehler said, waving the pistol. "Go! Get out. Now!"

Wesselmann and the other Gestapo agent hesitated. Across the way, the man who looked like a soldier threw back his great coat and revealed a small automatic rifle.

"Leave your windows open," Koehler said. "I wish the pleasure of this execution myself. You will hear the shots."

The look from the back-up man by the car was icy. He raised his weapon to indicate that orders needed to be followed. The two Germans took a final glance. Then, with an air of resignation, they turned and stepped into the Ford. Wesselmann was in the driver's seat. He cranked the engine. He backed the car away, then turned it. The beams from the headlamps caught Koehler squarely.

Koehler gave them a final wave with his pistol. The Ford turned and found its path through the trees and away from the burial ground.

Koehler watched them go. He looked at the man standing guard at his car. He looked at Cochrane. He looked back among the trees and could still see the lights of the Ford as it departed. It was still in hearing distance.

Koehler raised his pistol in the air. Cochrane watched disbelievingly.

Koehler aimed the pistol toward the treetops in the heavily wooded section. He fired the pistol twice. Then he fired a third time, a would-be *coup de grace.*

Cochrane's gaze found Koehler's. The gaze was as heavy as the moment.

Koehler turned and flipped the manacle keys to his assistant.

"Unlock him," he said.

The other man holstered his sidearm and came to Cochrane.

"Sorry about all that, sir," the man said in English. "I'm Corporal Willie Johnson. British Army. I was captured a year ago. I'm officially dead, also, if it makes you feel better."

"I'm not following," Cochrane said.

"It will all make sense, soon," he said. "There's work to do first."

Koehler came to Cochrane. They stood face to face. "I am not your friend and I am not your savior," Koehler said. "So don't for a moment think that I am. You wounded me with your transgression against me with my wife. That's over and done. You can help me now with something precious. And I can help you."

In the background, Cochrane again saw a movement in the Benz. Just a head. He couldn't see more. Then he realized. The person in the Benz *was* female, as he had first thought.

"First things first," said Koehler. "Pineapple."

"Pineapple?"

"Pineapple," Koehler said again. "As Herr Dulles suggested."

"Pineapple, mate," said Johnson.

After a long moment while Cochrane processed the fact that he was not going to be killed, he mumbled, "Pineapple. Jesus Christ!"

Koehler was already in motion. He went to the boot of the Opel and opened it. Cochrane looked in and gagged. There was the body of a dead man in the trunk. The dead man was wrapped in bloodstained sheets.

"Come on," Johnson said. "Nothing we can do for this poor bloke. We bury him here. He was a British aviator. Died in a crash after the air raids. If someone comes back to check the grave, they'll be able to tell there's a body down there. If they want to run tests, they can. It will take them days to figure he's not you, Mr. Cochrane."

They pulled the dead man from the trunk of the Benz. The dead man was naked, bullet wounds in the chest and the head: dark red blood around the wounds, the eyes half-mast, one unfocused the other shattered and still oozing puss. He appeared to have been no more than twenty-five when he died.

Cochrane drew a breath. He shifted into gear. His hands and wrists ached. But he and Johnson carried the corpse a few feet to the grave. Then they laid the dead aviator into it as gently as they could. The body settled in sideways and at an awkward angle. They let him rest in that position, though. Cochrane fought back a churning stomach as he looked at the dead man.

Johnson picked up a shovel and threw dirt in.

"We don't have much time, mate," he said. "Come on. Give us a hand."

The 'us' meant Cochrane, not Koehler. Cochrane pitched in. He was dying of thirst but at least not dying. Johnson picked up on it and found a canteen in the Opel and offered it. Cochrane glugged it down.

Koehler stood by the Benz. "All right, Herr Cochrane," he said finally. "Come here."

Cochrane walked to the Benz.

"It is I who summoned you through the office of Mr. Dulles. I am keeping my part of the arrangement. Mr. Dulles continues to receive coded notifications from this end. Now you will help us keep the deal. There is something for you to personally convey first to Switzerland, then to the United States. You will do that."

It was a statement, not a question.

"That's the arrangement I'm aware of," Cochrane answered. "That's why I'm here. What am I supposed to do?"

Koehler opened the back door of the Benz.

Cochrane stared in. Nothing could ever have prepared him for this day and this moment.

His eyes settled upon a frightened teenage girl in a fur cap and a pale blue scarf. She looked up at Cochrane with terrified eyes.

"This is my daughter," Koehler said. "In this foul world, she is the most precious thing I have. She is the only thing of intelligence and beauty that remains for me, the only thing I love. Her safety is paramount. But she is also carrying something from me to Mr. Dulles."

"I understand," Cochrane said slowly.

"I am entrusting her to you and to Mr. Dulles. She has a valid passport. It is American. Her new last name is Wagner, same as the great composer. Mr. Dulles and Mr. Donovan provided the passport. Eventually, she will go to live with family in the United States. If she doesn't reach her destination, or if she is harmed or taken advantage of in any way, for whatever reason, sometime in the future, even if it is long after the war, someone will find you and kill you if you are alive. It may not be me, but someone loyal to me will find you and kill you. Clear?"

"Clear," Cochrane said.

"If she arrives safely, you will be forever in our debt. Consider carefully which you would prefer."

Cochrane nodded. "I'll do my job," he said.

"Even if she were to stay here comfortably for the duration of the war," Koehler said, "the Red Army of General Zhukov may well reach Berlin before the American army of Patton or Eisenhower. If the Russians arrive first, every young German woman will be shot or hanged or raped. So you will take my girl to America. She has family there. An aunt, an uncle and cousins. They live in the state of Wisconsin. Do I need to say more, sir?"

"No, sir," Cochrane said. "I promise you. I'll get her there."

Koehler turned to the frightened teenager in the back seat of the car as a light cold rain began. "Introduce yourself," he said to Cochrane.

Cochrane spoke to her in German. "I'm William Cochrane from the United States of America," he said. "Herr Koehler is your father?" he asked.

The girl looked at Koehler and then at Cochrane. She nodded almost imperceptibly.

"I will do everything I can to make sure you arrive safely in America," Cochrane said, still in German. "I will get you to the family that awaits you. I promise."

The girl said nothing.

"She was active in a foolishly romantic anti-Hitler dissident group in Munich," Koehler said. "It was called White Rose. The Gestapo is looking for her. There's no time to waste. By my calculation, you can be across the border at Basel in three to seven days after you leave Berlin. That's all. Be careful. Good luck."

Koehler reached to his daughter in the back seat of the Benz. The girl leaned forward. They embraced. The girl cried. Then Koehler pulled away and handed the car keys to Cochrane.

"We will lead you back to Berlin where you will stay overnight," Koehler said. "This car and the other you see here are registered to the Naval Ministry. Stay behind me and you will not be stopped. Another vehicle will be ready for you later in the week. At that point, leave Berlin immediately."

"I'll do that," said Cochrane.

Cochrane watched as Koehler and the British POW went to the other car. Cochrane slid into the driver's seat of the Benz. The girl, wise and well instructed by her father, slid low in the back seat.

Cochrane turned as the other car pulled out to take the lead. He spoke to his passenger in German. "You're all right? You're ready?" he asked.

She nodded.

"Frightening, isn't it?" he asked in his kindest voice.

She nodded again.

"It's *all* very frightening," he said in German. "For everyone. Me. You. Everyone in the whole damned world. I think we'll do all right. I think we'll be okay. May I ask your name?" Cochrane finally asked, still in German.

She ignored him at first. She adjusted her fur cap and made a small pillow from a pale blue scarf. She settled in to sleep as Cochrane took the wheel and drove.

"Frieda," she said eventually. "My name is Frieda."

Chapter 42

**Berlin
February 1943**

They drove through the night back toward Berlin, the British POW named Johnson at the wheel of Koehler's car, Cochrane's Benz close behind. Sleet was intermittent and there was newly formed black ice on the road, making the journey slow and treacherous.

At one point as they neared the German capital, there was a military checkpoint, marked with a heavy roadblock and sudden bright lights. Soldiers, having little else to do in the darkest watches of the night, stopped both cars and surrounded them.

Cochrane counted quickly. There were six soldiers. Cochrane had heard of such squads, the positioning of which changed hour to hour overnight. They all bore rifles and battery-powered lanterns. They were looking for infiltrators or black market smugglers or anything else that swam into their nets.

Cochrane's heart was in his throat. Frieda rustled in the back seat of his car.

"Stay down," Cochrane said in German. "Pretend you're asleep."

Frieda rolled over, turning her face away from the windows.

Cochrane drew a breath. He watched what was transpiring in the car ahead of him. Johnson was keeping quiet. Koehler had a sheaf of papers, probably forgeries, that appeared to impress the soldiers. He was pulling rank, Cochrane thought to himself as his stomach was set to explode, and he was doing a good job at it.

One of the soldiers lost interest in the first car and wandered to the second. He came to Cochrane's window. He peered in, then shined the lantern in Cochrane's face. He gestured that Cochrane should roll down the window. Cochrane obeyed and gave a weak tired smile.

The soldier was a thirtyish private. He didn't look very smart and thus, to Cochrane, was dangerous and unpredictable. He shined his lantern first in Cochrane's eyes, and then on the female body in the back seat.

"What's this, your drunken whore?" the soldier asked.

A breath full of booze assaulted Cochrane. The man was obviously drunk on duty. "Why don't you lend us your slut for an hour? We'll fill her holes with more fucking than she can handle, hey?"

Cochrane opened his mouth to answer the extreme vulgarity with righteous indignation. But at the same instant, Cochrane's eyes caught movement around the car in front of him. The detail of soldiers was quickly stepping back, weapons lowered. The lieutenant in command of the soldiers was saluting obsequiously and his sergeant was quickstepping to the thug at Cochrane's window.

In two seconds the sergeant's hand landed on the shoulder of the drunken private. The sergeant grabbed back of the private's uniform and yanked him away. He shoved him backwards away from the car. The private fell hard into some rocks and ice. The sergeant kicked him.

"Hey, you stupid *arschloch*, shut up!" the sergeant snarled. "That's Naval chief of intelligence in the lead car!" The sergeant whirled and sharply saluted Cochrane. "Everything is very good, sir. This private will be discipled. Drive carefully."

"Sehr gut, Feldwebel. Danke," said Cochrane with all the courtesy he could muster.

From the lead car, Koehler made a hand gesture to Cochrane that the second car should follow.

There was another half hour of driving. They stopped at the building where Cochrane had his two temporary rooms. As the cars waited, Cochrane quietly went into the building alone. The last thing he wanted was to draw Heinz or Greta into the events of the early morning.

His key had been taken from him by the Gestapo and never returned. He turned the knob hard on his door. The lock broke with a loud snap that echoed through the ground floor. The electricity was still out. He stepped in and lit the lantern. He packed everything he could into a single suitcase and abandoned the rest, careful to take the case that contained his extra cash and escape passport.

He was back on the street within ten minutes. It was 3:00 AM. The neighborhood was black, except for the car lights. Koehler was standing protectively by the car where his daughter slept, his back against the car door, a Luger in his hand and pointing downward. Cochrane was convinced that Koehler would shoot anyone unauthorized who came near the girl. He respected that.

Koehler gave Cochrane a nod when Cochrane returned.

"I'm taking you to a safe house. They are expecting you. It's run by a woman named Frau Schneidhuber. Anitka Schneidhuber is a personal friend. You'll be respectful and stay with her till summoned?"

"Of course," Cochrane answered. "As if I have an alternative," he thought to say, but didn't.

"Your exit from Berlin is being arranged. Be patient. It will be dangerous." His tone changed. "Officially, you are dead, unless you are recognized or until they exhume the man we buried. Frieda? They will be looking for her."

"I understand."

"Do you have a backup passport? I'm told you do."

"I do."

"Use it," Koehler said.

Fatigue was crashing down on Cochrane. He was unsure how long he could stay awake. Idly, he thought back to the nighttime drive with Sergeant Santini which felt as if it had happened several years ago. He wished he'd had whatever chemical uppers that Santini had been snorting, but he didn't. So they pressed onward, Johnson now at the wheel of Cochrane's vehicle.

They drove for another quarter hour through the dark quiet streets of Berlin, detouring once because of rubble and running into another checkpoint, this one with more than a dozen soldiers, including two SS who seemed to be in charge.

Whatever real or forged papers Koehler was flashing, they must have been beauties, Cochrane thought, because they eased their way past danger once again.

They went around a few more corners and landed in a residential section of the city, again not too far from where he had once lived. They stopped in front of a single family house. The POW stepped from the Cochrane's car, looked both ways, gripped the gun that was under his coat, then went to the door.

Johnson knocked softly.

In a ground floor parlor a dim light illuminated. The front door opened.

A wide woman in a heavy coat loomed into view. She looked to be in her fifties. A wild crown of matted gray hair framed her face. She wore pants and had a large wide belly. She gave a nod to Koehler and said little. Cochrane could hear that she spoke German with an Austrian accent.

Koehler stepped from his car. He came back to the trailing car and retrieved his daughter. He put an arm protectively around her, steadied her and walked her into the safe house. The woman, Frau Schneidhuber, nodded that the cars could stay where they were.

They entered the house. The woman closed the door. Corporal Johnson carried in two suitcases from the second car, one belonging to Frieda, one to Cochrane. Two orange cats were sprawled on the floor in front of a dying wood fire on a grate. One of the cats was too stout to move. The other was too disinterested.

Corporal Johnson smiled to the cats and left the suitcases near the smoldering fire. Cochrane whispered thanks to the Englishman. He might have forgotten from the fatigue and lost all his tools of border crossing if the suitcase had disappeared.

As Cochrane tried to stay out of everyone's way, he noticed a chair by the window where Frau Schneidhuber had been sitting in wait. There was a well-thumbed copy of *Berlin Alexanderplatz*, on a side table, half open and face down. Next to that was a copy of Kafka's *Metamorphosis*. The woman's reading tastes were not just curious, they were currently illegal. A phrase from the latter work – which Cochrane had once read, or attempted to read, in English - bounced into Cochrane's delirious brain: *As Gregor Samsa awoke one morning from uneasy dreams, he found himself transformed in his bed into a gigantic insect-like creature.*

The image continued the surrealism of the moment.

On a wall in a corner right by a window was a yellowing portrait of Hitler, presumably present to keep the local snitches happy.

It was nearly 4:00 AM. The night would end in exercises in pantomime as few words were spoken. Frieda's father led her to a makeshift sleeping alcove on the first floor. He embraced her and let her settle onto a cot. There was a blanket. He covered his daughter and pulled the blanket up to her chin. Frieda returned instantly to sleep.

Then Koehler turned. He cautioned Cochrane to stay indoors as much as possible, if not entirely. He further advised Cochrane that he would be back as soon as the proper arrangements could be made. A day or two should be allowed, maybe a week at most.

Cochrane nodded but by this time was borderline delirious.

Koehler and his bodyguard stepped from the house. Johnson gave Cochrane a wink. Frau Schneidhuber closed the front door and locked it with an oversized key. There was a sturdy lock on the door with a steel panel around it, the lock much newer than the door. When her visitors were gone, she also dropped a long wooden bar across the door.

She turned to her overnight guests and, continuing in German, pointed out the kitchen, the water closet and a small table near the fire which contained several bottles of liquor. Then she led Cochrane up some narrow uneven steps to another makeshift cot that was crammed into a musty hallway on the second floor.

"Für dich, mein Freund," she said. "You speak German, I'm told."

Cochrane nodded. He spoke German and these arrangements were much better than an unmarked grave in the woods.

"You will be safe here," she said, "unless there is another air raid. There is no shelter nearby, so we may all be killed if bombs fall. If no bombs fall, we are all safe."

Impressed with her logic, Cochrane collapsed onto the cot. He was unconscious and into a deep state of sleep so fast that he never remembered closing his eyes.

Chapter 43

Munich
February 1943

In Munich, a more horrendous series of events transpired.

Those who remained active in the White Rose group delivered the sixth and final leaflet to buildings in Munich. They mailed copies to influential members of the military and the government. They ran off duplicates on copying machines and sent them to other cities through trusted couriers. As a special insult to Hitler, the White Rose distributed the pamphlets to Linz where Hitler had spent his youth. As a further affront, they smuggled the final leaflet out of the country to the French resistance in Strasbourg. It was passed along underground routes and several thousand copies were eventually scattered over Germany by Allied planes.

In the early morning hours of February 18, Sophie Scholl and her brother Hans were leafleting throughout the University of Munich. They carried a suitcase filled with leaflets through the main university building, leaving handfuls of their work at key intersections where students and faculty would find them in the morning. Jakob Schmidt, the custodian who had been shadowing them, suddenly appeared and confronted them. Schmidt, who had left school at age eight and never looked back, remained an ardent Nazi.

"You two! You're under arrest!" Schmidt barked.

At first they laughed. Schmidt was an ignorant little ape of a man. How could anyone take him seriously? The laughter didn't last long.

Gestapo agents were already on campus. Schmidt phoned them. The suitcase of printed matter was seized as evidence.

The Gestapo handcuffed Hans and Sophie and led them into an unmarked van. They were driven away. Later in the day, the SS arrested Willie Graf. The next day they arrested Christoph Probst. The Gestapo took all of them to Wittelsbach Palace. The

Palace in central Munich had once been the residence of the Wittelsbach monarchs of Bavaria. These days, however, it was Gestapo headquarters in Munich.

The first thing the interrogators asked for was a list of names. "Other members of your treasonous group," asked the Gestapo of Hans and Sophie.

The philosophy student and the biology student refused to cooperate. The recriminations were swift and brutal. The torture began within two hours of their arrest.

Chapter 44

**Berlin
February 1943**

Bill Cochrane was a young man again. He sat on the front porch of the house in Virginia where he had grown up. He was having a wonderful conversation with his father about the great baseball pitcher, Walter Johnson. He felt a hand on his shoulder. A woman was gently saying, *"Mein Herr? Mein Herr?"*

Cochrane's father laughed. "We don't speak German in Virginia," he said. "We fought a war with those Huns and we don't have to speak German."

"Mein Herr?" came the woman's voice again. "It's afternoon."

Bill Cochrane's eyes flickered open. His father, long since dead, waved good-bye and went back into the dream. The dream dissipated and went to wherever in the psyche they lurked.

Cochrane sat up groggily in a strange house in Berlin. There had been no air raid overnight, so he was still alive.

Frau Schneidhuber was leaning over to speak to him, a kindly smile on her wrinkled face, kinship in her deep blue eyes. "Mein Herr, it's already afternoon," she said in German.

Cochrane's sleepy gaze fixed upon her. He blinked like a fighter who had been dazed but was coming around. There was a clock on a nearby table. He focused on it. It said 2:38 PM. Midafternoon indeed.

"God..." he said.

"I have some tea, some canned fruit and some bread," she said. "You are welcome to anything I have."

Cochrane sat up on his elbows and came awake fast. "Where's the girl?" was the first thing he asked.

"Frieda is downstairs," she said. "Reading."

"Good," Cochrane said, relieved. "Good."

He struggled to his feet. The previous day, which started in a trailer, continued in more than one car, reversed itself at a grave

267

site, included a burial and then brought him back to Berlin, played out at sixty miles an hour. His head pounded. He asked himself: was he really alive?

"Some tea would be good," he said.

"I thought as much," Frau Schneidhuber said.

He noticed that she was wearing a silver chain around her neck. On the chain was a large key. He recognized it as the key to the front door. She took his hand and led him downstairs.

Frieda was sitting on a worn sofa in the parlor. She had borrowed the resident copy of Kafka's *Metamorphosis*. She was buried in it, her sharp eyes shooting across line after line.

There was a log smoldering in the grate. Someone had been out because there were some other scraps of wood that had been collected and set by the fire. That, or someone had given them to the fraulein. No matter, she made tea.

"Good morning. Good day," Cochrane said in German to the girl.

Frieda raised her eyes, looked at him blankly, then lowered her gaze and kept reading.

"Is that my only greeting, Frieda?" he asked with some irony, still in German.

No answer.

"I'm putting my life on the line to get you to Switzerland," he said in English, mildly piqued.

She looked back to him. *"Sie schnarchen wie eine Säge, die Holz schneidet,"* she said.

He wasn't certain what he had heard. *"I snore?"* he asked.

"She's right," Frau Schneidhuber said in German. "You snore."

"Sorry," he said.

"We don't care," the proprietress said. "My husband Fritz used to, also."

Cochrane was about to ask where her Fritz was but the woman's eyes indicated the portrait of a young soldier who was in a World War One uniform. Her gaze said everything. Nearly two million German soldiers had died in the first great war and Fritz had been one of them. He wasn't here right now and was not expected back.

"Argonne Forest," she said without emotion. "Killed by the French. Do you like your tea strong?"

"Anything you can do would be fine," he said.

She served tea and bread with loganberry jam. Cochrane devoured it. His eyes fell upon the picture of Hitler by the window. The lady of the house was no one's fool. She followed his eyes.

"The Nazi block captain, the gauleiter, served in the war with my late husband," she said. "He knows what I think. He knows about my books. I keep the picture in the window and he doesn't see anything else. We disagree on Hitler but we are friends."

"Does he know you have guests right now?" Cochrane asked.

"No," she said after a pause. "And even if he does, he doesn't. That's how it works."

Cochrane finished his tea. Without being asked, Frau Schneidhuber stood, went to the heating coil, retrieved the tea pot and poured Cochrane a second cup. All this while Frieda flipped pages of Kafka and ignored them both. The girl was in her own world, or more accurately the world of the great Prague-born author. Kafka had been born near the Old Town Square in Prague, at the time a major city of the Austro-Hungarian Empire. His parents were German-speaking middle-class Ashkenazi Jews. And then there was the content of his work. There were more reasons that Kafka was on the Nazis' proscribed list than there were unmarked graves in the Argonne Forest.

Cochrane finished his second cup of tea.

"I want to show you something," Frau Schneidhuber said.

She drew Cochrane to a small cabinet near the kitchen sink. There were shelves and drawers. "Left side, bottom drawer," she said. "Open the drawer, take a look."

Cochrane obeyed. There were a pile of rags that looked as if they were used for cleaning.

"Prowl," she insisted.

269

Cochrane rummaged through the soiled rags. Then she helped. She reached down and pulled the cloth material out of the drawer. Beneath them there was a collection of pistols: German and Czech, most at least twenty years old.

"They work and they're loaded," she said. "They were with my husband's things when his final box of belongings was shipped back to me. In 1926. Eight years after the war ended. Weimar efficiency. You should take a gun," she suggested. "If you kill a Nazi before you leave the country it won't bother me a bit."

Cochrane reached in. He selected a Czech pistol. Sure enough, it was loaded. It did not show much use. It had recently been lubricated, also. Frau Schneidhuber said that once a year she took a bus out to the most remote western edge of the Tiergarten in Berlin and fired away at vermin. She always picked a Sunday morning, she explained, because there weren't many people.

She gave him a handful of bullets. "In case of trouble," she said. "The others I keep. Someday the Red Army will come to my door if I'm not dead first from English bombing. I will be ready. I do not wish to be raped by filthy Russian peasants or live under Bolshevism. The first soldiers who come to my door will not live under it either."

Carefully, Cochrane put his Czech pistol and the bullets in his coat pocket.

"I'd ask how long you'll be staying in Berlin," Frau Schneidhuber said, "but it would be a pointless question, wouldn't it? You don't know."

"No, I don't," he said. "And thank you for the weapon."

"To your good health," she said with no small sense of irony.

Frieda remained silent through all this, not even glancing up.

Cochrane went to his bag and opened it. Nothing had been touched. He found fresh clothes and a razor. He piled his books and the box of dominos on the table. Frau Schneidhuber watched, then volunteered a piece of soap for shaving. He asked if he could wash. She said yes. She warmed some water in the tea kettle on the

270

grate. He closed the door to the tiny chamber where there was a toilet and a narrow standpipe above a drain that served as a shower. He cleaned up as best possible. The water from the pipe was frigid.

He began to wonder anew about the Tavern Wittgenstein and why he couldn't locate it. Dulles had urged him to go by at least once. He still felt that it could be important.

When he came out again in twenty minutes, Frieda was examining his books. She raised her eyes and looked at him.

"These are yours?" she asked in German.

"Those are mine," he said. "You may read them if you wish. The ones in German, of course."

Her eyes narrowed. He caught an air of mischief. She reached to the one by F. Scott Fitzgerald, *Tender Is The Night*, in English.

She scanned the opening page. "What's it about?" she asked in German.

"It's a tragic story about a young actress and a couple she knows," he said. "It's set in the south of France in the 1920s."

"So the people in it are French?"

"No. They're American," he said.

Her eyes rose to his again. "I'd like to read it," she said.

"It's in English," he said.

Frau Schneidhuber watched with a smile.

After a moment of thought, "I know," Frieda said, effortlessly switching to English. "I speak English, too."

"You speak English?"

"Why do you assume I don't?"

Stunned, "How do you happen to speak English?" Cochrane asked.

"My father taught me."

"Why?"

"So I could go to England. Or America," she said. "So I could leave Germany."

"He's been planning it for a while?" Cochrane asked.

She went back to her reading.

Cochrane sat down at the table with her. "Jesus," he muttered.

"Jesus?" Frieda asked, looking up again.

"It's just an expression," Cochrane said.

"'Jesus,'" she repeated. "Is that what you say when you're angry? Or surprised?"

"Some people do."

"You do," Frieda said. "I heard you say it before."

"You learn quickly," he said as a compliment.

"My teachers always told me that," she said.

Frau Schneidhuber laughed indulgently. "'Jesus.' Not a polite expression, Frieda," she said.

The German lady came around to a position behind Frieda. She placed her unsteady hands on Frieda's shoulders. Two of her fingers were crooked and there was a scar on the back of her right hand. "This is a very special young lady," Frau Schneidhuber said, again back in German. "You will take good care of her, I know."

"I will indeed," said Cochrane.

Frieda returned to her reading, setting Fitzgerald aside and returning to Kafka, who better fit the mood. The day passed uneventfully.

Chapter 45

**Berlin
February 1943**

As Frau Schneidhuber prepared to go out to go shopping the next morning, Cochrane gave her a hundred Swiss francs. She returned two hours later with fresh bread, dried meat, canned vegetables and real coffee. Cochrane stayed indoors all day, lest he be spotted by the block gauleiter and arouse suspicion.

Frieda stayed in also. There was no new communication from her father. Cochrane and Frieda were in a holding pattern. That was the bad news. Or maybe it was good news, the absence of anything bad happening being good. Again the notion crossed his mind of making a final pass at finding the Tavern Wittgenstein. He needed to decide if the risks outweighed the potential benefits.

Instinct and training told him to give it one more try. Caution told him not to.

Factored in: he would need to carry his pistol and need to take Frieda with him. There was no way he could allow her out of his sight for any significant passage of time.

Frau Schneidhuber had a radio. It was a primitive crystal set but it worked. The fraulein, Cochrane, and Frieda huddled around it toward nine in the evening and tried to pick up the BBC. The Nazi Party had initiated a new station with a powerful transmitter to broadcast at the same frequency to drown out broadcasts from London. But saboteurs, probably local Communists who moved about Germany at night, kept bombing the local transmitter. So tonight the BBC was clear. Listening was illegal. They kept the volume low.

There was much about the great Russian victory at Stalingrad, and projections of how long it would take for the Red Army to begin its march westward.

In further war news, the German submarine U-268 had been attacked and sunk off the Atlantic coast of France in the Bay of Biscay. A squadron of Royal Air Force bombers had turned the trick. Another German submarine, the U-562, had been sunk northeast of Benghazi, Libya, by a combined assault of an RAF squadron and the British destroyers *Hursley* and *Isis*. Cochrane was tempted to smile over the victories at sea but quickly caught himself. He may have been in anti-Nazi company, but not anti-German.

The announcer in London then added that the Japanese destroyer *Ōshio* had been torpedoed off Wewak, New Guinea by the American submarine *Albacore* and sank under tow. Since the German defeat at Stalingrad, the momentum of the war had shifted.

"I hate wars," Frieda said in English, opening up. "I don't care if it's Germans or Americans or British or Japanese dying. I don't like any of it." She turned to Cochrane. "Why do men do it?" Frieda asked. "Why do men kill each other?"

Cochrane drew a long breath "I don't know," he said. "That's a good question. I don't know the answer."

She switched gears. "Have you heard any news from Munich?" she asked. "About my friends?"

"The White Rose?"

"Yes," she said. "Be honest."

"I know that three people were arrested. I don't know the names."

"Are they in a lot of trouble?"

"I won't lie to you. Yes, they are. It's very serious."

She sighed. Her eyes became moist and she bit her lip. "I should be there with them," she said. "I want to go back."

Cochrane shook his head. "No," he said. "There's only so much any one of us can do."

"I should go back to Munich," she insisted. "I'll admit my guilt! I want to stand trial with the rest of them!"

"That's not going to happen, Frieda. My paramount job is to keep you safe. Then I'm to get you first to Switzerland and then to America. You might hate me for this right now, but that's what your father wants. In my opinion, it's also what will be best for you. I promise."

"I don't want to be kept safe," she muttered.

"In this situation," he said sternly, "you do not get what you want!"

She sighed. For a long moment she sulked.

She looked to Frau Schneidhuber who gave her an admonishing glare also.

"The American gentleman is correct," the fraulein said. "You will not be returning to Munich any time soon. Those filthy Nazis would murder you."

"They're going to murder my friends, aren't they?"

Neither Cochrane nor Frau Schneidhuber would answer.

Then, "We don't know yet," Cochrane said. "That's the best I can say."

"That means 'yes,' doesn't it?" she asked.

"We don't know," Cochrane said.

Frieda sulked a while longer. Then she looked moodily at the wooden box with Arabic writing next to the books on the table. "What's this?" she asked at length.

"Dominos," Cochrane answered.

"What are dominos?"

"Open the box," he said. "It's a game. A game with numbers. You might like it."

She looked at the domino case for a second, then grabbed it. She spilled out four tiles. She looked at them with fascination. "It's a game?" she asked.

"It's a game."

"Do you know the rules?" she asked.

Cochrane nodded. "Of course I do," he said. "I'll teach you. Then we'll play," he said.

Grudgingly but with curiosity, she set aside her book. "All right," she said. "Show me."

Cochrane and the girl settled in and played. To no one's surprise, she quickly picked up the game and its strategies.

Chapter 46

**Berlin
February 1943**

Heinrich Koehler did not appear that day, nor was there was any message. Cochrane, feeling grateful, but shut-in, ventured out briefly in the afternoon. He saw nothing that indicated any Gestapo or surveillance activity in the neighborhood. Accordingly, he and Frau Schneidhuber decided that their teenage guest – she was sixteen, it turned out - could come out for some air that afternoon.

Even though he was officially dead, Cochrane knew that the Gestapo could be looking for him as well as Frieda. One never knew with complete certainty what the other side knew or what random event could give away a spy behind enemy lines. For this reason, he felt it was better if Frau Schneidhuber strolled with Frieda. He would walk ten meters behind them, pretend to be alone, and watch their back, armed with his Czech pistol. The visuals would throw off anyone looking for a foreign man with a teenage girl.

There was a busy street nearby with many small shops and merchants. Cochrane refreshed his wardrobe with a change of hats, a dark scarf and an extra pair of gloves. All the items were second hand, which was perfect. They wouldn't stand out as new. At one point they walked into a Konditorei for pastry and coffee.

Frau Schneidhuber said the pastry shop was attended only by local people. There would be no danger. She had been coming here for years and knew everyone, at least by sight. Unaccompanied strangers would stand out and the locals would avoid them. Cochrane and the girl were acceptable, she said, because they were with her.

Most of the customers of the Konditorei hated the government, she explained in a low voice, but they feared an invasion by the Red Army. Most of her friends knew the war was lost and hoped there would be an armistice before the Russians could invade. But Hitler still had his true believers and the Gestapo had its rats. So one had to be careful.

"I hate Hitler," Frieda said, loud and clear, at this juncture of the conversation.

Frau Schneidhuber hushed her immediately. Everyone in the café pretended not to have heard.

Frieda had ice cream. Cochrane bought tea for himself and his hostess, using his German money. While he was anxious to get out of Berlin, he also knew that patience was an asset and he needed to be certain that an escape car and fuel were prepared properly.

"Have you been to Berlin before, Herr Stykowski?" Frau Schneidhuber asked.

"I was here briefly in the 1930s," he said.

"Did you like the city?"

"The city, yes," he said. "The politics, no."

"You wouldn't have a spare cigarette, would you?" she asked.

He fished into his pocket and found one of his giveaway packs. He handed it to her. She opened it, took one, and handed the pack back to him.

"Keep it," he said.

"Really?"

"Really," he said.

"Danke schön."

"Bitte schön," he answered. There was a packet of matches on the table. He lit her cigarette.

"I came here in 1924 from Hamburg," she said. "I loved this city. I was a young widow; you know that. Berlin was a carnival. The night life. Oh, you wouldn't have believed it. Behrenstrasse. Friedrichstrasse. Die Jägerstrasse. Sometimes the night spots were packed three and four to a building. You wouldn't think there were enough people to fill them. But there were. There were so many lights it was impossible to see the sky. The singing, the dancing, it went on till dawn. I worked as a waitress at a little place, then at a bigger place. The owners let me sing sometimes, too, early in the evening," she said with a laugh, her pink-rimmed eyes flirting with his.

She lowered her voice to be less audible to Frieda. "I had myself some good times. Some special men. The colored musicians were wonderful in Berlin in the Twenties. I loved them all. Anything went. German girls went with American Negroes. Drugs. Homosexuals. People with special appetites in the boudoir. It was so lighthearted and gloriously debauched. I miss it."

"I understand," Cochrane said.

She lingered on her cigarette, probably recalling indiscretions she did not regret. Cochrane let her talk and reflect.

"Some people said it was depraved. Sinful. A disgrace to German civilization," she said. "I think it was a way of forgetting the humiliation of the Great War."

"I agree with you."

"It was a way to avoid what you saw at dawn."

"What did you see at dawn?" Cochrane asked.

"The real world," she said. "The whole city changed when the sun rose. Berlin was a war-ravaged city in the 1920s. Gray and grim. Dawn was when you saw the bands of hungry orphaned kids roaming the streets. Crippled and maimed war veterans were everywhere. Even when the sun was at its midpoint in the sky, Berlin was a cold city. I would come home before dawn and sleep past noon. I'd miss my husband horribly when I was alone. I'd bring home unfinished bottles of liquor that the customers left on the tables so I could get drunk. All the girls did it if they didn't have a man, and for most of us, there weren't enough men. They'd all been killed. I couldn't wait to go to my club around two in the afternoon to help set up and have a meal. Our owner was an American gangster named Gazzella. He sold cocaine. He was a good man. Beautiful face, beautiful voice. He could sing Puccini. He made sure all his girls got food and dressed like flappers. The club was my island. I avoided the ugliness which was Berlin in the daytime. I was a night person anyway."

"How do you happen to know Herr Koehler?" Cochrane asked, probing.

She smiled. "I worked at a place called 'Der Resi'," she said with a sly smile. "Did you know it?"

Cochrane laughed.

"Indeed, I did," he answered.

The "Resi" had been the nickname of a vast, luxurious dance-hall, Der Residenz-Casino.

"It was at Blumentrasse 10, if I remember," Cochrane said, "right near Alexanderplatz. Huge dance floor. Maybe two hundred tables."

She nodded. "Herr Koehler and his wife, Theresia, used to come in. Early 1930s. We became friendly. Later the city became ugly with Nazis. The place closed in 1939."

"And what did you do at The Resi?" he asked.

"My usual," she recalled with a shameless smile. "Danced on a big stage with all the other girls in a sequined dress that was usually barely decent and sometimes completely indecent. Used to show my breasts every night if I liked that audience. Waitressed tables wearing not much more than a flimsy silk robe. I loved it. The place was beautiful and I felt beautiful being part of it. Do you remember how the ceiling was made from reflective glass? There were four bars and even a carousel? Private rooms for couples who couldn't wait to get home," Frau Schneidhuber laughed. "Did you know Theresia, Frieda's mother?" she asked, glancing at the girl who was out of earshot fetching more ice cream.

"We met a few times," Cochrane answered, sticking with a basic truth.

"I like Theresia," she said. "Fine woman."

"Tell me," Cochrane said after a slight pause. "Does Herr Koehler know how you feel? Politically?"

"Of course, he does."

"And that's not a problem?"

"Berlin is complicated," she said.

Then a little wave of sadness overtook her. "Halcyon days," she said with a sniff. "Better to have lived them than to have missed them. But all gone now, right?"

"I'm afraid so."

"Are you carrying the pistol I gave you?"

"Yes, I am," Cochrane said, suddenly alert and rock-still.

"Is it loaded?" she asked as she dreamily frowned and plucked imaginary lint from the front of her coat.

"Yes, it is. Do you see trouble?"

"No. I'm just asking," she said, her gaze returning to meet his. "These days trouble arrives before you can see it. You need to always be ready. You're a nice man. Decent. I hope you get home alive."

"Thank you," he said, his nerves settling back to normal.

Frau Schneidhuber fell silent. She drew a final labored puff from her American cigarette, then dropped it on the floor and snuffed it out with the worn toe of her shoe.

Cochrane watched Frieda return to the table, sit and devour her ice cream, which she took as a treat. For a few moments the world was normal: a man, a woman and a teenage girl were enjoying one of life's small pleasures. He wondered if he would have his own daughter one day. Cochrane smiled and said he admired Frieda's fur cap and pale blue scarf. They spoke German. Frau Schneidhuber's English was limited.

"Thank you," Frieda said. "It's me."

"What do you mean, 'it's me'?" Cochrane asked.

"I always wear my blue scarf and my silly cap," she said.

Cochrane's smile disappeared. "Did you always wear it in Munich?" he asked.

"Of course. Everyone knew me as 'the girl with the blue scarf and funny fur hat.'"

He thought about it for less than two seconds. He got to his feet. "Wait here," he told the two women. "Don't leave until I'm back."

Cochrane went to the first sidewalk merchant he could find who sold secondhand clothing. He purchased a deep maroon scarf and a black woolen cloth cap for the girl. The cap was a bulky one that would hide the contours of her face. He also bought a hair comb that she could use to pin up her hair. He was angry with himself for not having thought of this before.

It would have been foolish to ask Frieda to change her attire in the Konditorei. But he returned and walked the women back to the house where they were staying. Then he unveiled his new purchases and the reasons for their use.

Frau Schneidhuber supported him. Frieda understood.

They played dominos again that night. Frieda had developed a liking and a skill for the game. It offset her reading time and encouraged her to talk more. An hour into the games, there was a coded knock on the door: two short raps, a single, then three.

Frieda sat up. Frau Schneidhuber recognized the knock, too. It was Heinrich Koehler.

The fraulein went to the window to make sure Koehler was alone. From somewhere she had drawn one of the many pistols she kept. She held it downward in her left hand, then pocketed it when she was satisfied that there was no threat.

She went to the door. She lifted the barrier bar and undid the lock.

Cochrane held his breath. Something in him feared that Frieda would be taken from him before the assignment was complete. But the contrary was true.

Koehler had come to say good-bye to his daughter. He said he hoped that their separation would be temporary. Preparations were in place. Cochrane and Frieda would be on the move again the next evening. But there was a serious wrinkle.

Koehler felt that he was now under extra surveillance. He had slipped his leash to get here this evening, but it was important that Cochrane and Frieda be gone from Berlin.

"It is imperative," he said, "that you both get to Switzerland as soon as possible. The timing now might be urgent."

Cochrane said he understood. Frieda did too. Cochrane allowed Koehler a few minutes alone with his daughter.

When Koehler was set to leave, he gave the instructions for the next day to Cochrane.

There would be a car waiting in a car port at a certain address in the northwest section of Berlin. It would be ready at four in the afternoon, but Koehler recommended not leaving until sometime in the evening. There was a guest house two hours away which would accommodate them. Arrangements had been made.

"Who runs the guest house?" Cochrane asked.

"A friend who likes money," said Koehler.

"Black market?" Cochrane asked.

"Black market but trustworthy. A friend."

"All right," Cochrane said.

They would find maps and a flashlight in the car, Koehler explained. The flashlight would be between the seats and the maps had been stashed under the back seat floormat. One map was a standard road map of the area. The other was hand drawn and would lead them to their "guesthouse" for the first night on the road.

Additionally, there was an envelope with the maps, Koehler explained. It contained extra Reichsmarks and Swiss francs, pilfered out of some rodent fund in the Naval Ministry. There were two Lugers in the car also, loaded and ready and with extra ammunition. The guns were in the box of emergency road equipment in the boot. In the Third Reich, Koehler opined, what could be more essential emergency road equipment than pistols?

"And a key?" Cochrane asked. "For the car?"

"The key will be on top of the left rear tire," Koehler said. "If it is not claimed by tomorrow at midnight, the car will be withdrawn."

Cochrane understood. He had a window of eight hours to get out of the city with Frieda.

There followed a confidential conversation between Koehler and Frau Schneidhuber. Then as Koehler readied to leave, Cochrane drew him aside by the door within the small house. They spoke privately and in lowered tones in German.

"Just tell me one thing so that I know," Cochrane asked.

Koehler waited.

"Why me?" Cochrane asked. "Why did you choose me as the conduit to get Frieda out of Germany?"

Koehler smiled. "I have many trusted friends. The Gestapo, the SS, they would never suspect that I would employ a man I should hate. They would watch all my friends, but never an old adversary."

"Good thinking," admitted Cochrane.

"There's a second reason, also," Koehler said, allowing a pause. "You remember how you left Germany the first time? You were tough and brutal. An American cowboy, for better or worse. No one was going to stop you from reaching your exit. You killed people who stood in your way. You were hellbent on getting your job done. Against all odds and adversaries you did just that."

"Yeah. I suppose that's what happened."

"I admired that," said Koehler. "And I reasoned you might need to do it again."

The two men shook hands. Koehler hugged and kissed his daughter, then departed. Frieda sadly watched him go. Deep down, Cochrane felt that he would never again see Koehler alive. While he had every reason to dislike the man, his feelings were more positive than even ambivalent.

In the evening, they played dominos, all three of them. As the final game concluded, the Tavern Wittgenstein again floated into Cochrane's thoughts. He decided to mention it and asked if either had ever heard the name.

"Never heard of it," said Frau Schneidhuber.

But Frieda had stopped playing tiles. She stared at Cochrane.

"It's closed," she said. "The owner was murdered. About a month ago."

Shocked, "How do you know that?" Cochrane asked.

"Friends. From the University."

"In Munich?" Cochrane asked.

"White Rose had friends in Berlin," she said. "At Friedrich Wilhelm University. We used to go there. To Tavern Wittgenstein."

"Did you know about the murder only through your friends," he asked, "or also through your father?"

"I can trust you?" she asked.

"You can trust me, Frieda."

A long pause, then, "Both," she said.

She might have let it go at that, but then she added more. "The tavern is on a corner under a railroad bridge," she said. "It's open again under a different name. It's Bar Nuremberg now. A lot of soldiers drink there. Nazis. Other people too."

It was the 'other people too,' that captured Cochrane.

"Could you show me where it is?" Cochrane asked. "Tomorrow?"

"That would be easy," Frieda said. "If we are leaving Berlin, it's directly on our way. We can stop there."

Chapter 47

**Munich
February 22, 1943**

    In Munich, a special legal tribunal convened for the trial of Hans and Sophie Scholl and their friend Christoph Probst, the ex-Luftwaffe aviator. The government flew its favorite jurist, Dr. Roland Freisler, from Berlin to Munich to preside.

    Freisler was known as "Hitler's Hanging Judge." He was the personification of Nazi law, or more accurately lack of it. Earlier in his life, Freisler had earned the Iron Cross both 2nd and 1st Class for heroism during World War One. More recently, he had been an advocate of adapting the racist laws in the southern states of the United States as a model for Nazi legislation targeting Jewish people in Germany. Specifically, Freisler argued for establishing laws against sexual activity or marriage between races. He greatly admired American "Jim Crow" legislation and wished to import it to Germany to use against non-Aryans.

    The court held its session on a Monday. After three days of savage beatings at Wittelsbach Palace, the three defendants had "confessed" their guilt in the authorship and distribution of the White Rose pamphlets.

    Sophie Scholl arrived in court on crutches with a broken leg. She also had a set of bruises and cuts across her once-pretty face. Hans Scholl and Christoph Probst showed the evidence of beatings, also.

    Dr. Freisler declared the court to be in session. He read the evidence against the three defendants. Hans Scholl attempted to take full blame for the three defendants and asked for mercy on behalf of his younger sister and for Probst, the combat veteran who was married with two young children. Dr. Freisler angrily interrupted him after a few minutes and told him to sit down and shut up.

At the end of the day, Dr. Freisler pronounced the three accused to be guilty. They were sentenced to be executed by guillotine that evening. There was no jury, no process of appeal.

Hans, Sophie and Christoph accepted the sentence with serene dignity. Guards took the three condemned convicts by truck to nearby Stadelheim prison – where Hitler was once imprisoned - to await the implementation of their sentence. Execution time was set by Freisler's court for 6:00 PM that evening. Word reached the courtroom that other members of White Rose, including Alexander Schmorell and Kurt Huber had also been arrested. Nationwide searches continued for two dozen others, including Frieda Koehler and her friend, Ilse.

Robert Scholl, the father of Hans and Sophie, had been in the courtroom. He was allowed to see his son and daughter for a few minutes at Stadelheim. He embraced them and said he was proud of them for standing up to Nazi injustice. Sophie replied that she was proud to have done what she did.

"You will go down in history," Robert Scholl told his two children. "There is a higher justice than this."

Six PM arrived. A few heartbeats later, the blade of the guillotine fell three times.

At six fifteen, the government in Berlin announced that Hans and Sophie Scholl and their co-conspirator Christoph Probst were dead. The news of the executions were on German radio, a warning to others who might travel the same dangerous road of treason.

Bill Cochrane and Frau Schneidhuber made sure the radio was off that evening. There was no telling how Frieda might have behaved if she had known that her friends had been guillotined.

Chapter 48

Berlin
February 1943

    Pleased with the outcome of the trial in Munich, Kriminalkommissar Wesselmann stood impatiently in the falling snow in Berlin. It was late afternoon. Daylight was dying. He watched a team of four Polish women dig at the site where the American spy, William Cochrane, should have been buried.
    The weather had turned sharply colder across Germany and eastern France, in keeping with this being the coldest winter on record for a generation. Parts of the Rhine were freezing. So were many of the smaller rivers and lakes. Now the fresh earth of the gravesite had started to freeze also, slowing the work of the female prisoners with the shovels.
    Another POW, an elderly man who had once been a university professor in Berlin, stood nearby. His ankles were in chains so he couldn't flee. He was a translator who spoke German and Polish. There were two vehicles parked nearby. One was a private car. The other was a morgue truck. The driver of the truck, a civilian but not a prisoner, sat in the vehicle. The engine was off. The driver huddled against the cold.
    Wesselmann smoked. His anger was increasing. Big shots in the Naval Ministry were always pulling stunts on the loyal working grunts of law enforcement such as he. The big shots always thought they could fool "little" uncomplicated patriotic men such as Wesselmann.
    They pulled rank and used their well-connected friends to evade the law, act in poor faith toward the Third Reich, and get away with everything from rape to murder to defeatism. Often they conspired against the Fuehrer. Now Wesselmann was starting to hear troublesome stories about people in the military who were conspiring to kill Hitler. He also had picked up rumors about the "rat lines" that were developing after the so-called military defeat at Stalingrad. The lines would lead out of the country to the middle

east and then to south America, where well connected Germans, Nazis in name only, would take their money and live comfortably no matter who won the war.

These people were traitors and had no faith. Hitler had promised a miracle and would deliver one eventually. To a true believer like Wesselmann, this was clear.

But today, Kriminalkommisar Wesselmann was furious. He knew he had been tricked. He knew that Heinrich Koehler had been up to something when Koehler didn't allow him to watch the execution of the American spy. Now he was awaiting only the certified proof. Then he could go after Koehler, his seditious daughter, Frieda, and the American spy. Rounding up all three would re-ignite his career, he reasoned. Men were known to leap two ranks in the Gestapo overnight from such diligence.

After half an hour of digging, one of the captive Polish laborers unearthed a bare foot. The flesh was bluish white like porcelain. The ankle was twisted at an unnatural angle, both sprinkled with cold soil.

"Get down there in the grave," Wesselmann ordered through the interpreter. "Uncover the rest by hand!"

The diggers were down into the ground by about a meter and a half. With bare hands in the freezing cold the Polish prisoners threw dirt up to ground level. They cleared away the soil around the arms and shoulders of the corpse, then went to work on the head and face. Wesselmann smoked, waited and seethed.

Wesselmann finished his smoke. A nicotine kick shot through him.

"The face, the face!" he demanded.

Daylight was dying and the temperature was plummeting. Wesselmann had a terrible temper and was starting to lose control. He reached to his pistol and fired it into the air. Why couldn't the women work faster? No wonder these ignorant subhuman types had managed to get captured!

A few more minutes followed of intense digging in the grave. The body had settled sideways into the dirt, then it had been covered. The Polish women had to loosen the corpse and move it.

They threw more dirt from the grave to ground level, some of it scattering across Wesselmann's ankles. They tried to move the head but rigor mortis had already set in. That and some initial decomposition. Wesselmann knew a thing or two about corpses. He could already see that this man had been dead for a longer time than Cochrane would have been. The body had probably been frozen somewhere and then snatched by Koehler for his personal use.

The Gestapo agent lit another cigarette but he didn't get to enjoy it. The laborers cleared the face. Wesselmann could see it but could not get a good view. Still, the face didn't look right.

"Everyone out of the grave!" Wesselmann barked.

The Gestapo agent stepped down into the grave. He put his hands on the head of the dead man and twisted it so that he could get a good look. The body resisted. In a fury, Wesselmann twisted it harder. A bone in the neck cracked with a loud snap. Wesselmann glared. Then he spat. This wasn't the spy named Cochrane. Here was the proof! Koehler had had his own agenda. Now everything was clear.

Wesselmann stood and climbed out of the grave.

He turned to the driver of the morgue truck.

"Take this piece of frozen meat to the morgue!" he said. He followed that with a barrage of profanities.

He went back to his own car and punched the driver's side window so hard that it shattered.

There was a formal examination of the body the next day at a hospital. Wesselmann couldn't do anything further until the exam was complete and the results were on record. But the dead man in the grave had died of head wounds from a blunt object, not bullets. This was not Cochrane in the grave that had been specially dug for Cochrane.

Wesselmann might have exploded in a fury, but a thought came to him.

All of this was all coming together for Wesselmann as a major case. He could resolve this to his benefit or he could allow the case to defeat him and ruin his otherwise stellar career.

Facts: Heinrich Koehler was a leak in Naval security. His daughter was a defeatist and a member of the White Rose group in Munich. William Thomas Cochrane was an American spy who was in the country to assist them and perhaps facilitate their escape, most likely to Switzerland. One of the other girls who was on the run, the one named Ilse, had grown up with Frieda and probably had influenced her to become a subversive.

Wesselmann had done some research on Ilse that week. He had learned that she had a family home near Freiburg im Breisgau, the same city that the British had officially bombed.

Wesselmann added up all these conditional factors as he sat outside the medical examiner's office in Berlin. He came away with a clear picture.

He had a decision to make.

He could file a full report and escalate it, at which time some greedy superior in the Gestapo would grab the case, order a detachment of fifty agents, and resolve it by catching and executing the perpetrators.

Or he could take one or two trusted associates, Adelman and Bauer for example, and deal with this himself, earning inevitably a promotion and becoming a hero of the Reich.

There wasn't much of a choice. He postulated that the criminals would be taking the most direct route by train or car to Basel. He would need help. Adelman and Bauer, he knew, would be anxious to get in on the blood and glory.

He phoned Adelman and Bauer the next morning. There was a newly reopened bar in Berlin where a lot of his people now liked to spent time. It had recently belonged to a troublesome intellectual named Jacob Witte, who had named his leftwing drinking joint after Wittgenstein, whoever that was. But Witte had surrendered ownership and the place had been renamed. The place was now called the Bar Nuremburg in honor of the Fuerher's ascent. They would meet there.

After an afternoon standing in the snow and freezing wind, Wesselmann was pleased. He had a great plan. He would keep the details about the traitorous Koehler and his daughter to himself. He would resolve this intrigue through his own brainpower and reap the fabulous rewards.

Given the help of two associates, there was no way in hell that any of these unpatriotic fugitives would ever reach Switzerland.

Chapter 49

**Berlin
February 1943**

Cochrane waited as Frau Schneidhuber stepped through her front door and out into the street. She saw nothing that alarmed her. She turned and nodded to Cochrane who waited with Frieda. They were free to travel onward.

Each embraced the fraulein as they passed, each now carrying a single valise. They carried with them only what was most important. Behind him, Cochrane had left Frau Schneidhuber two hundred Swiss francs on the table by the fire, along with four packs of cigarettes. The lady didn't smoke, but she could barter.

Cochrane also stopped and looked both ways, seeing nothing that posed an immediate threat. He then half turned and nodded to Frieda, indicating that she should follow. She came to the sidewalk and stopped next to him.

They walked four blocks. They became aware of a noisy crowd gathered somewhere in the near distance. They continued two more blocks and were near the seat of government. They stopped short. To their right, toward the Brandenburg gate, there was a Nazi rally in progress, a big noisy blowout raising hopes and dreams of victory. The government was trying to throw off the stench of defeat that had flowed from Stalingrad.

Cochrane wondered how many more people on both sides would be slaughtered in the defense of a regime and philosophy that was rotten from the core out.

"I think we're good," he said. "Come along."

Frieda took his arm. Frau Schneidhuber had bought Frieda a pair of used shoes from a local shop, something a little more grown up than usual. While the SS and the Gestapo were busy looking for a man and teenager, they posed as an adult couple as they crossed Brandenburg Square. They continued along Unter der Linden until he spotted the university, which was not yet bomb-damaged and which was crawling with uniformed soldiers.

As they continued on a sidewalk past fringes of the rally, two men in suits and dark hats drew their mutual gaze upon them. They were squat and thick. They looked to be dumb as oxen and almost as smart. They stood motionless with their hands in their pockets studying, staring at Bill Cochrane and Frieda Koehler as they approached them, their four brown eyes giving away nothing.

One man was watching them closely, particularly Frieda, getting a good look at her face. Cochrane could feel Frieda's fear as she clung to his arm.

"Steady," he said quietly in English. "Just keep walking. Don't miss a pace."

Cochrane's Czech pistol was in his left side coat pocket, practically calling his name. He may have tried to re-assure Frieda, but he felt his own heartbeat quicken. He was ready for the day to end early with failure and bloodshed.

They came within a few meters of the two men watching them. The first man stepped forward and blocked their path. Cochrane continued to walk until they were almost face to face. The second man fell into a pace behind the first. Their hands were in their pockets. Against the cold? Or concealing weapons?

Cochrane stopped and said nothing. He was a moment from dropping his suitcase and drawing the twenty year old Czech revolver.

Then the first man smiled and tipped his hat. "Your daughter is very beautiful, sir," the man said.

"Thank you," Cochrane said. The other man tipped his cap also.

Bill and Frieda politely stepped around the two Germans, moving quickly so no one could get a good look. He noticed that Frieda kept her head down. Smart young lady. They kept going. Frieda tried not to laugh. These men had looked more like Gestapo than the real thing.

"Do you know the university here in Berlin?" he asked.

"I had friends who went there," she said. "They may have all been taken by the army by now. Or arrested. I haven't heard from any of them for months."

"So where's this bar?" he asked.

"Up ahead. You can see the railroad bridge from here. It's at the far end, street level," she said.

"Let's step it up a little," he said. "I'd like to get this done."

"I can find it," she said. "Walk with me."

"We're already walking together," Cochrane said.

"Sure. But you were leading me. Now I'm leading you," Frieda answered. "Come on."

A thick drizzle lay in the air. The moisture was their friend: it made observation from a distance more difficult. There was suddenly an eerie warmness to the mist. Where lights shone, the mist shifted in thin clouds. "How far do we need to walk?" he asked.

"Maybe half a kilometer," she said. "Follow along. I'll get you to Bar Nuremburg and you get us to Switzerland."

Chapter 50

Berlin
February 1943

Frieda led him straight to what had been the Tavern Wittgenstein. The entrance was through a metal door hidden under the train bridge. The small sign above the door that said "Bar Nuremburg" was new and handmade. They ducked in.

It was a fearsome place, noisy and crowded, filled with uniforms and swastikas, soldiers, SS and local police. There were very few women and everyone seemed to be bellowing in bellicose Prussian howls and barks. There was live music blasting: nothing organized, just groups of soldiers with squeezeboxes trying to outshout the next table with army ballads and so-called patriotic Nazi anthems. There were at least two renditions of the *Horst Wessel Song* going at once. Cochrane could have done without either or both.

Cochrane took Frieda's arm. He pulled her along so that they wouldn't get separated. This was the type of place where an unattached woman could get gang-groped and pulled to a table packed with soldiers. Cochrane couldn't have been more protective if Frieda had been his own daughter.

This place obviously wasn't what it used to be under its old name. The bully boys had taken over and driven out the old pink literary set. Cochrane doubted if he would recognize anyone in the place. He hoped to hell that no one recognized him.

The noise was overbearing. Cochrane led Frieda to the bar. A barman lurched in front of them. Frieda ordered a mineral water and Cochrane ordered a pilsner. There was a bowl of boiled eggs on the counter. Cheap eats: help oneself.

Cochrane leaned to her. He shouted close into her ear to be heard.

"We'll give it fifteen minutes," he said. "Then we'll leave."

"Why are we even here?" she asked.

"I'm going through some motions," he said. "It was the plan set in Bern. I have to at least make an appearance."

"Why?"

"I promised the man for whom I work."

"Is he American?"

"Yes."

"What's his name?"

"Allen."

She raised her scarf across her chin to shroud her appearance. She looked around.

"I hate what's happened here," she said.

"So do I."

The mineral water arrived. So did the beer. Frieda reached to the drinks and took a swig of the beer, causing Cochrane to doubletake and smile.

She looked as frightened as she had the first night he had seen her, a trembling teenager in the back of a car, with her father, a British POW and a dead aviator in a nearby trunk.

Cochrane raised his eyes. There were three barmen in total, all big and blond and Aryan. Police connections, he was certain. Behind them was an old discolored mirror with several cracks. It had a puncture mark in the glass about head high. The hole was round and ominous with dark stains rippling out from its center.

Cochrane had no sooner consumed half his beer and reached for a second boiled egg when he felt the body of a man come in hard behind him. The man jostled him.

The man slammed an iron hand down on the arm that Cochrane would have used to grab his weapon. There was music blasting, the soldiers were still doing tricks with the squeeze boxes and singing patriotic songs. *Lili Marlene* was in the air, even though Dietrich had long ago been wise enough to flee to Hollywood. Cochrane's heart nearly jumped up out of his throat because the man's grip on his was professional. It told him that he, Cochrane, wasn't going anywhere without this man's consent.

The man leaned in close to the American spy.

Something hard poked into Cochrane's back. It felt like a pistol, ready to blow a hole in his ribs and heart.

"William Cochrane!" said the man into Cochrane's ear hole from three inches away. He spoke English. "I'd recognize you anywhere, you fucking bastard! Tell the girl there with you not to go anywhere or make any move or they'll be worse trouble than you can ever imagine! Got it, you son of a bitch?"

"I got it," Cochrane said.

Frieda, a stricken look of horror on her face, froze. Cochrane put a hand on her arm.

"Stay there," Cochrane said to her in English. "Do what he says."

"Good!" the man said. "I'm not alone in here so be careful. There's more Gestapo in here than there are peanuts in a bag. So play it wise and you'll live to see the sun rise tomorrow."

The man paused. He slowly pulled the object out of Cochrane's back. The voice was starting to sound familiar. It had a New York accent.

"Now turn slowly and face me," the man said. "Don't say my name aloud and don't be surprised. Understand, you fucking meatball?"

Cochrane turned slowly. A moment later, when his fearful eyes focused, he found himself looking into the dark wise eyes of Irv Goff, former Lincoln Brigade commander in Spain, body builder in Coney Island, dinner partner at Luchow's a year and a half earlier and friend to both Allen Dulles and Wild Bill Donovan.

"Jesus God damned Christ!" said Cochrane. "You took a year off my Goddamned life if I even have a year left!"

Bill turned to Frieda and gave her an all safe signal. He gave his friend Goff a friendly shove. "You bastard!" he said.

"Yeah, well," Irv Goff said. "There are people around who'd like to take twenty or thirty years off both of our lives, okay? Got to be fucking careful, man. And by the way, watch out when you shove me. I've got enough artillery concealed on me to invade Sweden all by myself."

Behind them the beer-swilling local patriots stood and launched into a belligerent version of the *Vorwärts Vorwärts*, a sickening Hitler youth song, leftover from their misguided National Socialism-addled childhood. The true believers sang loud, clear, at attention and with stiff-armed salutes. They were all drunk as hell, seemingly impervious to any thought about the now inexorable march of the Red Army from the Volga to the Spree and the Havel.

Frieda simmered. Goff smoldered. Cochrane kept the collar of his coat up.

"I'd ask what you're doing here," Goff said, "but I know."

"How do you know?"

"Phone box a few blocks from here. I put my hand up to the ledge at the top. A little night bird visits on every day of the month divisible by three or five. Coded message. Only I know the key. How did you like my thumb in your back, you fucker? Felt like a Mauser, didn't it?"

"Keep the language clean, pal. The lady understands English."

"Yeah. I know she does. That's why I'm here."

"What the hell are you talking about?"

"Make nice. Follow me," Goff said.

They moved to a lonelier section of the bar even though the music was booming. "I'm told you're going on a trip. Want an extra passenger?"

"You?"

"Yes, sir. An extra wheelman to spell you when you're driving and an extra gun or two if you hit trouble. You better say yes, old friend. I'm training Italian partisans in North Africa and have to get to Geneva, then Tripoli. 'Monsieur D' in Bern said you were due back in his direction within a few days."

"How did you know all that?"

"Dot dot dot dash dash dash beep beep beep through the fucking stars at night. My friend who leaves me messages in the phone stall tells me when to listen. How else?" He drained a beer. "Listen, Bill. Who's the 'bastard,' by the way? I've hung around

SS Central here for five extra days hoping you'd turn up, man. So your damned car better be ready."

"I'm told it's ready," Cochrane affirmed. He shook his head. "Yeah, right. We'd be glad to have you," Cochrane said.

Goff was a warrior among warriors. Having him along was a no-brainer. He added punch, muscle, brains, artillery and didn't make mistakes. Cochrane finally relaxed enough to laugh.

"What happened to this place?" Cochrane asked as Frieda downed an egg. "Dulles said our people could come here safely. Now it's been taken over by the opposition."

"The usual Nazi tactics," Goff said.

"Murder," Frieda said softly.

Goff nodded. "Your girl here is no one's fool," he said. "She's correct."

Goff turned serious and bitter.

"The Nazi thugs walked in here around closing time one night around a month ago," he said. "A little musclebound Bavarian with black hair was the point man, though that describes a lot of them. He put a gun to Herr Witte's face. Asked him to name the anti-Hitler people in here while a couple of seven foot storm troopers blocked the door. He refused. So they shot him in the face. Point blank. Through the brain, between the eyes. That's the bullet hole you see in the mirror. Then they arrested his wife, shipped her to fucking Poland and took over the place. That's how it works under National Socialism. Charming, huh?

"This is so recent that Dulles doesn't even know about it," Cochrane said.

"Yup," Goff said. "Well, Allen knows now. I sent him word about a week ago. And I hope there's a special torture in hell for those Nazis who'd just walk into a place and shoot the owner." He glanced around and lowered his voice even further, "Christ Almighty, man! Wouldn't you just like to machine gun all these bastards right now and be done with it?"

Frieda could barely listen. She turned away. On the other side of her a young soldier gave her a smile. He tried to strike up a conversation. She turned her back to him.

"I see you're carrying suitcases," Goff said. "That tells me you're ready to roll. I've got one behind the bar, a suitcase. I still have a friend or two in this place even though I hope the Brits drop a bomb on it. What do you say? Eat a couple of damn eggs and let's get out of here. What's the girl's name, by the way?"

"I'll tell you later."

"Not much later, I hope," said Goff abruptly turning. "That's more *Geheime Staatspolizei* that just walked in. Gestapo. You know what? I'll bet I'm the only Jew in this whole fucking hellhole, much less the only Communist. Think of it: they'd like to kill me twice but could only do it once. Maybe I should kill a few of them first. Time to set sail, my friend. Forget the damned eggs."

Cochrane kept his hand to his face as he looked in the mirror. His eyes popped as he recognized Hans Wesselmann with what appeared to be two new associates with him.

"Come on! Shake a leg, meatball," Goff said. "Even I break a nervous sweat sometimes."

"Can you cover us to the door?" asked Cochrane.

"Sure can. Let's just get out of here."

Cochrane threw some paper money and coins on the counter.

Goff was a large sturdy man. Cochrane and Frieda, heads down, moved in his hulking wake with Goff being careful to block the view of Frieda. She had been wise enough to wear her new scarf and headgear. No more fur with pale blue.

They hit the street. They moved quickly.

Moments later they were lucky enough to find that rarest of commodities in Berlin, a free taxi. They took it to within two blocks of the carport they sought, exited the taxi and went the rest of the way on foot, staying close together, except when Goff dropped back, hoping to gun down any followers on a dark street. But there were no followers.

They found the car, a beaten up 1938 Benz. It looked as if it had picked up a dent for each month it had been on the road. It was sitting and waiting at the pre-arranged address on a side street off Ludendorff Strasse. The key, the maps and the money were all in place. Several dark windows overlooked the car from the adjacent buildings. Cochrane figured someone was keeping vigil from one of them.

They all climbed in.

Cochrane drove. Goff sat on the shotgun side with a Mauser across his lap. They reached the address for an overnight stay in Potsdam by 10:00 PM The venue was a small house on a dark street. It looked like something out of Hansel and Gretel, but without the witch.

The proprietor was a tiny man with a beard and thick eyeglasses. He mumbled and gave his name as Rudi. He registered his three guests with no questions asked, except he didn't officially register them. They were in a private home. Rudi's wife was a gangly gaunt pretty red-haired woman who looked as if she had escaped from a Tamara de Lempicka canvas. She was three inches taller than her husband and had a carving knife wedged in her belt. She ushered their car into a warehouse next door to keep the vehicle out of view. Once the car was stashed, Rudi walked out of the front of his house with a pistol to see if all was clear. It was. Then he came back indoors and smiled. His front teeth were gone, all of them.

There was an upstairs room for Frieda. The two men slept on the floor downstairs, positioned at different angles in the parlor in case there was intrusion during the night.

The parlor was filled with books in many languages, including Hebrew. Scattered on the walls were proscribed artwork. The owner of the house mentioned that he had been a lecturer at the university in Bremen until he'd been fired. When Cochrane and Goff laid out their pistols near where they slept, the man didn't bat an eyelash. He saw such artillery all the time. He said he would be up the next morning at six and would pack them a box of food. He hinted that if they were on the run, they should keep running. It all made sense.

Bill Cochrane, Irv Goff and Frieda "Wagner" were out of Berlin and on the road back to Switzerland. It seemed too easy and it so far it was.

Chapter 51

**Germany
February 1943**

They left the next morning before dawn. Goff knew the overnight police and SS work schedules. He theorized that their party of three would do well to be moving through the region just when the overnight shifts changed to morning. During that time, just before six a.m., the night shift was reporting back and the morning shift hadn't gone out to the streets yet. That meant there were fewer police on the streets. Gestapo was always a wild card, but most of them didn't like to freeze any more than anyone else.

Irv Goff sighed. Cochrane drove and Frieda rode in the back seat. Rudi had packed a box with bread and fruit and three jars of clean water.

Goff was in a mood to chatter.

"The Germans are a curious bunch of people these days," said Goff as Cochrane navigated miles of hilly icy roads at twenty-five kilometers per hour. "Get a bunch of them in a room together and they're all pro-Hitler," Goff said. "Well, they have to be, I suppose. But when you get the working people by themselves, you'll find that there's not much Nazi principle underneath, aside from the hardcore. They seem vulnerable and defenseless. You can bribe any of them, sometimes for not very much. A pack of cigarettes. A Hershey bar. Sad, really. They have a ferocious army and a crazed leader. They're a formidable opponent. But in the end, it's all going to come crashing down. The only question is who gets to Berlin first? Stalin's tank divisions, Montgomery's or George Patton's."

Cochrane considered it.

"I don't suppose you can blame them," Cochrane said. "Hitler and Stalin are similar sometimes. They believe that if you tell a lie often enough, people will believe it. The thing is, Irv, once the lie is exposed, what's left? Once it's clear that the war is lost, why fight, why die?"

"Good question," Goff said. "How many times can you get yourself killed? Just once it would seem to me," he concluded, answering his own question.

They drove for two and a half hours, Cochrane at the wheel the entire time. The day was clear once they were fifty kilometers south of Berlin. Clear but very cold. There was ice on the narrow roads. The last thing Cochrane wanted to do was end up in a ditch or a snowbank. Eventually, he found the type of spot he wanted by a bend in the road. "I'm going to pull off for a minute," Cochrane said. "I need to stretch."

"Think anyone is following us?" Goff asked.

"I haven't seen anyone. But that's one of the things I'm wondering, too."

Goff checked his weapon. "Okay," he said. "Do what you want."

They parked on a hilltop. They could see the road as it stretched before them and behind them. They were on a plateau with a lot of snow and frosted pines, which was what Cochrane remembered from happier times when he had been in Germany before the war. He had driven this way to take pleasure in the splendor of the countryside, the company of friends, the food, and the wine.

Cochrane stepped out of the car. Frieda looked at him expectantly. "It's okay. It's safe to get out," he said.

She opened the back door and slid out. She came around and stood next to him. Cochrane could see that while she accepted Goff, she remained wary of him.

The hilltop was free of the mist that often enshrouded the land in the late mornings. Cochrane had what he wanted, a view forward and back. There was a long view in both directions. Cochrane looked at it carefully. Goff stepped from his side of the car, paused, lit a cigarette and stood a respectful distance away from them, far enough to make it more difficult for a single sniper.

Frieda stepped closer to him. "I know what you're doing," Frieda said quietly.

"What am I doing?" Cochrane answered.

"You're studying the road," she said. "You can see if anyone is trailing us or if any danger is lurking ahead."

Cochrane smiled. "The kid's smart," Goff said.

Cochrane put his hand on Frieda's shoulder. "She's a *very* bright girl," he said. "Bright and brave. But we already knew that." He paused. "I'm honored to serve as her chauffeur." Lifting his eyes to his military friend, he added, "As I am equally honored to have you with us, Irv," he said.

"You're a good man and a good driver," Goff said, returning the compliment. "Let's just not wreck the day by getting us killed. How's that, meatball?"

"That's good. So we wait till we're in Switzerland before we start congratulating each other, right?" Cochrane said.

"Damned fine idea," Goff muttered.

Cochrane gave Frieda a short embrace around the shoulders. Then he turned his attention back to their surroundings. He reckoned they were five days away from the Swiss border, considering the driving conditions. It was a guess. That was if they were lucky. Five days away if there was no opposition or problem and an eternity away if any trouble emerged. Every kilometer was precious.

Cochrane's gaze returned to the terrain in front of him. Scattered houses and cottages reached into the distance. In a pasture a few miles to the east there was movement: a small herd of cattle with bales of hay scattered across a white landscape. Several houses flew Nazi flags. There was a long view down through a valley. Cochrane scanned to see if there were any military installations and found none.

He looked back to Goff who was still smoking but who had produced something very useful: a compact pair of binoculars. He was working the same terrain.

Cochrane gave him a moment. Then he looked back to Goff.

"You might as well tell me," Goff said. "What the hell's bothering you?"

"Something doesn't feel right. I can see us walking into a trap," Cochrane said.

"Why are you thinking that?"

"Instinct."

"Anything else? Keep talking."

"Those Gestapo people who came into the Tavern. I recognized one of them."

"You *what?*"

Cochrane explained what had happened on the tarmac in Marseille, then at the would-be grave site near Berlin. Wesselmann had been there for both. Then he had walked into the Bar Nuremburg with what looked like two new associates.

Frieda tuned into the conversation.

"We may be on the backroads," Cochrane said, "but I theorize that they're looking for us. And we're going straight toward Switzerland, which is what they expect us to do. Granted, they'll be watching the rail stations and they're spread thin. But anyone looking for us is going to be staked out somewhere along this road. The closer we get to Switzerland, the more likely we'll encounter someone. My feeling is they won't even stop to ask questions. They'll just open fire and ambush. We won't have a chance."

"I'm still listening," Goff said.

"On top of that, somehow we'd have to get past German security before we even get to Switzerland. I have a new passport and so does Frieda. But I'm not sure I trust it to get us through a Gestapo checkpoint. What about you? I have to think they'd love to catch you."

"Ha!" said Goff. "I'm probably one of the most wanted men in the country. Even if I hadn't done anything, I'm still a Hebrew."

"So we don't go directly into Switzerland," Cochrane said. "We go to France first."

"Whoa," Goff said. "That's all occupied territory to the west of us. Vichy."

"And if I'm recalling correctly, you've got some strong links with the French resistance. Maquis."

"Dulles mentioned that, did he?"

Cochrane grinned.

Goff's eyes twinkled. He dropped his cigarette and snuffed it with his boot. "Okay. That could be the case," he allowed.

Cochrane reached into the car. He grabbed the official map of the region. He looked at the roads.

"We'd need to detour toward Freiburg," he said. "Then go southwest and cross the border. The other side of the river is French. Is the Rhine frozen, do you know?"

Before Goff could answer, Frieda replied. "In this cold, probably," Frieda said.

"How do you know?"

"I used to visit this area in summer and winter. In summer we'd swim in the river. A bunch of us girls. We'd swim naked and the boys would spy on us. In winter we'd skate."

"So the river is narrow in some places?" Cochrane asked.

Frieda nodded.

"How narrow?"

The girl tried to remember. "Very. Eighty meters. Maybe a hundred."

"Do you remember the locations?" Goff asked.

"I think I do. I know where we used to swim and skate. That's where it was so narrow."

Cochrane and Goff exchanged a glance. Cochrane took a turn with the binoculars.

"There's just one thing," Frieda said.

"What's that?" Cochrane asked.

"My friend Ilse is from the Freiburg area."

"Who's Ilse?" Goff asked.

"Ilse was my friend in White Rose," Frieda said. "She fled. She knew they were looking for her and me. So she left. So she probably went home. They have a farm and a house. If we go in that direction, we can stop. Maybe we could stay. Maybe we can take her to Switzerland."

"My instructions are to get you to Switzerland," Cochrane said. "Not your friends."

"You're bringing *your* friend," she said, indicating Goff. "I cannot leave Ilse behind if she's in Freiburg. She'll be caught and executed."

Cochrane was about to argue against it again when Frieda continued.

"Ilse grew up in the region. If we can find her, she knows all the places where the Rhine is narrow."

"The kid's got a point," Goff said. "Let me have those binoculars for a minute."

Cochrane handed him the field glasses. Goff scanned the valley and the area where the road continued two or three kilometers ahead. Then he lowered the binoculars.

"Think you could set something up?" Cochrane asked.

"I'd need a day or two to set things up. That's *if* things *can* be set up," he said. "And I'd need a telephone to get things started." He paused. "But listen. There's a town up ahead. It has phone lines. That doesn't mean the phones are working, but we can find out."

"Okay," Cochrane said. "Everyone back in the car."

They stopped at a town named Madenburg, halfway to Leipzig. Goff found a phone in a small restaurant, made a call and waited for a call back. When he returned to the car and spoke simply.

"I made the contact," he said. "I'll know in a day. "We would cross the Rhine about ten kilometers north of Basel."

"The river is frozen?" Cochrane asked.

"They tell me it is. Who knows how it will be when we get there?" He paused. "There's a lot of Maquis activity south of Strasbourg, a lot of smuggling too. The local police are overtaxed and everyone is scared of their shadow. That could work well for us. Or it could get us shot. We'll see. Like everything else, it can go either way."

"You're always full of cheerful news, aren't you, Irv?" Cochrane said.

"Just look at the world around you, man," Goff said. "It's not like I imagine stuff."

They altered their route to steer more in the direction of France than Switzerland. Avoiding the larger cities also allowed them to avoid British and French bombers who now attacked German industries at all hours. Taking back roads avoided police surveillance but it extended the time needed for the trip. As for fuel for the old car, Goff could sniff out a black market dealer in almost every town in southern Germany. It was an admirable skill.

Everything went smoothly for a while.

Chapter 52

Germany
February 1943

    While the three travelers might have struck some of those they passed as suspicious, they paid generously at each overnight stop. Cochrane distributed packs of American cigarettes as needed. Goff worked the phones with coded calls to his accomplices in France. Increasingly they shared the driving. In some of the towns they passed through the stalls of street merchants. Cochrane bought books for Frieda, who was content to sit in the back seat and read. In the evenings, Cochrane and the girl played dominos, at least a half hour each night before they retired. They spoke English and German, switching back and forth interchangeably. From day to day, her English improved. From day to day, his German remained the same.
    One night he taught her a game that he had learned from Masud, the Egyptian gentleman who had sold him the set in Lisbon. Cochrane spread out the tiles face down.
    "Now turn one over," he said. "Just one."
    "Why?" Frieda asked. She always, it seemed to Cochrane, asked why.
    "A high tile numerically, double fives or double sixes, for example, suggests that tomorrow we will have a good day. Low numbers, double one, double two, suggests trouble may find us."
    "And the middle ranges?" she asked.
    "We are on our own," he said with a wink. "We will have to make our own good fortune."
    "That's a strange game," she said. "Why draw at all?"
    "Oh, we could do that, too," he said. "But then we would have no way to anticipate the next day."
    "Why can't the next day be a surprise?" she asked.

"It can be," he said. "But some days it's wise to know what awaits us." He paused. Then, "What about tomorrow?" he asked. "You decide."

She laughed. She turned over a tile. A five and a six. And sure enough, the next day went smoothly.

As they travelled, the odd twenty franc Swiss banknote to grease a palm here or there didn't hurt. Generally, people were sick of the war and hardships. In the town of Sangerhausen east of Leipzig, a war widow was happy to cook dinner for them and allow them to stay overnight in the rooms in which her children had grown up. She cursed Hitler profanely when his name came up. She hated the war and almost cried when Cochrane gave her several handfuls of German currency and two hundred Swiss francs which she could use on the black market.

A third day went by. Then a fourth. On the evening of the fourth, Frieda drew a low number. Double twos. And sure enough, midway through the fifth afternoon en route, there was a troubling incident.

They were in the habit of stopping every two to three hours to ease the pressure on the fragile engine of their Benz. They would stop on a plateau or overlook if they could find one and scan the area. It was a good idea to use the binoculars to see what was ahead and what might be following. Some days Goff would do the surveillance. Other days it would be Cochrane. Some days they would each have a look, just to be thorough.

On this afternoon, "Anything of interest?" Cochrane asked as Goff studied the view through the binoculars.

"Nothing," said Goff.

Goff stood as still as an iron statue, the only movement from him coming from the curl of white smoke that rose from his cigarette. His right shoulder was high as he held the field glasses to his eyes. His left arm hung down and his hand was submerged into a coat pocket. Cochrane assumed his hand was on his pistol, which was not a bad precaution.

"Nope. Nothing," Goff said again, relaxing slightly.

He took one step toward the car and froze. Something in the distance over Cochrane's shoulder arrested Goff's attention. He raised the glasses again, peered at the road where they had travelled. He studied it for less than five seconds.

"Vehicle," he said, sounding alarmed. Another moment. Then, with an edge, he added, "Shit! It's a police vehicle."

"Local or something more imposing?" Cochrane asked.

"Local."

Frieda's eyes were suddenly filled with fear.

"We all stay calm. No attempt to escape. That would make it even worse," Cochrane said. "I'll do the talking."

Goff returned to the car, as did Frieda. Cochrane had been correct. Goff had been holding his pistol. He shoved it under the roadmap in the front seat. He picked up an apple and tossed it to the Frieda, then another one to Cochrane. The appearance of normality could be a beautiful thing.

"Keep that weapon handy," Cochrane said, "but don't get trigger happy. The first shot that's fired on this journey and we'll be running like hell ever afterwards. Best to avoid conflict."

"Yes, sir," Goff said with another edge.

Moments later, a police car from a local town named Vogelstang slowed as it approached them. It came to a near stop on the side of the road, then abruptly turned in and parked near them. There were two local police in it.

They both stepped out. They had sidearms. They wore brown uniforms with a belt crossing their chests, plus black armbands with swastikas. They were local cops but muscular and intimidating.

The driver was a squat man. His partner was big and thuggish with a scowl, a scar across his cheek and a limp from God knew what.

"Papers?" the squat man asked.

Cochrane could almost feel Goff's heart beating. He sensed Goff was staying near his weapon. Frieda came to Cochrane and stood by him. The squat man looked down at her with menace, then smiled.

Frightened, she recoiled. He stopped smiling.

"Your daughter?" the cop asked.

"Close. Family member," he said.

"What's she doing with you?"

"We're out for a little drive."

"From where to where?"

Cochrane answered, "May I reach into my pocket?"

The cop said he could. But, "What are you doing here?" he asked.

"I am a foreign friend of the Reich," Cochrane said. "I have business with the Ministry of Finance."

"Doing what?"

"I'm afraid," Cochrane said. "That I can't tell you."

"Why is that?"

Cochrane handed him his passport and the letter of passage. The smaller man accepted it. The larger man moved to a position in which he could watch all three of them. He carried an automatic pistol. It was now drawn and he held it across his chest.

The twerp looked at Cochrane's passport, then his letter of passage.

He raised his eyes. "Who are your travelling partners?"

"This young lady is my niece," he said. "I'm taking her to see her mother who is Swiss."

"You're planning to cross the border?"

"We have every right and permission."

"Who is the gentleman with you?"

"An Italian soldier returning to his unit."

"He has papers for travel in the Reich? There is no Italian unit near here."

"He is returning through Switzerland," Cochrane tried

"You!" the cop shouted. "Come here!"

Goff stood his ground.

Cochrane turned. "Luigi! Don't keep these gentleman waiting. Come over and introduce yourself."

Goff was walking toward them but holding something in his pockets. One of the local cops raised the automatic pistol.

312

"Show the hands," the cop demanded.

Goff slowly withdrew his hands from his pockets. The one cop raised his weapon and aimed it at Goff's chest from a distance of ten yards. Cochrane was on the balls of his feet ready to attack and hit the weapon.

Then Goff spoke. "Do you fellows smoke?" he asked.

He had three packs of cigarettes in each of his enormous hands.

The cops looked at each other. The one with the gun lowered it.

"My friend doesn't have papers," Cochrane said. "His mother is dying from tuberculous in Italy. He's trying to see her before she dies. Have a heart."

On cue, Goff began to cry. He punctuated his sobs with bursts of Italian in Sicilian dialect.

Cochrane took the cigarettes and handed them to the policemen. They were frozen in place. He stuffed the smokes in their coat packets and patted each on the shoulder. Then, to seal the deal, he handed each cop a Swiss fifty franc note. They smiled.

"Thank you. God bless you. Heil Hitler," Cochrane said. He gave a salute and herded his passengers back to the Benz. He turned. "I assume we may go," he said.

The lead cop nodded.

Cochrane and Goff piled into the front seat of the Benz. Frieda slid into the back.

They pulled away. Neither Goff not Cochrane spoke for several minutes.

Finally, Frieda broke the silence.

"Jesus," she said. Both men laughed.

Chapter 53

Freiburg, Nazi Germany
March 1943

They had been driving for more than an hour around the back roads south of Freiburg when Frieda suddenly spoke.

"Slow," she said, as they went around a wide turn. Then, "Here! This is it!" Frieda said. She sat in the front seat. Irv Goff sat low in the back.

She indicated a narrow path for vehicles that diverged from the main road. It was covered with snow. There were tire tracks which appeared recent to Cochrane. He didn't know whether to take that as a good sign or bad. He was at the wheel of the Benz. He turned the car cautiously. Under the vehicle the snow crunched. Cochrane cut the speed to a crawl to avoid skidding or getting stuck.

Bare branches tipped with snow and ice rose on each side of them. The car continued for several meters. There was no room for another vehicle to pass, so Cochrane hoped they wouldn't meet one.

"You're certain this is the place?" Cochrane asked.

"I'm certain," Frieda said.

"The family home of your friend Ilse?" Goff asked.

"I'm certain," Frieda said. "I used to come here in summers before the war."

The blanket of snow around the structure rose and fell in waves, indicating either recent winds or recent footsteps. It was impossible to tell.

Cochrane raised his eyes to the rear view mirror. He ran two quick visual checks. The first was on the narrow pathway upon which they drove. No one was following. The second was on Goff behind him. Goff looked apprehensive. From the corner of his eye, Cochrane could see that Irv had his gun in his hand, positioned across his lap.

"You all right, Irv?" Cochrane asked.

"Couldn't be better," Goff, who could have been better, answered. The car continued up an incline of about twenty meters. Three quarters of the way up the vehicle lost its traction. The wheels spun. The rear of the vehicle fishtailed.

Goff reacted quickly. He opened his door. He shoved the pistol in his pocket and quickly stepped behind the car, put his hands on the boot and gave it a powerful shove. The wheels found their grip again and the car surged up the hill to a crest, Goff continuing alongside it with a steady jog.

"There's the house!" Frieda said with excitement.

A small cottage behind a broken gate came into view. It looked recently abandoned. The front door was slightly *entre'ouverte*. A small pane of glass by the door had been smashed.

Cochrane stopped the car and cut the engine, knowing he had to save every half teaspoon of fuel. Frieda opened her side door. Cochrane put a hand on her near arm, stopping her. Goff walked to the front door of the house. His weapon was concealed.

"We need to proceed carefully," Cochrane said. "And be ready for what you might find. Is Ilse's family Jewish?"

"What difference does it make?"

"None to me, Frieda. But the Nazis have been in this area for two years."

"Ilse's father was a veteran of the first great war. He was being allowed to run his farm."

"In the past, perhaps. More recently, who knows? When did you see Ilse last?" he asked.

"Last month. But she would have come here to get her Swiss passport."

"Be careful," Cochrane said.

Their eyes met.

"Do you understand what I'm saying? And what I'm not saying," he pressed.

"Yes," she said.

"You asked me two days ago if I trusted you and when I would prove it," he said. "That moment is now."

He reached within his jacket and pulled out a second pistol, a Beretta, which had been in the trunk of the old car. "Have you fired a gun?" he asked.

"Everyone has."

"You know how to shoot?"

"Yes."

In front of them, they saw Goff knocking at the front door to the house. There was no response from within. Cochrane handed the Beretta to her. "Keep it in your pocket. Use it only when you have to and use it wisely. We agree?"

"We agree," she said. She accepted it. She gave him a small nod and a faint smile. She put it in the left hand pocket of her coat.

"Okay. Let's go," Cochrane said.

They both stepped out. Goff stood next to Cochrane. "I don't like what I'm seeing, I don't like what I'm feeling," Goff said.

"I would suggest you watch the car, Irv," Cochrane said. "Frieda and I will go to the door. I don't know whether that house is empty or if it contains and entire Panzer division. I am certain that we will know in short order."

Cochrane scanned for recent tire tracks or footprints. Still, he couldn't see anything conclusive.

"Why don't I wait from cover?" Goff suggested. "No point giving away my location."

"Fine idea," Cochrane said. Both men looked around. They both spotted a thick strand of trees about twenty yards away from the car. Goff nodded toward it. "Perfect," said Cochrane.

Goff walked toward the stand of trees by stepping backwards in their new tire tracks. Cochrane admired his caution. Goff reached the trees then broke off a large branch which he lay on the ground. He took a crouching position behind it. He raised a gloved hand and waved to indicate he was set in position.

Frieda and Bill Cochrane stood before the door to the Kleinman's house. He pushed it and it gave way with a creak. He stepped in first. He felt a sinking feeling. There was furniture overturned, signs of a struggle. He looked for signs of blood but saw none.

Frieda called out. No response. There was a salon to the left, flanked by a flight of stairs. There was a kitchen in front of them. Frieda went to the kitchen. Cochrane paced carefully to the living area. He cocked his head to see if he could hear anything, people in hiding, for example. He wasn't sure whether he had heard something significant or not. It could have been a branch scraping the roof or it could have been a floorboard. But there was no mistaking anything when he heard Frieda scream.

He bolted to the kitchen. He found her by a window that looked back over an area behind the house. She was sobbing uncontrollably and held her face in her hands. He wrapped an arm around her and she screamed again. Her body language indicated something she had seen through the window.

Cochrane pulled back a shade. He grimaced. There were two bodies in the backyard. A man and a boy. He was still staring out the window in horror when he heard the front door open. He reached to his weapon, pulled Frieda out of the line of any fire, and turned.

"Bill?" came a voice. "You okay? I heard the girl scream."

"Come have a look," Cochrane said.

Goff came to the kitchen window and looked out. There was no shock on his face, just anger. He held his gun at his side. "Fucking hell," Goff said in a low voice.

"You stay with Frieda. I'll go take a closer look."

Cochrane walked around the cottage to the carnage and stopped short. It was worse than he could have seen from the kitchen. The father of the family was dead in the snow, as he had seen. So was the boy, Ilse's brother. They had been shot. The executions had been point blank in the face, swift and lethal. In its way, though, it barely approached the other horror. On a long branch near the back of the cottage, not visible from the kitchen window, hung the body of the woman of the house.

Cochrane winced. He looked at the path of footsteps in the snow. He counted three victims and three executioners. Cochrane processed it quickly. It had all the earmarks of a Gestapo execution. Three armed thugs and a defenseless family. He hypothesized that a squad had arrived to look for Ilse. Then, not finding her, they tried to extort her location from her family. When the family wouldn't give her away, if they even knew, they hanged her mother and shot her father and brother.

Cochrane put his hand to his mouth and walked back to the house. He entered. Goff had calmed Frieda slightly but the girl was still in tears. Cochrane sat down next to her on a ragged sofa in the salon. Goff went back to the front door. He remained inside but stood guard.

Cochrane let Frieda talk. She sobbed. She cursed. She refused to leave. She began to talk about burying the family or of waiting there until Ilse turned up.

"I'm sorry," Cochrane said. "That's impossible."

"We have to do what's decent," Frieda said.

"What's decent is to get you to Switzerland and then to America," Cochrane said. "That's the best thing we can do." He paused. "I didn't see a girl out back. Perhaps Ilse went elsewhere. Perhaps she's already in Switzerland," he said. "She has a Swiss passport?"

"Yes."

"Then maybe she's already there, Frieda. That's the best we can hope for."

Frieda's expression became very still. She thought for a moment.

"Come on. We need to leave before anyone comes back," Cochrane said.

"There's a crawlspace here," Frieda said. "We used to hide there when we were kids."

Picking up the implication quickly, "Show me," Cochrane said.

They passed Goff and exited the front door. They went around to the side of the cottage where there were some loose boards beneath the frame of the house.

318

There are minutes in everyone's life that are made up of more than can be lived at the time they occur. These were surely some of them. No sooner had Cochrane and Frieda pulled a nearly catatonic Ilse from the filthy crawl space beneath the house, the two teenagers embracing and Frieda trying to stifle her friend's screams, than Goff came around the side of the cottage like a madman.

"Bill!" he said in as low a tone as he could muster. "They're back. Two of them! Gestapo!"

"You're sure?"

"I'm sure!"

Cochrane came fast to his feet. "Stay with your friend," he said to Frieda. "You have that Beretta?"

Frieda nodded.

"If Irv and I don't come back, use it as you need to."

Frieda nodded again. She pulled the pistol from her coat. Ilse looked at Cochrane with an expression that would stay with him forever. Goff took a quick angry look at the three dead people in the back area. He signaled that he would return to the front of the house from which he had come. Cochrane signaled that he would go up the other side. Unspoken between them was the desire to get the visitors in a crossfire.

Cochrane came to the side of the house. He held his weapon aloft and peeked around the house. Goff had been correct, there were two of them. Long coats, fedoras. Mulish and sadistic looking. There was an old French car behind the Benz, something they had requisitioned or stolen. As Cochrane studied them, they had the doors of the Benz open and were inspecting it, poking through books that Frieda had left in the back seat. One of them pulled out her suitcase.

Unexpectantly, Frieda arrived beside Cochrane. Ilse was with her. At first some anger flashed in Cochrane. The girls were taking an unnecessary risk by being there. Then Cochrane thought again. He pulled Ilse close to him.

"Did you see the men who came before?" he asked in German.

She nodded, still half crazed.

"Tell me if those are the men," he said.

Ever so slightly, she peered around the corner. She recoiled. With wide eyes, she nodded. She held up two fingers.

"That's two of them?" he asked.

She nodded again.

He signaled to the girls to step back a few paces. Then he looked again and the two Germans had stepped away from the car. They were each carrying their pistols by hand and were in the open space between the two vehicles and the cottage. They were about twenty meters away.

Cochrane stepped out enough to give himself a good line of fire. With no warning, he aimed and fired. He hit Adelman full in the chest and a half second later pulled the trigger a second time. Adelman was screaming, wounded badly but not dead. But the second man, Bauer, was already in a crouching position from having seen Cochrane jump out from the side of the house. Cochrane's bullet missed completely.

By instinct Cochrane's aim went back to Adelman. The second shot hit him in the chest, too. But Bauer's shot came close. It shattered the wood a foot from Cochrane's head. Shards and splinters flew across his face as he ducked back behind the house. He might have been killed, but he heard Goff shout from the other corner of the cottage. There was a barrage of bullets and then return fire. Cochrane reached his weapon around the corner again, looked, and saw the Gestapo agent dancing backwards from the impact of Goff's shots.

Cochrane fired two more shots and dropped the man.

Goff emerged. So did Cochrane. Adelman was bleeding profusely and gasping. He was lunging for the gun he had dropped. Goff reached him first, grabbed the gun and kicked the fallen man in the head.

He turned to Cochrane. Goff was crazed. "Stay away from me, Bill, God damn it," he said. "I'll finish this."

Cochrane knew to give Goff the space he wanted.

Goff dragged and pushed each of them to a propped up position against their car. They were both still alive and had some struggle in them.

"You did this to this family?" he screamed at them in German. *"You did this?"* he howled. "You won't do it again!"

He walked away from them and then returned from the barn area with a canister of gasoline. "Sons of fucking bitches!" he screamed in English. He doused both the men in gasoline. He stepped back as they looked up at him with imploring eyes. He took out a pack of cigarettes and lit one.

"Bastards!" he screamed.

He took a deep draw on his cigarette and threw the match on the gasoline. They ignited in screams and spasms. Their car went up in flames and died with them.

He stepped many meters from the car and came to Cochrane's side. Frieda assembled there too with Ilse.

Goff was strangely calm again.

"There," he said. "That felt real good. Let's get to France before the fucking flames draw a fucking crowd!"

"Will your resistance people be ready?" Cochrane asked.

"I need to make one phone call along the way. They'll be ready. Let's move."

Chapter 54

Germany and France
March 1943

From there, leaving the burning auto behind them, it might have been considered a downhill run. They drove at a foolhardy speed across the southwestern region of Germany. The sky was clear but there were icy patches. Once, when Goff was at the wheel, the car skidded off a narrow road and was only returned to service by all four travelers getting out and pushing. Frieda, being the lightest, was at the wheel to guide the vehicle back onto its proper path.

There was little time to dwell on the horror of the afternoon. All of them knew that there were huge potential hazards with crossing into France. Odds were that not all of them would survive. Worse, time was of the essence. Goff's French contacts would only be out between one and two thirty on this frigid morning. They would be waiting across the Rhine on the outskirts of a town called Village-Neuf.

Cochrane was at the wheel for the final half hour, navigating a winding back road heading south parallel to the river. They were in an area that Goff knew well. He had made similar crossings before, he explained, though by makeshift raft, not across ice. But the two female passengers were growing impatient.

Eventually, they ditched the car. They grabbed what bags they could carry and continued along on shoe leather. The footing by the edge of the road was treacherous, as was the cat and mouse game with local police. Fortunately the area was remote and police patrols were minimal. Black market people, by spreading around some hard currency, had made sure that certain patrols were minimal.

"Which way is the river narrower?" Cochrane asked the girls.

They both pointed to a stretch to the south. There were a few lights from Village-Neuf across the water to peg the location. Goff gave a nod of agreement.

"Come on back up to the road," Cochrane said. "It will make our footprints more obscure. Go as fast as we can. Let's move a hundred meters."

The girls were surprisingly fast. Ilse led the way at a moderate sprint. They arrived at an area where the path to the river was partially obscured by a stand of trees. Frieda went second, Goff third, Cochrane fourth. Cochrane was also positioned as the lookout. Every twenty meters or so he would look over his shoulder. Eventually he saw what he didn't want to see.

On the hill above the road, he saw a car, a single pair of beams, then a second, then a third, fourth and fifth and a couple more. He stopped counting. German police, a local militia or Gestapo. It didn't matter. They had somehow left a trail and were being followed.

"Cross the river! Now!" Cochrane said.

They made their way among the trees. Frieda stumbled. Cochrane tried to pick her up by the arm. He stumbled. Goff grabbed them both. He steadied them. They continued through the snow and a tangle of underbrush until they reached the edge of the river and the ice that covered it.

"I'll go first, Cochrane said. "If the ice supports my weight, we'll be okay. I'll go on the far right side; Irv take the left. Keep the girls between us. But spread out. We don't want too much weight on any stretch of ice."

"The ice will be solid," Ilse said. "When it got this cold when I was young a hundred people could skate."

"My French friends are up the bank to the right," Goff said. "There's a road by the river. Go up there. Our friends will find us if we don't find them. The code word is, *'égalité.'* Say it loud and clear and with some conviction or you might get shot."

Cochrane went onto the ice, slipped and fell hard. But the ice held. He got up and slide-stepped about a hundred feet from Frieda. Ilse went closer to Goff. In the yellowy moonlight he could see them, dark conspiratorial figures moving low across grayish-black ice.

They were halfway across the frozen river when an armada of vehicles flooded the German side of the river, the area that they had just left. The Benz that they had abandoned had marked their exit. They had managed to stay downriver by a hundred to a hundred and fifty meters. But now car lights swept across them.

Shooting began. There was a stray shot or two at first from their pursuers, then a fusillade. Cochrane knew that the four escapees were the targets. He could hear bullets hit the ice several meters to his left. He figured he was at the midpoint of crossing the river. He tried to run but the ice was rough and uneven. He kept falling. He glanced to his left. His three cohorts were still moving. They had maybe about fifty meters to go. It was impossible to know.

Then a number of things happened at once. A staccato blast of machine gun bullets blasted from behind and swept across the ice. They hit about ten feet apart and went around Cochrane, one hitting to his right, the other to his left. They missed him completely. Then there were tracers sweeping down the lake, more machine gun fire and then two flares from the German side. Suddenly it was as bright as day, only worse.

Cochrane stopped and drew his pistol. He lay low on the ice and fired two rounds. The headlights from the German side were still flooding the lake. Suddenly in the full glare of two beams, he had the horrifying thought that none of them would make it to the French side alive. He hoped his shots would draw fire so at least the girls could make it across. He heard no shots from Irv's direction. He feared that Goff had been hit and possibly killed.

He zigzagged in and out of a shadow but when another shot came it was far off. He was near the riverbank. He glanced to his forward left and saw Frieda arriving on the riverbank. Ilse was in front of her. Ilse turned and extended a hand. Frieda grabbed it and the two girls were safely ashore.

Cochrane fired again. Then all hell broke loose from the French side of the river! Cochrane had no idea who was there in their support or how many there were, but the resistance had arrived with automatic weapons.

They had positioned themselves with cover, Cochrane assumed, and now, using the illuminated headlights as targets, were throwing barrage after barrage of bullets across the river. The armada of pursuing cars were now on the dangerous end of a shooting gallery.

When the first barrage hit, Cochrane could hear screams from the German side. Several cars were hit, two of the fourteen headlamps went out, then a third. The German guns redirected from the four escapees to return the fire.

Cochrane scurried to his feet, slip-stepping on the ice and moving forward, first in the edge of beams, then beyond them. A stray shot came very close to him. It buzzed by his head. The ice in front of him was pockmarked with bullet holes. He looked to his left and saw the two girls but no Irv Goff.

He struggled forward, slipped and fell again, almost lost his bag, but continued onward. He was within ten meters of the shore when two bullets hit within a meter of him. He expected to be zipped by a third, but no shot came. The gun battle across the river continued, however. Single shots came from rifles, fusillades from automatic weapons.

He looked to the shore and saw a dark figure come down the riverbank to the girls. He recognized Irv Goff's hulking figure. Cochrane was the only one of them still on the ice.

"Bill? You okay?" Goff called.

"I'm all right!"

"I'm getting the girls to a car!" Goff called back.

Goff took each by an arm and hustled them up the shoreline. Two Maquis figures emerged from the darkness, stooped low. Cochrane could see the outline of three vehicles. The shoreline was alive with French gunmen hunched behind trees. There was one car moving without headlamps. Goff protectively pushed the girls into the back seat.

Cochrane arrived on the shore, clutching his bag. At some point on the ice, he had banged his knee. He staggered. His foot landed on a tree branch thick with ice and he stumbled and started to fall. From somewhere out of the darkness two arms appeared. They were strong as a bear's. The arms steadied him, held him up and caught him.

Cochrane looked up into a bold ruddy face. "*Francais libres*," the man said. Free French. The man was maybe fifty-five. He wore a heavy dark sweater and a makeshift helmet. He was broad and powerful. He had a boy's pale face, but with wrinkled skin.

"Américan," Cochrane said. Then, trying to remembering, he said, "*Liberté.*"

"Eh?"

"*Égalité!*" Cochrane corrected.

The ruddy face laughed. "*Blessé?*" the Frenchman asked.

"*Non! Ça va! Pas blessé.*" Not injured.

"*Allons!*" the man said. Let's go!

The man hustled Cochrane to the lead car. There was a driver waiting. Goff stood in front of the back seat, shielding the two girls with his body. His pistol was in his belt. From somewhere he had acquired a carbine.

"You good?" Goff asked Cochrane as the Frenchman attended the doors.

"I'm good."

"Take the passenger side in the front. Maurice is our driver."

As Cochrane circled the car on a throbbing knee, Goff's gaze was intent on the Germans on the other side of the river. As Cochrane opened his door to get in, Goff suddenly snarled, "Fucking bastards!" just loud enough for Maurice to hear and laugh. Then Goff, crouching near the car, raised the carbine and got off six fast shots. He hustled into the car at the same time as Cochrane. Their doors slammed in unison.

As Maurice pulled away, Cochrane saw a hothead French kid of maybe eighteen run forward to a crouching position above the riverbank and open up on the other side with a machine gun. The other cars quickly cranked their engines, the French kid finished his volley, ran and jumped in a car and everyone sped away in different directions.

"Any casualties?" Cochrane asked. There was another carbine at his feet.

"I think it was clean. No one hurt," Goff said. "Not on this side, anyway. The other side, I think they got their noses bloodied. Look, I think our side fired five hundred rounds into a hundred foot area where they parked. We must have hit something."

"How many people did you have?"

"Maybe a dozen. I don't know," Goff said. "Let me ask you something."

"What's that?"

"Have you ever been so glad to see a dozen Communists in your life?"

Cochrane laughed and allowed that he hadn't. But his gaze was still on the river and any potential pursuers. Faintly, he thought he saw a familiar figure that had followed all the way from the other side.

"Son of a bitch," Cochrane muttered.

"What?" Goff asked.

The vision of Cambulat and Skordeno filled Cochrane's mind, as well as that of a thousand other Gestapo atrocities and unpaid debts. He reached to the carbine at his feet. "This thing loaded?" he asked.

"Wouldn't be much use it if wasn't," Goff said.

Cochrane grabbed the carbine and opened his door. "Have Maurice wait fifty to a hundred meters up the road," he said. "I've got some business."

"Don't get killed, meatball," Goff said amiably. "Your weapon has six rounds and the first shot is already chambered. Have fun."

The van slowed. Cochrane jumped out. He took a position in the snowy bushes along the side of the road. Maurice cut his lights and eased around a bend, leaving Cochrane in the near darkness. Everything was strangely silent, then Cochrane could hear footsteps. They belonged to a heavy angry vicious man who was so maniacal in his devotion to his filthy job that he had come all this way in pursuit.

He stopped thirty meters down the road. He raised an automatic pistol and sprayed bullets in the direction in which the van had disappeared. At the same time Cochrane took aim.

Wesselmann was walking forward now. Then he must have sensed something. He stopped. He cocked his head. His eyes were probably adjusting to the dim night. He drew a second weapon and from what Cochrane could see, which wasn't much, he sensed danger in Cochrane's direction.

Cochrane squeezed off a first shot and must have winged Wesselmann, because the figure in the dark staggered backwards, but began to fire the second firearm. Then Cochrane squeezed off a second shot, then a third and a fourth. He thought he saw Wesselmann sprawl, or spin or maybe he dived for cover. But he disappeared into the shadows of some frozen trees.

Cochrane waited for several seconds, then turned and ran. No shots came after him. He looked ahead toward the van and saw another figure standing in the road. At first he was torn with fear, but then he recognized Irv Goff, who was also holding an automatic rifle.

"Come on," Goff said. "Got to move, Bill."

"It was Wesselmann. I don't know whether I got him or not," Cochrane said.

The van doors opened and they slid in. This time Goff was up front next to Maurice and Cochrane was in the back seat with the girls. Maurice had a heavy foot and got them out of there in a hurry.

Several minutes passed. There was a heavy silence in the vehicle. Finally, Goff turned to Cochrane.

"You got him, all right, meatball," Goff said.

"How do you know?"

"From where I stood, from my angle," Goff said, "I saw his head explode."

Several seconds passed. "Jesus," Frieda said.

Chapter 55

Vichy France to Switzerland
March 1943

From there, the strategy was basic: get as far away as fast as possible and don't look back. Maurice was a prince of a driver with a touch of a daredevil tossed in. He wore a beret and a heavy scarf up around the lower half of his face. He knew the backroads and drove by the moon, never stopping, infrequently slowing. They were about five kilometers northwest of Basel, but Maurice had no use for normal border crossings. He had his own way of getting to Switzerland. He drove parallel to the city on secondary roads, then cut sharply and went through a farmer's field as the sky was lightening with dawn. The next thing anyone knew, they were in commercial neighborhood which sold farm products.

Cochrane knew the fix was in and was highly appreciative of it. Maurice drove into a barn. He hustled them all out of his car. There was a milk truck waiting. A new driver greeted them with a cigarette and a nervous tic to his left eye. Cochrane, Goff, Frieda and Ilse crowded into the back of his truck. Then the milkman was out the rear door of the barn and soon on another street that had no connection to the first.

The other street had a high brick and cement wall on its other side, topped with broken bottles and barbed wire. The milkman wore a pistol. He drove parallel to the wall, then stopped and tooted his horn twice. He indicated that everyone should step out. Cochrane glanced at his watch. It was 5:47 on a freezing morning.

The boundary between France and Switzerland ran down the middle of the street. The milkman looked at the wall, which bordered the Swiss side. He found the spot he wanted and pushed in the bricks with his foot. The bricks tumbled into Switzerland and left a hole. The milkman took the two bags from his passengers and threw them over the top of the wall. Someone on the other side caught them.

"*Allez. Allez! Vite! Vite!*" the man ordered.

The girls went first through the hole in the wall. A pair of confederates on the other side pulled them through. Cochrane went next. Goff was last. They were in Switzerland and it felt great.

They dusted themselves off. One of the Swiss replaced the bricks in the wall while the other hurried them along to a local street. The group of four was on the outskirts of Basel. They were near the end of a line for the bus that would take them into the city. They trouped to the bus stop. The first bus of the day was waiting. Its driver was sitting in it, getting his purse and tickets ready. There was also a conductor. The transit men looked at the four passengers strangely but said nothing. They had seen stranger things in the past and knew not to ask questions in wartime with Vichy France just on the other side of a six foot wall.

Cochrane produced Swiss francs for the fare.

At six o'clock in the morning, with Swiss precision, the bus pulled away from the curb. There were two other passengers. The route took them to the main train station in Basel on the appropriately named Centralbahnstrasse. They took the first available train to Bern and arrived shortly after 10:00 AM. They took a taxi to Allen Dulles's headquarters.

Dulles was standing in front of the building, smoking his pipe, arms folded across his chest on a sunny but clear morning.

Cochrane and Goff stepped out of a taxi. Dulles looked at them and glanced at his watch, as Cochrane paid the driver and threw in a fifty franc tip as a gesture of international understanding.

"What took you so long?" Dulles asked.

"Are you telling me you were expecting us?" Cochrane asked, stopping in his tracks.

"In fact, I was. Oh, hello, Irv," Dulles said, giving Goff a wink.

"How did you know we'd be here today?" Cochrane asked.

Dulles shrugged. "My spies are everywhere," he said. "Dot dot. Dash dash. Beep beep. Quite a mess you fellows left on the west bank of the Rhine. The Gestapo can barely understand what happened. Well done! Congratulations."

Dulles then made a fatherly fuss over the two girls and led everyone into his residence. One of his contacts in Provence had just shipped him two bottles of Remy Martin and a celebration was well in order.

Chapter 56

Bern, Switzerland
March 1943

As the next few days passed in Switzerland, Bill Cochrane had a strange sense of having dreamed the whole encounter in Berlin, which of course he hadn't. It had happened, he had lived it. Frieda, Ilse and Irv Goff were also in Switzerland, the latter champing at the bit to get back to North Africa.

There were several days of debriefing for Cochrane in Bern, most of them at the complex at Herrenstrasse. The other OSS employees had taken special note of him. They knew he had done something important and were treating him with great deference and calling him, "sir," though they had no idea what he had done.

He didn't mind. He took time out on his third day back, however, to pick up the watch for Laura at Monsieur Lesser's emporium. Through a coded message to General Donovan in New York, Dulles confirmed that Cochrane had returned from his mission alive and well, exhausted but uninjured and victorious, and would soon begin a trek home in a roundabout manner. Donovan personally phoned Laura in New York to convey the good news. He spoke quickly on the call, lest she hear his voice and immediately assume the worst after he identified himself.

The death of Hans Wesselmann of the Gestapo cast its own strange shadow. Cochrane gave Dulles a full report of what he had seen and heard. Messages from a well-placed source in the

331

government, Frieda's father in other words, continued to come through the nighttime blips. The purloined material focused on placement of troops, locations of Wolf Packs in the Atlantic, the movement of naval defenses from the Pacific region around Murmansk, and the strengths of various units in Normandy. But because Wesselmann had kept his own counsel on Koehler, little written record remained of the latter's suspected "defeatism" and contact with the OSS.

In the meantime, however, information still came through and the OSS in Bern had a new tool for deciphering. Not only had Frieda brought two code books, but she had memorized the intricate mathematical formulae and the sequences which her father used. Dulles's people were thus able to use her numbers and calculations to unzip and decode messages almost on the spot. Over the next few days in Switzerland, she made a written record of everything she knew. Her knowledge was turned over to Dulles's POW code decipherers.

"You know what I've learned from all this, Bill?" Dulles said, watching Frieda patiently explain some numbers and sequences to the OSS code breakers.

"What?" Cochrane asked.

"Never underestimate a smart sixteen year old girl," he said.

"That was apparent from the first time I saw her," Cochrane answered.

The information flowed well until late 1943 when her father was ordered back to sea and the espionage operation abruptly ended.

Ilse made contact with her extended family in the Zurich area. Dulles asked Cochrane if he could escort the girl to Zurich where the family would meet her and take things from there. He was happy to do so. Frieda Koehler meanwhile was installed courtesy of a local matron with an appropriate Swiss family. The father was a music teacher and the mother was a violinist with the Bern Symphony. The house was filled with books and had a piano.

It was perfect placement. Frieda started going to a Swiss lycée in Bern. She excelled, to the astonishment of no one.

Irv Goff's orders would include a return to North Africa. It was a no secret that the events that had started with Operation Torch would soon morph into an invasion of the boot of Italy. Dulles had big plans for Goff and appointed him to be the OSS liaison officer to the Italian Communist Party. Even before even leaving Switzerland Goff started drawing up training programs that would use anti-Fascist Italian volunteers to wage guerrilla warfare behind the German lines in northern Italy. When the United States Fifth Army of Lieutenant General Mark Clark began moving north after invading Italy in September of 1943, Goff's guerillas ambushed several of the SS units in retreat. As a side activity, since he could never remain inactive for too long, Goff created an infiltration team that parachuted fifty radio operators and meteorologists into enemy-held areas to provide daily weather reports for the Allied air forces. Working with the Italian Communists, Goff built the most effective intelligence operation in northern Italy.

One day in late April Cochrane turned up at Herrenstrasse and was ushered into Dulles's office. "Don't even bother to sit down," Dulles said. "Good news for you and some bad news."

"What's that?" Cochrane asked.

"You're on your way home!"

Apprehensively, Cochrane answered. "I assume that's the good news. What's the bad news?"

"You're going the long slow way," he said. "I don't want to risk sending you back through Portugal. There's always the chance the Gestapo is watching the route you took to get here. Plus Lisbon has descended into low comedy. I have reports of the Duke and Duchess of Windsor dining and golfing there with a banker named Ricardo Espirito Santo. Richard the Holy Spirit. The Huns have a hare-brained thing called Operation Willi: a plot to kidnap the abdicated king and use him for propaganda. God knows, no one would spend good money to ransom an idiot like that. Churchill would probably pay the Germans to abduct 'David' and his promiscuous domineering missus and shoot them. The Duchess had a long affair with Von Ribbentrop, you know," said Dulles, who had as fine a taste for scandal as anyone.

"So where am I going?" Cochrane asked.

"Italy," Dulles said. "By train and truck. But you'll have your dominos partner with you and Captain Goff as your personal bodyguard. I told you it was both good and bad."

It was. The time had come for Goff to head back to North Africa and he was doing it by a slow route, too. But Goff had designed the route.

Together, they took a train to Ticino in Switzerland, then enlisted partisan smugglers whom Goff knew in the low stretches of the Italian Alps. They boarded a truck which crept down the western coast of Italy, staying in rural communities either with partisans or local mafia. The route worked well and the food was great when there was any. No one was shooting at them and Goff took great pleasure in telling Frieda stories about Brooklyn, New York and teaching Frieda useful phrases in Italian. Cochrane gave away the last of his American cigarettes and never took his protective eyes off the girl whom he was taking to the United States. When possible, he bought new books for her and for himself at book stands and second-hand stalls.

"If I get to America, what books will I be allowed to read?" Frieda asked Cochrane one night.

"Not 'if,'" he corrected, "*when* you get to America you can read whatever you want."

She pondered it for a moment. "What music will I be able to listen to?"

"Anything you wish."

"Kurt Weill? Al Jolson? Jazz?"

Cochrane bristled slightly. "No one ever has any right to tell you what you can or can't read or hear," he said. "Don't ever forget that, Frieda."

"So America is perfect?"

He shook his head. "No," he said. "We are far from perfect. But we try to address what's wrong and improve as a nation. And most of us try to be receptive to new ideas: new books, new art, new music."

"And new people?"

"And new people," he said. "You in particular."

She thought about it, grinned and went back to her latest book.

They arrived in Naples on April twentieth. There was a Portuguese ship there picking up cargo, a freighter captained by a pro-American OSS operative. Dulles had arranged passage for two people in separate staterooms. Frieda and Cochrane split with Irv Goff at that point. Goff gave Frieda the "biggest hug in the free world," as he called it as they parted, then was ready to take off. Cochrane felt that he sensed some deep avuncular affection from Irv toward Frieda. But that would have made sense. Cochrane and Goff exchanged a firm handshake.

"See you in New York sometime, meatball," Goff said. "After the war. Maybe at Ratner's."

"We'll do that," Cochrane affirmed.

Goff flew to Algiers where the Allies continued to hold the North African coast. Dulles later confirmed to Cochrane that Goff had arrived safely.

The freighter upon which Cochrane and Frieda had passage sailed unmolested through the Strait of Gibraltar but then went out into the open Atlantic. It continued to Bermuda, the British colony, arriving ten days later, though not without spotting unidentified periscopes twice along the way.

The next day after arrival in Bermuda, Cochrane and the teenager in his custody flew to New York, passing above the Statue of Liberty, which made Cochrane choke up for a moment.

General Donovan sent a Jeep to Idlewild to retrieve them.

Laura was waiting for Bill at the gate. She rushed to him and embraced him when he stepped through. Donovan had also contacted Frieda's aunt and uncle from Wisconsin, the family that Frieda had come to live with. Not surprisingly, their last name was Wagner.

Donovan took everyone out to dinner at Sardi's the next night. By wonderful coincidence, Al Jolson was in New York, having recently returned from entertaining American troops overseas. Donovan and Jolson knew each other. The former called the latter over to his table and introduced Jolson to Frieda, who was stunned to meet the man whose music she adored but whose work was banned in Fascist Europe. Jolson shook her hand and sang a few bars of *California Here I Come* to her, much to the delight of the rest of the diners, and to Vincent Sardi, the proprietor, who stood nearby and beamed.

"Wow!" Frieda said to General Donovan after Jolson returned to his own table.

Donovan patted the teenager on the hand. "Get used to it, Frieda," he said. "This is America. Things like that can happen here."

At the same dinner, without saying anything, Cochrane pulled from his pocket the gorgeous watch he had bought in Bern from Monsieur Lesser. He placed it on Laura's wrist. She said nothing, either. But she leaned to him and kissed him. Donovan gave them both a wink. The General was enjoying his evening.

"By the way, Laura," Cochrane finally said. "Irv Goff says hello."

"Oh? You saw him, did you?"

"Yes. It's a story for another day," he said.

"I'm sure it is."

The next day, those who had gathered at Donovan's table at Sardi's began to go their separate ways.

Bill Cochrane received two months paid leave, a high medal from the OSS, plus a personal letter from President Roosevelt. The time off was more than necessary to unwind.

*

In his first days back in New York, Bill Cochrane behaved much like a man who had suffered a death in the family. The events surrounding his return to Berlin had hit him much harder than he had understood at the time. He spent much time buried in his books, indulging in an occasional imported Havana cigar and enjoying his whiskeys. What bothered Laura was the distant look she often saw on his face when he didn't know she was watching.

It was as if he had seen far too much while in Nazi Germany and was unable to forget the worst of it. He was able to tell her the story of Henrich Koehler, at least part of it, and how he and Irv Goff had transported a remarkable girl named Frieda and one of her brave young friends out of Hitler's inferno. But he didn't offer many details for years, and Laura didn't ask for them.

Eventually though, over the ensuing weeks, the imagined vision in his mind's eye of Wesselmann's head blowing apart from bullet he fired. He hadn't seen it when it happened, but he would see it for the rest of his life as it played out in his mind. But at least the immediate shadow began to lift over the summer months of 1943..

Bill's gracious good nature returned. His spirits perked up, that distant look disappeared and he turned his attention back to his work for the OSS. There was, after all, still a war that needed to be won.

Chapter 57

Washington D.C.
July 1943

Bill Cochrane saw Frieda again one more time in July of 1943. Some OSS people phoned him from Washington and said that Frieda was in the US capital for a few days. The girl was going back out to the Midwest to live with her relatives. For safety's sake, she was going to assume a new identity, as was their family. There had been some ugly threats by some crackpots in the American Bund and one could never be too careful. Those were all the details that General Donovan would give Bill Cochrane, aside from the fact that the threats had to be taken very seriously. The Wagner name wasn't going to work. The cover of the final new identity would be thorough, be lasting and run deep.

But in Washington, Frieda asked if she could say goodbye in person to the man who had guided her to America and safety. The answer from a grateful OSS was yes.

Cochrane packed a few business items in a new attaché case and took a train from New York to Washington. He and Frieda met for lunch at the Hay-Adams Hotel. She was suddenly looking more grown up and announced that she would soon turn seventeen. They enjoyed a fine meal and a good conversation. But after a while the talk became strangely stilted, as if there were now things that Frieda didn't dare discuss. On a more upbeat note, Frieda mentioned that she had exchanged air letters with Ilse, who was summering in Interlaken, Switzerland, with her extended family. The two girls hoped to stay in touch and get together again after the war. Whether or not that happened, was not something that Bill Cochrane ever learned. As for news of her father, either Frieda didn't have any, wasn't giving any or there was none to give.

Lunch ended. Frieda needed to leave for her home in the Midwest. Cochrane had new discussions scheduled with General Donovan in New York. They both stood. There was an awkwardness. They looked at each other. A kiss would be too much, a hug not enough, a handshake too formal. Suddenly, the inhibitions fell away and they embraced each other long and hard. She pulled away.

"Good luck to you," Bill Cochrane said. "I hope it turns out as well as it can for your father. I like to think there's some goodness in everyone."

"There's goodness in him. Only I can see it," she said. "Or remember it. He risked everything to get me out of Germany. I can always say that in his behalf."

"Yes, you can. We'll try to keep in touch," he said.

"Goodbye for now," she said. She turned to go.

He watched her. Then he stopped her.

"Oh, listen, Frieda," Cochrane said, reaching for the attaché case that he had carried from New York. "I nearly forgot. I have something for you. I think you should have this. Keep it as a souvenir, a good memory, I hope. Consider it a private understanding between us, a talisman, perhaps something that will continue to bring you good fortune in the future."

Cochrane opened the attaché case. He reached in. His hand settled on the wooden case of dominos that had travelled with them across Europe and across an ocean.

"The dominos?" she asked.

"The dominos."

"I never thought I'd see these again," she said.

"There were many times I thought I'd never see home again," he said. "I'll tell you something that I will tell to very few people. When we were landing at Idlewild from Bermuda, I had to hide my eyes from you. I looked down and saw the Statue of Liberty in our final minutes in the air. I had tears in my eyes. Not very attractive if a man cries, you know."

"I've seen other men cry and I saw you. You turned away but not fast enough," Frieda said. "I remember the moment. You patted me on the shoulder and said, 'See? We did it.'"

"I might have known," he said. He shook his head. "Jesus," he said with a grin.

"Jesus," she mimicked. Then they both laughed.

"Frieda, I promised the gentleman I bought these from in Lisbon that I'd pass them along to the right person at the appropriate time," Cochrane said. "That person is you. I think they guided us to safety. Now you're new to America. May they guide you in your new country. Here."

He held out the box.

"They should go to your son or daughter," Frieda protested.

"I have neither at this time," Cochrane answered. "I'd give them to my son or daughter if I had one, but I don't. So there. Please. No more discussion. Take them. I insist."

Frieda smiled, accepted them, made a motion to leave, then turned back. She leaned to him and put an arm around him and kissed him in the cheek. She stepped away, then mischievously sat down again.

"Okay," she said. "Join me. One more time."

Sitting together in the busy dining room, Cochrane watched as Frieda slid back the top of the case of dominos. The tiles lay face down in the container. She selected one, withdrew it from the pack and clasped it in her hand without looking.

"This is for both of us," she said. "For the rest of our lives. Are you willing?"

"I am if you are. Go ahead," Cochrane said.

"All right."

She placed the tile on the table. She turned it over. It was the double six. They looked at it and laughed.

"We're going to be fine. Both of us," he said. "You're going to have a wonderful life. Take care of yourself."

"You too."

She stood again. She leaned forward and they embraced a final time. Then she pulled away. "Thank you," she said. Her eyes were moist. "For everything."

Frieda turned. Bill Cochrane watched her leave the restaurant. She went through the door and was gone. The silence she left behind almost took the air out of the room. Through the window, he could see her on the street, striding purposefully toward her next destination, wherever it was. There was a chaperone waiting outside, a Captain Mildred Curtis from the Women's Army Corps. Captain Curtis joined her. The captain often worked with the OSS to keep an eye on adolescents. Captain Curtis took Frieda to a military Jeep that was waiting.

Just as a Jeep had picked him up in New Jersey several months earlier and brought him into the world war, a US Marine stood by a similar vehicle. He opened the door for the young lady who approached. Cochrane watched Frieda charm the young driver. The Jeep's flashers were on. Cochrane got a final glimpse of her as she stepped into the vehicle: tall and strong with a beauty and intelligence that glowed from within. Essentially, another man's lovely daughter. Eventually, Cochrane hoped, Frieda would be the equal partner of a man who would love and respect her.

The Marine closed the door and hustled around to the driver's side. He pulled out into the Washington traffic and was gone within seconds.

Silently, Cochrane left the Hay-Adams. He found a taxi which took him to Union Station for the train back to New York. As for Frieda, she wore her new identity as a cloak, presumably against the past and possibly against the future.

Bill Cochrane often thought of her over the many years that followed. But he never heard from her and never saw her again in his life.

Chapter 58

New York City – Manhattan
October 23, 2019

At Logan's in Tribeca, Caroline Dawson – Bill Cochrane's daughter - sat enthralled as Ellen McCoy, the historian, finished the story that had centered on her late father. They had been there for three hours. The lunch staff had changed to the dinner staff.

Ellen McCoy had been speaking almost nonstop and Caroline had rarely thrown in a sentence sideways.

"So you never knew of any of this?" Ellen asked.

"No. I know a lot about my father and his career. But I knew nothing of this story. It's completely new to me. It's stunning." She paused. "May I ask how you knew so much when I didn't?"

Ellen smiled. "I'm an historian at the University of Illinois," she said. "I've done a lot of research," she said. "Library of Congress. Freedom of Information Act. Declassified documents that are now online. Plus tracing you down, of course."

"But what prompted you?" Caroline asked.

A pause of several seconds, then, "Frieda Koehler was my mother," she said. "She passed away in 2008. She was eighty-one years old. She became a professor of mathematics at the University of California. I followed her into academia."

Caroline considered it. "And your grandfather? If I may ask? Heinrich Koehler?"

"It didn't work out so well for him," she said. "He was captured by the Soviet Navy in the final days of the war. He surrendered his ship rather than have his men be killed. He was taken prisoner by the Soviets and taken back to the Soviet Union. He died in a Soviet labor camp in 1952."

"Oh," Caroline said. "I'm sorry."

"*Are* you? At one time, Heinrich was an ardent Nazi."

"I won't make judgments," Caroline said. "Not after hearing your story."

There was an awkward pause. Ellen was suddenly aware of the time.

"Oh," she said, "I've talked a blue streak. It's after five. I need to go meet my family. They're all lucky enough to be American, by the way," she said. "Thanks to Frieda, thanks to your father, and thanks, strangely, to Heinrich." A beat, then, "We wanted to give you something from my mother. From Frieda."

Ellen reached to the shopping bag by her side and withdrew a small package. It was gift wrapped. Caroline guessed what was coming.

"For me?" Caroline said.

"Absolutely. May it bring you the same good fortune that it brought Frieda and our family for the last seventy-six years. It's only proper that it should now go into your hands. Do you have a daughter?"

"I do."

"Then you should pass it along to her someday, also."

"I can't say 'no,'" Caroline said. "Not after listening to you today."

"Then don't. Our family owes its very existence to your dad."

Caroline removed the gift paper and slid the aging box of dominos from its wrapping. She gazed upon it almost as if it were magical, and in a way it was, to have travelled so far and survived so long. She touched the wood which still bore the markings in English and Arabic that had once attracted the attention of her father in wartime Lisbon in the shop of a gentle soul named Masud.

She slid the top open and reached for a tile. Before she could turn it over however, a waiter accidentally nudged her arm in passing. The tile slipped from her hand and came to rest face up on the table.

It was a double six.

Spiritually speaking, Bill Cochrane's return from Berlin and Frieda Koehler's journey to America were finally complete.

THE END

Author's Notes:

Thank you for reading *Return To Berlin*. Your comments and thoughts are welcome. You can reach me at Nh1212f@yahoo.com.

This was, of course, a novel, but a novel based on fact and history. I've taken some historical liberties, which is a nice way of saying that I've fictionized some events. But I've tried my best to remain true to the overall truth of the era, the story and the characters. I like to write smart historical fiction and hope I have succeeded here.

I've probably read more than five hundred books on the 1930s and 1940s over the course of several decades, most in English some in French. Particularly of value here were *A Noble Treason* by Richard Hanser, originally published by G. P. Putnam in 1979. The book told the story of the White Rose revolt against Hitler and Nazism. Also valuable was *Germany's Underground, The Anti-Nazi Resistance* by Allen Dulles, first published in 1947. A companion piece, for obvious reasons, would be *Allen Dulles, Master of Spies* by James Srodes, published in 1999. I note also *Histoire de la Gestapo* (1962), by Jacques Delarue, *Berlin Diaries, 1940-1945* (1987) by Marie Vassiltchikov, and *Opposition and Resistance in Nazi Germany (Cambridge Perspectives in History)(2001)* by Frank McDonough. Credit also goas to the late Ada Smith for her description of Berlin in the 1920s.

For specific research, I used the websites of the BBC, the CIA, and The New York *Times* as well as those of *Wikipedia, Encyclopedia Britannica, History.com, The Holocaust Encyclopedia* of the United States Holocaust Museum and The *Atlantic* as well as scores of others. Believe me, this was not uplifting stuff.

*

Many real people populated this work of fiction. The reader may be interested to know the real life fates of some, aside from Allen Dulles and William Donovan whom you know about.

Julius Streicher, the virulent Nazi who published what was perhaps the most disreputable newspaper of the Twentieth Century (quite an accomplishment, I might add, in light of some of the stuff I've seen over the years) was captured by US forces in May of 1945. He was convicted on the charge of crimes against humanity in a trial of major war criminals before the International Military Tribunal at Nuremberg. He was hanged in Nuremberg on October 16, 1946.

Galeazzo Ciano, the Italian foreign minister, who was in bed with his mistress when the Allies invaded North Africa, was dismissed from his post by the new government of Italy when Mussolini was overthrown. Ciano and his family fled to Nazi Germany on August 28, 1943, afraid of being arrested by the new Italian government. Hitler's people returned him to Italy and Mussolini's administration. He was then formally arrested in Italy on charges of treason. He was tried and found guilty. On January 11, 1944, Ciano was executed by an Italian Fascist firing squad. As a final humiliation, Ciano was tied to a chair and shot in the back. Some accounts, however, had it that Ciano managed to twist his chair around at the last minute to face his executioners and shout, his final words, "Long live Italy!"

Field Marshal Friedrich Wilhelm Ernst Paulus, who commanded Sixth Army during the Battle of Stalingrad, presided over the ultimate defeat and capture of about 265,000 German military personnel, their Axis allies and collaborators. Under Soviet imprisonment, he was "re-educated" about Communism and Fascism. After the attempted assassination of Hitler on July 20, 1944 by several other generals, Paulus became a key critic of the Nazi regime while in Soviet captivity, appealing by radio from Moscow to Germans to surrender. Later, he was a witness for the prosecution at the Nuremberg Trials.

During those trials a journalist asked Paulus about the Stalingrad prisoners. He told the journalist to tell the wives and mothers that their husbands and sons were well. Paulus, for whatever reason, had a loose grip on the truth: almost all of the German prisoners died in Soviet captivity.

Paulus lived in Dresden, East Germany from 1953 until 1956. He worked as the civilian chief of the East German Military History Research Institute. He died February 1, 1957, fourteen years and one day after the surrender at Stalingrad. His body was returned to Baden-Baden, West Germany, where he was buried next to his wife, who had died eight years earlier in 1949. She had received the ring he had sent home after his capture in 1943 but they never saw each other again and were never reunited until after both were dead.

Paulus' top military aid, Colonel Wilhelm Adam was also "re-educated" at an "antifa" (anti Fascism) school in the Soviet Union. He later became an officer in the East Germany army. He authored a book titled, *With Paulus at Stalingrad*, in which he explained that "the Second World War started by Hitler's Germany was a crime not only against the peoples attacked by us, but also against the German nation, did not occur to us. And because of this, we did not recognize the deeper reasons for the defeat on the Volga, superiority of the socialist state and social system, whose sharp sword was the Soviet army."

Colonel Adam died in Dresden (East Germany) in 1978.

Irv Goff was a real person, also. After the Second World War, Goff became the American Communist Party's district organizer in New Orleans, Louisiana. He worked for Henry A. Wallace, FDR's Vice President before Harry Truman, on Wallace's 1948 presidential campaign. Goff agitated for African-American voter registration and was active on behalf of Civil Rights in the segregated American south, often his putting his life at risk. The famed journalist Studs Terkel interviewed Goff about his wartime experiences as part of his Pulitzer Prize-winning work, *The Good War*. Goff died on May 17, 1989 in Los Angeles, California. He was buried in Arlington National Cemetery, a unique American hero.

The identity of "B. Traven," the author of *The White Rose*, remains a mystery long after the author's death, despite the success of *The Treasure of Sierra Madre*. He may have been Ret Marut, as cited in this work, but may also have been a man named Otto Feige or yet another man named Traven Torsvan or even someone named Hal Croves. He might have been one of them, all of them, or none of them.

In 1946, the American film director John Huston arranged to meet "B. Traven" in Mexico City to discuss the upcoming filming of *The Treasure of Sierra Madre*. Instead of the presumed author, a man showed up at the hotel and introduced himself as "Hal Croves." The man claimed to be a translator from Acapulco and San Antonio. Croves presented a power of attorney form purportedly signed by "B. Traven," allowing him, Croves, to represent Traven's opinion on everything in connection with the planned filming. Croves was later present as the technical advisor on location during the shooting of the film in Mexico in 1947.

John Huston wrote in his 1980 autobiography that he had at first guessed that "Croves" might be "Traven," but he came to the conclusion that Croves was not the author. However, according to Huston, Hal Croves played a double game during the shooting of *The Treasure of the Sierra Madre*. Asked by the crew members if he was Traven, he always denied it, but his denials were formulated in such a way that crew members came to the conclusion that he and B. Traven were indeed the same person.

To this day, the mystery remains, as do many theories, the most bizarre of which holds that Traven was the illegitimate son of Kaiser Wilhelm II. Other lines of "thought" put forth the notion that B. Traven was the pseudonym of the American writer Ambrose Bierce, who went to Mexico to fight for the Mexican Revolution in 1913 and disappeared forever. Added to this was the rumor that Traven was the American writer Jack London, who theoretically faked his death in 1916 and then moved to Mexico and continued writing his books. See? There is nothing new about wacko conspiracy theories.

Both the latter theories seem unlikely. London died in 1916, His friends and family attended his funeral. And Bierce would have been eighty-two years old at the time of the first Traven novel.

Gauleiter Paul Giesler, whose harangue in Munich ignited some of the final open resistance to the Hitler regime, incited some of the worst violence during the last chaotic days of Nazi Germany. The violence was directed against "defeatists" and those seeking to surrender their districts without pointless destruction.

On May 8, 1945, the day that the Nazi capitulated to the Allies, Giesler and his wife committed suicide, fearing capture by American troops as they fled Berchtesgaden. Preceding him in death was Dr. Roland Freisler, "Hitler's Hanging Judge," who oversaw the sham trial of three White Rose members as well as many other victims during the Nazi era.

On the morning of February 3, 1945, Freisler was conducting a court session when United States bombers attacked Berlin. The Americans targeted government and Nazi party buildings, including the Reich Chancellery, the Gestapo headquarters, the Party Chancellery and the People's Court. Hearing the air-raid sirens, Freisler adjourned his court and ordered that the prisoners before him be taken to an air-raid shelter. He stayed behind to gather files before leaving.

A sudden direct hit on the court-building at 11:08 caused a partial internal collapse, with Freisler being crushed by a masonry column and killed while still in the courtroom. Freisler's body was buried in the grave of his wife's family at the Waldfriedhof Dahlem Cemetery in Berlin. He was so hated that his name was left off the gravestone. A foreign correspondent reported, "Apparently nobody regretted his death."

Among the files Freisler tried to grab was that of Fabian von Schlabrendorff, a July 20 Plot member who was on trial that day and who was facing execution. (Von Schlabrendorff had also once smuggled a time bomb, disguised as a bottle of Cointreau, onto the aircraft which carried Hitler back to Germany. The bomb detonator failed to go off, however, most likely because of the cold in the aircraft luggage compartment.) Postwar, he went on to be a prominent and respected jurist in West Germany. He died in 1980. His life was extended by thirty-five years thanks to the American bomber crew who snuffed Friesler.

Hans and Sophie Scholl were real people and key members of the White Rose. They were executed by the Hitler regime, as was Christoph Probst. Willi Graf, Alexander Schmorell and Kurt Huber were also arrested and executed.

With the fall of Nazi Germany, the White Rose came to represent opposition to tyranny in the German psyche. It was lauded for acting without interest in personal power or self-aggrandizement. In February 2012, Alexander Schmorell was canonized as a New Martyr by the Orthodox Church.

The square where the central hall of Munich University is located has been named Geschwister Scholl Platz after Hans and Sophie Scholl. There is a monument to them. The square opposite to it is Professor Huber Platz. Two large fountains are in front of the university, one on either side of Ludwigstraße. The fountain in front of the university is dedicated to Hans and Sophie Scholl. The other, across the street, is dedicated to Professor Huber. Many schools, streets, and other places across Germany are named in memory of the members of the White Rose.

One of Germany's leading literary prizes is called the Geschwister Scholl Preis, (the Scholl Siblings Prize). Likewise, the asteroid 7571 Weisse Rose takes its name from the group. The White Rose was also the subject of the opera *Weiße Rose* by Udo Zimmermann. There is an opera by Peter Maxwell Davies and a 2017 organ piece by Carlotta Ferrari. A German language movie, *Die Weiße Rose*, was released in 1982. It won the German Film Award for Best Picture.

The atrium where they were arrested still stands at the University of Munich, as does the courtroom where they were convicted. Most Germans and much of the world now know their story.

And a final note: There were other prosecutions of White Rose members. One was a young woman named Traute Lafrenz.

Ms. Lafrenz had studied medicine at the University of Hamburg in the summer semester of 1939 at the age of twenty. After the semester she worked in Pomerania, where she met Alexander Schmorell. In May 1941, she moved to Munich to study. There she met Hans Scholl and Christoph Probst. She and Scholl had a romance in the summer of 1942.

In late 1942 she brought the third White Rose flyer to Hamburg and redistributed copies with a collaborator named Heinz Kucharski. When Hans and Sophie Scholl were arrested in Munich in 1943, Lafrenz also fell under the suspicion of the Gestapo. Hitler's police arrested her on March 15, together with Alexander Schmorell and Kurt Huber.

During her initial interrogation, Lafrenz disguised the full extent of her involvement in the leaflet distribution. She was sentenced to one year in prison on April 19, 1943. After her release she was re-arrested by the Gestapo and imprisoned again. She spent the last year of the war incarcerated. Trials kept being postponed and moved to different locations because of Allied air raids. Her trial was finally set for April 1945, after which she probably would have been executed. Three days before the trial, however, the Allies liberated the town where she was held prisoner, thereby saving her life.

In 1947 she emigrated to the United States. She completed her medical studies at Saint Joseph's Hospital in San Francisco, California, becoming a doctor. She married an American. After moving to Chicago, she served from 1972 to 1994 as head of Esperanza School, a private, therapeutic day school serving students with developmental disabilities between the ages of 5 and 21. She has been involved in the anthroposophical movement in the United States for more than fifty years. In 2019 she received the Order of Merit of the Federal Republic of Germany.

At this writing in November of 2019, Traute Lafrenz – at age 100 - remains the last living member of the White Rose. An interview with her can be found on You Tube at https://www.youtube.com/watch?v=QMk6kumX0yM . She lives on Yonges Island near Meggett, South Carolina, in her adopted country.

She and her peers deserve our respect and gratitude. They also deserve to be remembered forever.

Noel Hynd

November 13, 2019

Hans and Sophie Scholl with Christoph Probst, Munich 1942.

Espionage Thrillers by Noel Hynd

Revenge
The Sandler Inquiry
False Flags
Flowers From Berlin
Truman's Spy

The Enemy Within
The Russian
The Cuban Trilogy
Firebird
Return to Berlin

Eisenhower's Spy   **(May 2020)**
Judgment in Berlin **(October 2020)**

Kennedy's Spy   **(May 2021)**

Non-fiction – Baseball

The Giants of The Polo Grounds
Marquard and Seeley
The Final Game At Ebbets Field

Printed in Great Britain
by Amazon